NEW LANARK
LIVING WITH A VISIONARY

C A Hope

First published in Great Britain as a paperback original in
2014 by

Marluc

www.completely-novel.com

ISBN 9781849144698

Printed and bound by Lightning Source International
Front cover produced by ronindreamer
All rights reserved
Front cover Artwork by Lane Brown
Back cover photograph of New Lanark by C.A. Hope

For my beloved sons with all my love.

Contents

New Lanark Living With A Visionary
the Second book in
The New Lanark Trilogy

Introduction

In the first frosty days of January 1800, Robert Owen and his wife took up residence in the heart of New Lanark, Scotland.

At only twenty-eight years of age Owen became the Senior Manager of the largest cotton mills in Great Britain.

After fifteen years of living under David Dale's benign ownership, the New Lanark villagers eyed their new master with barely concealed animosity and suspicion.

The country was financially crippled by the war with France, starved by poor harvests and beset with social unrest.

Undaunted, Owen set out to satisfy the demand for profits from his English partners while implementing his personal vision of creating a harmonious, industrious community.

Softly spoken, his youthful appearance belying a wealth of experience, he set to work straight away laying down new rules and scrutinising every aspect of not only the machinery and buildings but of the employees themselves.

Seen through the eyes of the people who lived there, this is the story of the unfolding social changes which took place in New Lanark in the first years of the nineteenth century. All the true events have been meticulously researched, as have the lives of Owen, his family and contemporaries.

Chapter One

"If to be feelingly alive to the sufferings of my fellow-creatures is to be a fanatic, I am one of the most incurable fanatics ever permitted to be at large."
William Wilberforce

August 1800

Mountainous black clouds rolled across the sky above Lowland Scotland, rumbling and booming with thunder claps. Every flash of lightening illuminated sheets of torrential rain plummeting to the earth, hammering on slate roofs and flattening crops.

It was the darkest hour of the summer night but candlelight seeped from cracks in many shuttered windows throughout New Lanark. Babies cried in fear of the sudden reverberating crashes and old and young alike, although exhausted from their labour in the mills, struggled to fall asleep in the oppressive humidity and noise of the storm.

A man burst from one of the doorways and ran down the cobbled street, holding his jacket over his head against the downpour. He was making straight for the dark bulk of New Buildings, splashing through bubbling puddles and wrenching open the street door to enter the pitch-black stairwell and pound on the first door.

'Enough! I hear ye!' The physician's dishevelled figure appeared, barefoot, in a loose nightshirt, his long brown hair straggling around his shoulders. Holding a candle high, he

1

peered at the soaked young man in front of him. 'What's happened? Who are you?'

'Joe Scott, sir, Please come ... it's ma wife, Ah'm feart fer her ... she's bin taken bad. Please come richt awa'!'

'Is she an employee of the mills?' Mr McGibbon was loathe to venture out into the storm.

'Aye ... she works in the school ... Mrs Scott, Fiona Scott.'

'What ails her?'

'She's gie hot ... an' her heid's bad.' When the doctor made no move, Joe pressed on. 'Her babbie's due ony day, but tha's no' the problem ... Ye ken ... we ha'e three ither weans an' she's ne'er had ony bother. Ma wife's ne'er ill, man, but noo she's all swelled up an' no' talkin' sense ...'

The doctor noted the desperate tone and nodded, 'Very well. Wait here.'

With that, he shut the door, plunging Joe back into darkness.

He groped his way to the main door and stared out at the lashing rain, a fearful restlessness bunching the nerves in his stomach, creating waves of nausea. Breathing deeply of the damp, earth-scented air, he struggled for control.

In the final years of David Dale's management, the Mills provided the village residents with a medical man and Joe felt renewed appreciation for such a benevolent master and, despite the many changes being brought to bear on the workforce by the new owner, Robert Owen, this service was being continued.

The last time Joe needed help, he had been forced to walk up to Lanark but that was for his mother, many years ago.

The memory made him shudder.

On that freezing night the doctor could do nothing for old Marie Scott. The following dreadful, agonising days while they watched her die were amongst the worst of his life.

And now Fiona was ill.

Fiona was everything to Joe; he had loved her from the moment he first saw her and could not imagine life without her beside him. Other people fell ill, other men's wives died ... not *his* wife ... it was simply unthinkable. Yet, it was there, the shocking reality that Death could knock on anyone's door at any time and wreak havoc.

His eyes alighted on the manager's house across the road, its roof gleaming silver in every flare of lightening. Owen and his wife were asleep not a hundred yards from where he stood in turmoil and it was common knowledge that she was also expecting a child. Joe's conscience pricked. Mrs Owen was well provided for by her husband, she could rest all day, whereas Fiona worked for twelve hours in the school room as well as taking care of their children.

His heart beat faster. Mental pictures of companionable evening walks with Fiona swam before him. Her expressive dark eyes, cheeky, serious, alluring, or earnestly looking up into his when she impressed on him how they must never take their shared life and love for granted.

He recalled a snow-laden winter's night when she confided in him how much it scared her to feel so happy, that she was sure something would happen to take it away from them.

Was this what she foresaw?

His thoughts grew darker until he was abruptly snapped back into the present by McGibbon's footsteps behind him. Having hastily tied back his hair and donned breeches and boots, the physician was still wrestling with his braces.

'Take this and lead on!' He thrust a leather bag at Joe and set about buttoning the cuffs of his billowing shirt sleeves. Then, casting a rueful glance at the rain, he whirled a cloak around his shoulders and they both launched into the thunderstorm.

After the clamour of rushing along the street and up the stairs, it felt suddenly quiet and still in the Scotts' shadowy room.

Fiona lay in the inset bed, flushed and listless. Bessie, their elderly neighbour, was sitting at her side, a mournful expression crumpling her features. Joe's brother, Cal, slouched in a chair by the empty fireplace, his fringe stuck to his thin face, clammy with sweat, and in the other large inset bed, behind tightly drawn curtains, the three little boys were finally asleep.

With Bessie holding a lamp for him, McGibbon made a careful examination, noting Fiona's swollen ankles, puffy, blood-shot eyes and her obvious discomfort at every touch. He called for extra blankets to be placed in a pile at the foot of the bed to raise the patient's feet and rolled up the light cotton sleeve on her left arm.

'I shall let a vein breathe,' he told them, beckoning for the weak flame of the whale oil to be brought nearer while he searched for his box of lancets. 'It will relieve the pressure in

3

her body and release the ill humours.' He clicked his fingers at Joe. 'A bowl!'

Joe reached for a bowl in stunned silence, his hands shaking.

'Aw Christ!' Cal stood up, alarmed, 'whit's he daen tae her?' His voice died away at the sight of the silver blades in the physician's hand.

It was Bessie who replied, 'Blood-lettin', son. Ye mak yersel' useful an' fetch some mair watter ...'

Cal snatched up the bucket and fled.

McGibbon was experienced in his craft and Fiona gave only a gasp at the first incision, allowing the flow of scarlet to gather into a globulous mass in the bowl. Then Bessie was instructed to wash her down with cold water every four hours and urge her to drink as much as possible.

'Is the bairn all richt?' Joe asked, accompanying McGibbon back down to the street.

'At present, but I would prefer it if Mrs Scott did not have to endure child birth while she is so obviously fatigued. That is my main concern. Keep her in bed, keep her as cool as possible, I will visit again tomorrow.'

'But whit's happened? Why is she ill? Is it a disease?'

'It is not infectious, Mr Scott, do not worry about it spreading. However, it can be a very serious condition. I have seen these symptoms in other women near their time.'

'Is it because she wis werkin'?'

'I doubt it. It can happen to ladies of the highest birth who have maids in attendance.'

'And they recover? It dis nae hairm the bairn?'

McGibbon looked directly at Joe, speaking slowly and seriously.

'If we can keep her fever down, we have a chance of both your wife and the baby surviving. The next few days are vital. Should she suffer any fits or seizures, send for me immediately.'

Before Joe could say another word, the doctor walked briskly away into the gloom.

'If,' thought Joe, 'Why did he ha'e tae say *if*? Dear God ... seizures ... ' he threw his head back, squeezing his eyes shut to block out what was happening; it was a nightmare.

The storm was receding, allowing shifting pools of moonlight to glimmer through gaps in the clouds. Distant rumbles of thunder were now barely discernible above the roar of the River Clyde churning through the gorge below the village.

Joe swiped his hands across his face to dash away tears and strode back up the stairs.

'Ah blame Mr Owen,' Bessie sniffed, wringing out a flannel in cold water and dabbing at Fiona's swollen feet. 'She wis tired oot wi' all the werk at the school an' then came hame tae clean the hoose afore the inspections tomorra.'

'Aye, blame Mr Owen,' Cal said scathingly, yawning. 'Why not? Every yin blames him fer a' an' sundry the noo.'

'Weel, Ah ken ye like the man, though there's gie few who share yer opinion,' Bessie persisted, 'but we ne'er had this carry on when Mr Dale was in charge. It's yon Mr Owen who's gi'en us mair hours on the factory flair ... clerks coming tae oor doors tae see if the linen's washed or the stove's blacked! It maks fer a load o' werk fer housewives.'

'McGibbon telt me it's nuthin tae dae wi' werking,' said Joe, wearily, all too aware of how tired he was and how quickly dawn would be upon them: he doubted he could sleep. 'An' ye can jist tell the inspectors tae leave us be tomorra, she can nae be disturbed. She's tae be kept cool sae let's pray the thunder's taken awa' the heat.'

The Scotts' prayers were not answered and they opened the shutters to find bright blue skies bathing the washed valley in sunshine, a fine mist rising from the river.

It was going to be another scorching day.

***

Anne Caroline woke to the chimes of the mill bell signalling the start of the working day. It was six o'clock.

For a moment she thought she was dreaming but on opening her eyes she immediately recognised the shape of the window and furniture of the main bedroom in the New Lanark cottage. It was still strange to be sleeping in this room because it used to be her father's private domain.

5

Turning her head against the smooth cotton pillowcase, she stretched out a hand to touch the empty space beside her. The sheets were cold. Her husband was a very early riser and in the first few weeks of their marriage it distressed her to find herself alone but now she was growing accustomed to his ways.

Robert Owen was a man of such energy that he simply could not achieve all he wanted to do in the number of hours most people considered to be a full day. So, since childhood, he assumed the habit of waking early and providing himself with more time to spend on his personal reading and pursuits before joining the rest of society.

Relieved to find bird song replacing the drumming rain and thunder of the night, she pulled the covers tightly around her shoulders and slipped back to sleep.

When she re-surfaced it was to see the stocky black and white clothed figure of her maid placing a water jug on the wash stand.

She sat up abruptly, pushing her cloud of wavy brown hair from her face and rubbing at the back of her neck; it was stiff and sore.

'Oh dear, Toshie ... I fear I have slept too long.'

'Ah'm sure there is no hurry, madam,' the older woman drew back the curtains, flinching at the sudden flood of light. 'After the crashin' an' bangin' o' the storm last nicht ye needed tae rest awhile longer.'

Chiding herself for being so lazy, Anne Caroline reached for her bible. She prayed for forgiveness and asked God to give her the strength to overcome the fatigue which plagued her during these months of pregnancy.

'When I am dressed and downstairs,' she thought, 'I will meet the next challenge of the day.'

The day did not improve.

By eleven o'clock when Owen had still not returned, Anne Caroline found herself gazing out the window at the dazzling sun flashing off the symmetrical lines of window panes in the mills.

An uneasy expectation pervaded the entire village, seeping into her subconscious. She felt as if she was waiting, but what was she waiting for? All the excitement of packing up from

England, travelling north, being with her father and sisters again and then the joy of discovering she was with child, was replaced by the dawning reality of having reached her final destination.

Although they returned to Scotland at the start of the year, she spent all the winter months with her father in Glasgow and it was only after living in the village for the last few weeks that this realisation was causing concern.

This small stone house, planned by Dale as a country cottage for the family to enjoy for occasional holidays, was now her home. She acknowledged her father's generosity with gratitude and, being situated right in the centre of the mill village, it was extremely convenient for Owen to conduct his business. However, it was hardly the sort of place Anne Caroline ever envisaged as her matrimonial home.

Being raised in one of the most gracious and opulent mansions in the city of Glasgow and accustomed to the variety of company and entertainment which her high social circle afforded, living in this little house was very poor in comparison.

For the hundredth time, she cast an eye around the parlour and wondered what her friend Rosemary would make of its meagre size, plain plaster walls and simple furnishings. She ran a finger down the edge of the curtains, drawn back into wide sashes. The printed fabric was faded by the sun, the once vivid blues were bleached grey, the polished floorboards rustic beneath their layer of cloudy wax. All the furniture had been chosen by her aunt, as had the lamps and rugs, wall hangings and chinaware.

The basic arrangement of the rooms was adequate for their needs but Anne Caroline realised she should be bringing her own, and her husband's, taste to the decor. It was a daunting thought and she wished she could consult with her friends in Glasgow.

The front door opened and footsteps sounded in the hallway.

'My dear,' Owen cried as she ran towards him. 'Business matters took much longer than I expected, I hope you have not waited for my return before eating?'

He stood before her with the same slight smile and earnest expression which captured her heart on their first meeting. A great weight lifted from her shoulders; what did it matter if the rooms were not as she would like them to be? Or if her wealthy city friends considered the house small and cramped? The answer stood infront of her: nothing mattered more than being with this delightful, attractive man and knowing he loved her as much as she loved him.

He exuded such a quietly fascinating air that despite his unremarkable features and slight frame he instantly commanded attention. Owen was no dandified charmer, he cared little for fashion although, like everything he did, he presented a neat, professional appearance at all times.

In his company once more, Anne Caroline was ashamed at fretting over inconsequential issues.

She smiled at him brightly, rewarded by the deeply affectionate look in his eyes.

'And did your meeting go well?' she asked.

'In some ways, yes. We have made a start at inspecting the workers' rooms and, it must be admitted, there is a good deal of resistance. I will press on! This is a remarkable and special place. I knew it from the first time I visited. I recall thinking how, of all the places I have seen, I would prefer this community to try an experiment which I have long contemplated putting into practice.'

'An experiment?' Her tone was teasing. 'A strange description! I hope it is not too extreme?'

'It will mean more changes to the way people here are used to working ...' he was glancing at the clock on the mantelshelf. 'and *living* for that matter, but it will be so much better for everyone when it is implemented.'

'More changes! What sort of changes?'

He gave her one of his candid, naively innocent looks. 'For the better. Better in every way.'

She was perplexed. 'But these mills are doing so well, you said so yourself? Many, many visitors have sung their praises and my father is justly proud of this whole village.'

'I have nothing but respect for your father, you must be aware of that?' He took her hand tenderly in his, 'however, I want to do things differently. As you are aware, that is why your Uncle James and Mr Kelly could not continue in their positions.'

Anne Caroline did not wish to linger on this topic. While staying in Glasgow she witnessed the anguish it caused to members of her family when the news of their dismissal, for that was what it was, reached Glasgow within the first month of Owen taking up the reins.

While she knew nothing of business matters, he confided many of his personal ideas and plans for the village during their tedious journey north from Manchester. She didn't pretend to understand all his theories but was entranced, as perhaps only a wife can be by her beloved new husband's enthusiastic, vehemently explained principles.

Yet, she had always envisaged Uncle James being included, providing her with many occasions to enjoy the company of Aunt Marion and her infant cousins.

She simply smiled and changed the subject, ringing the bell for Cooper, the housekeeper, to order a tray of food to be prepared.

For most of the population of New Lanark, Robert Owen was either regarded with animosity or fear, but for one person, he was the answer to her prayers.

For years, Mrs Cooper bore her duties as house-keeper in New Lanark to the Dale family with fortitude. Hers was a difficult role to play due to sudden bursts of extreme activity followed by long periods of depressing loneliness. She would keep it in good order for months at a time with no employer even setting foot over the doorstep. Then word would arrive from Glasgow that the Master was arriving at short notice, or the whole Dale family were about to descend and she would be sent into a frenzy of bed making, food ordering and all the preparations required to receive up to ten people, including attending staff.

Throughout the previous autumn and into the winter, the New Lanark house remained empty. Cooper slept in her attic bedroom and ate her meals alone at the kitchen table. Fires were regularly set and lit but the light of the flames danced around static rooms, the furniture draped with dust sheets, vases bare of flowers.

November and December were interminably long, spent mainly behind shuttered windows reading, sewing and praying. Too often, she would stand by the warm kitchen stove and listen to the suffocating silence all around her, hearing only her own heart beats quickening with a welling sense of panic.

On a couple of occasions she actually began penning her letter of resignation but within a few words she would pause and stare at the inky lettering with dread. How could she even think of being so foolish as to end her own employment, cutting herself off from a regular wage and comfortable accommodation? It terrified her to see how close she came to taking such drastic action.

As a widow with more than forty summers behind her and no savings or income, no relatives and only her experience as a housekeeper and basic cook to fall back on, the future looked bleak.

Then the joyous news arrived!

She was to prepare the house to receive Mr Dale's eldest daughter and her new husband: they would be staying indefinitely.

Indefinitely!

She thanked God fervently for understanding her plight and giving her the fortitude to overcome her weakness in the darkest days.

Cooper was so entirely swept along on this wave of excitement that she ignored all gossip about Mr and Mrs Owen, choosing to concentrate exclusively on presenting the house and her food to the highest standard.

However, there was one aspect of her new master which she struggled to dismiss and that was the well known fact that he was not a Christian. He did not worship in an Established Church and it was even rumoured he did not believe Christ to be the Son of God! Whenever this came to mind, she thrust it away and reminded herself that if Mr Dale, who was profoundly religious and a gentleman whom she held in the very highest esteem, could accept this heathen, then she would strive to follow his example.

After the Owens arrived from England there were even more improvements to the household. A further two staff were employed, a parlour maid and valet, and Mrs Owen provided a comprehensive guide of how she wished the house to be run. Having always longed to be given exactly these orders, Cooper could have wept with relief.

The only slight disappointment came from Mrs Owen's choice of menus. Cooper was an excellent cook, indeed she was originally hired on the strength of this skill. However, her new Master held a preference for plain food.

In his early childhood, Owen mistakenly ate dangerously hot flummery and the trauma still affected his eating habits and digestion.

'When it is only Mr Owen in residence,' Anne Caroline told her, 'Please do not prepare rich dishes. Mutton and oat broth for his main meal or some similarly simple dish such as bean and pea porridge or barley stew would be sufficient ... with a baked apple or other sweet fruit pudding or custard. This is what he prefers. Absolutely no spicy, hot or heavily seasoned recipes. When I am here, we will discuss alternatives because, as you know,' Cooper had known Anne Caroline since she was a child, 'I share my father's enjoyment of good food!'

So, while her Mistress remained in the city throughout the winter, the housekeeper dutifully followed her orders and prepared the requested meals. It seemed unusually basic fare for a man of such high standing but to her amazement he ate it with obvious enjoyment and even complimented her on her 'fine dish'.

On the first occasion when she found herself alone in the house with just the Master to attend, Owen spread his papers on the desk in the parlour and worked late into the evening. She made a pot of tea and drew her chair over beside the range, opening the bottom oven for more heat. The dishes were done, a warming pan placed in the master's bed and the fires stoked.

For the first time in years, she relaxed.

'If this is how it is to be working for Mr Owen,' she thought, 'even if he is does not worship the word of Our Lord, I daresay I am truly thankful.'

***

David Dale stood on the terrace outside his new country dwelling and breathed deeply of the country air.

After giving the New Lanark cottage to his daughter and her husband, he had missed having a place to escape to from the pressures of city life. These longings culminated in the acquisition of Rosebank, a gracious, gabled country house set among gardens on the banks of the Clyde at Cambuslang, an easy carriage ride of just four miles from Glasgow. He felt immediately attracted to its fine features and chuckled when told it was designed by the Adam brothers, the same architects he employed for his Charlotte Street mansion.

Gazing out over the garden, apart from a scattering of bruised petals knocked from full blown roses, the peaceful scene before him gave no hint of the wild weather of the night before. No-one expected their first night in their new home to be accompanied by such a tempestuous storm. When the thunder grew from intermittent growls to great crashing, reverberating booms, Dale found his frightened daughters in the small parlour downstairs. With windows rattling at every thunder clap they drew back the curtains and curled up on the window seat to cry out at every lightening flash and marvel at the fierce rain sending water coursing off the roof, pelting the stone slabs on the terrace outside. The whole household was kept awake until the early hours, making the event even more memorable.

It was no surprise that his daughters were still asleep in their rooms but recalling their excitement and delight on exploring the house the previous day was a pleasure in itself.

He watched a furry bodied bumble bee buzzing between spires of deep blue delphiniums before his eyes were drawn to a blackbird running alertly across the grass nearby. Cocking its head to one side, listening intently, it suddenly stabbed its beak into the soft green turf and pulled out a wriggling earth worm.

Dale leaned his portly body onto his cane, easing his aching knees and enjoying the tranquillity of the scene. He remembered a conversation with Owen when they discussed the benefit of being close to Nature. It was taken for granted by most people that one felt better after a country walk or a turn around a city park, yet both men felt its buoyant effects were vastly over-looked.

The Lord God created the plants, insects and animals and if Man engaged with them, even for a short while, their presence caused a soothing effect, leading to a general feeling of well-being and a lighter frame of mind.

12

He was musing on these thoughts when Renwick came to inform him that his morning meal was now prepared.

'Breen suggests you may wish to eat in the Morning Room, Sir?'

'Aye, that'll be grand. It is a novelty for us all to discover how we will make use of the many rooms here.'

Renwick followed his master back into the shade of the house and along a wide flag-stoned corridor to the eastern most room on the ground floor. It was a sunny room, affording a pretty view onto formally planted low box hedging surrounding displays of scarlet and yellow snapdragons: a perfect place to enjoy his first meal of the day.

'Whit's the rush aboot?' Cook asked when the new maid came flying through the kitchen door after serving the master's porridge.. 'Is Mr Dale needin' something?'

'No.' the maid was shy, her flat child's face swamped by the frills on her cap, 'it was jist ... he spoke tae me ... asked me ma name, an a'!'

'I hope you were polite,' Breen said sharply. All the new servants were unknown quantities.

'Ah telt him ma name, Ah curtseyed, like ye telt me an' said 'Iris, Sir' an' efter he spoke, weel Ah didnae ken whit tae say ... in a' ma time in service up at the Hall, none o' them e'er spoke tae me.' She clamped her hands to her cheeks, feeling the heat of embarrassment. 'Mr Dale looked sae scary, an him a magistrate an a' ... but he smiled and his words were kind.'

Breen was checking off a list in her little notebook. She licked the end of her prized lead-pencil, a New Year's gift to her from Renwick, and made a final tick before turning her attention to Iris.

'You will find we have an exceptional employer in Mr Dale, few houses in the country have such a privilege.' She fixed the girl with a stern eye. 'If you work hard and give loyal service, you will retain your position with us. I may remind you that you, and all the new servants, are on a month's trial.'

'Aw.' cried Iris, 'ye'll no' regret takin' me oan ... Mrs Breen.'

Later, when Breen and Cook were alone in the kitchen, the back door and windows flung open for a draught, Cook stewed a pot of tea for them.

'Wee Iris is throwing herself in tae every task Ah give her,' Cook laughed, picking a selection of slightly misshapen melting moments off two baking trays and placing them on a plate.

'This oven's too hot a' the back,' she inspected her morning's work, 'I'll make a couple o' sponge cakes, they'll soon tell me how tae arrange the cooling plate, adjust times.' She plonked herself down at the table, tucking the tea towel in the belt of her apron and reached for a biscuit. 'How dae they taste?'

'As delicious as always,' Breen reassured her. 'Everyone has a lot to learn here, but, all in all, I believe we shall enjoy our times in this new residence.'

They smiled over their tea cups to one another and when Renwick came in with a query, insisted he joined them in sampling the biscuits.

A holiday atmosphere pervaded the house in the same way Breen recognised from the few occasions she visited New Lanark. This time, however, the surroundings were luxurious and along with the butler and Cook, there were enough staff to carry out their duties to the same high standard as she demanded in the city.

At midday, Dale received his first visitor to Rosebank, his business partner and friend from Catrine, Claud Alexander.

'My, you've chosen a charming place here, Dale!' he greeted him, clambering out of the carriage and stamping on the gravel to stretch his long legs after the journey. 'Damnably hot day for travelling!'

Dale was at the front door, waiting in the dappled shade of a mass of overhanging honeysuckle.

'Come away in ... come away in ... it is much cooler inside than out today!'

'Thank you, this heat reminds me of India. You expect to sweat out there but in Scotland it takes ye by surprise.'

After his drive from Ayrshire, Alexander was shown up stairs to refresh himself before joining his host in the drawing room. A light breeze wafted the curtains, gently swaying stalks of lavender and ferns arranged among a vase of scented white roses.

'I can see why you chose this house,' Alexander said, appreciatively, accepting a crystal tumbler of iced lemonade. 'Was the panelling here? or have you remodelled the room?'

'Happily the panelled walls in the hall and this, the largest of the two reception rooms, were here. However, a team of painters have worked their magic by covering it with this pale colour. I like it! What say you? My late brother's wife encouraged me to use a young designer from the city.'

'An excellent choice. It shows off your paintings magnificently. You have quite a collection and this little Nasmyth is a gem.' Alexander took a closer look at a small landscape in a gilded frame. 'And that's a fine engraving of the New Lanark Mills by ...' he squinted at the print, 'Robert Scott. I don't believe I have noticed these at Charlotte Street. New acquisitions?'

Dale lowered himself into his chair and, on seeing his friend's glass already empty, waved his hand to the footman, beckoning him forward to take an order.

'You'll take some more lemon, Claud?'

'Indeed, delicious.'

'Yes,' Dale continued the conversation, 'I enjoy looking at good works of art, whether in oils, enamel or wood. That writing desk in the corner is by a young man we heard about only recently. The marquetry is superb.'

Both Dale and his colleague in the Glasgow branch of the Royal Bank of Scotland, Robert Scott-Moncrieff, were keen supporters of up and coming talent. They were well placed to match wealthy merchants with houses to fill, with emerging craftsmen or painters to bring about a mutually beneficial relationship. If a particularly attractive piece came to his attention, Dale would often buy it for himself: he now had two substantial houses to furnish.

Having great wealth was a privilege and a responsibility to Dale. He earned it by his own sheer hard work and industry and knew he was fortunate, but he also wished to spread his money to those setting out in their trade and deserving of support. He did not consider it extravagant to spend twenty pounds on a yew wood dressing table for one of his daughters' bedrooms , because he knew the twenty pounds would enable the young joiner to feed and clothe his family while he created another exquisite piece of furniture.

How else would such intricate craftsmanship be funded, unless there were rich customers to buy their products?

After admiring the house and asking after each others' families, the gentlemen turned their attention to Catrine Mills.

'So, you think we have a buyer?' Alexander asked. 'The mills are going well at present, as you will be aware, but given the rising taxes being pressed upon us to pay for this terrible war, I am not sure how profitable the books will look this time next year.'

'I have been in correspondence with young Mr Kirkman Finlay, old James Finlay's son. Ye remember him? Fine fellow, died about ten years back? Shrewd textile merchant in his time. Well, his company is now in the hands of his son who is making it known he is keen to expand and wishes to purchase a large cotton mill. I made inquiries regarding Finlay's structure and financial stability.' Dale rested his head against the high arched back of his chair. 'These are extremely precarious times for many businesses, but Mr Finlay appears, on paper, to be capable of raising the required capital. Indeed, his affairs are in a healthier state than the Royal Bank!'

'So, it is as bad as the periodicals are shouting from their front pages? D'ye think the Bank will collapse?'

'All I can say is that my Glasgow office is probably supporting the whole banking system.' Dale smiled, crumpling his plump cheeks, 'the worst is hopefully behind us. If Mr Finlay's offer is good or even just reasonable and you and I are both in a mind to sell, I say we settle and be done with it.'

'D'ye know when they will be coming to survey the mills?'

'Not yet, I will notify you immediately, have no fear, my old friend. I am also given to understand that Finlay and Company will uphold the running of the school and the other facilities we have worked so hard to provide for the workers.'

Claud nodded thoughtfully. 'How is your son-in-law getting along down at Lanark?'

'These young lads! Both Kirkman Finlay and Robert Owen have yet to see thirty winters, a sobering thought that, eh? Together they have experienced less time on this Earth than I.' Dale sipped his lemonade.

'Aye, but then they have us auld dogs tae thank for the forethought and establishment of the mills in the first place!'

'I fear Owen has put a few noses out of joint but he is young and full of enthusiasm.'

Alexander arched his brows, 'It's true your brother left?'

'Oh aye, he's still raw on that account but I can see both sides of the issue. Owen is highly organised, he's implemented various rules to manage the works efficiently, stop pilfering, absenteeism and the like and that, I'm afraid, means hard work for the clerks and managers.'

'Ye infer your brother is lazy?'

'I see things as they are, not as I wish them to be. Let's just say James was used to the easy, quiet life and coping with change, so many changes, was too much for him.'

'Kelly would not be fazed by a bit of hard work, though? Why did he leave? A grand chap, I always thought.'

'Now William Kelly's a different man, entirely. He is his own man. I have spoken with him several times in the last few months, made introductions here and there, and he is preparing to set up mills of his own, at Rothesay. I can see him doing very well. He has too many skills and too fine a brain to remain under another's employ ... he would and *should* have left even had I not sold up.'

'And what of the children? the orphans? How does your new son-in-law deal with them?'

'As good as his word, thank the Lord! He shares our dislike of the practice of hiring infants and has stopped taking any more from the Poor Houses. And,' Dale nodded, thoughtfully, 'he genuinely holds their welfare as a priority. I can ask for nothing more.'

'Yet, if the rumours are correct, he is working them harder. A whole hour a day more?' Alexander narrowed his eyes. 'How does he justify that after proclaiming his concern for workers in general?'

'I agree with you, it is hard to stomach. Owen tells me he is as discomfited by it as we are but we must not forget, he may be the senior manager at New Lanark, but he is only a junior director and must dance to the Board's tune. Markets are difficult, men are being called to war and prices of finished cotton are plummeting. He must be under extreme pressure to keep production high to compensate.'

'Perhaps we had the easy times, eh, Dale? Before the French mischief, trade debacles and rocketing prices for the raw material? It will be a relief when Catrine is passed to another, I must admit.'

'Amen! I'm too old for the game nowadays, preferring to pass the time of day with my gardener in the hot houses or preach the Word of the Lord God. I too look forward to divesting myself of Catrine ... and my other mills.'

The conversation moved easily from topic to topic until the sun moved around to shine through the windows and reflect off the polished floorboards, dazzling Dale's eyes.

'Come,' he said, grasping for his cane, 'enough of business, let us take a walk around the grounds. Did ye hear the splendid news that I am to be a grandfather?'

***

While Dale and Alexander took a leisurely stroll along Rosebank's shady beech avenue, Calum Scott was suffering the unremitting glare of the sun beating down from a fathomless, deep blue sky.

His work at the Forge in New Lanark sometimes required him to accompany the wagon over to Wilsontown Ironworks, a few miles away over rough roads.

Today, it was Big Lachie's son, Kyle, who was driving the wagon. Kyle was everything Cal would like to be, darkly handsome, strong, confident and good company, which usually made the shy boy eager to please him, grateful for any attention. However, Cal's thoughts were so wrapped up with Fiona and the dreadful, sleepless night they had all endured, that he just sat in silence as they bumped and lurched their way across the moors.

Sweat soaked their thin cotton smocks and the loose fitting summer breeches stuck uncomfortably to their thighs. Beneath their hats, brims pulled down, their hair was damp, perspiration running down their necks.

'Yer no' the cheeriest lad at the best o' times, Cal, but ye tak the biscuit t'day.' Kyle grunted during their return journey, flicking the reins lazily to slap the back of the lead horse.

Cal squinted sideways at him, shifted in his seat and then carried on staring out at the shimmering heat.

A mile or so further along the road, Kyle mopped his face with his sleeve, asking, 'Dae ye ha'e the watter?'

Cal pulled himself out of his reverie and reached between his feet for the flag which they refilled at Wilsontown.

'Here, tak the reins ...' Kyle passed him the slippery leather straps and seized the water with both hands.

Pulling out the stopper and pouring it liberally over his face and into his open mouth he let it run freely down his neck.

'Mibbee ...' Cal said, falteringly, 'we should gie the horses a rest by that copse, there's a drap o' shade there?'

'Ah, the lad can speak!' Kyle laughed. 'A grand idea! The moor's a devil tae cross in all weathers, barely a tree tae break the wind nor the sun. Ah've heard men ha'e died here when the snow's bin blowing. It all looks the same, nothin' tae show ye where yer gaun.'

Not having driven heavy horses before, the feel of the powerful beasts under his control made Cal's heart pound. The ground was littered with boulders and it was too dangerous to risk damaging the wagon wheels to drive up close to the small stand of fir trees, but when they were near enough for the shadow to fall across the horses' heads, he reined them in to a halt.

'Neatly done.' Kyle congratulated him, jumping down from the high seat and seeking refuge away from the heat.

Cal carefully secured the brakes and tied up the reins before joining him.

'Ah hear yer brither's dae'n weel at his trade.' Kyle said, after taking another long drink and handing the flagon to Cal.

'Aye, he is.'

Kyle caught the flash of desolation whipping across Cal's face.

'Whit's the matter? Yer brither's a'richt ... is he no'?'

'It's no' Joe, it's his wife. She's bin taken ill. Bad like.'

Kyle was instantly alert.

Despite the passing of the years he still held Fiona in the highest regard. He saw her only a few days before, obviously heavy with child, yet still drawing his attention like no other lass he knew. She looked well, laughing and sharing gossip with other housewives outside the village shop.

'Whit d'ye mean ill?' he asked.

19

'She has a fever, but the medic says it's no' catchin', it's tae dae wi' her bein' aboot tae ha'e a bairn.'

'An' can they no' dae something aboot it? Has Mr McGibbon bin tae her?'

'Aye, Joe fetched him bu' he jist says tae keep her cool.' Cal's troubled expression worsened. 'We were hopin' the weather would turn but ...' he shrugged. 'She was awfy bad in the nicht an' Joe did nae want tae gae tae his werk this morn...' Memories crowded into his mind of his brother's whispered, choked endearments to Fiona before time ran out and he was forced to leave. 'She's a' swelled up, an sae drowsy. If it were the winter, Bessie says we could bring in snow an' pack it a' aroon her. She's seen it done afore, but wi' this hot spell, we can nae e'en keep the milk frae turnin' within the hour.'

They stood in the shade listening to the clouds of flies buzzing around the Clydesdales. The heat was overwhelming, stifling.

Then Kyle slapped him lightly on the arm.

'C'mon, Ah have an idea!'

Kyle let Cal drive the team until they reached the outskirts of Lanark, where he took back the reins and skilfully guided the heavy cart to the market place. The streets were crowded and loud; hawkers crying their wares, townsfolk bustling about their affairs and dogs and children dodging among the rattling gigs and handcarts. They drew to a halt beside a stall piled high with baskets bristling with crowing cockerels and chickens, a macabre rope strung above them hanging with dead rabbits and pigeons. Wasps zig-zagged their way between the bloody corpses.

'Watch the load, Ah'll be bak!' Kyle swung himself down into the throng and disappeared from view.

Within minutes, he returned, bearing a heavy wooden box and heaved it up onto the seat.

Cal grasped it and tugged it towards him.

'Jeez! It's awfy heavy!' he lifted the lid: straw. 'Whit ever is it?'

'Ice! I ken a boy, a poulterer, who werks wi' the fishmonger. He's alis got ice.'

As the horses made their way carefully, slowly, down the last steep part of the road into New Lanark, Kyle turned to Cal.

'When we git tae yer road end Ah'll stoap an ye can tak this up tae yer hoose. Din nae tarry mind, fer ma Da' will be wonderin' whit Ah've done wi' ye.'

'Aw, this is a braw idea, Kyle. Ah thank ye frae us a'...'

Kyle leaned close to him, 'Best ye din nae mention it wis me who thocht o' the ice, eh?' he winked. 'Yer brither might no' be sae keen on it if he thocht he had tae thank me, sae din nae tell him!'

Cal was in too much of a hurry to discuss the past problems between the two men, but nodded agreement and dragged the heavy box to the edge of the seat, manoeuvring it onto his shoulder.

'Ah'll be doon tae the Forge in twa meenites!' he called breathlessly, staggering off towards his tenement door.

Bessie fell on the ice with exclamations of relief.

Cal was no sooner out the door than the old lady was tearing an old sheet into squares and wrapping up handfuls of frozen chunks to lay them on Fiona's forehead, around her wrists and ankles.

A strong odour of fish soon began to permeate the room but it was of little consequence to Fiona. She lay drifting in and out of consciousness, shivering and sweating, moaning and restless and then as still as a statue. Bessie watched over her, having sent the little boys down to Mrs Young, a neighbour with more children than she could count so a few more made no difference, allowing her to give the whole day to observing the girl's every move.

McGibbon came and drew more blood, his pursed lips and clipped instructions fuelling Bessie's concern.

When the bell tolled the end of the day for the mill workers, Joe's younger sister, Rosie, came bustling in, desperate to help.

'They'll be needin' a meal,' Bessie told her, speaking in a hushed tone. 'D'ye ha'e anythin' in yer hoose ye could bring doon fer the men?'

'Aye, Ah'll away and get it. An' ye must be fair done yersel', Bessie. Did ye sleep at a' t'other nicht?'

'Och, Ah din nae sleep these days, Rosie. Ah git ma rest when ma mind's kept fu', no' when Ah'm lyin in ma bed.'

Rosie gave the old lady's arm a squeeze: it was not long since she received the devastating news of her eldest son's death in

Egypt fighting the French. 'Yer a strong wuman, Bessie Jackson, so ye are, an' we're that gratefu' yer here tae help us.'

Rosie hurried off to prepare her food and Bessie carefully unpacked some straw and scooped out the remnants of slushy ice. Removing the warm, sodden rags from Fiona's forehead and replacing them with cold ones, she looked down on her sleeping face.

'Haud on tae yer life, lassie,' she whispered. 'Yer too young tae die. Ma lad wis too young,' tears were blurring her vision as she smoothed Fiona's hair away from her brow. 'Ah'm auld an' done, let the Lord tak me instead. Ah wid welcome the peace.'

When Joe came home he was fearful to look at his wife. All the way down to the village he prayed she would be better and now was the dreadful moment when he would find out. Bessie moved away from the bedside to let him move closer, busying herself with laying bowls on the table and filling a jug with water.

'She looks the same?' Joe said flatly, kneeling down to kiss her on the cheek. 'Where did ye git the ice?'

'Cal brought it frae Lanark, Ah think it's helped a wee bit, she's no' bin moanin' since.'

Joe reached for Fiona's hand, 'Bessie? her fingers are no' sae big. D'ye see?' He lifted the loose bag of ice away from her feet. 'An' her legs? Are they better than when Ah left?'

Bessie humoured him and went over to the bedside, she couldn't say whether they were better or not but if it made Joe feel happier she wouldn't disagree.

Rosie brought a large pot of broth and some bread and cheese, setting them on the table and insisting Bessie ate with the men; she would sit with Fiona.

When Cal arrived back, exhausted, he brushed off Joe's thanks for finding the ice.

'T'was nuthin. Ah asked **Auld Bel** if she had onythin' fer a fever,' he handed Joe a glass stoppered bottle. 'Twa spoons mornin' an' nicht.'

Bessie rolled her eyes, having no faith in the Gaelic speaking, self-appointed apothecary. 'Bel's potions!'

Joe studied the murky brown liquid, 'Ye ken ... Bessie, Fiona speaks well o' the wuman, we can try it?'

Cal shrugged, 'It'll dae nae hairm.'

22

Joe administered the Highlander's herbal remedy, lovingly murmuring to Fiona that she was looking better and the fever would soon be banished.

The others sat dejectedly, chewing, tearing off bread and helping themselves to chunks of Rosie's oily, sweating cheese.

'Weel, we can jist pray,' Bessie said, hardly daring to hope. 'God willing, she'll recover.'

Cal did not believe in God, he was not sure what he believed in, but while his brother and sister were smiling encouragingly, he was not.

He felt a horrible chill deep inside. Joe was so desperate for Fiona to get better that he was deluding himself and even if the swelling was subsiding, she was still seriously ill.

***

At exactly half past seven the next morning, Owen met his new manager, Robert Humphreys, outside Mill One.

Humphreys, a dapper young man in a black jacket, cream breeches and polished riding boots, removed his hat politely in greeting, the sun gleaming on his pink bald head. He was an old colleague of Owen's from when they worked together at Bank Top Mill and was disliked in the village for much the same reason as Owen: he was not Scottish and he was enforcing the new regulations.

The previous evening, they agreed to walk up stream to where the water was diverted into the underground tunnel feeding the lade. Owen was fully aware that there were periods when the river level was so low it could not draw enough water to feed the great wheels which powered the machines. Dale informed him of the problem right from the start and Kelly had also been most insistent that Owen should understand the limitations of this form of power.

Setting off briskly, Owen explained to Humphreys that he did not feel the problem lay with the power source, it was a matter of making the most of all available water.

'Expecting to have sufficient water in the river all the time is unreasonable,' Owen said. 'Even in Scotland it does not rain every day or even every week although, I grant you, like Wales, it is a very wet country.'

'Perhaps, if we dug a pond and held a head of water to draw from in times of draught, that might ensure continuous production?'

They made their way up the steep bank beyond the Forge, just yards from the cliffs overhanging Dundaff Linn.

'I cannot see that as a practical solution The gorge is deep and cut through shale and old sandstone, it would be a massive task to quarry stone from here and anyway, beyond this wall, it is not our land.'

They paused to look back at the village, standing above the opening where the tunnel emerged to release water into the deep channel of the mill lade.

'Come,' Owen opened the gate in the stone boundary wall, 'we will walk up to the start of the diversion. I was studying the plans again last night and I believe I have a solution.'

Beyond the Bonnington Estate wall the path took them along a precarious route cut into the steep slope. To their left, the hillside towered above them and, dropping sharply off to their right, a sheer rocky cliff fell away to the river bed far below.

Humphreys was unnerved by the proximity of such a sudden and dangerous chasm. He walked behind Owen, hardly daring to take his eyes off the other man's heels, for to look towards the gorge made the possibility of falling into its jaws altogether too obvious.

'I take my hat off to the men who blasted and scraped their way through this land,' Owen said, admiringly. 'The tunnel is one thousand yards long, an incredible example of engineering.'

After walking for several minutes, the track led them downhill in a series of twists before opening on to a marshy meadow lying level with the river bed. Here, the Clyde showed a different side to her character, running wide and smooth, bordered by bull rushes and small bird-cherry trees, several of which were eerily shrouded in ermine moth webs. Bobbing sandpipers flittered among the rocks protruding from the shallows where shoals of silver minnows darted: a benign, gently rippling river.

'Here is our problem,' Owen pointed to the mouth of the tunnel. 'Unless we have at least two inches of water across this area it does not reach the outlet to the mills.'

Humphreys shook out his handkerchief and wiped the perspiration from his face while watching Owen balance precariously on the dry tops of otherwise submerged stones.

'There is a natural line of rock here,' Owen called over the gurgling water. He was delighted by what he was discovering and enjoying the opportunity to be out in the countryside. 'If this was reinforced and raised to create a higher barrier, a proper weir could easily be made. A considerable reserve of water could then be funnelled into the tunnel, even when the rainfall drops to poor levels.'

He jumped nimbly onto a large flat stone, only to find it moved under his feet, forcing him to leap to another one, almost tripping.

'Be careful!' Humphreys shouted, 'or you'll end up falling in!'

Choosing his stepping stones carefully, arms outstretched, he explored further out into mid-stream.

'Yes, this will work ...' Owen called over his shoulder. 'I am sure it will work!' He turned too quickly, lost his footing and stumbled, landing on his knees and half rolling under the water.

'No harm done!' he cried, laughing at his predicament, 'very refreshing!'

'My goodness, dear!' Anne Caroline exclaimed, when her husband walked back through his front door. 'You are soaking!'

Owen grinned at her, one side of his hair clamped to his head and hanging in rats' tails around his collar.

'I took a tumble in the river but I was in no danger!'

'Well, I hope your adventures were worth it?'

'Oh yes, I am convinced we will be able to harness more water for the mills, all I have to do is discuss the matter with our neighbours at Bonnington and the Miss Edmonstones across the water at Corehouse.' He pulled his jacket off and handed it to Murdoch, his valet. 'First, I must change into dry clothes and then I am meeting Humphreys in the office.'

His wife's face fell in disappointment. 'You are going out again, immediately?'

He was already on the stairs, taking the steps two at a time.

'The new machinery has arrived for Mill Two, I need to see it is properly installed.'

Anne Caroline returned to the front parlour and took a seat by the window.

Of course, he was busy but she rarely saw him except across the dining table for their main meal. It was not as if she didn't have a lot to do herself, but there was little which took her fancy.

She felt the need to pray. Her husband's views on Church attendance were very different to her own but he never stood in her way to follow her religion.

She pulled the bell cord for Cooper, quickly asking her to arrange for their carriage to be made ready; she wished to travel up to Lanark to Church.

This raised her spirits and when Owen paused at the doorway, attired in a dry shirt tucked into pale breeches, his waistcoat neatly buttoned, she stretched out a hand to him.

'I will be attending Church in town this afternoon and then I thought I might call upon Aunt Marion.'

He took her hand and kissed it, 'Do not over tax yourself. Although the air is fresher I fear there may be another downpour before the day is out.'

'Which is always good for your water wheels,' she smiled up at him.

'If my plans come to fruition they will never be idle due to the weather.'

'Then I wish you well with your plans, my clever husband.'

His lips curved, abashed by the compliment, then the absorbed, pre-occupied expression she knew so well returned to his features.

If hard work and diligence were to make the mills a success, they were in very good hands.

***

'Joe? Joe!'

Joe jerked awake in the chair, disorientated.

'Joe!'

It was Fiona's voice, low, urgent.

He lunged towards her across the dark room, 'Ah'm here ...'

'Aw Joe ...' she whispered, reaching for his hand. 'Whit's wrang? Why are ye no' in bed?'

He took her in his arms and held her close, at a loss for words. Just hearing her lilting Highland tones again constricted his throat with emotion and relief.

'Ah didnae want tae disturb ye,' he murmured. 'Ye've no' been well.'

'Ah feel awfy sleepy ... aye ...' her words slipped away and he felt her grip on his arm releasing. 'Din nae mind me,' she mumbled, turning on her side and curling up 'ye need yer sleep ... come tae bed ...'

He sat for a long time listening to her gentle rhythmic breaths. She was cooler, she was talking, she was recovering. He didn't cry out or laugh, there was no physical manifestation which could express his feelings but as he sat quietly on the bed he knew he had never been so relieved.

By the following afternoon, Fiona was sufficiently well to understand the gravity of her illness and effusive in her apologies for causing so much trouble.

'The mattress is ruined, Bessie!' she cried. 'It reeks o' fish an' there's soggy patches richt through the straw ...'

'Dinnae fret, lass. We'll get the men tae chuck it oot. Noo,' Bessie poured another pan full of boiling water into the little tin bath and stirred it with her hand: lukewarm, better than cold anyway. 'Here an' Ah'll help ye, ye'll feel better efter a good wash.'

Fiona was very weak, everything was a tremendous effort. She lowered herself awkwardly into the bath, clutching the sides, her knees drawn up, her long hair wrapped up in a turban.

'Ah'm sae big Ah'm feart Ah'll git stuck!'

'That babbie can jist stiy where it is until yer weel agin. Ye need tae rest an' git yer strength bak.'

'Ye'r sae guid tae me, tae a' o' us,' Fiona smiled her thanks, noting Bessie's strained, grey complexion. Following the devastation of her son's death, Bessie was being persuaded to leave the village and move in with her daughter, a kindly woman with children who could fill their grandmother's days. 'Whit will Ah dae wi'oot ye, Bessie?'

'Jist fine. Anyhoo, Ah'll no' be far awa', ye can gie me a shout if ye need me. Let's tak yin thing at a time, eh? Yer past the worst noo, nae hairm done.'

'But the bed?' Fiona was appalled at the state of the bedding. 'We'll need new blankets an a'. Whit will Joe say? An' me no able tae wark.'

'Ah'll ask aboot, there's bound tae be somebody wi' a spare mattress an' some blankets no' being used. When the next load o' bedding comes doon, ye'll be back tae normal.'

When Joe came home he was so pleased to find Fiona sitting up in the chair looking more like her old self that the subject of the mattress was of little consequence.

'D'ye think Ah care aboot the bed? Och, ma darling, whit's a new bed sae lang as yer weel agin.'

'But it's no jist the beddin' Joe, the cover an' the blankets are mingin'.'

'We can manage fer ane nicht on the hurlie bed an' Ah'll gang tae Lanark early in the morn an' buy us a new yin.'

'Bessie says we can mibbee borrow yin?'

The innocent suggestion, said with the best of intentions, sparked a violent reaction in Joe.

His head was turned away so the exasperated, hurt expression went unseen and he fought back a bitter retort. His nerves were frayed from worry and physical exhaustion, but it was deeper than just a few nights without sleep while Fiona was ill.

Nearly losing the woman he loved, with all the ramifications of bringing up his children alone, had hit him hard. It was a daily struggle to provide for them all and it seemed that no matter how hard he tried, he was still living on the lowest rung of society.

So, it came as a final insulting reminder of his incompetence to have Bessie suggest he couldn't even provide a new mattress.

He let the rage seep away, clenching his teeth and taking a long time to unbuckle his bootstraps.

'As Ah said,' he managed to keep an even tone to his voice, 'Ah'll git yin in the mornin' an' arrange fer it tae be brought doon.'

When he glanced back at Fiona he was met with a solemn, knowing look in her almond eyes.

'That'll be grand,' she said quietly. 'An' while yer aboot it, we need mair blankets.'

He nodded, holding her gaze as his rankled, prickly frame of mind receded.

'Tell me whit we need an' Ah'll git it.'

'Ah ha'e all Ah need,' Fiona said plainly.

Although Bessie was in the room, she was speaking directly, intimately, to her husband. 'Ah have ma Joe an' ma weans.'

Bessie kept her attention on the pot of soup she was stirring, a smile tugging at her lips. Many years married and their fourth child about to be born, yet these two were as wrapped up and besotted with each other as in their days of courting.

Then Fiona gave a little chuckle, breaking the serious atmosphere, 'Mind ... a bed that disnae stink o' deid fish wid be braw.'

A week later, Fiona gave birth to a baby girl.

Even in the powerful, painful throes of the last contractions, she was determined to protect her plump new mattress. The baby was born with her mother lying on an old blanket on the floorboards with Bessie kneeling beside her, cursing the rough timber pressing into her knees.

Laying the tiny infant in Fiona's arms, the old woman levered herself up to sit on the edge of the bed and both of them started to laugh at the absurdity of their positions.

'*Failte Sionaidh*,' Fiona welcomed her daughter, through joyful tears. 'Ah hope ye'll ne'er ha'e tae lie on a floor agin!'

Chapter Two

"Man is born free; and everywhere he is in chains."
Jean-Jacques Rousseau The Social Contract

David Dale and his younger daughters spent a relaxing summer at Rosebank. The family soon fell into a pleasant routine and their new country home was close enough to the city to allow frequent visits with friends.

Every day, except the Sabbath, Renwick instructed a footman to run up the hill and collect the newspapers from the Mail Coach. These, and detailed letters from his clerks and partners, kept Dale up to date with world affairs. He could choose his own time to retire to his comfortable morning-room and attend to business matters.

He enjoyed this more leisurely pace of life and pursued the sale of the Catrine Mills with Alexander's assistance, looking forward to the day when they could sign over the management and financial worries to Finlay & Co.

One area which still held heavy responsibilities was the Royal Bank of Scotland. He had been so involved with the branch from the outset, being the first Glasgow Agent for the bank, that it was a struggle to give up this particular position.

He was personally and emotionally involved with the Royal Bank, it was not just a simple directorship which could be ended by signing a letter of resignation. Had it not been for his friendship, nearly twenty five years ago, with John Campbell, a senior figure in the Royal Bank in Edinburgh, he would not have met Campbell's daughter, who became his beloved wife, Carolina.

30

He knew what the gossip-mongers whispered behind their hands when he was given the prestigious Glasgow agency, but he also knew their cries of nepotism were unfounded. He proved his worth, both as a husband and a banker. Let them say what they wanted, his little branch was now doing more business than the original east coast office and he was not ashamed to take a large portion of the credit.

Scott-Moncrieff, his partner in the Branch from its inception, was an admiral fellow; astute and the epitome of efficiency. Dale admired him as a colleague and cared for him deeply as a friend.

With the increasing hardship for manufacturing businesses and merchants in general, it was a thorny problem to know when the right time would come along to broach the subject of his retirement.

Scott Moncrieff was prone to take matters to heart and would become despondent and anxious over others' misfortunes. Just before his association with Dale, he was the Deputy Receiver General for the Land Tax, an important position, but after successfully fulfilling the post for several years, he was by passed for promotion to the full position. He took the rejection sorely and completely resigned from the Land Tax Office.

Working alongside Dale, who was both pragmatic and realistically optimistic, they balanced each other in personality and the partnership continued very successfully through many financially turbulent events.

Dale's inner strength, his calm, carefully considered influence, was drawn from his passionate religious beliefs. In his every action he wanted to better the lives of others and to him the most powerful way to make this happen was to preach the word of the Lord. While his work as a Cotton Master was decreasing, he devoted more time to providing sermons and counselling to the congregation of his church, the Old Scots Independents.

Naturally, in wondering about how to relinquish his duties with the bank, Dale turned to the Bible for guidance. He would remain for a while longer in the Glasgow office, in name at least, for this inspired confidence which was his main value, but he would slowly disengage from regular duties.

31

At the end of September, the Owens came to stay at Rosebank.

It was a long arranged visit to culminate with a gathering of friends and family to celebrate their first wedding anniversary. Dale had proposed the event and Anne Caroline agreed wholeheartedly with the idea. While she would occasionally visit her father at Cambuslang for a week or so at a time, her husband was usually too busy to leave the works and only managed a couple of days, here and there.

Their arrival was eagerly anticipated and as soon as the carriage was heard crunching over the gravel by the front of the house, Jean and her sisters hurried to the door with Renwick.

The hours spent rumbling over the roads were becoming more tiring for Anne Caroline as her pregnancy progressed and she begged their forgiveness and asked to be excused to lie down for a spell.

'Can we sit with you, dear?' Jean asked, 'while you rest we can tell you all that has been happening.'

'Of course,' Anne Caroline said, smiling at their hopeful faces. 'Just please do not be affronted should I fall asleep.'

Jean linked her arm with her elder sister and led her away towards the staircase. Mary and Margaret jostled together in a flurry of colourful muslin and lace, vying with each other to take her other arm; little Julia tripping along behind, determined to be included.

Dale looked at Owen, standing in the midst of the organised chaos in the hallway.

'The Lord has granted us a most wonderful afternoon. Join me for a walk around the garden before the chill sets in?'

A few minutes later, when Anne Caroline looked out of her bedroom window, she caught sight of the two men making their way slowly down the length of a long herbaceous border. Owen's taller figure, slender in his long brown travelling cape, leaned attentively towards the stocky, older man. They would pause, point out a bloom, an especially attractive grouping of colours or fine specimen plant, their gestures wide and expansive, growing easy in each others' company.

The sight pleased her immensely. She adored her father and was deeply in love with her husband so their growing friendship and mutual respect warmed her heart.

Outside, the sharp autumn scent of burning leaves blended with the sweet perfume of late blooming moss roses. A breeze rustled the foliage on mature oak and beech trees, sending the first gilded leaves floating to the ground. The quietness was only disturbed by an occasional plaintive bleat from a distant flock of sheep and the soothing, rhythmic coos of wood pigeons.

The white washed country house with its distinctive crow-stepped gables and bay windows, sat amongst lush green gardens. It was a very different world from New Lanark's enormous stone buildings, crowded tenements and cobbled streets. It seemed to embody Dale's retirement from the hustle of mills and commerce, yet he was not quite ready to leave the stage as a mill owner and merchant.

'I have some business matters I would like to discuss with you,' he said, turning to Owen.

'Of course, Sir, I am at your service.' If Owen was surprised it did not show in his voice, nor his expression.

They continued on their path to complete the circuit of the formal flower beds before Dale led the way back into the house. Calling for coffee and sweet biscuits to be brought to the drawing room, they took seats on either side of the fireplace and settled into deep conversation.

Stanley Mills in Perthshire was again on the agenda.

Following George Dempster's plea for Dale to invest in this beleaguered cotton mill on the River Tay, Dale was researching the business. It was now in the hands of James Craig and a potential new partner, James Mair, who were looking for substantial capital to rejuvenate the factory.

He relayed all he knew to Owen, confiding in him that he was already planning to outlay a sum of money for the rebuilding of the mill which was destroyed by fire the previous year. Now, his dilemma was whether to increase his investment.

Owen raised many valid questions and the more they looked at the matter, further possiblities and uncertainties arose.

Eventually, with the room glowing gold with the setting sun, Jean came tentatively to the hall door.

'Papa, Mr Owen, please excuse me interrupting ... it is late and Anne Caroline is now well rested ...'

33

'We will change for dinner, then,' Dale beamed affectionately at Jean. 'My! The Lord has blessed me this day! It is a treat for me to have all my family here!'

Owen rose from his seat, bowing his head politely; he was honoured to be considered part of the family.

It was also personally gratifying to know Dale sought his opinion on the Stanley enterprise. He decided he would make his own enquiries and do his utmost to furnish Dale with properly informed advice.

Over the days which followed, the two men enjoyed a visit to Glasgow together. They met with mutual colleagues and, much to Owen's satisfaction, spent time in the Tontine Rooms where they took coffee with some of the most influential city merchants and brokers.

Owen was already well known among Glasgow businessmen, having engaged in an association with their companies on behalf of the Chorlton Twist Company. To be seen with David Dale gave added kudos to his new position of senior manager at New Lanark, engendering confidence in him amongst the older merchants. Most of the men around the crowded booth were well past middle age and Owen's youthful presence brought new life to the discussions.

At Rosebank, Dale and Owen were often to be found talking earnestly on both commercial and philosophical subjects while enjoying rambles on the banks of the Clyde or sitting by the log fire late into the evening.

'Look at them now,' Anne Caroline whispered to Jean one afternoon as they dabbled with paints on the terrace.

To take advantage of an unseasonably mild day, a table with two chairs was arranged to give a view of the most colourful area of the garden and the girls were enjoying capturing the scene.

'They have made several circuits of the lawn,' she continued, 'and now returned to the new seat under the chestnut tree. They are so absorbed in their words that they never so much as glance this way.' She was smiling happily. 'Who would have believed it a year ago?'

Jean agreed, licking the end of her fine water colour brush and smoothing it to a point before touching it lightly to a little pot of hard blue paint.

'Your husband certainly has a great deal to say. Papa spends much of his time listening, but he seems content.'

'Dear Robert has so many ideas and projects,' Anne Caroline laughed, fondly. 'I have never known a man so full of enthusiasm. He has complete conviction that he can execute all the plans he devises! I confess, he is sometimes so consumed with purpose to fulfil a task that he barely sleeps, yet he remains full of energy and never complains of fatigue or ill health.'

'And you are enjoying married life?' Jean's young face was full of anticipation.

'Oh yes, very much.' Yet, as she uttered the expected words, memories flew into her mind: lonely hours of feeling trapped within four walls without her family, her husband engrossed in work, the nausea of early pregnancy. Hastily brushing them away, she turned instead to the happy aspects, of which there were many.

'I cannot tell you how wonderful it is to know I am bound in Holy matrimony to a man I hold in such high regard.' She looked across the lawn to Owen. 'Perhaps the joy comes from knowing he feels the same?

'When I first fell in love with him, as you know, Jean, there seemed to be so many obstacles to our being together that I was unable to feel truly happy.' She sought the words to express her thoughts, 'I was delighted by him, excited to know he returned my feelings but, well, there was always a cloud of bittersweet worry where our relationship was concerned. Then, ever since our wedding, that angst completely disappeared and I can love him fully and freely knowing we are always going to be together.'

Jean gazed wistfully at her sister, 'Oh, I do hope I meet a gentleman who makes me feel the way you do about Robert.'

'I'm sure you will!' Anne Caroline told her cheerily. 'Why Jean, you are far prettier than I am and you have a wit and charm which will captivate any man!'

'I know of no man I wish to captivate,' Jean sighed.

'Gracious, you are not yet sixteen, you have many years to find your special person.'

'I was thinking that myself, not a week ago. However, it struck me that any husband I do find in the future, must be alive and walking around now, for he will be my age or older.' She applied herself to painting again. 'I found that a strange notion, but nevertheless true.'

'I remember thinking very similar thoughts at your age and, of course, now that I am with Robert, I can ask him all about his life before we met. Do you know, I was only an infant in the nursery when he was already leaving home to make his way in the world?'

'Well, he is several years older than you...'

'Only seven years. He was still but a child when he left his parents to venture out into the world, although he did move to live in his brother's house in London. He will celebrate his thirtieth birthday next year and I intend to mark the occasion!'

Jean pushed back her long hair, neatly tucking stray curls behind her ears and wrapping her shawl more tightly while she scrutinised her picture.

'I would like to marry a man who has black hair and 'eyes like glinting sapphires'! Just like in the novels!' Jean giggled, her childish sense of humour rising to the fore, making her sister laugh as they used to before her marriage.

Owen heard the laughter and looked fleetingly towards the house, pleased to see his wife in such good spirits.

He was relating the ongoing struggle he was experiencing in trying to inspect the New Lanark housing and Dale was encouragingly interested in his plan.

'I believe,' Owen continued, 'that we should look after our workers as well or indeed a great deal better, than we care for our machines. Too many employers believe they will produce more profit if they have the very latest machines. A huge amount of time and money is poured into these wood and metal contraptions and great attention paid to the gears being oiled and the work rooms kept immaculate. Yet they neglect the operatives!'

Dale nodded, following the argument. 'It is what I have been saying for years. It is essential that the employees eat properly and are given sufficient time to rest.'

'Indeed, sir, but not only would their welfare be improved by wholesome food, but if their beds are free of lice and their linen clean, they will feel well and fit for their duties.'

They mused over the best way to ensure the housing could be maintained and Owen set out his intended course of action.

'I have discovered that it is not just the Highland folk who are living in squalor, in fact, many of the rooms in Caithness Row were amongst the cleanest and best appointed in the village. It is right across the board; Irish, Scots and English incomers all have both excellent housekeeping regimes and, perversely, terrible ones. Nests of rats, brimming, putrid toilet buckets! Chickens and, I do not jest, a milking cow!

'Even gaining entry to witness the state of the rooms has proved hazardous to my managers. Repeated efforts were made in the most serious areas and although the men have no quarrel with my plans, they are not present when my clerks demand entry which is, by necessity, carried out during working hours.

'I'm afraid to say that some of the housewives become quite wild, barring the doors and even threatening to throw their slop pans over the poor men as they try to uphold their duty. So, I am going to arrange for each staircase to elect a supervisor, one of their own, who will make a weekly report on the cleanliness in their dwelling.'

'Well,' Dale raised his eyebrows, 'that is brave, indeed! I look forward to hearing of this adventure!'

Undeterred, Owen launched into explaining his other current project: building a weir to supply constant water into the mill lade.

On the penultimate day of their visit, 30th September, guests arrived to attend a luncheon in celebration of Robert and Anne Caroline's first wedding anniversary.

Many were of David Dale's generation, like his Charlotte Street neighbour Archibald Patterson, but there were also the younger society set including Rosemary Peckham and her husband, the Tennants and both father and son from the Mackintosh family with their wives.

Rosebank hummed with the babble of many voices, its gracious panelled rooms shining with hundreds of candles and the latest in design of painted glass oil lamps. It proved very congenial to hosting large numbers, with double doors spread wide to allow the guests to flow at will from dining room to drawing room.

Jean, Mary and Margaret took turns entertaining the company with recitals on the grand piano, ending the evening with a delightful duet from the older girls accompanied by a song from Margaret and little Julia.

'You are looking so well, dear Anne Caroline,' Rosemary gushed as she kissed her goodbye. 'Please send word as soon as you arrive at Charlotte Street and I will call on you.'

'I shall, although it will not be for several weeks.' It was arranged that she would return to her father's house for the birth so she could be attended by the eminent physician, Mr Palmer.

'Until then,' Rosemary embraced her warmly, transferring a cloud of sweet perfume. 'I pray it will all pass smoothly. It is our lot in life to bear children.' She paused, as if she had said enough before adding, 'I am again with child, but please do not spread it abroad ... it was only confirmed last week.'

Anne Caroline's face lit up with the news but she quickly composed herself, 'Good bye, Rosemary. I shall certainly send a note the very moment I arrive. We will have much to talk about!'

***

Owen did not spend his time away from New Lanark on purely social pursuits; several very good contacts were made which could lead to orders. He was in the manufacturing business and was constantly on the look-out for new buyers, whether overseas, where the larger orders lay, or at home. It was all useful trade in these months of depressing news from the War Office and ever decreasing European markets.

An interesting conversation with a gentleman who owned a large grocery retailing business in the centre of Glasgow inspired fresh ideas for supplying cheaper but better quality produce to the mill village. Also, at the end of the evening reception for his anniversary, he spoke for some time with George MacIntosh and learned of the gentleman's intention to tour the Highlands the following summer. The expedition was partly for business and partly for pleasure, but he would be visiting Perth and travelling north to Sutherland.

Since hearing of these plans, Owen's active brain kept returning to them. The Mills at Stanley were near Perth and

MacIntosh was also a partner in his father-in-law's other Highland mill, Spinningdale, which lay north of Inverness. He acknowledged the importance of this connection and stored it away to decide whether to act upon it, or not, nearer the time.

It would certainly be sensible to visit and actually see Stanley and Spinningdale if he were to advise Dale on them. It would mean a lengthy time away from New Lanark and the task of physically negotiating the mountainous roads to reach his destination was rather a daunting thought. However, with a companion like MacIntosh who held a shared interest in the mills and who knew many of the landed gentry along the route, perhaps it was a journey he could undertake.

After an early start, the Owen party arrived back in the village before the end of the working day and Owen lost no time in getting straight down to work.

While Anne Caroline retired to her bed to rest, her husband called an impromptu meeting of his senior managers.

How was the new machinery performing? What progress was being made on costing out the construction of the weir? How many of the tenement rooms, badly damaged by tenants and abandoned, were now being repaired?

The mill buildings were casting long, inky blue shadows in to the gathering dusk before Owen turned down the wick in his desk lamp and left the office to walk the short distance home.

Cooper met him in the hallway, awaiting his instructions.

'Ah, Cooper!' Owen smiled at her, 'I wished to ask you ... the meat and vegetables you prepare, where do you buy them? At the village stores?'

Shocked by the question, Cooper's already pallid face drained completely of colour.

'No, Sir. I do not. Is there something wrong with the meals?'

'Oh no, not at all. I assure you, they are delicious.' He rubbed his chin, looking at the floor for a moment, pensively. 'Why do you not purchase the goods here? Surely it is easier to walk only a few yards than trail up the hill?'

The housekeeper was now growing flustered.

'I walk up to Lanark two or three times a week, that is all, Sir. I place my orders and the items are delivered.'

'But there is a butchery and a green grocery within the village, why not give them my custom?'

'Oh Sir, you would not thank me for the meat or poultry sold here!' Cooper was aghast. 'I could not place ... *that* before you or my Mistress.'

'You have charge of the purse for this house, would it not save us a considerable amount of money?'

'Goodness me, no, Sir! I beg your forgiveness but it is quite the other way around.' She drew herself up, appalled that he was accusing her of mismanaging the household budget. 'If it is the cost of the food that troubles you, I assure you the shops and market in Lanark are very much more reasonable and, what is more, the goods are fresh and far superior.'

Owen nodded, thoughtfully. 'Thank you, Cooper. That is what I thought might be the case.' He saw her relax slightly but her pinched lips and stiff posture still bristled with resentment.

'Now,' he smiled beguilingly, 'I would very much like to eat whatever you have prepared this evening.'

She nodded solemnly and was turning away when he added, 'Cooper? Please do not feel my questions were in any way a reflection on the service you provide. I was merely looking for confirmation on what I had already deduced for myself.'

His words took a little of the sting out of Cooper's hurt feelings and she calmed herself by laying out his supper tray, paying particular attention to serving only the most tender slices of beef.

Eating his meal in the comfort of the warm front parlour, Owen told his wife about his latest plans to enhance village life.

'My dearest,' Anne Caroline cried, amazed by her husband's new endeavour. 'The Company will provide the *groceries* for the villagers? May I ask why?'

Owen finished the last mouthful of roast beef and wiped his mouth delicately with the serviette.

'It is the obvious thing to do.'

'You are a mill owner, Robert, not a green grocer.' She changed her position in the chair, rearranging the folds of her heavy linen gown to cover the obvious bulge beneath the material. She could feel the baby kicking and was faintly embarrassed in case her husband might notice. 'Why make more work for yourself when there are already shops in the village?'

He answered good-naturedly. 'The shop keepers down here are very aware that they can charge whatever price they wish for their wares. I have looked at the goods and would never wish to buy them so why should the villagers?'

'But they do, everyday.'

'Only because there is no alternative. After working all day or with children to attend, the notion of walking up that steep hill to town is not appealing. Then, of course, they would have the long descent carrying their purchases. No, it is much easier for them to buy from a supply in the village, but this means they pay for inferior food.'

'It is a fine and admirable thought but how would you manage to run a shop as well as everything else?'

'Good heavens, no!' He laughed out loud. 'I would, or rather the New Lanark Twist Company would only buy the supplies, wholesale. The shop would have its own managers.'

He warmed to his theme, telling her how the Company already bought in large quantities of beef, mackerel, potatoes and all other food stuffs for over four hundred orphans in Mill Four.

'Do you think your partners in Manchester would agree to this enterprise?' Anne Caroline asked.

'That remains to be seen. It is an idea, and I must accept that it may be something for the future for at present I am much too taken up with the mills. However,' he yawned, 'I strongly believe that the Company would reap higher productivity from a man who has nourishing food to eat. I intend to make it possible for all the inhabitants of this community to enjoy decent food at prices they can afford.'

***

When longer hours of darkness reigned over the land, the hedgerows gave up their harvest. Country folk and animals alike sought out glossy purple brambles and crimson rosehips, carefully gathering mushrooms and fungi with confident, experienced eyes before either frost or maggots tainted their bounty. The skies lost the chattering, wheeling swallows to be replaced by flocks of fieldfares and redwings greedily combing the meadows or flocking in rowan trees, stripping the scarlet berries.

During shortening days the woodlands rustled with birds and red squirrels, at night, badgers and foxes criss- crossed each others' paths, heads low, scenting and sniffing their way. Nests no longer held broods of hungry chicks, they were now places to bundle together and shelter through the coming winter.

By candlelight, before work on a wet morning, the Scotts wished their faithful, much-loved neightbour and friend a fond farewell with tears in their eyes. Making her promise to visit regularly, they hugged her in turn, each murmuring a personal goodbye. Bessie was the first person they met in New Lanark and over the years she became part of their family.

Anne Caroline boarded the carriage to drive up to Glasgow on a very wet October morning. Holding a large black umbrella over their heads, Owen escorted her from the house.

'I shall travel up next week,' he said loudly over the rain hammering on the cab roof, supporting her as she climbed aboard. 'Please give my regards to your father ... rest and stay well, my dear wife.'

'I will miss you terribly, Robert, but will just tell myself that we will be together again very soon.'

He kissed her hand, squeezing her gloved fingers tightly, then stood aside for Toshie to scuttle over from where she was sheltering and pull herself up into the carriage.

Owen remained standing on the road, a slightly built figure under the wide umbrella, his hand raised in farewell until the horses were out of sight.

Further along the village, high in the tenements, Fiona was sitting on the rug in front of her stove, peeling potatoes. It was taking a long time for her to overcome the effects of her illness, followed so rapidly by the birth of her daughter. After two months away from the school, she presented herself at the School Manager's office. He knew Fiona and listened to her plea to resume earning but could not grant her permission to return.

The young woman before him was thin and pale, hollow cheeked. Her usually luminous eyes were dull, grey shadows as dark as smudges of coal ringed her eyes and between her brows, lines showed her strain.

'Mr Owen is very strict that no person should be put to work who could be considered unfit to carry out their duties,' he told her. 'Rest, Mrs Scott, and come back to see me in a month.'

Fiona cursed as she reached for a bunch of carrots, viciously slicing off the limp green leaves and laying them aside to add to soup.

She was angry and worried and blamed Robert Owen for how she felt.

Not only was she not deemed well enough, which she sometimes acknowledged might be true, but Mr Owen's new rule regarding child workers was a second blow to the family income.

With mounting bills for winter clothes and provisions, Donnie was keen to earn for the family and despite initially not wanting their son to enter the mills, Joe agreed he could apply for a job.

'Jist tae see us through this wee bit, mind?' Joe said sternly.

Yet that small avenue to a few more pennies a week was denied them when Donnie came running home, crestfallen and near to tears. Mr Owen was no longer engaging children under the age of ten years.

Fiona wished she could suddenly regain her health but although she could tackle more and more each day, she would become shaky and dizzy after exertion. Often in the middle of the day she would be forced to curl up under her shawl on the bed, Sionaidh tucked in beside her, dozing.

She knew Joe was concerned, both for her and for his dwindling savings account.

In a fit of pique she threw the carrots into the washing bowl, spraying soiled water across the rug.

Davey started giggling and little Robbie scrambled off his chair and trotted over to the mess, plunging his hands into the water and splashing merrily. Seeing his mother was upset, Donnie went to her aid, roughly pushing his little brother away from the fireside and knocking him backwards, arms flailing, his head taking a glancing blow on the chair leg.

For a second there was silence, his mouth wide, then his screams joined the rest of the noise and disorder.

Over this racket, came two loud knocks at the door.

'In the name o' the wee man!' Fiona clutched at her head, eyes flashing round the room. This was not an inspection day, was it? No, there was word that they were now to be carried out by a neighbour, but no-one was yet selected, so it could not be that.

Baby Sionaidh started crying and Fiona snatched her up, holding her against her shoulder, and wrenched open the door.

'Whit dae ye want?' she shouted, glaring.

The two men on the landing took a rapid step backwards, hit with the full force of screaming infants and a fiery housewife bellowing at them.

'Mrs Sarah Rafferty? Wife of Sean Rafferty?' one asked, tentatively, his expression showing that he clearly did not think this was the woman he was seeking.

Fiona's confusion began to clear and she stared at the men with rising alarm. Brilliant red jackets and black shakos, glinting with brass, declared their profession as soldiers.

She was shocked. Both their sudden appearance and the mention of her sister in law took her breath away leaving her speechless.

Her legs began to shake.

'Naw,' she managed at last. 'There's nae body wi' that name here. Ye ha'e the wrang hoose.'

The older of the two men, an officer, was assessing her carefully, his eyes narrowing as he asked, 'May I have your name, please?'

'An' whit business is it o' yours whit ma name is?' Fiona responded with spirit. If these men were after Sean, for that could be their only reason for calling at the door, they would receive no help from her.

'The tenant for this room is listed as Mr Joseph Scott,' the officer continued, 'Are ye Mrs Fiona Scott?'

Fiona held his penetrating stare; his eyes were as sharp as blue ice beneath sun bleached lashes, startlingly pale in contrast to his weather beaten, deeply tanned skin. Thoughts of Bessie's son flicked momentarily into her mind; the scorching heat of Egypt, men like these fighting for their lives ...

She kept her lips firmly sealed.

Drawn by curiosity, the children quietly swarmed around their mother's skirts, eager to see the finely dressed soldiers.

Without looking away, he spoke slowly and precisely, 'I have a warrant to arrest Mr Rafferty. Mr Rafferty's wife is Joseph Scott's sister an' this is her last known address. I must warn ye that ye are impeding His Majesty's officers in their duty if ye dinnae answer ma questions.'

With these chilling words, Fiona was forced to speak. Using the excuse of rearranging her baby in her arms, she dropped eye contact, murmuring. 'Aye, I am Mrs Scott, but we hav'nae seen nor heard frae Sarah fur o'er a year.'

'Yer married tae Joe?' the officer said suddenly. 'Fur truth?'

Her attention jerked back to him and to her amazement she saw tears swimming in the man's eyes, a broad grin spreading across his face.

He snapped his heels together, touching his temple in salute and bowing his head. 'Lieutenant Samuel Scott at your service, ma'am. I am Joe's brother.'

***

Joe came home tired and wet. He barely noticed how tidy the room was or the combed hair and washed faces of his sons, but he looked appreciatively on his wife's happier face.

'Ye feelin' better, lass?' he asked, kissing the top of her head as she sat in the chair nursing Sionaidh.

'Aye, Ah am that.' Her lips curved in a suppressed smile. 'Ah'll be daen the dinner when Ah've feenished wi' the babbie, then we'll ha'e some peace.'

Joe swung the swee over the coals, holding his hands out to the warmth, his back to the room. After a few moments, he looked over his shoulder at his three little boys playing and talking in hushed voices on their shared bed, the curtains half drawn.

'It's awfy quiet in here? has somethin' happened?'

'Naw, they're jist bein' guid lads ... mak the most o' yit!'

Fiona had warned the children not to breathe a word of the soldiers' visit, threatening them with the bogey man if they told their father.

45

After introducing himself, Sam suggested springing a surprise on his brothers and Rosie by coming round to their lodgings after work. Fiona agreed and threw herself into clearing up and making a large pot of soup. There was little else in the house to offer the gathering, so she penned a neat note to Rosie. Without mentioning the reason, she asked if Rosie could please bring down some cheese, bread or anything else she had to spare.

Donnie and Davey took the note up to Rosie's room and left it on her table, making sure it was in clear view as soon as their aunt came home from the mill.

Night came early, merging with the dreary rain which fell all day, shrouding the valley and holding the coal smoke low over the village. Cal came through the door coughing, his chest wheezy and tight.

'Ah'm fur ma scratcher ...' he announced to his family, shrugging off his soaked jacket and hanging it on the hooks behind the door.

'Whit time is it?' Fiona asked, anxious to delay Cal from undressing straightaway.

'Ah dinnae ken? It's sae driech oot there it's bin like evenin' since midday.' Cal sat down to untie his boot laces, his nose was running and he kept sniffing and clearing his throat.

'Ye should eat afore ye sleep, Cal. Ah'll dish it up noo.'

Handing her sleeping baby to Joe, Fiona started to lay out the bowls. Where was Sam? Perhaps he wasn't going to come at all? A terrible thought struck her, perhaps it wasn't Sam?

For a moment she was quite upset, humiliated that she believed the man's words. 'Och, whit does it matter,' she told herself, 'no hairm done an' all ma hoosework's feenished.'

She glanced at Joe and saw him watching her. 'Whit?'

'Yer deep in thocht,' he replied, tilting his head to one side enquiringly. 'Whit's up?'

As she opened her mouth to speak, heavy footsteps could be heard coming up the stairs. They stopped outside the door and then came two sharp raps.

'Ye expectin' someone?' Joe asked, bundling the baby towards Fiona.

'And who wid Ah be expectin?' she smiled, bursting to share her secret.

It was Cal who reached the door first, standing in his stocking feet, coughing.

Looking back on the moment, Joe realised that he recognised his brother immediately, but it was so unexpected to find him standing in full uniform in the doorway that for several seconds they all just looked at one another.

Sam spoke first. 'Hello Cal ... Joe,' he nodded to each of them, searching their faces for recognition. 'I ken it's bin a lang time but it's me, Sam ... yer brother.'

'Sam?' Joe gasped, caught like a statue in mid stride, then he rushed forward and hurled his arms around him and suddenly the three brothers were hugging and crying and slapping each other on the back.

Fiona stayed by the fire, tears running down her cheeks. Donnie and his brothers clapped their hands and jumped up and down on the bed, whooping with excitement, even if they were not too sure who this distinguished army officer was, or why their parents were laughing and crying at the same time.

The ecstatic welcome was just winding down when Rosie came up the stairs. She was weary and dishevelled from working on the big frames all day and also annoyed at being required to turn out into the nasty weather to run this errand for Fiona. So, when she entered the Scotts' room, she was scowling, holding out her contributions for the meal.

'Rosie!' Sam cried, 'Why lass, yer as pretty as a wee doll!'

Rosie recoiled from his advances, intimidated by the military uniform. 'Whit ever are ye thinkin', sir?' she said sharply, 'How d'ye ken ma name?'

Then she saw who it was and shrieked with delight, throwing herself into his out-stretched arms, like a child to its parent.

All fatigue evaporated.

The rest of the evening was spent in a rush of gabbled questions and chatter. Rosie ran home and brought Gerry down to meet his brother in law and Sam regaled them with tales of far off lands.

The simple meal was consumed with as much fervour and enjoyment as if it had been a banquet. Cal brought out the ale he usually reserved for his evenings' fishing, his face flushed with excitement as he offered it around the table.

They talked of their mother and their crippled sister, little Meg, both now buried beneath the turf on the hill above the mills. They marvelled at how different they all looked since they last sat around a table together. Much amusement and play was made of the fact that Joe was now taller and more muscular than his 'big' brother.

Jumping up from their chairs, they stood back to back to show Joe to have a good two or three inches on Sam in height. Both men were strongly built and the family resemblance could not be mistaken. Awkwardly, this also illustrated Cal's short comings and although the noisy banter scarcely paused, Fiona saw the grin on his face freeze into a forced, pained expression before he reached to take a long drink from the ale flagon.

She quickly averted her eyes, feeling his hurt and being acutely aware that the he must not see her pity.

Instead, she studied the two older brothers. Joe's yellow blond hair was cut short, whereas Sam's, tied back in a black ribbon, was long and bleached in white streaks by the sun, reminiscent of Joe in his early years at New Lanark. She gazed at them, remembering her first glimpses of her future husband when he laboured on the construction team. Would she have been so infatuated with Sam? Their features were similar, even the timbre of their voices, although Sam's Scot's accent was softened and anglicised.

No, it was something else in Joe, beyond his surface, physical appearance which captured her heart.

'Why did ye join the army?' Rosie asked Sam, 'Did ye plan tae join when ye left us?'

'I was in a bad way efter the fight wi' Da', an' at first I thought I would go back an' kill him. The hate I felt was terrible ... what he did to Meg ... an' all o' us. I wanted to take him by surprise and finish the job.'

Joe nodded, understanding, not condemning.

'I was badly beaten' Sam continued, 'bruised, ma head bleeding,' Rosie stifled a cry, 'but I found a place tae sleep in a barn an' the farmer's wife gave me some food. I told her I needed work an' her man gave me a ride on his cart up tae Hamilton. It was there, efter a few weeks o' grafting in a stable-yard that I saw the red coats o' the Scottish Rifles recruiting in the square. From that day, the 26th Rifles or as we are properly known, the Cameronians, have been ma life.'

'Ha'e ye killed a man?' Donnie piped up, awe-struck by his new uncle.

'I have, laddie, in the line of duty. Every time is like the first, it's no' something ye get used to, but ... I have to obey orders.'

'Yer a Major noo, sae a reckon ye gie the orders noo.' Cal said.

'I'm no' a Major!' Sam looked aghast. 'A Lieutenant, an officer, aye, an prood o' it ... but no' a Major.'

'Och Sam, we're sae proud o' ye...' Rosie leaned across the table and stroked his uniformed arm. 'We thocht ye were a Major because that wis whit Tam telt us.'

'Tam?' Sam looked around his family with raised eyebrows. 'Who's Tam?'

'Tam Murdoch?' Joe said. 'He's a pal o' mine and came back frae the war in a bad way ... lost an arm ... He sed he'd spoken wi' ye, that ye served together ... and that ye were a Major.'

Sam frowned with concentration. 'A wee man? Curly hair?'

'Aye.'

'I mind the man and whit was said, how could I forget for he told me aboot ye all? but he was nae a Cameronian! It was in Weymouth we met, och, I can nae remember his regiment ... the Scot's Greys?'

Joe shook his head, 'Ah din nae ken, Sam. yer a' jist scarlet jaikits o' the military tae me!'

'I seem tae mind his cap ... aye, but he told me you were well and making a fine life here at the mills but I din nae ken why he said I was a Major?'

'Nae matter!' Joe raised his tumbler. 'Ah drink tae ye, ma brither, we all dae, fer we are that prood an' happy tae see ye!'

They toasted his health and then their own, laughing as they clashed their assorted tumblers together.

'Anyhow,' Sam cried, 'In the army there's always someone above ye and our commanding officer's a guid man. When I joined it was Sir William Erskine, he was a hard man, but fair wi' it. The last five years it's been Sir Charles Stuart but things are changing, Stuart's leaving and we're to have a new Colonel. I tell ye, the war with France is forcing things tae change.'

49

'Ye've done awfy weel tae be an officer,' Gerry said with admiration. 'Ah gather there's gie few who manage tae achieve tha' frae the ranks.'

'I grant ye! But I cannae take all the credit, the Lord must have been caring for me. A lot was to dae with just working hard and staying with the regiment,' he rubbed a hand over his face, 'not getting killed ... but I've had a lot of luck as well. The first Major I was under took an interest in ma education. I owe him!. That was on the first voyage to Canada ... he put me in the company of a well read soldier and ordered me tae be able tae read the Bible when we made land. Ye ken, in the Cameronians, ye receive a Bible as soon as ye join, sae we all had them, but few in the ranks could read them.'

'Fer truth?' Joe cried, 'ye could read by the time ye landed?'

'Oh aye, there was plenty o' time! It's a lang voyage! I was a bit slow wi' some of the longer words an' did nae always understand them, mind ... but when ma turn came to read a passage at the garrison in Quebec ... I did it!'

Sam told them of the years of marching around Canada, to and fro between Quebec and Montreal and outposts along the Niagara river and then by ship to St John's in New Foundland. He skipped over the tortuous first years and his rise to Colour Sergeant, the culmination of his ambition and far more than he could have expected.

'So there I was, fair made up with meself as a Colour Sergeant. That's the end of the line for a man like me, the top o' the ladder. Ye ha'e to be born wi' a silver spoon in yer mooth or at least a faither wi' wealth and friends in high places tae purchase ye a commission. Then luck or Fate or whit ever ye fancy tae call it, looked kindly on me.'

'Whit happened?' Donnie squealed, enrapt with his new hero.

Sam ruffled the little boy's hair affectionately. 'Och, it's a lang story, anither day, eh?'

'Aw ... tell us?'

'Well, let's just say there were many events o'er the years an' each one lead me up tae where I am this day. As I say, luck or fate?' He laughed to make light of his achievements. 'It started wi' a big hungry bear ... ' Donnie and Rosie both took a sharp intake of breath, hanging on his every word.

50

'The bear was at a Niagara where there's a mighty river,' he pulled Donnie on to his knee, 'and the river runs through a gorge, just like the Clyde runs here, but it's gie wide and deep ... with thick forests all aroond. Wolves and bears prowl and howl in the forest!' Sam opened his eyes wide, playing up his story for his new found nephew. 'America lies on the south shore of the river and Britain held the north. Well, a few years back, the British made a treaty to hand o'er our fort at Niagara to the Americans and all was going well ... until one hot day.' He paused for effect. 'The garrison children were playing outside and there was a cry that one o' the wee boys was missing.

'Dozens o' men were sent oot and was nae it jist ma luck tae suddenly spy the lad in a glade? Pure chance! He'd wandered off into the woods to follow a bear ... and that bear was nae happy when it heard everyone hollering and trampin' aboot in his wood. No' happy! He reared up on his hind legs and roared then ... dropping tae all fours he came bounding towards us! There was no time tae load ma rifle so I snatched up the lad and stood very still. That's whit we were told tae dae and ... it worked! The grizzly stopped, sae close I could see the dust on his fur an' his shiny black nose wrinkling as he sniffed the air then he turned awa' an' walked off into the trees.'

'Oh!' Rosie whimpered, flushed with excitement. 'Thank the Lord ye were spared an' Ah can see ye safe and weel with ma ane eyes!'

'Aye, I prayed hard with gratitude that nicht, I can tell ye. It turned oot the boy's faither was a Captain and he showed his gratitude by giving me a commendation.'

'He made ye an officer?' Cal asked.

'No no ... it disnae werk like that but ma name was noted and he ... *thanked* me, personally.'

Sam suddenly went quiet.

There was too much to relate on their first reunion. It would seem like boasting to tell them how the Captain rewarded him with money; money which eventually paved the way for him being able to take up the rank of Lieutenant when it was offered to him.

'Enough of me!' he cried, 'I want to know about all of you.'

As the siblings made a start at filling in their lost years, Fiona tidied away the remnants of food and forcibly removed Donnie to join his sleeping brothers. A weariness was creeping over her from the afternoon of furious activity and she sat down quietly on the edge of the children's bed, changed Sionaidh into clean linen and settled her to her breast.

A sense of unease began to grow: no mention was being made of Sean Rafferty or Sam's original reason for coming to New Lanark.

Then, when everyone suddenly realised it was very late and stood up from the table, Joe said, 'How did ye ken we were here? Did ye gae back tae Douglas?' he smacked his hand to his forehead, 'Ah'm forgettin', Tam telt ye we were here!'

Sam was buttoning his tunic, 'I requested to join the division being sent up to Lanark to try an' find ye all, and then, when I read my orders, I saw I had business in this village.'

Joe was smiling, 'Weel, that wis handy! Did they jist tell ye where Ah lived at the office, then?'

Only Fiona noticed the moment's hesitation.

'Aye, they did.' Sam grasped Joe's hand in both of his, 'It's grand tae see ye again, and yer braw family. We must talk again soon, tomorrow?'

Cal was drawn into the arrangements and the brothers agreed to meet the next evening at the Tavern in Lanark.

'Whit a day!' Joe sighed, when he finally dropped onto the mattress beside Fiona. 'Sam. My, it's like a miracle.'

'Ye must be fair pleased,' Fiona whispered, 'efter all these years apairt.'

He raised his arm to encircle her and she cuddled close in his embrace.

'Joe? There's summat Ah should tell ye aboot when he came tae the door.'

'Mmn?'

She took a deep breath, 'Ye ken Sam telt ye he had business in the village? Weel, his business wis at oor door. He's seeking Sean Rafferty.'

Joe's eyes flew open and she felt a spasm of alarm run through his body.

'Jesus!'

'He asked me straight, wis Ah Sarah? Weel, Ah ken noo that he knew fine well Ah wisnae, but he wis wi' anither soldier sae mibbee he had tae act a' official like.'

'Whit else did he ask?'

'Ah cannae mind but the army ken this wis the last place Sarah lived, an' they ken she's merrit tae a deserter. Aw, Joe, whit'll we dae?'

Joe searched the darkness for the answer, the euphoria of the evening completely blown from his mind.

Eventually, exhausted, he murmured, 'Nuthin. We'll dae nuthin.'

***

The housekeeper's office at Charlotte Street was designed with a large interior window giving a view to the kitchen door and directly into the scullery and laundry. This allowed Breen to keep an eye on her servants from her seat, yet, with the door closed, afford privacy for any confidential conversations.

It was into this little room that she invited Toshie to join her to share a pot of tea on the afternoon following Anne Caroline's return to Glasgow.

A maid presented the tray and withdrew, closing the door behind her.

'It's a pleasure to be here again,' Toshie said, taking a seat beside the small coal fire. 'I swear that road frae Lanark grows longer every time we travel. I slept like the deid last night.'

'Are you uncomfortable in New Lanark?' Breen poured the tea.

'Och no, well, not throughout the summer months but the last few weeks have seen ice inside the windows and it's been awfy damp. I make sure the linen's aired by the fire every evening before the bed's remade, but it's a constant battle.'

'Mrs Owen is well, though. You have no concerns? Is there anything I should be aware of to make her more comfortable? Anything you require?'

'We are very well catered for here, Mrs Breen.' Toshie took a sip of scalding liquid and quickly replaced her cup on the saucer to cool.

Breen's office reflected the care she took in the entire house. The light oak chest of drawers was polished like glass, the key rack above it similarly shone, each label positioned to show the lettering, every key gleaming. Above the little fireplace, placed symmetrically, four brass candlesticks held new tallow candles.

'There is a tranquillity to Mr Dale's residences,' Toshie continued. 'Both here and at Rosebank. I fear that is missing at New Lanark.'

'How is that?'

'Well, at the risk of sounding uncharitable, Cooper is no' the most generous minded woman, perhaps that has something to dae wi' it? However, there is also an atmosphere to the place, the whole village ... I'm afraid the people have nae taken to Mr Owen. Not taken to him at all.'

'Yet he seems to find favour with Mr Dale,' an important endorsement in Breen's eyes, ' and, of course, our own dear Mrs Owen. I find it hard to believe that there could be anything to dislike in the young gentleman.'

'Oh, I agree,' Toshie reached for her tea cup again, before thinking better of it as her tongue explored the growing blister on the roof of her mouth. 'He is charming, I have seen it for myself at close quarters, but he drives himself very hard and I imagine he expects others tae work wi' the same dedication.'

'Does Cooper find this too demanding?'

'No, or at least she would never admit it,' they both smiled, 'she is just against him because he does not attend the Church. It's not so much in the house, the maids are maybe a bit dour when he's at home, but that's because their parents are villagers and it's the villagers who show their hard feelings. Ye ken whit like it was in Mr Dale's day? He would barely set foot outside the door than people would be smiling at him, trying to catch a few words from him. Now, I've seen them turning in their steps and walking away rather than bump into Mr Owen.'

'That's a shame.' Breen lifted the tea pot to refill their cups and on seeing Toshie's was virtually untouched, asked, 'is it not to your liking?'

'A little hot. I will wait a while.' She settled back in the chair. 'Mr Owen is making a lot of changes down there, that's what it is all about, I think. His plan to make checks on the cleanliness in all the workers' houses is very unpopular. I've heard shouting and swearing! As loud as you like!'

'Goodness me! from Mr Owen?'

'Oh, good heavens no! From the tenants. They can be a wild and fiery lot, some of the women have a vocabulary you would never expect to hear from a female.' She winced at the memories. 'Mr Owen never raises his voice.'

'Perhaps he'll think better of continuing these inspections?'

'I would nae hold your breath,' Toshie laughed. 'He's a rare one! As long as my mistress is happy I shall bless the Lord and trust in Him to sort it all out.' She took another taste of the tea, deemed it safe and turned the conversation to Breen's arrangements for preparing the house for a new baby.

***

Cal wandered along the line of horses tethered outside the Tavern. It was bitterly cold and he was glad of his heavy jerkin and thick wool scarf while watching sparrows and pigeons vying with mice to glean fallen oats, carelessly discarded from nose-bags.

He never came up to the old town by himself and wouldn't have dreamt of going inside the inn unless in company so he was filling in time outside, waiting for his brothers.

His experienced eye picked out the well bred animals from the working beasts, and he moved from one to the next noting their condition, the tack and how they reacted to him patting them. Some were very head shy, pulling back violently when he raised his hand, a sure sign of ill treatment. Others were so old or worn down that they didn't even register his presence, but there was a beautiful jet black gelding who pricked up his ears and nuzzled gently at Cal's arm when he smoothed its fine coat.

'Hey, Cal!'

He looked up to see a pony and trap rattling down the hill with Joe holding the reins and a plump young woman bouncing in the seat beside him.

When they came to a halt, Cal took hold of the pony's bridle.

'This is a bonnie wee beast!' he couldn't help saying, admiring the grey Highland pony with its flowing, exceedingly long, black mane and tail.

'Steady as a rock!' Joe grinned at him. 'Please meet Miss Melanie Ewing,' he turned to the girl, 'ma brither, ma *younger* brither, Calum.'

Cal politely doffed his cap and Melanie smiled sweetly from under her bonnet, her podgy cheeks dimpling.

'We're meeting her Da' here, he asked me tae bring the cart doon fur him sae they can drive on tae Nemphlar afore it's too dark. Ha'e ye seen 'im aboot?'

'Naw,' Cal fiddled with the buckles on the harness, aware of Melanie's round, inquisitive eyes focused on his every move.

'Tam no' wi' ye? Ah thocht ye were tae esk him?'

'Ah tried ... but ye ken whit he's like?' Joe jumped down from the cart, looking around him. 'Ah'll tell Sam he jist disnae want tae be reminded o' his soldiering days.'

'Did ye ask him why he thocht Sam wis a Major?'

Joe nodded, turning to Cal with an overly frank smile. 'Aye, he wis muddled in the heid when he came back, is all ... Ah, here's Mr Ewing!'

Cal recognised the earnestly honest expression on Joe's face and threw him a sceptical glance, letting him know he was not fooled. Whatever the reason for Tam's mistake, Joe was not saying.

No sooner was the Ewings' pony and trap trotting away into the darkening streets, with Melanie waving and smiling, than Sam came striding into view.

Finding an empty booth in the corner of the noisy, bustling tavern, Sam insisted on paying for a large jug of ale and left them to push his way through the crush to place the order.

'Afore he comes back,' Joe said quickly, leaning close to Cal, 'Ye should be warned tha' he'll mibbee ask aboot Sarah.'

'He kens she's merrit an' awa' frae here.'

'Aye, but Fiona telt me that wis why he chapped oor door in the first place ... he wis sent tae arrest Sean.'

'He ne'er said onthin' aboot tha'! D'ye ken Fiona's richt?'

Joe gave him a withering look, 'She's richt. Wheesht, he's comin' back. We'll see if he brings it up again.'

Sam was confident and loud, unbuttoning his uniform jacket and lounging back, eager to hear more of their time at the mills. They talked of Joe's long apprenticeship and his wish to move his family to a better home and Cal's love of the countryside and horses.

'And whit aboot ye, Sam?' Joe asked. 'Ye happy tae stiy in the army?'

'Aye, fur noo. It's a young man's life, hard going, fierce. We're here fur the winter but then we'll be sent awa' again.' He shrugged, 'If I'm spared the next few years, I fancy buying some land, settling doon.'

'Where?' Cal was interested. A rush of thoughts raced into his mind: working with his brother, tending the land, running his own team of Clydesdales ...

'Anywhere! the world's a big place!' Sam took a long drink. 'Canada's gie like Scotland in parts, if you keep on guid terms with the Iroquois.'

'Whit's tha'? A bear?' Cal was enthralled.

'Naw, they're the natives that live in the woods an' plains. There's six tribes, they call themselves the Six Nations or Iraquois but they're all a bit different. They can look awfy fierce but I respect them an' can understand that they must be mad as hell to have white men seizing their land.'

Sam told them stories of the half naked, tattooed men who skulked invisibly among the vegetation, their heads sometimes shaved to the skin, or decorated with eagle feathers.

'I've only ever seen one squaw, a young woman. Och, she wis the loveliest creature! I can see why they keep their women hidden away.'

'Ye dinnae fancy gettin' merrit yersel' then Sam?' Joe asked.

'I fancy the notion but,' his eyes flashed, guffawing, 'I've known a good few lassies an' would like tae know more. Women seem tae like this gold braid an' it's gie tempting tae take advantage!'

Cal was embarrassed. He didn't want the conversation to turn to him if lassies were the topic.

'Will ye be stiyin' in Lanark,' he said, as casually as possible. 'If ye say yer here through the winter, then?'

'Mibbee no' Lanark, aroond the area though. There's some things tae be done.'

The atmosphere at the table changed. Sam sat forward, frowning, gripping his tankard and staring at the dregs of ale in the base.

'Ye better know, if ye din nae already ... I'm in charge o' hunting down deserters an' the duty's fallen on me to find Sean Rafferty, oor Sarah's man.' He could see from their faces that they already knew. 'I could've given the task to someone else, but ...' he shrugged again. 'Rafferty was released frae prison on conditions, an' he knew he was committed to the service of the King.' Sam rubbed his hands over his face. 'Whit sort o' a man is Rafferty?'

'He's Sarah's husband.' Joe told him. 'Ye cannae ask us tae help ye, Sam. She's bin through sich a lot an' whitever we think o' him, he's oor brither in law in the eyes o' the Lord, he's also faither tae oor kin.'

'They have bairns?'

'Aye, a lass an' a wee lad.'

After their cheery laughter and fast, enthusiastic exchange, they sat in silence, downcast.

Then Sam cleared his throat and took a deep breath before asking, 'Is she happy wi' him?'

Cal just grunted. Memories of his sister's heartbroken sobs were as strong as her ecstatic, shining smiles where the Irishman was concerned.

'Ah cannae say if she's happy or no,' Joe said slowly. 'But Ah tell ye this, she chose tae be wi' him, tae leave us, an' all she knew at the mills. She gathered up her babbies an' wouldnae be persuaded tae stiy. Happy or no', that man means the world tae Sarah, an' Ah'll no' be a pairt in his undoing.'

Cal looked from one to the other. 'Whit wid happen tae him if ye find him?'

'He would be put to trial, military trial, for he had been passed to us from the jail.'

'Sae?' Cal persisted, he wanted to know the worst. 'Whit wid they dae wi' him?'

'The jail again, or hard labour or ... possibly deported to Botany Bay.'

'Ah've heard they hang deserters?' Joe said solemnly.

'Depends whether he's seen as a deserter. That's for the court tae decide.'

Joe leaned across the table, looking earnestly into Sam's eyes. 'Fer yer sister's sake, mon, can ye no' jist drop the matter? Say ye cannae find him?'

'I have ma orders,' Sam felt the rising antagonism in both his brothers and heaved a sigh. ''Tis Rafferty who has committed the offence, no' me. Dinnae gae blamin' me fur his wrong doings!'

'Ye say ye chose tae tak the joab o' huntin' him doon?'

Sam nodded.

'Then can ye no' jist gie it tae anither yin?'

Sam nodded again, saying slowly, 'Aye, but they may not be sae gentle aboot their business.'

A pall of bad feeling brought the evening to an end and they parted outside with less effusive affection than the previous night. Sam walked off towards his billet in the Bloomgate and Cal and Joe struck out along the Wellgate.

Bracing themselves against the cold breeze, each of them struggled with the problem.

Unwittingly, Sarah, the one member of the family not present, was the centre of attention. Her choice of husband threatened to drive a wedge between her newly reunited brothers, causing a fricton which they could already sense.

Joe kicked at the ground, sending a spray of stones scattering into the shadows.

'Damn Rafferty! Damn him tae hell! He's caused nought but pain in this family frae the first. Mibbee it wid be fur the best if Sam found him ... get him oot oor lives.'

Cal tramped along beside him; winding their way down the hillside to New Lanark beneath the undulating grey light of the moon.

The raucous tavern and Sam's stories of peculiar tribes and faraway lands unsettled the young man. A strong desire to love and respect his new-found brother conflicted with the realisation that Sam was virtually a stranger.

Cal was suspicious of strangers.

Turning his mind to another subject, he asked, 'Sae, oot wi' it? Afore we met Sam, ye were nae tellin' the truth aboot Tam.'

'If Ah tell ye, yer tae swear niver tae tell anither soul?'

'Ah swear!'

'It's a lot aboot nuthin ... but Tam dis nae see it like that. He didnae lose his airm fighting the French.'

Cal stopped dead in his tracks, mouth gaping.

Joe gestured to Cal to keep walking. 'Och he fought battles ... he's as brave as they come. He telt me fer the first time aboot nearly starving in the snows in Flanders an' fearsome charges at the enemy. He sed his regiment wis supportin' the Duke of York!'

The brothers exchanged a look of admiration for their friend: assisting Royalty in the thick of war.

'Tam sailed hame wi' life and limb, as he telt me, praying tae God fer saving him.'

'Sae whit happened tae his airm?'

'It were an accident. In a field in England while they were training. Years efter being in battle.'

'An accident? Weel ... why did nae he say?'

'He thocht he wis gaun tae die an' wanted his Ma an' Pa tae be prood o' him. Thocht it wis a grander story tae be wounded in battle than crushed under a canon during practice ... in Engand. He made up a lot of things ... said whitever he wanted 'cause he thocht he'd soon be deid. He wis ashamed o' his carelessness.'

'Ashamed? Away! He's nuthin' tae be ashamed o'.'

'Whither we think sae or no, that's how he feels. It's better we say nuchin.'

'Ah'll no' breathe a word.' Cal said quietly, plodding along. He knew the feeling of shame all too well.

Even when he told himself it was not his fault that he was beaten and treated cruelly throughout the terrible months he spent away from New Lanark, he still wanted to keep them hidden: secret.

It was with relief that he glimpsed the rows of smoking chimney pots in the valley below him. Their familiarity brought warmth to his heart, easing his anxiety.

He wished Sarah no ill, nor Sam, nor Tam, but their lives were so unlike his own that he couldn't even begin to resolve their dilemmas.

Tomorrow the sun would rise, he would go to the forge, stoke the fire and carry on as usual.

***

On a frosty November afternoon, the fire crackled and hissed below the magnificent carved mantelpiece in the drawing room of Dale's city mansion. On one side of the hearth, snoring gloriously, the master of the house dozed in his cushioned chair. On the other side sat his elderly sister in law, Margaret Dale, her be-wigged head bowed low in sleep, blissfully unaware of her open mouth, dribbling slightly.

Around them, Jean and her sisters were trying to amuse themselves with books and embroidery or taking it in turns to practice new pieces on the piano with the soft peddle firmly depressed.

The whole family were spending the day in a state of expectancy since being informed that Anne Caroline was confined to her room; the baby was on its way. This was earlier than anticipated and a message was immediately dispatched to Owen.

No-one could settle to their routines and the main meal was eaten out of necessity rather than enjoyment, their thoughts and attention focused on any signs of someone approaching with news.

Even the customary walk on the Green was postponed, despite Giggs becoming quite cross with Julia and Margaret for wasting one of the few dry, bright days of the autumn. The girls simply refused to leave the house in case they missed the great occasion, appealing to their father to be allowed to forego their constitutional.

Dale relented, believing the baby would arrive soon and the walk could then be enjoyed. However, as the hours passed by, his eldest daughter's cries could be heard becoming more and more desperate, even through the solid walls and long corridors of the great house. When their aunt arrived to join the vigil, not wishing the younger girls to become alarmed, she suggested they all gather in the drawing room to play the piano, sing songs and pass the time together by the fire.

It was into this quiet domestic setting that Robert Owen arrived from Lanark.

'Good evening,' Owen went straight to David Dale who was just waking up and attempting to push himself out of his chair to receive his son in law. 'I made haste as soon as I received your note,' he shook Dale's proffered hand and nodded his head politely to Mrs Margaret Dale and his sisters in law. 'What is the news? May I beg your leave to go straight to my wife's side?'

'There is no news yet,' Dale informed him. 'It is best to leave the women folk to these matters and remain here with us.'

Owen's expressive face was shadowed with concern. 'It has been a long time ... is everything all right? Is the doctor in attendance?'

'Babies take their own time to enter the world, Mr Owen,' Margaret Dale said, soothingly. 'The physician is perfectly content that there is nothing untoward and, of course, Mackintosh is with Anne Caroline ... that maid has many years of experience. Please do not worry yourself unnecessarily.'

Dale called for hot chocolate drinks to be brought, the lamps and chandeliers were lit, the fire replenished and the windows shuttered against the dark evening. It should have been a pleasant and restful interlude but they were all growing increasingly apprehensive. None more so than Owen who, normally calm and unruffled in his manner, paced the room clasping and unclasping his hands, too preoccupied to join in with the conversation.

A knock on the door heralded Renwick, ushering the surgeon into the room.

'It is a boy!' Palmer proclaimed. 'A healthy boy!'

Owen seized the man's hand, 'Thank you, sir, thank you! May I see my wife?'

'You may.'

Owen rushed into the hall and was already at the foot of the grand staircase when the doctor continued. 'Mrs Owen is very tired, it has not been an easy delivery. She will require a great deal of rest but I expect her to be fully restored before the end of the month.'

Anne Caroline was, indeed, exhausted.

'Robert!' she cried feebly, 'We have a little boy. Oh, my dearest husband, we have a son, our very own son.'

'Oh! There he is ... ' Owen kissed his wife and gazed upon the little bundle in her arms. 'I could not have imagined a baby to be so small and so ...' he beamed at her, eyes bright with emotion, 'pink!'

She laughed involuntarily, catching her breath in a gasp: every muscle in her body ached. Intense sensations of love and overwhelming relief surged through her, throwing caution and propriety to the wind.

'I surely thought I was to die, Robert.' Tears brimmed in her eyes, 'the Lord has saved me and blessed us with a son.' She raised a hand, weak and trembling, stroking back her husband's hair and tracing a finger lightly down his cheek, 'Oh ... how I love you.'

Toshie was busy by the washstand, not wishing to intrude on the intimate scene. She was worn out. There had been times during the day when she feared for Anne Caroline but now it was over, the baby was born and although the infant was smaller than she would have liked, it appeared to be perfectly healthy.

Owen's hair had grown long in recent months and now fell around his face, catching on his high collar. He pushed it back behind his ears, leaning close to his new son, tenderly drawing the shawl away to look upon his face. Anne Caroline lay back, gazing on them both.

For a moment, they were not Mr and Mrs Owen, he was not the owner of a large cotton mill with thousands of people in his employ, they were simply a man and a woman, amazed by the miracle they created together.

Watching them out the corner of her eye, Toshie thought how young they appeared in the cosy, dimly lit bedroom. Memories of attending her previous mistress, Anne Caroline's mother, blurred with the present scene.

Lives came into being and passed on.

'God Bess you,' she murmured.

***

In January 1801, Great Britain officially embraced Ireland and became the United Kingdom.

All the arguments and hopes which filled the newspapers and coffee houses when the Bill was passing through Parliament the previous summer, came bubbling to the surface again. It remained to be seen whether this amalgamation of the countries would bring anything other than theoretical peace to the rebellious Irish.

War continued to rage on the continent with Austria and the Russian Empire battling against newly revolutionised France. Taking advantage of Napoleon's absence they at first succeeded in forcing the French troops to retreat. However, hearing of the defeats, Napoleon returned, abandoning his regiments in Egypt and immediately taking charge of military affairs. He wasted no time in dispatching General Moreau to force the Germans into signing an armistice.

Napoleon's superior military planning took him into the Alps, where he personally joined the front lines.   Crossing the mountains on a mule, he used clever strategies to empower his troops to complete winning campaigns in Italy, compelling the Austrians to withdraw.

The social chaos and financial cost of the war in these European countries impinged harshly upon Britain's trade. Dale spent a great deal of the winter closeted in meetings with his fellow directors of the Glasgow Chamber of Commerce. Scottish merchants were caught in a constant struggle to find new markets and maintain competitive prices while both their customers and suppliers fell away as fast as taxes were raised.

Throughout the coldest months, Anne Caroline stayed in the comfort of her father's house with her new son, Daniel. Owen visited regularly, becoming a familiar figure among Dale's friends and colleagues. His enthusiasm and quick wits made him interesting company at dinner tables, business functions and even in the offices of the Royal Bank of Scotland, where he could often be found with Scott Moncrieff.

When Owen was in Glasgow, a tangible relief could be felt amongst the inhabitants of New Lanark.

Their new employer's plans to improve their lives were still creating a great deal of bad feeling. The task of inspecting the workers' lodgings was slowly being passed to the occupants themselves. While this was supposed to alleviate the conflict, it was turning out to be a difficult process to implement.

In general, the tenants who naturally kept their rooms in order, complied quite happily, but those who took domestic dirt and disorder for granted, were determinedly set against being judged by their peers. For many, especially the Highlanders, it was hard enough to cope with living in such a heavily populated, industrial community. They were used to peaceful glens with a patch of land around their croft to grow food or keep animals and the freedom of great swathes of countryside to roam and hunt.

Living cheek by jowl with hundreds of strangers was as difficult to adjust to as the fourteen hours spent in the mills every day.

Slowly, with Owen's uniquely patient encouragement and absolute faith in his orders being carried out, less and less households barred their doors.

His initial concern for the fabric of the buildings and the serious overcrowding within each room was also being overcome. By setting teams of men to renovate and fit out rooms which were vandalised and abandoned, he was able to offer them to families where several generations were presently squashed in together. Instead of twelve bodies sharing the space, this could bring it down to six, making it easier to comply with his new regime of hygiene.

The most disgruntled members of the village chewed their tobacco and complained that this arrangement meant the Company could ask for double the rent, where the same family used to only pay for one room. However, no such grievances were heard from the individuals who found themselves enjoying a better standard of living.

Rosie took on the job of checking the rooms which opened off her own tenement stairwell. She volunteered readily, comfortable in the knowledge that, apart from the Shearers in the basement, most of her neighbours were friends and competent housewives.

Armed with the special little book and pencil she was given for the purpose, she wrote a clear report on the state of each room on the day of inspection. She was proud of her duty and tripped up and down the stairs each week, knocking on the doors as if she was the housekeeper of a grand mansion.

Early in the new year, Sam Scott turned up to see Joe at Ewing's yard and announced he was leaving again. Although this parting was only expected to be for a month or so rather than years, it still left a void.

Each of the siblings reacted in a different way.

For Joe, it caused uneasiness because he was sure Sam was pursuing his orders to find Rafferty. It played on his mind. While chiselling and sorting stone, walking to his work or driving the pony and trap, he found himself forming arguments both in favour of capturing Sean and also for leaving him at large so he could live with Sarah.

Cal reflected on how exciting his elder brother's life must be and in contrast, how pathetic his own simple existence must seem to someone who fought battles and travelled to exotic places.

It was not that Cal was jealous of Sam's experiences, for the very thought of the rough, violent life in the army filled him with horror. It was the realisation of how dissimilar they were which he found disappointing. During their long separation, any time he thought of his brother he saw him as an extension of himself, just older. Perhaps more like Joe or Sarah in personality. So, it came as a jolt to discover his own flesh and blood to be a bold, strident man with weathered skin, searching eyes and a loyalty to his regiment so unyielding that he chose it before his sister's happiness.

Rosie's reaction was one of delight at having her brother in her life again, already filled with excited anticipation for his promised return.

Everyone she spoke to was informed of Sam's startling arrival in New Lanark. No soldier had ever been so brave, marched across such dangerous lands or risen more swiftly up the ranks. Suddenly, she could rightfully lay claim to a close connection with this handsome, scarlet clad Lieutenant of the 26th Scottish Rifles, the Cameronians.

This brought her more status on the factory floor than Jenny Moir's uncle being promoted to under gamekeeper at Bonnington Estate, and far exceeded Tillie Smith's doubtful claim to being the illegitimate grand-daughter of a nameless Earl.

If Sam was away seeking to bring Sarah's husband to justice, Rosie felt little compassion for Sean. Like Joe, while she did not wish her sister any more heartache, she believed Sean Rafferty should take his punishment. If that meant he was banished to the ends of the earth then Rosie would shed no tears.

In April a warm spell of settled weather enticed blossom trees into flower and the first of the year's midges danced over rivers and lochs. In the towns and cities, the streets bustled once again with handcarts, hawkers and beggars.

There was better news regarding the war with reports spreading daily of a naval offensive against Holland.

'Splendid news!' Dale boomed across his study to Owen, slapping his hand down on the broadsheet spread out in front of him. 'We have victory at Copenhagen!'

'Aha!' Owen was as delighted as Dale. 'Now we can break up this League of Neutrality Russia forced upon us and properly enforce a blockade of France.'

'Indeed, the seas will be ours again.' Dale sat back, thoughtfully. 'It appears it was the notorious Vice Admiral Nelson who won the battle. At least he has done one thing right for he lacks any of the morals I would expect of a man in such a high position.'

'Nelson does appear to have an unconventional private life,' Owen mused. 'We can be thankful he carries out his naval duties somewhat better.'

'I pray for his poor wife,' Dale said quietly. 'She is a lady of great dignity to withstand the humiliation of having her husband living openly with his mistress. Not only that, Lady Emma Hamilton is married and they have set up home as a *ménage a trois* ... with her mother living with them. I ask you? They have a child now! Dear Lord, what a sinful household that poor wee soul will be raised amongst. What God forsaken society do they inhabit?'

'I believe Lady Hamilton received little or no education,' said Owen, 'and is using the one asset she possesses to better herself in life. Unfortunately, her pretty face has led her into the wrong company, being passed from one man to another. I understand from my wife that they are the most famous people in Britain today.'

'Astounding,' Dale shook his head. 'But I do not believe Lady Hamilton is an innocent victim, nor stupid. The depravity of human nature never fails to sadden me. I shall pray for their salvation and preach the word of the Lord in every effort to save others from such a sinful path.'

Owen decided it was time to change the subject.

'Sir, as you know, we are leaving for New Lanark tomorrow and I would like to speak with you regarding your northerly ventures, Stanley Mills and Spinningdale.'

'Ah, yes. Speak away!'

'In conversations with Mr George MacIntosh I hear that he is travelling through the Highlands in the summer months. I would like to propose, if it suited both yourself and that gentleman, that I would accompany him. It would allow me to see, on your behalf, the state of the businesses and then I can report to you more fully on my return.'

'An excellent plan, my dear fellow. Have you put it to MacIntosh yet?'

'No, sir. Perhaps you would like to broach the subject? He may not wish to have me as a travelling companion and it would be easier for him to refuse if I was not present. Do you not agree?'

Dale roared with laughter. 'Believe me, if MacIntosh did not want you with him he would have no trouble telling you to your face! However, I shall speak with him ... leave it with me.'

The next day, after fond farewells to both family and Charlotte Street's faithful servants, the Owens boarded their carriage and set off along the familiar road to Lanark.

Sharing the duty between them, Anne Caroline and Toshie held the baby reverently in their arms, bracing themselves through especially bumpy parts of the journey. The infant was usually placid and biddable but the constant movement of the coach often brought lusty cries.

After one ear-splitting outburst, Toshie cast a fearful eye to her master. Most gentlemen would be grinding their teeth and shouting over the din, ordering something to be done to appease the infant and stop the racket.

Owen caught her glance.

'Take no heed on my account,' he smiled. 'Babies cry.'

Awaiting their arrival in New Lanark, Cooper made strenuous efforts to ensure the house was warm and the baby's sleeping arrangements, a cot in the master bedroom, were as gracefully arranged as possible. She was nervous of very small babies and, her bedroom being directly above the cot, hoped Master Daniel was a sound sleeper.

Within a few days the household found their duties fell into a routine and soon Anne Caroline felt suitably relaxed to take short walks around the village or join her husband conducting tours of the mills.

Owen was eager to show his wife the latest improvements, point out where changes were proposed and ask her opinion of the cleaner streets. Sometimes, they would host a select group of visitors, providing refreshments and arranging with the teachers to put on a recital from the school children. Owen was particularly in his element on the factory floor discussing the merits of his new methods and machinery while his wife entertained the ladies of the party.

The tourists always enjoyed their visits and Owen took great satisfaction from their comments. He was as aware as his under managers, and even his own wife, that he was not generally liked within the village, but he knew he must persevere. The upgrading of his little community was only just beginning and yet the benefits could already be seen.

One morning, a week or so after returning from Glasgow, he set off early for a meeting with the Edmonstones at Corehouse regarding the ongoing plans to build the weir. The river was running low following prolonged dry weather, necessitating the closing of the sluices to Mill Three. He wished to invite the two spinster sisters and their estate manager to accompany him to the riverbank and discuss the problem while it could easily be demonstrated.

Anne Caroline stretched luxuriously in her bed.

Bird song carried in through the open window along with the muffled rumble of heavy horses pulling a load up the hill behind the house. Her mind wandered lazily between choices of outfits for the day and arrangements for her husband's thirtieth birthday.

She had already spoken to her father regarding holding a surprise celebration at Rosebank and he welcomed the idea whole heartedly. But who to invite? would a luncheon be best or now the days were longer, perhaps an evening dance?

She also wished to procure a special present for him but was finding it hard to think of anything he would like yet did not already own. This subject had been discussed at length with her sisters and Rosemary before leaving the city and remembering her friend's words brought her to mind.

News of Rosemary's new baby daughter arrived the previous day and although a quick, congratulatory message was immediately dispatched, another, more personal letter required to be written. How delightful it would be to raise their children together over the coming years.

Anne Caroline was roused from her thoughts by the boisterous shouts of workmen. Startled, she realised she must have dozed off. She sat up, dazed, her eyes darting to Daniel's cot: he was still fast asleep.

He was such a good baby, his last feed was just before sunrise. She had nursed him quietly, happily accompanied by her husband's rhythmic breathing from where he slept beside her and the melodious dawn chorus echoing among the woodlands cocooning the village.

She looked at the wall clock.

No, that couldn't be? She could not have been sleeping all that time?

Throwing the covers aside, she ran to the cot.

Daniel lay in his tightly wrapped shawl, eyes closed, his black lashes fanned on his cheeks. Perfect.

She held her breath,

He was perfect.

Perfectly still.

Her eyes bulged in terror, a scream growing within her, causing her whole body to shake. She grasped her baby and pulled him to her, knowing the truth straightaway but her brain refused to accept what she was seeing ...

Holding him close, she rushed to the door gasping and screaming for Toshie. She knew it was no use, she could scream for help, beseech God in her desperate cries, but no-one could help her.

Baby Daniel Dale Owen was dead.

Chapter Three

"Tears are the silent language of grief."
Voltaire

Joe slung his satchel over his shoulder and left Ewing's yard to set off along the grassy track towards New Lanark. With less than a month to go before the summer solstice, the evenings were light enough to work until late and he was satisfied to be making good progress on his latest commission.

Passing the meadow, he noticed Melanie leading their cow towards the byre to be milked. She raised her free hand and waved, walking slowly through the knee high grass as if wading through a lake; moths and pollen rising like a mist around her in the low rays of the setting sun. Joe returned the wave and walked on, his footsteps muffled among the lush green grass scattered with drifts of rich yellow buttercups and blue forget-me-nots flowering above a carpet of starry white daisies and swathes of clover. The flowers stirred memories of his sister, Sarah.

He missed Sarah.

Images swam before him of her as a child; grinning up at him, gap-toothed, her golden hair crowned with daisy chains or trails of honeysuckle. She could never resist plucking a pretty bloom to tuck behind her ear, even as an adult.

'Hey! Joe!' Hidden in the half light, the figure of a man scrambled to his feet from his seat on the craggy roots of a tree.

'Sam!'

The brothers slapped each other heartily on the back, grinning broadly.

'I didnae want tae disturb yer work,' Sam said, brushing at the moss and grass on his breeches. 'I've bin waiting here thinking ye must pass by. If ye'd not come soon I was heading doon tae the mills.'

'It's grand tae see ye,' an anxious note crept into Joe's voice. 'Did ye find oor Sarah?'

'No. Not a sign o' her or her man. I've put in a report but I can nae say that will be the end of it, Rafferty's still an absconder. He'll be in a city somewhere, hiding among the crowds, but we followed every avenue we could think o' and turned up nothin'. He's maybe changed his name or left the country. It's no' up tae me now, I'm no' longer charged wi' finding him.'

'Whit d'ye mean?'

'The regiment is moving out, we have our next orders. We are sailing to Egypt.'

'Egypt?' Joe was immediately fearful. 'How lang fur?'

'Och, din nae look sae worried!' Sam flung his arms wide and shrugged. 'As lang as it takes. A year? Mibbee two?'

'An' when d'ye gae?'

'In the morning.'

'Whit! But Rosie an' Cal will be wantin' tae see ye ... an' wee Donnie ... but Ah wager he'll be sleepin' the noo ...'

'Say ma goodbyes fur me? I can nae be doing wi' goodbyes.'

Joe nodded. 'Weel, Ah'm fair pleased ye came tae see me afore ye left.'

'I wanted tae give ye this,' Sam pulled out a money bag. 'Tak it Joe, I want ye an' the family tae have something frae me.'

'We dinnae need yer money.' Joe was offended. 'Ye've earnt it yersel', keep it.'

Standing in the dusk, Joe saw the sudden hurt on his brother's face. For all his swagger and smart uniform, a forlorn, vulnerable expression changed Sam's features.

'Please, Joe. Jist tak it. Put in yon saving's bank in the village. I ken ye din nae need it ...' his mouth twisted as he wrestled with emotions, brows drawn down. 'But ... I need ye tae tak it. I promised mesel' I would help ye all, Ma, Sarah ... wee Meg ... an' I didnae. I left ye all. You ... you Joe, you took care of them. Ye've done a grand job an' money can niver take the place o' all the years ye've spent keeping the family.' Sam shoved the bag into Joe's hands. 'Give some tae Rosie an' that sappy man o' hers, an' yer lass can find a use fur it wi' all yer bairns. Use it.'

Reluctantly, Joe lifted the flap of his satchel and dropped the bag inside. It was heavy.

'Ah'll keep it fer ye then, till ye come bak.'

Sam took a step closer, 'No ye won't,' he said harshly. 'Listen tae me, Joe, ye'll mak guid use o' it. Ye say I've earnt it? Aye, I have, an' sometimes I thought the task would kill me. They pay me fer puttin' ma life in the way o' danger an' they gie me board and lodging, clothe me, train me ... Ye want tae know how I became an officer, well, I'll tell ye. I didn't care if I lived or died, I threw myself into the army with all ma heart for I had no one else to care aboot. They say I was brave ... huh! A brave man is a man who knows he may be killed, feels the fear o' it and yet carries on anyway. No' me, I did nae care so there was no fear, no bravery.'

'Whit did ye dae?'

'I was always pushing mesel', if summat needed doin', I did it. We were at sea, making a short crossing near New Foundland in a convoy of four small ships an' we were spotted by a French frigate.

'It was gusty, rain lashin' in oor faces an' heavy cloud makin' it gloomy. They were always on the look-out for more ships, as was oor navy, an' we knew they were gaun tae have us ... take us prisoner.'

Sam swallowed, tense. 'We were the smallest in the convoy so to protect the others we changed direction and sailed towards her. Richt enough, they were fast upon us, canon fire across the bow, no' tae damage us but we got the message! We only had six canon and fired ... kept firing ... Och it were fierce ... hurling ropes an' swarmin' bodies on the deck. It was all screamin' an' creaking, shots being fired an' choking on gun smoke ... we were under orders tae hold oor positions and fire but wi' the rolling waves ... the shots were wasted. With swords drawn it was hand tae hand an' they were nae daft! It was the officers they were aimin' fur an' oor Captain went doon!

'A young Major was standing beside the Captain when he fell. Poor lad ... he was shakin' ... frozen wi' fear. I could see he was to be the next under the Frenchie's sword an' threw

73

mesel' across the deck to reach him, managin' tae cut doon his attacker moments before the blow fell. I'll ne'er forget the look in the Major's eyes; sheer terror. He was jist a lad, more used tae garrison duties, organising parades an' escortin' the Mayor's daughter in the ball room ...

'The next thing, he'd disappeared! There was nae time tae e'en think ... I was that mad at the thocht o' losing the ship that I jist kept slashing at all comers.

'The wind was growin' an' I saw the ropes breaking loose. I thocht we were tearing awa' from the French ship until I saw they were desperately cutting themselves loose. The big frigate's sails were billowing, pushing it side on into the rising waves and in danger of capsizing if it stayed strapped tae us.

'It was the weather ... or God, as some would have it, who saved us that day! Seein' their vessel sailing away from us, the French soldiers stranded on our deck surrendered themselves.

'I found oor young Major below deck, cowering in his bed, an' the other officers were either deid or sorely wounded ... sae, I took command and we limped for land.

'The official report stated I saved the Major's life and due to the serious condition of more senior officers, I was recognised for assisting in holding the ship for the King. It recommended me for a commission.' He grunted. 'The other officers were also promoted ...' he winked at Joe, 'The young Major made Captain.'

Joe was listening in stunned silence.

'Weel,' Sam grinned, sheepishly, 'ye wanted tae know how I was made an officer.'

'Ah dinna ken whit tae say. Ah'm tha' prood o' ye.'

'Jist doin' ma joab! Noo, it's near dark, ye'll be missed at hame. Mak sure ye use tha' money ... get ma nephews claes an' books fer their lessons. Buy something pretty things fer yer bonnie wife! If ye din nae ...' he laughed to break the force of his words, 'I'll be mighty angry wi' ye when I return!'

Joe knew when to give in, taken aback by the strength of feeling in Sam's voice.

'Whit aboot yon land ye wanted tae buy when ye leave the army?'

'I'll see tae that when the day comes.'

The bell in the clock tower in old Lanark started tolling the hour: eleven o'clock.

'Ye had best get hame,' Sam said again, brightly, determined to part on a high note despite the under current of raw emotion.

'Aye. But ye tak care o' yersel', Sam! Din nae leave it sae lang!'

They embraced warmly, outwardly cheerful, then Joe set off at a brisk pace down the shadowy lane into the valley.

Sam listened to his footsteps receding into the night until they became indiscernible among the gentle breeze rustling the hedgerow.

He looked at the dark shifting shapes of nearby trees and then far away to the horizon, black against a silvery grey night sky. This was his homeland; soft, lush, fragrant. Breathing in the scented Scottish air, he savoured the memory and wondered if he would ever see his brother again.

***

Cooper stood in front of the range watching for the first signs of the milk starting to foam and boil. It was oppressively hot in the kitchen even with the door to the scullery and the back door propped open to allow a draught.

She dabbed the sweat from her forehead, smoothing stray hairs back under her muslin cap and sighing from both the heat and the turmoil within her mind.

In the weeks since baby Daniel died she was tortured with feelings of guilt. Had she done something wrong to cause the tragedy? Was the house not clean enough? The bedding not aired sufficiently? The infant's linen tainted in some manner by her method of laundry?

Worst of all were the recollections of her uncharitable thoughts when, drained of energy, she was roused from her sleep in the early hours of the morning by his hungry cries. How could she have been so selfish?

She sought forgiveness in prayer at every opportunity and forced herself to be even more diligent in her work. Witnessing her employers' personal distress was eating away at her, creating a physical discomfort which banished her appetite and left her tossing and turning through the night.

On noticing Cooper's dreadful pallor and visibly trembling hands, Toshie enquired after her health. This kindly gesture was greeted with a curt rebuttal and stoic silence, inviting no further mention of her condition.

The milk began to rise up the sides of the pan and was skilfully drawn to the side in the nick of time before overflowing.

The new minister from Lanark was coming down to the village to take the Sunday service that afternoon and Cooper was anxious to attend. Perhaps, she could seek a private word with him and he could offer her comfort by guiding her to enlightening chapters in the scriptures.

Upstairs, Anne Caroline was also preparing to leave the house. She too, wished to hear the minister's sermon.

After the devastating shock and accompanying tears and hysteria, Anne Caroline bore her grief quietly.

Her initial reaction had been to run to her father. She yearned for his warmth and wise words, to be enveloped in his protective arms, lay her head against his familiar broad chest and breathe his distinctive cologne, as she used to as a child. However, within a few days of Daniel's death she realised her place was with Robert. He was just as deeply affected by their son's death, only he masked it by his masculine desire to lessen her misery.

Letters from her father and sisters arrived almost daily, sending affectionate, supportive messages and inviting her to come 'home' whenever she wished. At first, she could not muster the strength or willpower to even reply but when she did, it was to thank them for their kind thoughts but she simply could not bear to leave her husband and travel to Rosebank.

'Home' was now with Robert in New Lanark.

Only Robert saw the intensity of her loss.

Alone together, he would hold her as she sobbed, his young shoulders taking the burden of their bereavement as he struggled to remain strong for them both. Each knew the other's pain and sharing this personal tragedy so early in their married life brought a new found closeness.

Her days were spent waiting for the moment when she could drop the social etiquette of formal mourning and lie in her husband's arms, letting the tears flow; talking quietly together in the privacy of the marital bed.

Every day, she thanked God for Robert's endless patience.

It soon became clear that she was pregnant again. When she told him she was carrying another baby she admitted her mixed feelings; pleasure in knowing a new life was growing within her but fearing for the health of the infant and concern that no matter how wonderful it was, it could never replace Daniel.

However, as they talked, Robert's natural optimism persuaded her of the many reasons they were fortunate to look to the future.

'Losing our first born will forever be a tragedy to us, my dearest,' He told her fondly, reaching for her hand and lacing his fingers between hers while they lay in bed. 'He cannot be replaced, nor should we even expect that, for he was as individual as you or I.' She moved her head on the pillow to see his strong profile in the moonlight. 'It is right to feel this pain,' he said slowly, the curved sihouette of his eyelashes glistening, 'for we cared for him so very deeply and he will not be forgotten, but our new baby must not suffer from comparison. He or she must be seen for themselves. Our early years mould us for the rest of our lives so we must strive to raise our child to feel only love and happiness, not burden it with our sorrow for the passing of its brother.'

Her husband's words brought comfort but she also sought solace in the words of the Lord and spent long hours reading passages from the Holy Bible. Despite his own views on the Church, Owen understood the importance she placed in her religion and arranged for the Mill's chaplain to visit his wife every afternoon.

Today, the minister from St Nicholas' Church in the old market town of Lanark was addressing the village congregation.

Dressing formally, with a delicate black lace veil draped from her hat to partially conceal her face, Anne Caroline took her place in the front row of the large meeting room. Toshie accompanied her and at her mistress's insistence, Cooper was invited to join them so the household sat together.

The villagers noticed Mrs Owen's presence straightaway because she usually worshipped 'up in Lanark'. Tongues wagged, whispers rippled through the crowd, pitying her for her recent loss, appraising her clothes and demeanour but also criticising her husband for not being supportive.

Anne Caroline heard snatches of their hurtful remarks and wished they knew how wrong they were about their employer. The very fact that he was not there, sitting beside her, coloured their views which made it hard to explain. It was on leaving the service and receiving warm, compassionate looks and smiles that she became aware of a new role she could play, one of intermediary between her husband and the people in their community.

It was obvious they liked her yet just as clear that they disliked Owen and his new managers. She knew the reasons for these attitudes. Most of the residents of the village held her father in such high esteem that just by being his daughter gave her a privileged position. Unfortunately for Owen, it was not only his lack of religion which counted against him, it was his sweeping, unwelcome changes, including extending their working hours and prying into their home life.

Maybe, she wondered, when she left the meeting rooms and walked towards her front door, maybe she should always attend the church services in the village? Instead of staying for weeks with her father in the city or at Rosebank, she should be here, living amongst the community and supporting her husband.

It was a bold thought. While Owen was working wholeheartedly to produce the results demanded of him by his partners in Manchester, she was continuing to see the little New Lanark house as the temporary holiday residence it was in her childhood. Now, since this personal tragedy, the reality of her life was becoming clearer. It was not enough to decorate a few rooms or hire new staff, this was not a game she was playing for a few months.

When Owen came home later that evening, he found Anne Caroline writing letters in the parlour.

'How are you, my dear?' he asked, going to his desk and neatly flicking through a pile of papers in search of a particular letter.

'I am a little better.' She watched him objectively, noticing how tired he looked, his rather long nose accentuated by the angle of the daylight from the window, a lock of hair falling untidily across his cheek.

Then he looked up, half smiling; the expression immediately animating his face, sparkling in his eyes.

'Indeed, you look more relaxed.'

She laid down her quill. 'I am beginning to see beyond the darkness. For the first time today, my mind was not completely absorbed with Daniel.' She hurried on, 'I feel a little guilty admitting this to you, or even to myself, for it seems as if I am forgetting him, which I am not, not at all ... but I think I am beginning to come alive again, for I fear I almost died myself ...' there was a catch in her voice, 'on that awful day.'

Holding the letter to one side, he gave her his full attention.

'It will become easier to bear.'

She drew a lace edged handkerchief from her cuff and dabbed her eyes, 'I pray to Our Lord God for strength.'

Owen pursed his lips, 'If it comforts you to do so,' he said, softly, 'but I am sure you will find your own strength.'

She did not argue that any strength she might find would be God given, instead she lifted the lid of her writing slope and placed her papers inside, saying, 'You must be hungry, shall I ring for something to be brought?'

Cooper took the orders for a light meal to be prepared for her master and hurried back down the stairs to the kitchen. Her plan to speak with the minister had not transpired but his sermon provided much food for thought and she was in a more comfortable frame of mind. She was also relieved to notice her mistress in better spirits.

Slowly, the Owen household was starting to recover.

***

During the heat wave of early summer, production at New Lanark was seriously curtailed. In the worst periods only Mill One could be kept supplied with a sufficient head of water, necessitating Owen to take the unprecedented decision of keeping the jennies running throughout the night.

The practicalities of organising extra shifts for workers from the other mills to be put onto unfamiliar machines caused lengthy delays and interruptions. Owen was on call to deal with many of the problems, day and night, knowing all stages in the production line due to his experience in Manchester.

Actually working on the factory floor gave him the opportunity to assess the efficiency of his workforce, firsthand.

He was satisfied with most of what he saw yet became increasingly concerned by other aspects. In particular, he was ill at ease with the use of the very young orphans.

From the start of his management, he stopped the arrangement of bringing in paupers from city hospitals and Poor Houses and refused to hire children less than ten years of age. However, true to the assurances he gave Dale, those infants who were already apprenticed to New Lanark remained in employment.

His Manchester partners would not entertain Owen's proposal to spare the orphans from the work rooms until the age of ten, declaring it unreasonable: if they did not work, then the Company should not be expected to provide their board and lodging.

So, there were still children of no more than five or six years old scurrying between the machines, their bare feet white and slippery with cotton dust. They were tired and fractious, bickering between themselves; their tiny faces pinched, dark rings round their eyes.

Owen felt responsible for them, disturbed by colluding in their situation. Although he gave strict instructions that none of his Boarders were to be struck or mistreated, he was fully aware that when his back was turned some Overseers disobeyed his rules.

'I would dearly like to remove all the little ones from the work rooms,' he told Anne Caroline one evening when he joined her by the fireside. 'It is just not right for them to be among all that noise and dust for so many hours. When I see the older children who have spent all their lives in the factory, I see so many who are deformed or barely grown, with stunted limbs and poor health.'

'But they have the best of food here,' Anne Caroline said, surprised. 'My father was most insistent on that issue.'

'Oh yes, I grant you, in comparison to the scraps and gruel they would be given in a Poor House or begging on the street, they certainly enjoy nutritious meals. Yet, they spend every day working indoors.'

She looked at him quizzically, 'Compared to other mills, I understand that they have a better life than others.'

'Just because it is better than the others does not make it right. There are mills with putrid air where sixteen hours of labour are imposed! Deplorable! Today, I saw one infant asleep on his feet. That is not only wrong, it is dangerous practice.' He sighed. 'The dormitories are very crowded as well. It is most unsatisfactory having them crammed in together, three in a bed. I have proposed the addition of a new building to house the orphans.'

'You are going to build? Where? The village already fills all the available space on the hillside.'

'I have identified an area beside New Buildings. It should be simple enough to construct in the same manner as all the rest and if my partners are agreeable, I will push ahead with these plans before the year is out.'

'Goodness!' his wife smiled, lovingly. 'Another building in New Lanark. Papa will be most intrigued to learn of this development.'

Owen nodded emphatically, his eyes on the glowing coals in the grate, his mind on the latest sketches. 'I am sure he will approve.'

'Shall I inform him in my next letter, my dear?'

'Perhaps we should wait until I hear from Manchester that the matter is decided ... I should know within the week so we could tell your father when we visit Rosebank.'

Anne Caroline agreed and the conversation turned to their plans for the coming month. She would be staying with her father while Owen went off on his Highland expedition with George MacIntosh to visit Dale's northerly mills.

She was looking forward to being with her family again despite poignant memories of her last sight of them when she carried Daniel out to the carriage for the journey south.

Their vacation to Rosebank in May for Owen's thirtieth birthday had not taken place. Having kept the planned celebration a secret from him, Anne Caroline made no mention of it. Then, in one of his letters of condolence, Dale referred to 'informing all guests of the cancellation of your luncheon party.' Owen was touched by his wife's thoughtfulness but understood that any sort of frivolous gathering was unthinkable at such a sad time.

Rain is never a stranger to Scotland for very long. All four mills were back in full working order when Owen gave Humphreys his final instructions before boarding the coach to travel north.

'I am greatly looking forward to seeing Papa again.' Anne Caroline said to Toshie, settling themselves into the cushioned seats, 'I do not believe I have ever been parted from him for such a long time.'

Owen climbed into the carriage and took his place beside his wife.

'I am also looking forward to this visit,' he patted her arm, 'Your father is one of the most conscientious and kind-hearted men I have ever met.'

Anne Caroline slipped her hand into his, leaning against him for support as the carriage lurched forward.

'He is a true Christian,' Owen continued, much to Toshie's surprise. 'He does not merely give lip service to the ideals of his religion, he conducts his whole life in a good and charitable manner, respecting the rights of others with forbearance and understanding.' Owen sighed, looking out onto the passing countryside, dripping and dull beneath a shifting sky. 'Many simply purport to be Christians, or followers of Islam, using these great beliefs as a cloak of respectability with little heed to actually adhering to their values in day to day life.'

Anne Caroline gave his hand a squeeze, knowing this statement most probably stemmed from a recent letter from the Rev Mackenzie, a prominent member of the Lanark clergy. It was a shame, she thought, the Reverend felt the need to criticise her husband purely on the grounds of his non attendance at Church.

Inevitably, tears were shed on being reunited with her family for the first time since losing Daniel. The gentle, compassionate expressions on her sisters' faces and her father's strong embrace cut through her resolve to remain composed but it did not matter. They were all affected by the tragedy and, as a family, they were all grieving. Simply being surrounded by their mutual understanding and shared sorrow gave them all comfort, allowing their natural feelings to be shown without embarrassment.

After the emotional greetings, everyone relaxed.

Toshie was delighted to be back among the Dale household. Renwick proposed a toast of welcome to her at the servants' evening meal and she looked at the familiar faces around the kitchen table and beamed with happiness. She was worn out from long months of sadness and sparse living at New Lanark. To be with Breen and Giggs again was a joy. These were her friends, as close to family members as she knew, and the relief of being with them gave physical pleasure.

Dale was feeling the same comfortable contentment.

The devastating news of baby Daniel's death had shocked him deeply. Not only was it so unexpected but it left him with a terrible despair for his beloved daughter, knowing he could not be with her to offer prayers and guidance from the scriptures. He wrote to her often, sitting for hours at his desk in the hushed morning room, looking with unseeing eyes at the flower garden outside the window while trying to convey his support and love through carefully chosen quotes and advice. After the first few weeks of receiving replies of barely a few words, she shared the news of her pregnancy.

Seizing the news of this happy future event, he became more hopeful of her successful recovery. He knew how her mother struggled after the untimely deaths of their own infants and how the births of subsequent babies brought her some relief.

Dale's strong paternal instincts were being forced to take second place. She was now a married woman and, unless invited, he should stand back and let Owen take over the responsibility. This, it appeared, was not misjudged, for the young couple were surviving this dreadful personal loss and he was delighted to witness their affectionate relationship was as strong as on their previous visits.

That evening, among the delicious aroma of Cook's roast beef, with soft candlelight glinting on highly polished mahogany and silverware, Rosebank's dining room buzzed with conversation. Jean and Margaret regaled their elder sister with anecdotes of the intervening months and Mary and Julia were eager to join in, their exuberance tempered by shyness in Owen's presence.

Owen sat on Dale's left and the two men kept up a lively exchange throughout the meal. One topic rolled easily into the next, each enjoying the other's point of view and knowledge, whether on the proposed route for the Highland tour or the new lodgings for the orphans to be built in New Lanark.

***

News of the proposed construction work in New Lanark soon reached Joe's ears. Ewing was gathering up teams to carry out the work and he wanted Joe to take charge of twenty men.

'Sae ye'll be werkin' agin in the village?' Fiona asked, eyes shining.

'Aye, t'would seem sae.'

It was late in the evening and they were sitting at the table with Cal, eating reheated barley stew. In the shadows, away from the single lamp on the table, the children were already asleep in their bed behind the curtain.

'Aw Joe, that'll be grand! Ah'll see ye mair an' ye can tak yer midday meal here wi' me an' the babbies.' She playfully ruffled his hair. 'Ah didnae think Mr Owen wid be building, no' like auld Mr Dale. Is it anither mill?'

'Naw. Ewing showed me the plans, it's a row o' tenements tae be tacked on tae the end o' New Buildings but the stairs are no' the same. There's only the yin doorway. It's fer the orphans frae Mill Four, or sae Ewing says. Owen's efter telling every yin that the weans need mair room.'

Fiona pulled a face, 'That's no' like 'im? Wi' all these rules tae mak sure there's nae stealin', long oors in the factory an' frae Rosie's stories, alis pushin' folk fer mair werk ... an' noo he's spendin' money on a new hoose fer the bairns?'

'That's whit Ewing telt me.' Joe laughed at her cynical expression. ' Ah din nae care whit the building's for, ma darlin', Ah'm jist awfy pleased the werk is comin' oor way.'

'He's no' as bad as folk say, ye ken.' Cal said thoughtfully. 'When he calls by the forge he talks tae us, proper like, no' jist rappin' oot orders.'

'Och, ye jist like 'im 'cause he wis polite tae ye.' Fiona said, bluntly. 'Whit aboot all the bother he pits me tae wi' cleanin' the hoose fer fear o' yon Mrs Letham findin' bugs in oor room?

Or yer poor sister, werkin' sae lang at the jennies tha' she's no' able tae keep her eyes open fer a gossip o' an eve?'

Cal shrugged, using his finger to wipe up the last morsels from his bowl.

'There's hardly any weans at the classes efter the mills stoap noo,' Fiona continued. 'An' those that come alang are too weary tae learn. Ah hear all Mr Owen's fine words aboot schooling when he's bringin' roond his toffs, but that's in the day time when he's showin' aff the rooms. There's mibbee a quarter o' the pupils at nicht than there were in Mr Dale's day.'

Cal liked tending the visitors who came to see the village.

'There's bin a gie lot o' carriages doon this year,' he said. 'Big Lachie and Kyle mended a wheel fer yin an' Ah helped wi' the horses.' He chewed for a while then added, 'The groom wis saying whit a guid place we had here, an' how he'd heard his maister speaking highly o' Mr Owen.'

'That's fine fer him tae say!' Fiona tossed back her long hair. 'Ah'm jist awfy glad the Owens ha'e gone awa' fer a while. We can rest easy tha' he's no' goin' tae be watchin' whit we get up tae every day.'

'Humphreys is still here,' Cal reminded her. 'Gerry telt me tha' they've tae keep reports on everything sae Owen can read them when he's back.'

'Aye, Rosie wis saying ...' Fiona stood up and started to gather up their wooden bowls and spoons, dumping them into the wash basin. 'D'ye ken Rosie's all richt?' The two men looked at her questioningly. 'D'ye no' think she's doon in the mooth?'

'Ah cannae say Ah've noticed but noo ye ask, aye, she wis quieter the ither nicht.' Joe glanced at the water bucket; nearly empty. 'Ah'll fetch mair watter.'

Cal reached for his jacket, 'Rosie's jist tired. Like us a'. Tis Sabbath t'morra sae Ah'm gaun oot tae fish noo.'

'See if ye can catch yin?' Fiona called after him, 'Gie it tae Rosie?'

'Aye richt! Mibbee if Ah catch twa ...' he flashed an uncharacteristic grin and Fiona waved her hand at him, smiling.

Family: why did she always have one of them to worry about? As soon as Donnie's cough improved she was mashing a yarrow leaf poultice for a rash on Davey. When the rash cleared there was Sionaidh's lack of appetite and she was still not showing any sign of trying to crawl. Robbie, on the other hand, was always up to something, playing rough and hurting himself. Then one of Joe's eyes became red and sore, running with tears until she discovered a piece of grit beneath his eyelid. At least Cal was well at the moment, perhaps due to the potions Auld Bel gave him for his chest or maybe just because the weather was better.

So that left the problem with Rosie.

Cal returned in the early hours of the next morning with three fine brown trout. Having only fallen asleep a few hours before the others were rising, he clambered into the children's bed as soon as they woke and pulled the curtain across, immediately dropping back into a deep sleep. This was a regular occurrence, developed out of many heated arguments, allowing him to spend Sunday mornings catching up on his rest.

Fiona found the fish and decided to take one up to her sister in law.

'Gerry an' his sisters are oot ...' Rosie greeted her, smart in her pale pink muslin Sunday dress, her hair plaited and coiled stylishly around her head, ready for her bonnet.

Fiona feigned surprise. Gerry and his two sisters, who shared their room, were known to visit their elderly aunt in Mantilla Row every Sunday morning and she had been watching from her window to see them pass by in the street below.

'Cal's still asleep but he'd want ye tae ha'e this.' Fiona handed her the fish, wrapped in a piece of cloth. 'He caught three last nicht an' we'll niver eat them all afore they gae aff.'

'My! Cal's a clever lad!' Rosie exclaimed. 'When they need tae feed a banquet up at Bonnington Hoose, Ah've heard tell they net the river. They should jist ask ma brither.' She swung the kettle over the fire. 'Ye'll tak a cup? They'll no' be lang an' then we're awa' tae the Church.'

Fiona took a seat at Rosie's table, noting the pretty embroidered tablecloth and a centrally placed pottery jug arranged with pink campion and a variety of grasses.

They spoke of Rosie's duties as 'Bug Hunter' for her stair, of the weather, the sudden lack of mice since 'Mrs Maclean doon the stairs' died and her room was cleaned out and of Gerry's frustration with the new managers.

86

'If it's no' a list o' this, it's a new report on that ... they seem tae think he can dae five things at once.' Rosie turned suddenly away, wiping at her cheek.

'Is everythin' all richt wi' ye?' Fiona asked gently.

Rosie squared her narrow shoulders, blinking rapidly to clear her eyes. 'Ah'm jist bein' stupit. Ah have a grand husband an'... we dinnae struggle fer pennies tae live, Ah'm lucky.' She gave Fiona a wavering smile, her chin crumpling as a tear escaped.

'Tell me? Whit's happened?'

'It wis Ella upstairs ... wee wuman, droopy eye, wi' six or seven weans? ye ken her? her husband's in the store rooms?'

Fiona nodded, making encouraging noises for her to continue.

'Weel, Ah wis telling her she needs tae tak a turn in brushing her steps, her neighbours have bin complaining tae me tha' she's a lazy bisom ... which she is.' Rosie took a deep breath, 'Ella gets all high an' mighty wi' me ... shoutin' an' swearin' an' then, when Ah telt her tae haud her tongue, she shouts oot that if Ah had bairns Ah would nae be sae mean spirited. An' then she calls doon the stairs efter me, "Or mibbee yer mean spirit is why yer man disnae gie ye babbies!" Rosie's cheeks flamed with the memory.

Fiona was horrified, '*Sgriosail* ! Och that wis a terrible thing fer her tae say! Tak nae notice!'

'It wis nae jist whit she said, it wis ...' there was a long pause. 'We've bin wed some years an' Ah thocht by noo we wid ha'e a bairn. Ye ha'e four an' look at oor Sarah, every time she lay wi' that Sean she fell.'

'Some folk tak their time, ye niver ken when ye might find yersel in the family way.'

'Ah didnae used tae think aboot it, but e'er since ye had wee Sionaidh ... an' wi' all an' sundry talking aboot the Owen's bairn, then Ella upstairs stuck her twa pennies in ... Ah think on it all the time.'

Fiona tried to comfort her until Una, Gerry's oldest sister returned, then she made her excuses and left.

There was nothing she could do to help Rosie have a baby, it was in God's hands, but now that she knew what the problem was at least she could lend a sympathetic ear.

***

The evening before Owen was to leave to meet MacIntosh and travel north, he sat by the fire with his father in law discussing the future of the mills at Stanley and Spinningdale. Owen was already familiar with the financial situation in both establishments as well as having studied many documents laying out the labour force, building stock and machinery. Neither of the mills was returning a profit and both showed serious problems, yet there was a real need to maintain the employment and housing which they provided, especially in remote Spinningdale.

'It is, and always has been, a philanthropic venture,' Dale conceded. 'At least at Stanley there could be alternative livings to be made on the land in that neck of the woods. Although, I hear the poverty is so great that the Duke of Atholl has opened public kitchens for the deserving poor.' He murmured a prayer for these unfortunate souls. 'The port in the nearby city of Perth has excellent facilities allowing the movement of goods with ease. It's far better placed than New Lanark in that respect.'

'It would certainly be more economic if New Lanark was closer to a harbour,' Owen agreed. 'Last winter the roads were almost impassable at times and I am led to believe it was actually a mild season compared to many in recent years. What a shame we cannot send the cotton down the Clyde!'

Dale chortled, 'Now that would be grand. Out of the mills, into boats and sailed down to Glasgow. I fear the Clyde does not have the character of the Tay or Thames. Its crashing waterfalls and rapids could never be tamed to act as a canal, more's the pity.'

Owen smiled, 'I am pleased to say I am managing to tame a small part of it. I am nearing agreement with the Misses Edmonstone at Corehouse to construct a weir upstream of the lade inlet.'

'Are ye, by Jove!'

'They are concerned for their privacy, I believe. They have taken the notion that hordes of workers will use the weir to cross the water and trespass on Corehouse estate.'

'Well, there is that possibility.'

'I have assured them that I will make strenuous efforts to ensure this does not occur. It really is vital to have a good head of water supplying the wheels continuously. We cannot sustain the required output if only one of the mills is in service, even if I keep it running throughout the night.'

'And you have been forced to do this?' Dale asked, watching Owen's solemn expression.

'Unfortunately, yes, sir. It was not ideal.'

'No, I have never agreed with working in the darkest hours of the night. These hours should be spent at rest.'

'I agree, entirely. However, my partners in Manchester are most insistent that all orders are fulfilled on time.' Owen sat forward, relieved to be sharing his frustration with a like minded businessman. 'It seems it is not enough that I have improved the output, the machinery and even the fabric of the village buildings. They press me for more! I am a junior partner and obliged to carry out the orders of the board but at times it is extremely aggravating to have to put all my attention on making money.'

'And what would you rather be putting your attention on, if not profits?'

'Oh, profits are essential, I understand this and am determined to give them the returns on their capital which they desire. However, this does not and *should not* be based on increasingly long hours of drudgery. I am convinced that I can maintain high production without wearing out my workers but, so far, their demands occupy so much of my time that I have yet to be able to implement my own plans. As I keep reminding Mr Atkinson, New Lanark is the largest cotton manufacturer in the United Kingdom and I intend to keep this high status.' He paused, marshalling his thoughts into words. 'I suppose, my irritation comes from the fact that I am being thwarted by both my fellow business partners and the villagers themselves.'

'And how are the children faring? The paupers in Mill Four? I trust they are still attending lessons regularly?'

'Ah, the children. They are all progressing well and, of course, when the new Nursery Buildings are built, they will enjoy even better conditions. The teachers and assistants in the school continue to do their best in the time allowed and the excellent Mrs Docherty supervises them in her kindly manner.

It is the village children of whom I despair. Their parents seem ignorant of even the basics of care and treat them in a most irresponsible, reckless way. Bruises and black eyes are far too common.'

Dale stretched his legs, 'Are the infants not exceedingly tired if they are working the fourteen hours you now implement?'

'As I mentioned to you, Sir, I was against this extension in working hours but was over-ruled. It is my firm belief that the experiences of early childhood influence and form our characters and I am working towards the day when there are no children under ten years of age in my mills.'

'But if they are not working, they will run amock. You cannot have these young people spending their days idly looking for mischief! They need to be usefully employed, bring in money for their families, learn the word of Our Lord and learn a skill.'

'They would not be idle, they would attend school.'

'They already attend school.' Dale reminded him.

Owen did not wish to offend him. 'The system you devised was very beneficial but, as I am sure you will agree, it had its limitations. After a heavy day of toil, these young students can barely stay awake long enough to learn their letters.'

'In my day, they did not spend so many hours in the workroom.' Dale raised an eyebrow, fixing him with an ironic look. 'They attend their scripture lessons, I hope? And the Sunday services?'

'They do,' Owen confirmed. 'I have no wish to deny them access to any of the world's religions. Yet, this fact does not seem to have registered with the Reverend Mackenzie of Lanark.'

Smothering a yawn, Dale decided against embarking on a religious discussion. His son in law was a clever young man, of that there was no doubt, but his admitted agnostic views were far removed from Dale's own staunchly Christian beliefs.

Early the next morning Owen and his valet bade farewell to everyone at Rosebank and embarked on the first leg of their journey. He was taking his own carriage up to Glasgow where he would meet George MacIntosh, whereupon they would travel north together in MacIntosh's magnificent touring chariot.

Chapter Four

"My heart's in the Highlands, my heart is not here,
My heart's in the Highlands, a-chasing the deer,
Chasing the wild-deer, and following the roe,
My heart's in the Highlands, wherever I go."
    Robert Burns

Shifting beams of sunlight pierced through the banks of cloud rolling over lowland Scotland. Here and there, showers fell in veils, creating distant rainbows and leaving the next shaft of sun to sparkle on fresh puddles and dripping leaves.

Through this changeable weather, MacIntosh and Owen settled into the coach seats and enjoyed their steady progress along the streets of Glasgow. It was not long before the coachman could allow the team of four matching greys to find their rhythm, unfettered by city traffic or pedestrians, and move smoothly out onto the open country road heading north towards Stirling.

The roof of the black travelling chariot was piled with luggage, with further bags stowed under the exterior rear seat. The gentlemen's valets squeezed into this space, rugs over their knees, grateful for the provision of a cover to draw over their heads when it rained.

Trees waved their wet branches in the wake of the passing carriage and the occupants looked out upon enclosures of rising crops, farmyards spotted with ducks, horses hitched to carts, smocked figures moving busily at their tasks. The black arrows of swallows swept low over open pastureland, before whisking up, their beaks bristling with insects to feed newly fledged young in dazzling displays of midair acrobatics.

Thousands of miles away, Sam Scott was surrounded by a very different scene.

Egypt.

Sweltering, dusty, glaringly bright Egypt.

He recalled hot days, even weeks, to contend with in Canada but nothing like the intense heat of Arabia in midsummer.

He lay in the shade of a canvas awning, one of hundreds of soldiers waiting for their orders, listening to snatches of conversation and feeling the sweat run from his body. His stomach was churning and his head ached. In this stifling air every movement was an effort, even breathing. He glanced at the men around him, similarly motionless, their heads propped on folded jackets, their boots, breeches and stockings piled at the side, arms laid loosely away from their boiling bodies.

There was talk that the water supply was tainted; perhaps the reason for their sickness and lethargy? He reached for his water bottle, so thirsty that he didn't care if it was poisoning him.

The liquid was warm, not unpleasant but leaving a strange aftertaste. He took another swig: what the hell, it was wet.

This was the regiment's third day on land after months at sea and the longed for relief of leaving the cramped confines of the ship was already wearing off. Sam raised his head to crane out over the camp seeing only pale shimmering images of tents with white stony ground below and brilliant blue sky above.

All living creatures sought the protection of any patch of shade, no matter how small, except the moving shroud of flies buzzing over the latrines.

Sam closed his eyes and turned his head gingerly to one side, trying to find comfort from the pain within his skull, another bout of nausea rising in his stomach.

'Please God,' he murmured to himself, 'let me be well again before we're called to duty ... or let me die.'

***

'Delighted to make your acquaintance,' Owen shook his host's hand.

'Likewise, my dear sir, any friend of MacIntosh is welcome in this house,' David Smythe, the current Lord Methven, gave a hearty handshake belying his grey-haired, elderly appearance.

He indicated the staircase behind him. 'Please ... you will wish a little time to yourselves after your journey and we will meet again in what? An hour, shall we say?'

This was the second night of their expedition and if Owen was impressed by the mansion in which he stayed at Stirling, he was astonished by Methven Castle on the outskirts of Perth.

He cried out in amazement at his first glimpse of the imposing five story structure rising out of rolling parkland. Solidly built in a square, with a tower at each corner, this castle had been the Smythe family home for nearly one hundred and fifty years and, McIntosh briefed Owen before they arrived, it stood on the site of the original twelfth century castle lived in by Margaret Tudor, daughter of England's King Henry V11.

Owen was shown to a bedroom with a lavishly draped four poster bed taking prime position. On the marble topped wash-stand, a brightly painted Chinese water jug was filled, a clean hand towel neatly folded at its side. The walls were festooned with tapestries and gilt framed paintings which, viewed beneath the high painted ceiling, emanated an air of times gone by: understated and slightly faded luxury.

He washed while Murdoch unpacked his trunk, then lay back on the bed and recalled the journey. So far, it was surprisingly easy and uneventful, with the bonus of finding MacIntosh excellent company, regaling him with the problems his son, the chemist, was having with an Irish company stealing their patented bleaching powder and anecdotes about the various landed gentry with whom they would be lodging.

It boded well for the rest of the tour.

Dressed for dinner in a formal shot silk evening suit and starched white cravat , Owen descended the sweeping staircase looking forward to the second evening of his Highland adventure.

Lord and Lady Methven were saying goodnight to their baby daughters in the drawing room and Owen was grateful to McIntosh for informing him of the near quarter century disparity in age between husband and wife.

'The Lord's wife is a beauty!' MacIntosh had beamed. 'Her grace and fine features were even noted by the bard Robert Burns when she was just a lass: "The evening sun was ne'er sae sweet, as was the blink o' Phemie's ee." She is the daughter of

Murray of Lintrose but known around these parts as the Flower of Strathmore.'

Lady Euphemia was Lord Methven's second wife and her glossy dark brown locks, smooth features and slender figure presented such a youthful picture that, had he not been forewarned, Owen would have mistaken her for being the Lord's daughter.

'It is fortunate we are in residence,' Euphemia smiled at Owen, 'we spend a great deal of our time in Edinburgh.'

Owen nodded, recalling her husband's profession: a Judge.

'You are from Wales, are you not?' her eyes sparkled, flirtatiously. 'What brings you to Scotland?'

Owen was delighted to tell her and the evening passed very pleasantly, especially when he found the food to be plain, easy on his weak digestion. Sometimes, when dining away from his own table, he struggled with rich or heavily spiced dishes. He did not wish to appear rude in leaving the food uneaten, but neither did he want to fall ill in a stranger's house.

When the meal was drawing to an end, Euphemia rose from her chair and bade them all good night, leaving the men to their discussions among the candlelight.

'I am sure you two gentlemen are very weary from your day's excursion,' their host said, patting the head of a large deer hound, one of three who wandered at will around the room. 'But I would beseech you to join me for a dram in my study for a short while, eh?'

It was true, Owen was tired, however, there was nothing he liked more than intelligent conversation. Persuaded to take a small measure of malt whisky, the gentlemen relaxed by the fire where the hounds joined them, spreading themselves on the floorboards like grey rugs. They debated the hoped for Treaty to bring an end to the war with France, the crippling taxes being levied to pay for it and the latest breakthroughs in manufacturing.

Owen also aired his views on looking after the workers with as much diligence as factory owners gave to machines. Methven was intrigued, drawing parallels between Owen's plans and the philanthropic work already achieved by David Dale.

Encouraged by such a receptive audience, Owen went into finer detail about New Lanark until MacIntosh fell asleep and his snores grew too loud to ignore, at which time the evening was brought to a close.

The next day, Owen was relieved to discover they were within just a few miles of Stanley and MacIntosh suggested they should stay at Methven Castle for several days. This would allow them to survey the mills, visit merchants and brokers and take advantage of the opportunity to explore Perth before moving north.

Lord Methven was agreeable to this extension to their visit and offered them the use of his coachman and Landau to navigate the narrow local roads.

'Usually,' MacIntosh told Owen when they set off to view Perth's busy port before visiting the mills, 'I see Sir George Dempster when I'm in the city. However, he is expecting us to stay with him at Skibo, his estate in Sutherland. He is passionate about improving the health of the land, quite the agriculturist! '

'Sir George was Member of Parliament for Perth, was he not?' Owen asked, noticing the townsfolk gawping at them and pulling their children out of the way as they rolled past.

'Aye, that he was. Always has a mind to bring employment and prosperity to the Highlands. It was Sir George who invited Richard Arkwright up from England all those years ago. He held a reception for him in Glasgow which, of course, Dale attended, leading to the founding of your mills.'

'I heard this story. A very fortunate meeting!'

'Sir George also brought Arkwright up here, to Perth, and showed him the site where he proposed to build another venture at Stanley. Arkwright invested in it and greatly enjoyed the visit, being made a Freeman of Perth for his generosity.'

'We passed other mills, just a few streets back? I saw lades running water down to the Tay, right beneath our wheels.'

'We will take a walk around the streets one day for there is much to see that will interest you, I am sure. Wool is the main industry here but I would say leather ranks high as well ... and whisky!'

Owen glimpsed the wide, sluggish waters of the Tay when they paused to admire Smeaton's imposing bridge. He wondered if the river was as massive upstream beside Stanley. Surely, there was no problem in keeping the wheels running at these mills, unlike New Lanark.

Leaving the busy streets of Perth, the road dipped and turned, snaking around hills and clinging to the sides of the valley while keeping close to the west bank of the river.

'Look now!' McIntosh instructed. 'ye see there! Bleachfields! More than eighty acres. These are the Luncarty bleachfields of my old friends Sandeman and Turnbull.'

'Are we to meet with them?' Owen enquired, peering out of the window. 'I already know of this business. They produce the finest bleached cotton on the market.'

'Aye, it's a grand venture, but alas, the founders both died about ten years ago. William Sandeman was one of the first investors in Stanley, bringing with him a great deal of local knowledge and experience of the cotton trade. He was a very trustworthy man, deeply religious ... a Glasite. His brother, Robert, was so taken up with his church matters that he left the business ! And a damned fine business it was! William's new partner, Hector Turnbull, moved up to Luncarty from the Lothians where he was with the British Linen Company's bleachfield at Saltoun. He was younger than Sandeman but they hit it off straight away! Indeed, their children, of which there were in excess of *thirty* of them ... became closely entwined and now there are at least five marriages between Turnbulls and Sandemans!'

'Well, goodness! How opportune to have these bleaching fields so close to the mills,' Owen laughed, his eyes scanning the flattened land, pale with cotton.

A couple of miles further along the road, MacIntosh raised his cane and knocked twice on the carriage ceiling.

'We will stop here,' he told Owen.

'Here? There is nothing here but some trees and a hamlet.'

They climbed out and the older man took Owen by the elbow, guiding him along the rutted road.

The coachman reached for his pipe, nudging the groom beside him. MacIntosh was tall and broad shouldered, brightly dressed with yellow breeches and white hose, a shining red silk waistcoat beneath his open frock coat. Beside him, Owen appeared almost a youth, slender in a grey knee length, tight fitting coat, neatly buttoned above white breeches. Both men wore polished buckled boots with heels, hampering their progress across the uneven ground: an incongruous sight.

'Come, humour me!' MacIntosh cried. 'We will only walk to that break in the trees ... and take in the scene.'

"And then it all became clear," Owen wrote to Anne Caroline that evening. "It was a most glorious sight! Far below our vantage point, the great curving river was flowing towards us, abundant energy for any mills and there on the northern bank was a mighty stone building as similar to our own Mill One at New Lanark as I have yet to see."

On closer inspection, Stanley's mill had one major difference: it was constructed of brick.

'Why is this?' Owen remarked when they disembarked down in the valley beside the mill. 'The lower portion of the walls are stone, yet as it rises the walls are brick.'

'At Arkwright's insistence!' McIntosh laughed. 'The bricks were made here, adjacent to the mill! He wanted to stamp his English heritage on the enterprise. The construction drawings were adapted, but the overall aspect of the mill is pleasingly Scottish apart from the materials.'

They were greeted by the works manager, James Craig, and it being a warm, dry day, they strolled around the site admiring the mill lade, corn mill and the original tunnel constructed half a century before by Lord Nairne.

However, there was no escaping the focus of the visit: the site of the burnt out East Mill. The foundations and piles of rubble from the destroyed building lay testament to the devastating fire of less than two years before. Builders were making a start on the reconstruction but there was a long way to go.

'Right!' said Owen, rubbing his hands together. 'Shall we go inside, gentlemen? There is much I would like to see on behalf of Mr Dale.'

***

'Weel, wid ye credit sich a thing?' Bessie cried, clapping her hands to her cheeks and staring up at Fiona from under her

97

bonnet brim. 'Ah mind tellin' yer man on the first nicht he arrived in the place that this wis gaun tae happen!'

Fiona was laughing, jiggling Sionaidh in her arms, 'Weel, it has! Whit dae ye think?'

'Och, it's grand ... jist grand! Can Ah gie it a wee try?'

Fiona handed her a wooden bucket,'That's whit Ah've bin waitin' here in the street fer ye tae dae. Ah wanted tae catch ye as soon as ye came doon the hill sae ye could gie it a try.'

Very carefully, the old lady set down the bucket and clasped the pump handle of the new water stand-pipe. After a few attempts, the first drops spurted from the spout, each accompanied by Bessie exclaiming to God of the miracle she was witnessing.

'Och lass, this must mak a big difference tae ye all. Why, ye can run doon yer stairs an' be bak wi' the watter afore yer e'en missed!'

'It's bin here fer aboot a week noo an' Ah still can nae believe it's sae easy.' Fiona switched her baby onto the other hip, ready to pick up the filled bucket. 'Noo come up an' ha'e a blether, it's getting gie nippy oot here an' it's startin' tae spit wi rain.'

'D'ye ha'e yer washin' oot?' Bessie asked, tripping along beside Fiona, aware that she was no longer strong enough to help her carry either the baby or the bucket. 'Ah'll gie ye a haun tae bring it in.'

All down the streets, flapping lines of clothes and bed linen were being reeled back in through windows, shouts for wayward children echoing off the rapidly emptying road.

There was much to catch up on and Bessie's visit had been invited by Fiona for several reasons.

With the children squabbling around them and cups of sweet tea to sip, Fiona told her about Sam returning and how well Cal was keeping, happier too after striking up a friendship with another lad who was keen on fishing. Then there was the new building project in the village which Joe could be working upon and the changes in her own job meaning shorter hours because there were fewer children in the evenings.

'Ah din nae want ye tae be a stranger tae us, Bessie,' she said quietly. 'Mrs Young is guid wi' the bairns but Ah miss ye here tae ask advice an'... weel, jist tae ha'e a blether like.'

'Ah didnae want tae bother ye. Yer alis sae busy an' Ah ken ye like tae be alane wi' yer man at any time yer no' werkin'... sae, Ah didnae want tae intrude.'

'Away wi' ye, yer niver 'intruding'' Fiona gave her an involuntary hug. 'Yer lookin' fine though, Bessie. Livin' wi' yer dottir is suitin' ye?'

'Aye. Ah can be o' use there. She's aboot tae ha'e her sixth babbie.'

'When's tha'?'

'Twa months frae noo. She's prayin' fer a lad, efter the five lassies.'

'Bessie? D'ye think ye wid be able tae come tae me agin fer anither babbie?'

'Ha'e ye fallen agin, lass?'

'Aye, but Ah can nae mind how far on it is.'

Fiona burst out giggling, her cheeks flushing scarlet. Lowering her voice for the children's sake she whispered, 'Like ye say, Ah'm alis busy an' one month runs in tae the next an' weel, Joe's bin at hame mair this summer.'

Bessie's button eyes twinkled mischievously, 'Din nae say anither word! It's grand news.'

'Ah hope Joe thinks sae, an' all!' Fiona's smile froze on her lips, the mirth disappearing in an instant. 'Och, Bessie, Ah've jist minded Rosie.'

Quickly, hoping to couch it in terms Donnie and Davy wouldn't understand, Fiona told her about Rosie. They were still mulling over the best way to break the news of a forthcoming niece or nephew in the kindest way, when Cal came home. He was fond of Bessie, looking on her as the grandmother he never knew, so he stayed to chat for a while before wrapping up some food and placing the package in his bag.

'Ye still fishin' then, laddie?' Bessie asked.

'Aye, best pairt o' the day.' He topped up his bottle from the large flagon of ale he kept on the top shelf of the dresser and jammed the cork home. 'Ah'm aff tae the river.'

'It's rainin'!' Bessie said.

'Guid fer the fishin' ... the fish are already wet! Cheerio!'

As soon as the door closed, it opened again and Rosie popped her head inside.

'Bessie! Mrs Young wis sayin' ye were here!' Rosie pulled out a chair and dropped into the seat, kicking off her clogs and rubbing at her ankles. She was drained from her long shift.

'Sae tell me,' she said, 'whit's bin happenin'?'

Before Bessie could answer, Donnie said, 'Bessie's comin' tae stiy agin when Mam has the new babbie.'

The silence which followed spoke volumes.

***

In the end, Owen required a second visit to Stanley mills to satisfy himself of being able to answer any enquiry made of him by his father in law.

Then, after a full day of meeting fellow mill owners and businessmen in Perth, Owen and MacIntosh set out from Methven Castle early on a promisingly sunny morning. They would be revisiting their hosts on the return journey so the farewells were brief and cheerful with a great deal of banter about being lost in mountain mists or plunging to their deaths in treacherous ravines.

'These quips about the danger of the Highlands seem unfounded,' Owen mused. 'The landscape here is similar to my home at Newtown and also Lanarkshire or Derbyshire. I admit I am surprised, because I felt considerable trepidation at the thought of this journey when it was first proposed.'

'Aha! That is because we are not in the Highlands yet!' MacIntosh gestured to the scenery. 'If Kinnoul Hill, behind us,' he pointed to a substantial wooded hill beyond Perth, 'is a minnow, wait until you see the mighty Atlantic salmon!'

It was seventy years since General Wade ordered a three hundred strong working party to construct the road to Inverness. The surface was still intact although peppered with repairs and potholes due to the challenging terrain. On either side, moorland and reedy, bob-cotton spangled bog gave way to expanses of woodland and rocky outcrops. The coachman slowed the horses to a walk in several places to safely negotiate tight bends and steep slopes.

'Good gracious!' Owen suddenly cried out, excitedly. 'The land seems to have risen above our heads!'

MacIntosh knocked on the ceiling and the horses were drawn to a halt so everyone could disembark and admire the magnificent sight lying ahead.

They were nearing the ancient city of Dunkeld, a thriving market place and regarded by many as the gateway to the Highlands. Its proud cathedral, partly ruined, was almost as large as the town itself, squatting on the far bank of the Tay. It was cocooned by towering, tree clad hills on every side. Servants and gentry alike, everyone who caught their first sight of the place was enchanted.

Rising into the clouds on the far, high horizon, misty peaks of craggy mountains were visible. Owen shivered; were they to traverse these giants?

'We will be taking the low road, never fear, dear boy,' MacIntosh assured him. 'Mind you, that will still be taking you nearer to God than you'll ever have been before, I wager!'

On reaching the banks of the Tay, they once again disembarked for the perilous ferry crossing. The river was running low but the stiff currents and deep pools loomed as a hazardous barrier and Owen felt physically scared as he watched the horses being coaxed onto the ferry; their eyes white ringed, ears flat back.

'There's much talk of a bridge being built!' McIntosh informed him when they jumped aboard behind the carriage and clutched the vessel's railings. 'The Duke of Athol is minded to bring Telford up for the job.'

'I doubt he will have it built before our return journey,' Owen muttered through gritted teeth. 'Perhaps there is a different route to take when we come back?'

'Oh aye, there is!' McIntosh beamed. 'It's longer, of course, and not near so stimulating!'

The ferry lurched away from the bank, chains straining and Owen cast him a fearful look, taking a tighter grip on the rails.

However, as soon as they were safely on the north bank he admitted to feeling exhilarated by the experience and from the servants' grinning faces and boisterous manner, he was not the only one.

While the horses rested, they sought refreshment at a hostelry and Owen took advantage of the warm sunshine to wander down to the market place among the locals. It was fascinating to encounter the native people in their own land, bringing home to him how different life must be for the Highlanders working in his mills.

He watched their expansive gestures while haggling for goods or calling out their wares, the noisy children playing on the streets, naughtily teasing cats or running among ducks being herded to a pen, skilfully dodging the smacks of enraged adults shouting curses through toothless mouths.

Over the time he had been at New Lanark, he signed off several good workers who were taking up arms with the Cameronians and being curious about the Lanarkshire regiment he read a little of its history. Looking around now at the white washed, terraced houses and the Square thronging with people, he was reminded of an account of dreadful blood-shed in this very place. It was the Lowland regiment, the newly formed Cameronians, who the King sent to hold back the Jacobites.

He looked at the locals' black hair and sun burnt faces, shrewd, pale blue eyes under dark lashes and occasionally a gloriously ginger haired individual came to view. No wonder these proud people held resentment against the English. Not only taking over their country's governance but building roads to carry soldiers deep into the Highlands to suppress more uprisings and now, throwing them from their lands to replace them with sheep.

Owen's smart clothes attracted much attention, marking him out as a foreigner and he was soon surrounded by a gaggle of inquisitive children. He could not understand their language but smiled at their funny little expressions. They bounced along beside him on barefeet, squinting through long tangled hair, loose smocks swinging around their sun-browned limbs.

He felt stuffy and over-heated in comparison, running a finger around his high cravat to ease it from his throat.

Throughout the following days, they made their way slowly through deep glens, shadowy forests and across vast expanses of wind flattened moorland. It was heavy work for the horses but the occupants were happy to alight whenever the coachman deemed necessary.

The two valets, unknown to each other before the trip, were now firm friends. They fell into a routine of helping each other care for their masters in strange households or inns, exploring the countryside together during frequent stops along the road. MacIntosh enjoyed a brief walk to take in the new horizons, find a conveniently private bush to relieve himself behind and then return to the comfort of the upholstered seats to take a snooze.

If they were stationary, Owen preferred to stay outside the coach. He now wore casual clothes through the day, dispensing with his restrictive high collared shirts and cravats, and donning his stouted footwear suitable for scrambling among the rocky terrain or meandering on a loch shore. Finding an outcrop or fallen tree trunk, he would sit and contemplate the scene around him, letting his thoughts run free.

The peace and quiet was exhilarating.

Only natural sounds disturbed the silence: breezes rustling in the flower filled grassland, larks soaring above, mere specks, singing their hearts out, the occasional mew of a heavy winged buzzard making lazy circles in the sky. Often, herds of red deer could be seen grazing in the hills or lying low among the vegetation, almost invisible until they moved.

On the last leg of their journey, the weather broke and the party arrived at Skibo Castle thoroughly worn out and damp.

George Dempster greeted them at the bottom of the entrance steps, a small army of servants clustered behind him.

'Come in ... welcome!' His beaming red face peered into the carriage. 'My you're lookin' all-in! We will have tae see tae that!'

Having heard of Dempster's reputation for entertaining, Owen braced himself for the coming adventure.

***

In Rosebank, the Dale household looked out through blurred wet windows at the dripping garden and pursued indoor pastimes, bemoaning the lack of sunshine.

Beneath the scorching Arabian sun, Sam Scott could only fantasise about rain falling on green grass. He was in a world of heat, dust and sand. The searing headaches he suffered on landing in Egypt were abating but poor provisions and foul water were taking their toll on everyone. He received his orders and galvanised his men with his usual blend of cajoling and bullying, acutely aware of their weakness from chronic vomiting and diarrhoea.

French troops held the heavily fortified city of Alexandria and despite losing the leadership of Napoleon when he returned to France, they were still succeeding in retaining this vital harbour. The Cameronians were charged with reinforcing the British army before a concerted effort could be mounted to take back the city.

They marched through the night using the brilliance of the moon and millions of stars to light their path. When the first silver rays of morning radiated across the eastern horizon, the shout went up to pitch camp, sending everyone to their designated task, eager to have it completed before sunrise.

Attending the regiment were dozens of arab men and boys in floating robes, their heads swathed beneath white keffiyeh which were drawn closed across their faces so only black lashed, curiously light eyes surveyed the Scotsmen.

Sam knew little of the Islamic faith but grew accustomed to their devout chanting and rhythmic, murmuring prayers, especially at sunrise and sunset. No matter how busy the camp was or how urgently they might be required to assist with food, water or raising canvas, the Moslems rolled out their mats and knelt in prayer.

By the time the heat began to build for the day the soldiers dusted off their grimy jackets, polished the badges on their shakos and jammed them on top of greasy hair to present for parade.

Noting the lines of red eyes and haggard, unshaven faces, Colonel Gordon kept his speech short before dismissing the ranks with orders to sleep.

Throwing himself down on his mat, Sam eased off his boots and thanked God Alexandria was only one more day's march away.

'Whit are we daen in this place?' the man beside him groaned, returning from the latrines. 'Ah've left most o' mesel' in yon cludgie ...'

'Ye nae better?'

'Cramps like the Deil hissel'stabbin' ma guts ...' Already stripped to the waist, the soldier curled up, clutching himself, panting.

'We'll get ye tae Alex an' get the physicians tae tak a look at ye.'

'If Ah mak it.'

'Aye, ye'll mak it. There'll be guid watter, mattresses an' no' jist auld goat tae eat. Ye'll see.'

Sam spoke boldly, as if it was a certainty, though he had no idea at all what lay ahead of them: which was just as well.

***

Anne Caroline rustled along the polished oak floors of the upper landing, the hem of her gown catching on her pink satin pumps. Having spent some time with Toshie perfecting a hairstyle combining the new fashion for a smooth, tight bun at the nape of her neck, then applying hot tongs to create short rippling curls around her face, she swung her head from side to side, enjoying the sensation.

'Papa?' She knocked lightly on the open door to her father's study.

'My dear, come in!'

'Another letter from Robert!' she waved a sheet of paper. 'He is greatly enjoying his tour of the north and writes most humorously of his adventures.'

Dale's face was wreathed in smiles. It was excellent news but his pleasure was in seeing his daughter's face alive with enthusiasm, smoothing away the anxious, downcast lines of the last few months.

'So, what has he to say?' he asked, rolling the blotter over his signature before leaving his desk and ushering her to a comfortable seat overlooking the garden. 'Sit with me and tell me his news.'

Since arriving at Rosebank, Anne Caroline often sought out quiet times with her father. They would pray together and discuss verses from the Bible, applying the teachings to her terrible loss and seeking to find a way to heal the pain of bereavement. As always, Dale knew where to find the most comforting passages, urging her to look to the future, the wonderful gift of her unborn child and the blessings bestowed on her by God.

She looked tenderly on his dear face as he spoke, drinking in his calming presence, sensing his deep, paternal affection. The special bond between them which was forged after her mother died remained as robust as ever.

If she doubted their closeness since marrying and leaving his house, she was reassured that nothing had changed, in fact it was stronger. Now, when they conversed it was as two adults freely stating their point of view. Although he was her father, she no longer depended on him for protection or a home and he also felt this subtle change in their relationship.

'Does he mention Spinningdale?' Dale asked, referring to the letter.

'Only to say he has visited the mill, but this is dated a week ago and he is still a guest at Sir George's estate. He tells of evenings spent with music and singing, saying they rode estate ponies through wild countryside and saw eagles and stags.'

She read some paragraphs and they laughed together at a reference to Dempster's invitation to Owen to join him at the card table.

'For all Dempster may enjoy a game of cards,' Dale said, charitably, 'he owns the nickname Honest George for good reason. He's one of the few men in politics who can't be bribed. A fine man! He continues to lobby to improve the lot of his tenants up there, which is why Spinningdale exists at all.'

'I remember seeing him when I was a child.' Anne Caroline recalled. 'Tall and handsome in his wig and silk cravat.' She wrinkled her nose, caught up in the memory. 'He appeared very large ... on the night all those poor Highlanders stayed with us in Glasgow. It was a thrilling time!'

'Aye, it turned out well, lass. Many of those homeless wretches you saw that evening are still at the mills, thanks be to God, engaged in useful employment.'

'Perhaps you could come and stay with us at New Lanark, Papa? I am sure the villagers would be pleased if you gave a sermon there again. I would certainly like that, very much.'

'The village belongs to your husband now, I wonder if it would be such a good idea for me to return?'

'But of course, it would be a splendid idea! When the baby is born ... maybe in the warmer months of the coming spring? Oh, I should love you to visit us.'

He patted her hand, 'We'll see, my dear.'

'Oh,' she turned the corners of her mouth down, 'when you say that, it means it will not happen ...'

He chuckled, casting her a wry look, 'Not necessarily, but I gather that there are still some problems among the workers regarding the new management. Owen is confident he can overcome these obstacles and when that is the case, if you should both wish me to visit, then I would be delighted.'

The clocks in the house rang out the hour.

'Three o'clock already? I will leave you to your correspondence,' Anne Caroline kissed his cheek, preparing to stand. 'It is very pleasant being here and I am so comfortable, I can hardly believe I have not known this house all my life.'

'It has that air to it, has it not?' Dale levered himself from the seat, grappling for his cane which had slipped to the floor.

His daughter instantly reached for it, turning the smooth wood in her hand and admiring the familiar gold top.

'Perhaps this vacation from New Lanark has come at just the right time,' she said, seriously. 'There are no domestic pressures or arrangements to make and it is so enjoyable being with you and my sisters again ... and visiting friends in the city.' She looked directly into her father's understanding eyes. 'I am feeling stronger every day. Thank you.'

'Bless you, you are your mother's daughter, my dear girl.' Both physically and in expression, he could see Carolina standing before him. Where had the years gone? It was surely yesterday that his sweet wife looked at him in that way, seeking strength, bravely struggling to overcome tragedy. 'Trust in the Lord, take each day and live it as He has shown us, follow the path of Righteousness. Life is hard, sorrowful and sometimes filled with pain but these difficult times are just as important and just as much a part of Life as the happy days.'

He put his arm around her shoulders, walking her to the study door. 'It is only by knowing adversity that we truly appreciate good fortune.'

She smiled ruefully, 'I have good fortune, Papa. When I look at the poor people in New Lanark or think on the horrors of the war, I realise how lucky I am ... yet, the ache of loss is still hard to bear.'

'And you will bear it. The Lord God will give you strength, He understands your sadness ... you are not alone.'

When her sisters were released from their lessons with Mr Craig, the tutor who visited from Glasgow, they hurried upstairs to prepare for their walk and find bonnets and capes.

They were accompanied by Giggs and Toshie, not just out of any fear for their safety or propriety but because the maids enjoyed the exercise as much as their young mistresses.

A stiff wind caught at their skirts, dipping the brims of their tightly tied hats, the ribbons flying out around their heads.

'D'ye ken yet how much longer you will be staying with us?' Giggs asked, raising her voice as her words were whipped away.

They were walking at the rear of the party, bracing themselves against each gust.

'A week or maybe more, I believe. Mrs Owen is planning to go up to the city tomorrow and stay the night at Charlotte Street. She is calling on Mrs Pemberly and that lady has arranged for them to attend an afternoon recital. Before returning , the mistress is also taking the opportunity to have fittings for new maternity gowns.'

'There are items I'm needing frae the hoose fur the bairns,' Giggs said. 'If I draw up a list, can ye bring them back wi' ye?'

'Aye.'

'Living between two households can be very trying,' Giggs confided. 'If the truth be told, I prefer Charlotte Street tae this place but the master is set on spending all the summer months here.'

'I see a difference in him from our last visit. He has awfy trouble with his walking now and seems ... not frail, no, but jist not sae strong.'

'It comes tae us all.' Giggs nodded, tugging her cape back into order.

'If we're lucky tae live that long!'

'I pray every night for Mr Dale's health. It'll be a sad day when that fine gentlemen is called to his maker.'

'Och, don't dwell on such a dreadful thought. I should nac have said anything.'

They turned into a sheltered lane lined with overhanging chestnut trees and walked on the carpet of flattened daisies and dandelions between rutted wagon tracks. The damp grassy edges were tall with fluffy headed meadow sweet and willowherb growing through grasping flowering bramble and stinging nettles. Sweet scents mingled with the pungent aroma of woundwort. Butterflies flittered between the blooms in patches of dappled sunlight, splaying their iridescent wings to show off exotic, vividly coloured patterns.

Out of the wind it was warm, quiet, the sudden peace encouraging the younger girls to pause every few steps to watch the antics of a wren foraging quietly in the thorny thicket or follow the trail of a clambouring beetle.

Anne Caroline was walking ahead, listening to Jean describing the virtues of the latest novel she was reading but when they stopped to wait for the others, she turned and looked back.

Mary was laughing about something, throwing her head back, her loose curls shimmering around her shoulders. Behind her, the maids were smiling and all around them were the soft sounds of insects humming, bird song and rustling leaves high above their heads.

This moment is good, Anne Caroline thought.

***

The next day Anne Caroline and Toshie went to Glasgow.

It was strange to be in Charlotte Street without her family and Anne Caroline was pleased when Rosemary accepted her invitation to dine with her after they both attended an afternoon violin recital.

'The house is swathed in dust sheets except for this room and my bedroom,' she cried, when they entered the drawing room, followed by a senior footman who remained in the reduced staff in the city house through the summer. 'I am beginning to regret my decision to stay the night.'

'Perhaps I should not have arranged the seamstress?' Rosemary asked anxiously.

The friends had maintained a faithful and intimate exchange of letters since Daniel's death, making their meeting earlier that day as easy as if they had never been apart.

Rosemary's new infant daughter was thriving and the apple of her mother's eye, yet she refrained from mentioning her, or her son, not wishing to cause Anne Caroline any discomfort. Like all the Owens' friends, she was shocked by their tragic loss and in turn, very relieved to hear they were already expecting another baby.

'Oh no,' Anne Caroline reassured her, 'I am grateful to you for recommending someone for I am in dire need of new outfits. The fashions change very quickly nowadays and it is bad enough to feel so ungainly and to dress in one of only four suitably large frocks. Their lines are all woefully jaded which does not help my mood.'

'It is important to dress well, dear Anne Caroline, especially while you are with child.'

Rosemary's ample figure was becoming increasingly matronly despite being encased in tightly laced corsets. Having succeeded in marrying well and taking up the role of wife and mother, she was now turning her attention on becoming a figurehead in her social set. She wished to be looked upon as a lady who others craved to be associated with and would clamour to be included in her circle.

'We do not do much in the way of socialising in the country,' Anne Caroline told her, 'and I would not wish to flaunt expensive gowns in front of the paupers who are our neighbours. A new day dress? Maybe something suitably simple yet pretty for entertaining the wives of Robert's guests in the afternoons ... and a new skirt and cape for Church.'

'It is warm enough these days to enjoy the light gauzy materials.'

'With a matching stole? I would feel too naked in some of the frocks I see.'

Rosemary was taking a turn around the elegant room, 'This really is a most wonderful house. I am content in my own until I see these sumptuous fabrics and *objets d'art.*'

A meal was served to them at a small table in the drawing room and they talked companionably while they dined.

Downstairs, Toshie found herself to be the centre of attention, even taking the audacious step of sitting in Breen's chair at the table. Of the half dozen staff, she knew four of them quite well and enjoyed the evening telling tales of her time in Manchester, the morose Mrs Cooper at the mills and how agreeable it was at Rosebank.

Fiercely loyal to her mistress, not one word was uttered regarding the family's bereavement, nor the awkward, hostile attitude the mill workers showed towards Mr Owen. These were lower servants and she felt very protective of the young couple having seen them both distraught in the most devastating period of their marriage.

The next morning, Rosemary returned to Charlotte Street in her handsome little gig, followed by an inferior covered wagon bearing the name Holroyds. The seamstress alighted along with several junior assistants carrying boxes and rolls of material.

'Good gracious!' Anne Caroline greeted her, 'You appear to have brought an entire drapery shop with you!'

'This is Mrs Hendry, she works wonders with a needle.' Rosemary glanced around the scurrying figures, 'Where is she now? Oh, there she is in the hallway ...' A tall young lady hurried into the room carrying two bulky carpet bags. 'She is in the employ of the Holroyds, d'you know them? Of course you do, for my Mama told me they were recommended to her by your own mother. I have been using Mrs Hendry for the last year, she is one of their best and she is greatly sought after in the highest circles. My dear, Mrs Jacob told me about her ... and you know how pernickety *she* can be?'

Anne Caroline's lips curved in a smile at her friend's remark but her expression changed when the seamstress approached.

'Mrs Owen,' Mrs Hendry bobbed a respectful curtsey.

'Do I know you?' Anne Caroline looked at the woman quizzically. 'Have we met before?'

There was something very familiar about her delicate features, large blue eyes beneath dark brows and pale golden hair, but especially in the way she moved and held herself; straight backed, almost defiant.

An awkward pause ensued.

Mrs Hendry glanced away for a second and then, giving out a soft sigh as if coming to a decision, she met Anne Caroline's gaze.

'Aye, Ma'am.'

Rosemary was agog, 'Well, pray tell us, Mrs Hendry?'

'Ah'm frae New Lanark, Ma'am.'

Anne Caroline's brow puckered, then a wide smile spread across her face, 'Now, I remember! You worked in the house!'

'Aye, Ma'am.'

Anne Caroline nodded, pleased to find her memory was serving her well. 'And you are the sister of Mr Joseph Scott, are you not? Don't tell me, I will recall your name! My sisters and I enjoyed such happy times ...' she turned to Rosemary, 'my father presided over her brother's marriage. I was very young at the time but it has stayed with me. Yes, I have it ... Sarah!'

Rosemary laughed, 'Ah, you are mistaken in her name, for this is Mrs Mary Hendry.'

Anne Caroline looked non-plussed, 'Do you have a sister who resembles you closely? I know it was several years ago but I must admit that you are the image of the girl I knew in the village.'

'No, you are not mistaken, ma'am, for I use the name Mary now ... since marrying ... Mr Hendry.' Sarah's mind was frantically searching for a plausable excuse. 'Ma husband prefers ma middle name, Mary, but ma Christian name is Sarah, richt enough.'

Rosemary was losing interest in the conversation and, eager to browse the new patterns and array of fabrics, she moved away to smooth her hand over a roll of turquoise taffeta, murmuring, 'Sarah or Mary, I shall continue to call her Mrs Hendry.'

'Well,' Anne Caroline said, surveying the stylish young woman and noting her discomfort. 'There is no need to feel embarrassed for you have obviously done very well for yourself, Sarah ... Mrs Hendry. My father's wish is for all his workers to better themselves and you are clearly a shining example.'

Somehow, Sarah managed to maintain her composure.

Ever since leaving New Lanark she lived under a shroud of dread for the moment when someone would recognise her and this encounter was unnervingly unexpected. She often visited Mrs Pemberly's home in Kelvinside and presented herself for work at Holroyds that morning believing today's appointment would be the same as all the previous ones. Even when she was informed that she was to take two assistants with her and meet

Mrs Pemberly at a different address, she had no idea where they were going.

It was only a chance comment by the coachman, referring to the privilege of attending 'Mr Dale's gracious residence,' that her heart began to race. Surely not *the* Mr Dale? Her previous employer and the owner of the mills where she worked as a child? The gentleman in whose house she enjoyed some of the happiest days of her life as a housemaid?

When the party disembarked and she was informed Mrs Pemberly was with Mrs Owen awaiting her arrival, she braced herself and planned her course of action.

It was simple.

If she was recognised, she would lie.

Deception was a large part of Sarah's life and it came easily to her, so she would just smile and say they were mistaken.

Mrs Mary Hendry was a needlewoman in Glasgow, employed by a respectable city merchant and married to John Hendry, a woodworker. The Sarah Scott they were confusing her with was an illiterate mill girl who married an Irish rebel and moved away from her family several years ago.

How could one, possibly be the other?

Anyway, she decided, it was years since she had any direct contact with Mr Dale's daughter so it was highly unlikely that anything would be mentioned.

And then she came face to face with Anne Caroline Owen.

Any notion of dishonesty evaporated when Sarah found she just could not bring herself to continue the deceit. Yet, as soon as she admitted her true identity, she regretted it, trying to cover herself by asserting her married name.

The encounter upset her enormously.

She was still dismayed by the incident when she walked home through the quiet evening streets. Being a country girl at heart, she hated living in the city amongst the stench and over-crowding and it pained her to be raising her children in this filth. What was worse was the knowledge that their pretence could be discovered at any moment, leading to grave consequences for them all.

Her husband, Sean, or John as he was now known, still regularly attended clandestine meetings with other Irishmen; sometimes disappearing for days or weeks at a time. His work was intermittent and the family only managed to survive from day to day due to the wages she brought in by working at Holroyd's. The strain of this arrangement caused regular, blistering rows.

Sarah was no longer the submissive wife she had been when they were first married and living in New Lanark. Now, she stood up for herself, but, to her astonishment, her husband responded with new found respect.

The sun was setting by the time she reached the humble row of thatched cottages in Townhead where the family rented a room. Having struggled with how to relate the day's disturbing events, she decided to say nothing of her meeting with Mrs Owen. It was best that way.

She saw Sean sitting on the doorstep rubbing polish into his boots, her son on one side, copying his father, and her daughter on the other.

'Ma!' Cathy shouted, bouncing up to greet her mother.

Sean glanced up, shaking his black hair away from his face. Their eyes met and he winked.

'Yer an awfy man,' she told him, but her fond tone told a different story. 'God alane kens why Ah come hame of a nicht! It must be fer the bairns.'

As soon as she was through the door into the dark interior, she unfastened the fitted silk jacket and matching skirt, folded them carefully and laid them inside a kist before unlacing her kid skin shoes.

The room stank of burnt potatoes. Glancing to the hearth she saw a pot of vegetables bubbling above glowing peat, hissing as splashes escaped the pot.

Standing barefoot in her shift, she yearned to curl up and close her eyes on the wide, rumpled bed where they all slept. Instead, she picked up her shawl, threw it round her shoulders, winding it around her and tying the ends expertly behind her back. There was a lot to be done before she could sleep and then tomorrow it would start all over again.

Chapter Five

"Necessity is the plea for every infringement of human freedom." – William Pitt the Younger

Owen returned to Rosebank triumphantly.

The moment he emerged from the carriage, Anne Caroline felt a rush of pride. His skin was golden, glowing from spending so much time outside in the pure Highland air, alternately wind and sun burnt; his hair, cut neatly before departure, now curled over his collar and flopped in an unruly fringe catching on his brows and lashes. She appraised him anew, excited at hearing the familiar tones of his voice as if for the first time.

'I have missed you so much, my dearest Robert,' she cried, when they were alone in their room.

'As I have, you.' He took her in his arms, kissing her tenderly. 'The journey was extremely tiring, you would not have enjoyed that aspect.' He looked into her eyes, searching for the desolation which clouded her soul since Daniel's death and finding only hints of it behind her loving gaze. 'You are looking well. You have been all right while I have been away?'

'I feel a little more at ease, daily less anxious. There is much to keep me occupied here and there is always someone nearby to distract me from melancholy thoughts.'

'I am sure your family have enjoyed having you here and it was a comfort to know you were safe in your father's house.'

He kissed the top of her brown curls, hugging her against him.

'Oh Caroline,' he sighed, 'it was a remarkable experience but I admit it is a relief to be finished with the confines and discomforts of the carriage. I swear I can still feel the motion of the springs even as I stand here on this rug.'

She took a seat at the dressing-table to hear his news while he freshened up and changed his rumpled travelling clothes for clean evening wear.

'The further north we went, the wilder the terrain. Even the people seemed freer in their movement and expression. Perhaps being so close to Nature? At the inns, despite being ramshackle and smelling strongly of peat smoke, we were welcomed and given warm hospitality ... on the whole, the mattresses were well stuffed and wholesome. I am happy to say I always fell readily to sleep! Of course, we were aware the peasants could see easy opportunities to make a few pennies from us.' He opened the doors on the mahogany wardrobe, searching for an evening jacket: it was pleasant not to be restricted to the same tail coat he was forced to wear every evening on the tour. 'MacIntosh's opulent carriage caused a commotion wherever we went and his horses were greatly admired.'

He shrugged on a dark brown jacket with satin trim, buttoning it neatly and adjusting the folds of his cravat so they tucked into the embroidered waistcoat.

Anne Caroline went over to him, smoothing a hand over his shoulder to remove a stray hair, enjoying their intimacy.

'So, perhaps it was not the frightful ordeal you anticipated?'

'There were moments! One day, we came to a narrow bridge, a drover's bridge, spanning a deep mountain stream. The width of the chariot wheels was almost exactly the width of the road. It was only due to the extreme skill of the coachman and his handling of the team that the whole cab was not lost over the side.'

'My dear! You might have been killed!'

'Fear not! We all disembarked and walked behind but there was much jubilation and cheering on reaching the other side.'

He rummaged around in his portmanteau.

'I brought this from Inverness ... for you.'

He gave her a small paper parcel tied with a satin ribbon.

'Oh, it is beautiful!' she held up a silver brooch set with coloured stones intricately fashioned into a thistle. 'Thank you! I shall wear it this evening.'

When they gathered with the family in the drawing room Owen bestowed small gifts on everyone. Each one had an accompanying tale, adding to the charm of the simple tokens.

For his father in law, he purchased a beautifully painted map of the area around Spinningdale which Dale accepted with a beaming smile, immediately wanting to know which of the hamlets Owen visited.

In all, the tour of the Highlands was a huge success and Owen was brimming with stories to share with his waiting audience. Dale was eager to hear reports on his mills and Anne Caroline and her sisters were full of questions about the great houses and families who gave him hospitality.

In the kitchen, Murdoch was being bombarded with similar questions..

'Did ye see the sea?'

'Aye.'

'Were the hooses grander than Mr Dale's?'

'Naw, weel, no' as grand as yon Glesgie mansion but mair like this yin. Though, Lord Methven's wis a muckle castle and the corridors in Mr Dempster's ran fur miles.'

'Whit wer' the lassies like?' a footman asked.

Murdoch laughed, his cheeks growing pink. 'As bonnie as peaches!'

'Whit did ye eat? The same as us or jist oatmeal orra time?'

'No' as guid as Cook's,' he cast a cheeky look to the rotund figure by the stove, 'an' in yin place the scullery wis running wi' rats ... an' there were chookies under the table aroond yer feet!'

The girls squealed and giggled.

'Did they a' speak the Gaelic?'

Cook and her two maids were rattling around putting the finishing touches to the dishes for the welcome home meal.

'Ah cannae hear mesel'think!' she shouted over her shoulder to the servants chattering around the table. 'Wheesht the noo, will ye! When the food's up wi' Renwick in the dining room Ah want tae hear all aboot it as weel!'

Breen came in, 'My goodness, what a hullabaloo! I take it you had a safe journey?' She looked pointedly at Murdoch who jumped to his feet.

'Aye, thank you, Mrs Breen.'

'Well, I'm sure we will hear all your adventures in due course. Right now, we need to have the meal served and the rooms set fair while the family are at their dinner.'

The Dale servants hurriedly scraped back their chairs and went about their business.

Breen paused beside Cook, saying in an undertone. 'It is good to hear such cheerful voices, both in the drawing room and here.'

'Aye, we have a happy hoose the nicht.' Cook stirred a generous dollop of cream into the mashed potatoes, tasted the results, added a couple more pinches of salt, tasted again and then indicated the dish be taken through to the table, asking, 'How lang are the Owens staying, noo he's back frae his gallavantin'?'

'Toshie told me this morning they were expecting to leave in a couple of days.'

Cook pushed stray hairs back under her cap.

'An' then we'll no' see Mrs Owen agin until the babbie's due?'

Breen nodded, 'Now, there's a thought.'

The kitchen was suddenly quiet, all servants having disappeared to their chores, leaving only the two older women standing beside the stove.

Cook lifted the kettle, judged the weight to be right for a pot of tea's worth of water and placed it on the range.

'We must pray tae God their next bairn is spared. Sich a tragedy,' she sighed.

'Some things are best not dwelt upon. It was God's will and we must trust in His divine wisdom.'

'Ma sister's second born died beside her in the bed, as they slept.' Cook said, visibly upset. 'She still says he's jist sleepin'.'

'Life can be awfy hard,' Breen squeezed her arm. 'Maybe it's not so bad to be auld spinsters like ourselves, when we see such pain for these mothers, whether rich or poor.'

Taking a deep breath to banish the memories of her grief-stricken sister, Cook busied herself with reaching for a tea pot from the dresser. Her fingers lingered over the plain white one but moved on to grasp the handle of her favourite, delicately painted with roses.

'Well, it's too late fcr either o' us tae hanker efter babbies.' she muttered. 'Ye can nae be in service an' be wantin' bairns.'

Breen smiled, wistfully. 'The thought of children always appealed to me.'

Then she gave Cook a knowing look, 'It was the thought of being wed to a man that did not appeal!'

***

The next morning Owen gave Dale his considered reports on the mills.

Stanley showed potential and the housing stock was in fair condition. He felt it could succeed if given further investment and with the close proximity of Perth harbour, it could soon return profits.

'My concern lies with Mr Craig, the manager. On my second visit, he invited me to dine with him at Stanley House. It is a magnificent residence and he seemed more preoccupied with its upkeep and his agricultural pursuits in its grounds than he did with the mills.'

'Was he forthcoming with facts and figures for the business?'

'I fear he is not one for paperwork, however, I was given the chance to spend the afternoon with his clerk and discovered much of what I needed in various ledgers.'

'And Spinningdale?'

'The workers are dejected and poorly managed,' Owen said forcefully. 'There is a generally bad feeling to the place as soon as you enter the doorway, making it clear from even the smallest child to the Overseers that they do wish to be there. The cleanliness and health of the people is appalling. On our brief stroll to view the housing we encountered disorder, waste and dirt at every turn. Nearly all are women and children. I was informed that this is always the case in the summer months due to the men having left to travel south for work in the fields or forestry. Even road building is sought as a preference to being employed in the mill!'

'It is as I thought,' Dale agreed. 'Yet there is no other business for them to make a living and without the means to feed and provide shelter for their families they would have to leave the area.'

'Perhaps that is what they should do? The accounts illustrate the lack of industry, showing a serious loss for the last eight

119

years and I can see no improvement in the foreseeable future.'
Owen ran his hand over his head in despair. 'Why, in the name
of goodness, was it not a woollen mill? The new fascination of
the landowners for sheep would have readily filled the stores
and perhaps the workers would be keener to handle local
produce from neighbouring land.'

'I argued this very point at the time of inception but my
partners were adamant that cotton would be more lucrative in
the long run.' Dale grunted, remembering the raised voices and
ardent reasoning of his colleagues. 'They were carried away
with the thought of recreating the successes of Manchester and
my own businesses in the Lowlands, quite blind to the
geography of the venture.'

'But handkerchiefs? Cotton handkerchiefs by the thousand ...
the order book is failing and with the loss of so many markets
in Europe I cannot see production levels, poor as they are, even
being maintained.'

'My role in creating Spinningdale was entirely to bring
shelter and work to that wretched part of Scotland. I did not
expect, nor need, financial returns. I most vehemently wished to
halt the seemingly inevitable emigration from Scotland.'

'The population is falling rapidly across the entire region.'

'Aye. Just today I read of the plight of the emigrant ship, the
Sarah. It sailed out of Fort William with nigh on seven hundred
passengers aboard, packed to the gunnels! I know you share my
abhorrence of the slave trade, the most inhumane of trades, yet
had these poor unfortunate Scots been slaves they would only
have allowed that ship to carry less than five hundred in its
holds! By God, where's the conscience in this land when we
treat our brethren in this ghastly manner.'

'Did the ship sail?'

'Indeed it sailed, for several weeks, to Pictou in the Americas
but made land with around fifty dead and countless others taken
ill and dying.' Dale shook his head, jowls wobbling. 'I pray for
the suffering of those souls. May the Lord God take mercy on
them and grant them Everlasting Life.'

They both fell silent for some minutes: contemplative.

Then Owen ventured, 'I gather there are calls for the
Passenger Bill to be taken through Parliament without delay. At

least the numbers will be limited and some control put upon the conditions aboard.'

'There should be no ships crossing the seas with their holds full of human cargo!' Dale exclaimed. 'Neither African nor Scottish! It is a sin against all that is Holy that one man treats another with such contempt! I read of the new plans to improve the barren land in the north but for the people there ... they know these mountains as their homes. Spinningdale was an attempt to keep them at least on their own soil.'

Owen could see Dale was becoming more heated with every word.

'I can only agree with you and applaud your intentions, Sir. I too am in disagreement with the whole notion of forcing families to leave the land of their ancestors.' He lowered his voice to a reasonable tone. 'While travelling, I heard some terrible tales of injustice. The Highlanders are proud of their ways. They are strong people with their own language and a long history of their own customs. It is very clear that they are still bitter against the English and I cannot blame them. Sir George Dempster gave me many examples of why they harbour this deep resentment, not just since Culloden, fifty odd years ago, but to the Union, a hundred years ago and long before that time as well.'

'What we as merchants and bankers see as progress,' Dale said solemnly, 'is also the raping and pillaging of a nation's way of life.'

'It is truly shocking,' Owen agreed. 'For pure greed, these country folk are being thrown out of their tenancies to make way for sheep. I heard of great swathes of land being burnt and sown with grass to feed hundreds upon hundreds of sheep. The tenants are redeployed to pull kelp on the coast, but not all wish that life.'

'And apparently, nor do they wish to work in mills.'

'It is my view, Sir, that, while it was a worthy experiment, you should dispose of Spinningdale as soon as you can find a buyer. Whereas with Stanley, I have laid out my figures for its necessary investment,' Owen reached for the papers on the desk beside him and passed them across to Dale.

The following day, both Dale and Owen's carriages trotted out of Cambuslang towards Glasgow. The gentlemen were meeting with MacIntosh and other business colleagues at the Tontine while Anne Caroline and Toshie were returning to Charlotte Street for the final fittings with Mrs Hendry and then to Rosemary's for the afternoon.

'Aha! Ye survived the tour!' Scott Moncrieff hailed Owen as they entered the busy coffee rooms.

Owen raised a hand in greeting, allowing Dale to precede him through the throng. Heads were turning, merchants and clerks alike swung in their seats: Dale was in Glasgow, perhaps a meeting could be contrived, a word in his ear as he passed?

'Indeed!' Owen called back, 'A thrilling and enjoyable experience in the main part!'

'An' that was just tolerating my company!' MacIntosh boomed, standing up to grasp Dale's hand and usher him into the bench beside him. 'We passed a splendid time, I am sure your son in law has related the stories.'

'There will be many more, no doubt,' Dale grinned, sinking his broad backside onto the seat. The aches in his joints eased in the warm summer temperatures and his digestive system was behaving today, allowing him to relax and join the company of friends in a way he used to take for granted in previous years. He thoroughly enjoyed business, all areas, from the excitement of planning new ventures to nurturing markets and promoting the products. When he felt well, as he did that day, he relished the challenges, sharing and drawing on his experience to advise others and make decisions.

Unfortunately, these days of good health were becoming the exception and when he was dogged by a lack of energy, heartburn and rheumatism, he was glad of having retired from most of his everyday affairs.

The four men discussed the pros and cons of selling up at Spinningdale and dissolving the company of Balnoe which they formed specially for the purpose of creating the northerly mill village.

'It's been ten years,' MacIntosh said sombrely. 'We've given it a good crack o' the whip. None of us could have foreseen the effects of this protracted war.'

'Aye, we tried.' Dale took a sip from his coffee. 'I'm still sorely concerned for the loss of so many Scotsmen leaving our shores.'

'If we could run factories in the same fashion as New Lanark, I am sure many more would stay,' said Owen. 'The fact that Spinningdale is so inaccessible makes it hard. I am pleased to say, and I am sure, Sir,' he glanced at Dale, 'you would agree, the Highlanders employed in the Lanark mills are hard workers and cheery souls. They just need to be guided and although Sir George can oversee operations from time to time, clearly the site managers have no regard for their workers nor the conditions they impose upon them.'

MacIntosh gave a snort, but said kindly, 'You give too much thought to the feelings of the paupers we employ. They make their own lives out-with the mill.'

'Yes, and we provide schooling and housing but these people are ignorant of how to make the best use of these facilities. It is not their fault, I am not accusing them of being wantonly slovenly, it is a matter of teaching them, showing them how to live better lives.'

Dale caught MacIntosh's eye; both men had heard Owen's views on this subject, regularly.

Owen noticed their exchange but did not take offence. 'I make no apologies for my words, and if I repeat them it is because I feel strongly.' He smiled, 'The Highlanders are used to living in stone crofts and running among the hills as and when they wished. They grew their own food by their doors and spent most of their time in family groups where they would care for each other. Of course, they hate being shut inside four walls and working from dawn to dusk amid heat and noise.'

'How else do we manufacture cotton, if not in mills?' Scott Moncrieff asked. 'The demand is huge, as you know.'

'Markets right across the world are demanding cotton and as a mill owner I wish to take advantage of it.' Owen admitted. 'That is not to say that this could not be managed in a more enlightened manner, which is my aim at New Lanark.'

MacIntosh looked at Dale's placid features wondering why he did not speak.

'Well,' he said, for him. 'Mr Dale has been doing this for years.'

Owen nodded, 'Indeed he has, but we cannot accommodate all the evicted Highlanders at New Lanark. I am making many more improvements and hope to impress upon the visitors who view my mills that these establishments do not need to be dreaded. They could and should be wholesome communities.'

For all his enthusiasm, Owen's buoyant mood took a severe check within hours of returning to New Lanark.

'It's the long light evenings,' Humphreys told him by way of explanation.

Owen was reading the report on incidences of drunkenness and disorder during his absence.

'McEwan *and* Bates? Both dismissed?' Owen showed deep disappointment. 'I spoke at length with Bates not two days before leaving. I was sure he grasped the fact that his behaviour was unacceptable and should he be found to be intoxicated and brawling again we would have no choice but to sack him. His wife is a Twister in Mill Three, is she not?'

'Yes, and a good one. She set about him, clouting him and shouting at him long into the evening.'

'And two others ... also given warnings?'

'As I say, there is greater opportunity for them to meet after work and fall into these bad ways.' Humphreys did not add that the workers took full advantage of the fact that the Owens were not in residence. Sloppy time keeping, lewd behaviour and, at times, complete absence from work caused numerous problems.

A medical report caught Owen's eye.

'A serious accident?' He quickly read the report. 'This Mr Dunn, is he recovering?'

'His arm was too mangled by the machine to be saved, but McGibbon was at the scene within minutes and made all the arrangements for him to be transferred to the Infirmary in Edinburgh. The last we heard, he is making good progress and should be back in the village very soon.'

'I will visit him when he returns, make sure I am informed.' He continued through the papers on his desk. 'Are we no further on with finalising the conditions for the weir? I expected to find a letter from the Miss Edmonstones' factor.'

'There was a letter, yes.' Humphreys riffled through the pile on his own desk. 'Here! Unfortunately they are prevaricating again. This time about the water being diverted on the Sabbath.'

Owen took a deep breath, forming a patient expression on his features. 'Surely I have already informed them that we would not be running the wheels on a Sunday? Unless in extreme circumstances?'

'I believe it is clarification of the 'extreme circumstances' which they refer to in the letter. Also, they make further remonstrations concerning the residents of the village trespassing on their land.'

'I will ask for another meeting with them. Really,' annoyance tinged his voice, 'I assumed we were finished with this discussion and was looking forward to proceeding with the project.' He turned his attention to the list of those tenants still refusing to allow inspections of their rooms. 'I see three of the rooms are occupied by the same family. They were from Glasgow, were they not?'

'Indeed,' Humphreys said. 'It's not for the want of the men folk trying to make them see sense. It's the two older women ... fierce in their opposition.'

'Then we shall move them,' Owen said, decisively. 'All the families who will not follow these guidelines will be moved to the edge of the village. It would be unfair for a good housewife to have her efforts contaminated by the stench and infestations of her wanton neighbours.' He looked up from the sheaf of papers. 'Make sure they are aware of the repercussions and if they continue to bar their doors this week, move them next week.'

Production figures were up, orders were up and the estimates for the construction of Nursery Buildings were awaiting his approval. The sum was less than already agreed with his partners so he immediately called for his clerk, Gerry, to draw up a formal acceptance and instruct the work to start straight away.

However, when he returned to his house after this long meeting, Owen felt deflated.

His wife noticed the lack of his usual optimism and asked the reason.

'Oh there is nothing of major concern, my dear,' he replied. 'When I was away, my plans for the future of these mills were forever in my mind. I can see it so clearly, how it could be ... how it *should* be.' He sighed heavily. 'Seeing the reality shows me how much there is still to be done.'

Anne Caroline murmured encouragement, telling him not to expect to do everything at once.

'Why put off these improvements?' he said, 'I can see no good reason for delaying a better way of life, yet, there are some people who are so stuck in how things have always been that they cannot open their eyes and see there is an alternative. A much *better* alternative.'

He told her of the Edmonstones and their worries regarding the villagers stealing or poaching on Corehouse estate and then of the tenants who refused to lay their homes open for inspection.

Cooper appeared to ask if there was anything they required.

'Perhaps a jug of hot chocolate?' Anne Caroline raised her eyebrows to her husband. 'My dear? Will you join me? I find a cup of hot chocolate very soothing'

Owen agreed, rising from his seat to tend the fire.

'You would not believe it of me, but while in the north, I enjoyed the whisky.'

'Gracious! I always thought you found it too strong?'

'After a day of exercise in the mountain air it did not seem to affect me in the same way. Sir George initiated me to the taste of several local distilleries and it was quite delicious. In very small amounts, I might add!'

Cooper turned on her heel and descended the stairs to the kitchen, sniffing her disapproval. Not only did the Master shun the word of the Lord, he imbibed strong spirits!

***

'Weel, the Owens are hame.'

Fiona looked up from her sewing to find Rosie standing in front of her. Since the mill bell rang out a few minutes before, there was such a lot of noise and activity in the street that she did not hear her approach.

'Sae Mrs Young telt me.'

Rosie sat down on the ground and pulled off her cap, flapping it in the evening air to free hundreds of specks of cotton. Just released from work, her face was still flushed from the overheated work room; speckled with fibres.

'Ye look all in?'

126

''Tis a lang day.' Rosie smothered a yawn. 'Ah telt mesel' Ah'd bake some loaves this eve but Ah hav'nae a notion tae dae onything but sit doon.'

Fiona made a final stitch and bit off the thread, holding up one of Robbie's little smocks.

'Gerry will be late the nicht.' Rosie's eyes were wandering aimlessly over the workers streaming home. 'He's alis late when Mr Owen is here.'

'D'ye want tae stiy wi' us fer yer supper?' Fiona asked, bent over her needle work again. 'There's plenty.'

'That's temptin'.' Rosie yawned again.

'Will ye no dae tha'!' Fiona teased. 'Ye'll ha'e me a' it an' efter the day Ah'v had, ma eyes'll close as quick as ye say blink!'

Rosie made a face. 'Ye dinnae ha' tae staun a' day wi' tha' infernal racket in yer heid. Whish -whish, whish -whish! It's still in ma ears the noo.'

'Naw, Ah had the bairns bawling and Mr Aitken tellin' me 'dae this' every time Ah drew breath.'

'Ah thocht ye liked the school room?'

'Och, Ah dae. It's jist havin' tae be there every day ... like onything.'

Rosie rearranged herself to sit cross-legged, modestly tucking her skirts around her barefeet.

'Seein' ye sewing brings Sarah tae mind. Ah wonder whit she's daen?'

'Probably havin' anither wean ...' Fiona caught herself, 'or sewing an' moanin' aboot bein' tired.'

'Ye can mention babbies, ye ken? Ah'm no' gonnae throw mesel' aff Corra Linn fer the want o' a bairn, sae din nae fret.'

Rosie's attention went to Sionaidh sitting contentedly in the basket beside them. She was a quiet baby, sometimes, Rosie thought, maybe a little too quiet and docile. She didn't want to say anything to Fiona or her brother but it seemed the infant often stared into space with a blank expression and she still made no effort to try and crawl. Picking up the well chewed clothes peg in the bottom of the basket, she waved it infront of the baby's face and was pleased to see the chubby fingers grasp it.

'Sometimes,' Rosie mused, 'I wonder whit it must be like tae be like Mrs Owen. She jist sits in tha' fine hoose a' day wi' servants at her beck an' call. Mibbee yin day ma Gerry will rise tae manager an earn a salary an' Ah can leave ma work an' sit a' day.'

'Ye wid get awfy fed up, ye can nae sit aboot an' dae nuchin'...'

'Ah wid gie it a fair try!'

'Here's yer man noo ...' Fiona nodded down the street.

Gerry was conspicuous among the other residents with his dark coat reaching below his knees and black top hat.

'There's guid news fer Joe,' he informed them straight away. 'Mr Owen's going ahead wi' the building werk.'

'Oh my!' Fiona flashed her wide smile. 'He'll be sae pleased wi' that! An' Ah'll be seein' him mair!'

Rosie held her hand up to her husband, 'Gie me a haun?'

He pulled her gently to her feet and she brushed at the dust and grit on her skirt saying, 'Ye've bin marrit nigh on ten year an' ye still want tae see mair o' him?'

'Ye see Gerry as soon as he steps oot the office!'

'Aye,' Rosie slipped her hand into Gerry's. 'It's grand. Ah can nae fathom how some wimen manage when their men gang awa' tae war. We see oors every day, an' Ah'm thankfu'.'

Gerry smiled sheepishly, 'Come an' fetch me some supper then.'

As the couple walked away, tall gangling Gerry and tiny barefoot Rosie, picking her way carefully beside him, swinging her cap, Fiona heard her say, 'An' t'morra, Ah'll esk Netta next door tae fire the stove early fer me an' Ah'll dae a baking fer ye.'

The street was emptying so Fiona called to her sons and started to gather up her belongings.

Swifts were soaring over the village, diving between the tall buildings and jinxing around the chimney pots. Their high pitched screams echoed around the valley while windows clattered shut and tenement doors banged. Twilight was descending, merging colours into shadows as another day at the mills drew to a close.

For a small space of time, nothing moved in the darkening village and then the first black and white snouts of badgers snuffled their way out of the woodland. Soon, they were joined by owls and bats, claiming the peaceful night as their own.

***

Sam left the camp and walked up a short incline to where a line of riflemen were positioned, their sights trained on the enemy below.

Behind him, stars still shone in the night sky, ahead, the approaching sunrise bathed the grey landscape in an eery, misty light. Silhouettes of two soldiers turned on hearing his approach, saluting him before resuming their duties.

He crested the hill and looked down on Alexandria.

The black, inky water of the port was crowded with small boats moving between half a dozen huge, full rigged war-ships. Trapped by the British blockade in the Mediterranean, their sails were furled tightly against towering masts, swaying gently at anchor in the harbour. Through the early morning air came the call to prayer, proclaimed from ornate minarets adorning mosques all down the valley.

Sam shivered.

This was an extraordinary, beautiful country.

As well as the Egyptians who worked and lived in Alexandria, there were thirteen thousand French soldiers confined behind the fortified city walls which lay barely half a mile from where he stood. After Hely Hutchison's victory in taking back Cairo, the Revolutionaries retreated to this vital port only to find they were unable to break out.

The Cameronians joined another thirty four battalions stationed both to the east and west, effectively cutting the French off from all supplies. Since arriving at the camp, they witnessed or actively participated in action every day, with each side continually mounting assaults on the other. Brutal skirmishes resulted in injuries for the British and their Turkish allies but brought about much more serious casualties and fatalities to the weak and disheartened French.

The French soldiers were almost unrecognisable now. Apart from the compulsory tricolour cockade, most of the regulation blue, red and white uniforms were long worn out and gone, supplanted by civilian clothes and jackets of every hue. Disease was rampant and the shortage of food meant Arab horses were the only available source of sustenance.

Their terrible plight was recognised and continually assessed by the British who knew it was only a matter of time before Menou, the Commander of French forces, would be forced to surrender.

A cool breeze fanned his cheek and Sam relished its caress. All too soon they would be victims of the burning sun once more, dazzled by its unremitting brilliance and their skin scorched within minutes if laid bare. He was newly washed and shaved, thankful for a ready supply of water from a spring nearby; the main reason for choosing this area in which to station the garrison.

He leaned against a palm tree, one of several surrounding the camp, his hand on his sword, eager for the whole business to be over. Yet, despite the hardships and danger, he felt invigorated to be serving on the front line in such an important battle. He wore his scarlet uniform with pride, ready for his orders, whatever the day might bring.

Two hours later, the Cameronians marched out of the camp to the beating drum, their flag held high against the startling blue sky, helmet badges glinting, rifles with bayonets fixed. Today, twenty regiments were attacking at the same time, all at different positions and each with particular aims to achieve. Orderly and immaculately in step, the British and Turkish forces converged on Alexandria.

Sam's heart was thundering in his chest, cheeks burning under the blazing sun as he squinted to focus on an area of collapsed wall, judged by the Colonel as wide enough to breach. With support from their canons pounding from the hill, the riflemen at the front dropped to their knees, firing at the French Guard to clear the way.

Then the bugles sounded along the lines of troops encircling the city and they started to run: scrambling over rocks, surging among buildings, ten thousand strong, screaming and roaring, firing, reloading, firing, reloading ... blades slicing.

Fear vanished and sheer survival took over.

Bellowing orders to six of his best men, Sam fought his way out of the main street towards a side lane which he knew lead to a barricaded building. Resistance was vicious and every step of the way was hard won by hand to hand combat. The anonymous mass of the Revolutionary Army became individual frantic human beings, pitiable with their bearded, starving faces and tattered uniforms.

Finally disengaging from the fray, Sam's band of scarlet soldiers dashed away from the main battle but soon realised with alarm that the intelligence they received was flawed.

Expecting soldiers, they now faced two canons, already primed and firing. This was the ammunition store, the target he was detailed to destroy, and his hand went involuntarily to the bag slung around his waist holding a firebox and flammable material.

Diving for cover, he forged forward; half crawling, half running between shacks, scaling walls and scampering along roofs, his men following. Dodging and weaving amidst the dust and chaos he vaulted over a wall, falling clumsily into an empty courtyard and instantly recognising the square black windows of the armoury. Within moments he was joined by several of his men and they set about raising a fire.

'Run!' he yelled, his voice harsh, shaking from exertion. 'Our job's done! Get out and God speed!'

Within seconds of clambering back onto the roof, a massive explosion ripped the building apart, showering rocks and debris over the fleeing men. The violent shock wave knocked them to the ground, killing the French artillery men in the street and pouring out plumes of billowing smoke.

From beyond this mayhem, bugles were sounding the retreat. Stunned, Sam dragged himself to his feet and with bleary vision, retrieved his hat from beneath a pile of bricks, jamming it on his head to shield himself a little from the merciless sun before gathering up his men and running behind them to escape the city walls.

A grim smile spread across his blackened face.

'Our job's done,' he muttered, over and over, until they were beyond the city walls, away from the screams and pandemonium.

He slowed to a walk, his breath coming in laboured gasps.

He was alive.

Thank God, he was alive and as far as he could tell, all his men were still with him. He wiped at the sweat running down his face, blinking at the saltiness stinging his eyes and was suddenly gripped by dizziness. Staggering slightly, he reached out to grab the man in front of him, noticing with surprise that his hand was as scarlet as his jacket.

The soldier glanced over his shoulder, open mouthed. 'Sir, yer heid! '

Sam's arm dropped to his side, his knees crumpling, knowing he was falling but unable to speak as a dark fog sucked away his senses ...

Chapter Six

*"Do not judge, and you will not be judged. Do not condemn,
and you will not be condemned. Forgive, and you will be
forgiven." Luke 6:37 NIV*

While most of Robert Owen's proposals for improving the
lives of his villagers were being thwarted by his Manchester
partners, the construction of the Nursery Buildings was moving
ahead as planned. Once again, New Lanark residents were
engulfed by the noise and dust of builders and the twisting
cobbled road leading down to the mills bustled with heavy
horses dragging wagons laden with building materials.

'Does it no' strike ye as odd tae be doon here agin? Wi' a' the
hammerin' and cairts o' stane aroon ye?'

Joe looked up from his work on the foundations, squinting
against the pale white light of the overcast sky to find Tam
watching him.

'Ah live here!' he shouted back, above the din. 'An' it's no'
that lang since we put up New Buildin's.' He jerked his head to
the towering block of tenements adjacent to the Nursery.
'Ye've no' bin doon here fer years ...' Joe pulled himself out of
the trench to stand beside his friend. 'Whit brings ye doon?'

Since admitting to his fabricated story about how he lost his
arm, Tam's behaviour towards Joe was wary at first, keeping
his distance. Slowly, this wore off and a new closeness formed.

Tam held up a sheaf of papers. 'This. A' the materials fer yer
joab. Ewing telt me tae run o'er it wi' ye.'

Joe's lack of education rarely held him back but when it came
to reading and writing he had fallen into the habit of relying on
Tam or Fiona.

133

'Ye could ha'e gi'en it tae me at the yaird.'

'Naw, weel ... aye, yer richt but there wis sumat else Ah wanted tae talk aboot, private like.'

Joe spread his arms to embrace the crowded street and rattling carts. 'An' it's gie private here!' he laughed, pulling off his dusty cap and slapping it against his thigh. 'Ah can barely hear ma ane thochts.'

'Ah didnae want Ewing tae hear, is all.' Tam leaned closer, waiting for the rush and rumble of a barrow load of sand to be deposited before continuing. 'Ye ken fer a couple o' years Ah've bin learnin' ma letters an' noo Ah'm keepin' the books fer Mistress Ewing's bakery as weel as helpin' oot wi' the office papers fer the yaird? An' bein' paid fer it an' a'.'

'Aye, an' Ah gather yer daen a grand joab.' Joe's eyes were flicking over his team of men labouring among the foundation stones.

'Miss Melanie has bin sae patient an' kind,' Tam laid his hand on Joe's arm, 'Are ye listenin' tae me?'

'Aye, Ah am, but Ah cannae staun here blethering ...'

'Ah'm no' jist bletherin'... it's important tae me, mon!'

'Whit?'

'D'ye think Miss Melanie wid marry me?'

'Whit?' Joe gave him his full attention. 'Ah didnae ken ye'd taken a fancy tae wee Mel?'

'An' why no'? ' Tam was defensive.

'Weel ... she's awfy young ...'

'She'll be seventeen years next month.'

Joe chuckled, 'Is tha' a fact? Maks me feel gie auld!'

'Ne'er mind aboot ye feelin' auld! Whit d'ye ken? She's sae sweet hairted an' seems tae like me. She's alis fussin' o'er me an' bakin' me special cakes. The patience she had when Ah wis startin' tae write an' learnin' ma sums... she's an awfy guid teacher! But it wis mair than that. Ah see it in her eyes, or is it jist me wishin'? Afore the army, Ah ken the lassies liked me weel enough but noo? Efter a', Ah'm crippled ... Ah'm jist feart it's 'cause she pities me?'

'Naw, it's no' that she feels sorry fer ye, dinnae fret on tha' score. She telt me months back how brave she thocht ye were, an' clever wi' it.'

'She did?'

'Aye.' Joe remembered the incident. 'She was makin' scones an' put some aside fer ye, saying ye needed feedin' up an' whit a braw friend Ah had in ye.'

Tam's face glowed with pleasure. 'Why didn't ye tell me?'

With a shrug, Joe slapped Tam on the back, making a move to end the conversation. 'She likes ye, Ah can vouch fer that but Ah cannae say ony mair. If ye care fer her, Tam, an' she's the lass fer ye, then ask her faither fer permission tae court her ... proper like? At the end o' the day it's Mr Ewing who has tae agree.' Joe jumped back down into the trench, 'Ah ha'e tae git on noo, tell me aboot yon list t'morra? guid luck!'

As he worked, Joe pondered on the unlikely union between his friend and the stonemason's daughter. Even if Mel returned Tam's feelings, her father would be looking to find her a husband who could step up to taking charge of not only the bakery but also his stone masonry business as well as caring for her spinster aunt. The relationship seemed doomed from the start.

'Mr Scott!' A lady's clear, high-pitched voice cut through his thoughts and the racket all around him. 'Mr Scott!' it came again, insistent.

Mrs Owen, with her maid beside her, was standing a few yards away, an incongruously feminine figure in her colourful dress and flower embellished hat. She raised a gloved hand to catch his attention.

He dropped his tools and leaped up onto the road.

'Mrs Owen!' he raised his cap, bowing his head politely.

'I trust you and your family are well?' Anne Caroline asked, appraising him with a slight smile. 'Is it not wonderful to see our little village growing once again?'

A heavy wagon drawn by six Clydesdales was manoeuvring its way towards them down the last stretch of the hill, accompanied by the clattering of poles being jammed under the wheels every few yards to slow its progress. All the men on the site were scrambling onto the road, clearing away buckets, tools and ladders amidst shouted directions to prepare for the delivery.

'Aye, indeed.' Joe agreed, nervous to have the mill owner's pregnant wife in such a potentially dangerous situation.

'I have been meaning to speak with you for some time,' Anne Caroline said loudly, 'however on each occasion I have been way-laid by other matters. I just wanted to tell you how pleased I am to know your sister is doing so well.'

Joe nodded, slowly. Had Rosie been promoted? She was now on one of the largest twisting machines in Mill Three, but surely she'd been working it for several months? Or was it her duties as a superintendent for her stairs? That must be it: Rosie was one of a minority who embraced Mr Owen's new rules.

'Aye she's a grand worker.' The noise around them was rising.

Anne Caroline plucked at the delicate folds of her skirt. 'I am delighted with all her designs. She has great skill with a needle, you can be very proud of her.'

Confusion showed openly in Joe's expressive eyes.

'Your sister, Mr Scott? Sarah?' Anne Caroline clarified. 'Now employed by Holroyds in Glasgow? Did she not mention to you that she has made several pieces for me?'

A loud clatter caused Anne Caroline to miss the look of shock on Joe's face as she glanced round sharply to see the massive horses forging towards them.

She swung back to him, 'I daresay that load is destined for here, so ...' she laughed, raising her voice 'I shall leave you to your work!'

Toshie was urging her mistress out of harm's way, making the labourers stand back to allow a path towards her house.

'Thank ye ...' Joe cried, 'Thank ye ... ma'am.' His brain would not function properly, suddenly filled with a hundred questions, none of which would form into coherent words before Mrs Owen was almost out of ear shot.

'Mistress Owen! Can ye tell me, please ...' he shouted across the crowd, 'is my sister well?'

Through the clamour he couldn't make out her words but her bright smile and nodding bonnet were answer enough and he raised his cap again in acknowledgment.

'In Glesgie!' Fiona said excitedly, when Joe told her the news. 'An' she's workin' as a seamstress. That's jist grand! it's whit she alis wanted tae duc. Aw, Ah'm that pleased fer her.'

Cal was very relieved to hear of Sarah's good fortune.

'Ye say Mrs Owen telt ye oor Sarah made her claes?' he asked. 'The claes she's wearing noo? Fer truth?'

'Aye, an' she said the name o' the place where she werks but fer the life o' me Ah cannae mind it. It wis sich a shock tae hear her name.'

'Kind o' Mrs Owen tae tell ye,' Fiona said thoughtfully. 'Och, Ah hope she's all richt, happy ... an' the bairns.'

She had moved a chair to the window to catch the last of the light and was sitting with Robbie on her knee, combing lice eggs from his hair. 'Ye'll ha'e tae dae, son. Let your brither up noo.'

Davey took his place. 'Can we gang up tae Glesgie an' see Aunty Sarah?'

'It's a lang way away,' Fiona murmured, scrutinising the close toothed comb. 'But mibbee Ah could ask yin o' the servants at Owen's hoose tae tak a letter fer her?'

'Sarah can nae read,' Cal said straight away.

'Ah ken tha', but Sean can.'

Joe was doubtful. He yawned, stretching out his long legs; it had been a heavy day's work. 'D'ye ken ony o' yon servants?'

'No' yet,' Fiona's attention was caught by movement in Davey's thick curls. 'But Ah'll mak a point o' it next time Ah see ony o' them in the street. They can nae all be as snooty as yon stuck up 'holier than thou' Mrs Cooper. Aha! ' she expertly pinched out a live bug, crushing it between her fingers tips. 'The heid-bugs ha'e no bin sae bad this year. But there's mibbee a handfu' o' wimen who can nae keep their bairns clean an' as fast as the rest o' us deal with oor weans, the ithers spread them aroon agin!'

'That'll be the next thing Mr Owen will be askin' the superintendents tae dae,' Joe snorted, 'peering at oor heids!'

'He wis in the school room fer a lang time the day,' Fiona said, 'Jist watchin' an' writin' in a book.'

The mill bell started to toll and Cal stood up, 'Ah'll away tae catch Rosie an' tell her aboot oor Sarah.'

'Tak the lads wi' ye?' Fiona asked, kissing Davey on the cheek as he squirmed off her lap. 'An' the watter bucket?'

Sionaidh was sitting on the rag rug at Joe's feet, he poked her softly with his bare foot, letting her play with his toes.

137

'Tam's sweet on wee Mel Ewing, he wis doon tae ask me if Ah thocht she wid wed 'im.'

'Tam an' Ewing's dottir?' Fiona burst out laughing. 'Ah can nae see that happening!'

'An' whit aboot a paur miner's son frae Douglas an' the bonniest lass in a' the Highlands?' Joe smiled at his wife, 'there's mony wid ha'e sed Ah had nae a chance wi' ye.'

Fiona came over to kneel in front of him beside Sionaidh, leaning up to offer her lips for a kiss which he readily supplied.

'Ah wis born tae be wi' ye, Joe,' she whispered. 'Ah knew it frae the first.'

He tousled her hair, 'Naw, ye didnae! Ye wid nae e'en talk wi' me tae stairt wi'.'

'An' ye ken fine weel why tha' wis!' She straightened her shoulders, indignant. 'Ah thocht ye were courtin' Sarah. Ah didnae ken she wis yer sister ...' her words trailed away on seeing the playful glint in his eye. 'Ye ...' she turned to their baby, 'yer Da's a rogue sometimes, ma darlin'! Ye watch oot fer men like him when ye grow up.'

The stairwell suddenly resounded with returning workers, doors banging, loud voices and jostling bodies: the usual end of the day routine. Above their heads, the floorboards creaked and muffled conversation filtered down to the Scotts' room but they were so used to it that neither Joe nor Fiona even noticed their neighbours while they talked between themselves.

Cal and the children returned without Rosie, saying she was tired and just wanted to go straight home.

'She wis pleased tae hear aboot Sarah,' Cal said, 'an' she'll be alang t'morra fer a proper blether.' He set down the newly filled water bucket. 'Gerry telt her last nicht tha' it's in the newspapers aboot the soldiers in Egypt.'

'Whit aboot them?' Joe's stomach lurched.

'They'll be hame soon. They won some muckle battle wi' the French, or sumat, an' the war in Egypt is o'er. Or that's whit Gerry seems tae be saying.'

Joe relaxed. 'Let's hope sae.'

Fiona cast a concerned eye towards her husband, feeling his anxiety as keenly as if it was her own. Was there ever going to be a time when all the family were well and without problems?

138

A few hundred yards away, Anne Caroline was leaning over her writing slope, engrossed in correspondence. She spent a great deal of time recounting everyday happenings to her sisters, friends and especially to her father, finding it a passable substitute to being able to speak with them directly. It also initiated the future enjoyment of receiving their replies which conveyed their presence right into the heart of her village home.

Gauging the evening light and her mistress's comfort, Cooper became scrupulously efficient in sending a maid up to refresh the fire and light lamps before the room grew too dark.

'Ah dinnae ken whit she finds tae say but she's still at it,' Senga laid two worn and ink stained quill pens on the kitchen table. Most of the barbs were removed revealing the shiny, well handled goose quills with just a short plume of white feathers.

Apart from Toshie, who was in the scullery starching lace, all the Owen servants were sitting around the kitchen table after their main meal of the day.

Murdoch scraped back his chair and retrieved the pen-knife from his bag hanging in the sculllery. 'Between the master an' the mistress, Ah'm fore'er dressing these nibs.'

Ena eyed the quills suspiciously. 'Yon's a white faither, sae where's a' the black stuff at the end come fae?'

'Geese ha'e black blood,' Murdoch said seriously. 'The faither's fu' o' blood an' it oozes oot when ye squeeze it ...' in a flash he pointed it towards Ena's face.

She screamed and jumped away from the table sending Senga and Alice into giggles.

'Och stoap teasin' the lass ...' Alice cried, 'din nae tak ony notice o' 'im, Ena. Ye dip the end in ink an' then ye can scratch yer letters on tae paper.'

Ena gasped, 'Sae it's no' blood?'

Cooper had heard enough nonsense, 'No Ena, it is not. Don't be so foolish.'

'Well,' Murdoch glanced up from his handiwork. 'It could be blood ... frae a fish...'

'Away wi' ye,' Senga pushed him on the shoulder, smiling. 'Ye've a story fer everythin'!'

For once Cooper joined their conversation, 'Cuttlefish, that's where the finest ink comes from, he's right.'

The servants looked in astonishment at the housekeeper. Her angular face, usually severe and unsmiling between her black bonnet brim and bow, became animated when she explained the intricacies of making different inks. From mixing soot with gum Arabic to the more complicated procedure involving oak gauls and beer, she was surprised to find a genuinely interested audience.

'It was a process I became very familiar with in my previous position. My employer required a constant supply and when Indian ink was difficult to come by it was my duty to ensure the wells were adequately replenished.' she concluded, leaning back against her chair.

'Perhaps ye could show me?' Murdoch ventured.

Cooper inclined her head graciously, 'Very well. When you return from Glasgow.'

Senga and Alice exchanged a quick glance; Mrs Cooper was showing another side to her, an interesting side which hinted of a life beyond these four walls and the Church.

Later that evening, Owen came home to be presented with a neatly tied bundle of letters.

'Please would you pass these to my family,' Anne Caroline asked, 'there is one for each and I would be grateful if you could post the one on top to Miss Spear.'

'Of course,' he laid them on his bureau. 'We owe a great deal to our mutual friend in Manchester.'

It was Miss Spear who introduced them in the first place.

'How long do you plan to be away, my dear?'

'Only a few days. It would not be worth the tedium of the journey for you to accompany me.' Owen took his seat on the other side of the hearth, loosening the cravat at his throat and relaxing. 'I have perhaps two days of meetings in the city and look forward to your father's kind hospitality in the evenings and then I shall return.'

The coal fire hissed in the grate and outside the windows the darkness of the late September evening was complete. Soon, autumn would be in full force, gusting leaves from the trees and silvering the landscape with frost.

Anne Caroline laid a hand across the growing bump beneath her dress; the baby was due in less than two months. She longed for its birth and feared for it in equal measures, not for the physical pain of the delivery but for the dread of loss if she were to lose this child as well.

Owen looked at her, sympathy in his eyes. 'We will soon be travelling to Charlotte Street together and I will remain with you until our baby is born. It will be more comfortable for you there through the winter months and, like last year, your father has already extended the invitation.'

Involuntary tears smarted in her eyes. 'I pray all will be well this time, Robert.' She turned her face away from him, discretely wiping her eyes. 'I'm sorry... I am reminded of our hopeful arrangements a year ago.'

She murmured a prayer beneath her breath.

Owen waited until she was composed again before leaning forward and extending his hand to her. She grasped it, smiling apologetically, embarrassed for weeping.

'We will remain hopeful ,' he said softly, squeezing her fingers, 'and I am sure all will be well.'

She nodded, holding his reassuring gaze.

In that quiet moment she could feel his love for her and his understanding as only he, her closest, dearest friend, could understand, and she drew strength from their unity.

***

David Dale was still in residence at Rosebank so Owen rode up to the city for appointments each morning and returned to the tranquil country house every evening. When he visited without Anne Caroline, the two gentlemen dined alone, the younger Dale daughters remaining with Giggs in the nursery for their meals despite Jean's remonstrations that she was now quite old enough to join the adults in the dining room.

Dale enjoyed having his son-in-law to stay and they would spend their hours together engaged in deep conversation.

'How are the pauper children?' Dale asked 'Are those wee black haired twins still with you?'

'Yes, I spoke with them just the other day.' Owen's eyes gleamed, a smile lifting his youthful features. 'I have further plans for the little ones. I aim to throw open the school to every child as soon as it can walk by itself, relieving the burden of childcare from the parents and thus allowing them to return to work.'

'And yet you no longer wish to engage infants in the mills. Without the natural progression of the older ones moving to the picking rooms, my dear boy, you will be over run with children in your school room! I had many hundreds in my day and we were forced to break their numbers down into different classes just to fit them all into the room. How will you accommodate them?'

'At first, I am moving the orphans out of their lodgings in Mill Four and they will reside in the new Nursery Building. Then, I propose to utilise their current dormitories as meeting rooms and more school rooms. In the future, I will build a purposely designed school.'

A wide grin spread across Dale's face, 'I have heard you speak of this before, but it would take a serious amount of capital and I am assuming your partners may not be so enthusiastic.'

'Now is not the right time to put this to them, I grant you, but I have long had these plans in my head and fully intend to succeed.'

In the lamp light of Rosebank's drawing room, Dale watched Owen recounting the measures he was taking to make slow but steady success in achieving a substantial reduction in pilfering from the company. The younger man was filled with a self confidence far beyond his years: he had thought the problem through, issued instructions for searching the perceived culprits and was single minded in expecting the desired results.

'The men know I am meticulous in keeping account of all materials.'Owen stated firmly. 'I do not threaten them with the courts, what good would that do? Send otherwise useful and trained employees to moulder in jail or be transported to the other side of the Earth? No, they are reprimanded and warned not to steal. It is only by them learning that their actions are wrong that they will change their behaviour. Only the most persistent offenders have been dismissed.'

'And your actions are having the desired effect?'

'Indeed they are. My Report Books are proof of the falling incidence of stolen goods, useful savings are being made. For many it has been a habit, a way of life taught to them by their parents and theirs before them. They have not had the opportunity of education or moral examples in life so are unable to appreciate the repercussions of their crimes.'

Dale grunted agreement. 'The enlightened philosophies of Rousseau and Voltaire are not lost on you, Mr Owen.'

'I first read Rousseau's work The Social Contract as a boy and it struck a true chord, "Man is born free, and everywhere he is in chains." It resonates all the more as I grow older.'

Dale chuckled, still seeing Owen as a youth. 'You are familiar with his Discourse on Inequality?'

'Ah yes, a very original and provoking work.'

'No wonder he became the darling of the French revolutionaries, but Rousseau's views on religion were blasphemous. The man swung from Catholicism to Calvinism, as it suited him, and his personal morals were lamentable.'

'Yet he cared for his fellow man. Surely, that is the important feature to all his work? Not which organised religion he chose to align himself with, or whether his children were born within the blessing of the church or on the wrong side of the blanket ... he devoted a great deal of time and passion to his fellow man, regardless of their class or creed.'

The frown deepened on Dale's brow. 'God rest his soul and grant him forgiveness and everlasting peace.'

'He spoke out most vociferously against the despicable trade in slaves and,' an expression of pleasure flitted across Owen's face. 'His beliefs regarding the education of children to prepare them as valuable, reasoned citizens are to be applauded.'

'As with Voltaire,' Dale said. 'However, at least he acknowledged the presence of a God and I can only agree with his arguments against the Papists of Rome.'

'Their essays on Man's freedom to choose and follow any religion without fear of persecution are brilliantly executed. The Church's power, intolerance and corruption causes more suffering and corruption to Man's life than Life itself. I strongly believe this myself, as you know.'

Dale took the remarks with an understanding nod. 'If God's word in the Holy Scriptures was adhered to, as I preach to my congregation, we would not have the pain and degradation of so many today.'

'Exactly! the main tenets of every religion are a guide to love and treat one's neighbours with kindness and respect, yet this has been contaminated and twisted to suppress the lowlier members of our society. You, Sir, are one of the few truly religious men I have encountered. You are sure of your beliefs, you do not require to alter my own to make you feel more secure. Across all the religions of the world, each believes it has *the* answer. If this gives comfort and support to the individual follower then I have no quarrel with those who wish to worship in that way, but if it presumes to denigrate another belief and kills and tortures in the name of its own God, then it is purely being used as a tool for Man's greed for power over others.'

They discussed the emotive and thorny topic of religion until it was time to retire for the night, each passionate about their own points of view.

'Ye needest to be very right,' Dale smiled benignly when they parted on the upstairs landing, 'for ye are very positive!'

Owen travelled back to New Lanark the next day bearing letters and small gifts from his sisters-in-law for Anne Caroline.

It was a stormy, wet day, making the ride longer than usual and he was tired and soaked through when he finally dismounted outside his home. Despite this discomfort, he pulled up the collar of his cloak and pressed his hat more firmly into place, bracing himself against the wind to inspect the new footings of Nursery Buildings.

Ewing's men were making good progress and in the fading light over two dozen men laboured among the mud and gravel, eager to complete the next line of the walls and raise the building above ground level.

Owen spoke briefly with Joe Scott, the most senior mason on site, then, satisfied that all was proceeding as he intended, he bid him good evening and turned to assess the scene around him, allowing the muscles in his legs and back to adjust to standing once more.

A favourite book of his childhood was Robinson Crusoe and now Owen felt he almost had his own island. Here he was, Laird of all he surveyed and in his own little kingdom he wished to make a difference to the lives of the inhabitants. The great words of philosophers on how to achieve unity and peace were alive in his mind but he had his own, particular, views on how to better the lot of his employees. He was in charge here, so he could put into practice all the ideas he knew in his heart would bring about a change; it excited him and filled him with energy.

However, as happened on his return from the Highlands a few weeks before, his purposeful, enthusiastic frame of mind became dampened on reviewing the latest communications from Manchester awaiting his attention in the office. There would always be problems, he understood that, but his optimism ensured he immediately explored solutions and remedies; he had no time for a defeatist attitude.

His partners demands for higher returns on their investment would have to dealt with, which inevitably would mean delaying some of his personal plans for the social development within the village but not cancelling them. This realisation raised his spirits again and Anne Caroline was pleased to have her husband return to her in a light, happy mood.

***

Autumn crept over the landscape undercover of incessant drizzling rain, swelling the Clyde into an immense cascading rush of foaming water. Leaves dripped from the trees and the sky emptied of its summer visitors, filled instead by a heavy haze of dusty coal smoke seeping from row upon row of chimneys clustered along the tenement roofs.

Huddled beside their hearths, the workers and their families returned to familiar winter routines. It was dark by the time they left the factory floor requiring oil lamps and coal buckets to be filled before closing the shutters and preparing warming barley stews or porridge to stave off the cold. Already weary from their work, they blundered through their chores amid jagged shadows and flickering light. Laundry was largely ignored, the few items which demanded to be cleaned hung in lines across the ceiling, damp and low over their heads.

Children and old folk helped where they could manage, aiming for the moment when they could all finally sit around the table and eat, clogs and boots cast aside. Later, with the infants settled beneath blankets, it mainly fell to the womenfolk to deal with any mending or cleaning, ever mindful of the weekly inspections, while the men dozed over their beer and pipes before exhaustion drove them to snuff out the candles and climb into bed.

On the hillside below the tenements, Mrs Docherty had her own problems attending to the pauper apprentices in Mill Four when the sun left the valley and winter approached.

Since Owen took over management, no new orphans were engaged from the Poor Houses in Edinburgh and Glasgow but she was still responsible for the welfare of over four hundred children aged between six and sixteen years of age.

Just as in Dale's time, the company provided the girls with warm winter smocks and shawls, the boys receiving knee length breeches and jackets. These clothes, together with linen under garments, socks and boots and an extra blanket for every bed, meant an enormous additional burden on the daily running of the dormitories. In the bowels of the great building, dangling above the mangles, sinks and tables piled high with soiled clothes, pulleys constantly groaned with washing. The heat from fires set beneath the cauldrons struggled to dry the clothes hanging limply in this steamy atmosphere.

This October was no different from the many she dealt with before, but Mrs Docherty sighed audibly while compiling her order for supplies. With dark days and biting wind came illness, already evident in the barking coughs and running noses of her charges. Small pox and the dreaded fever of measles were raging in the cities but amongst the wooded hills of Lanarkshire it was influenza which struck down the population. Ten children were too poorly to work, of which two or three were causing serious concern.

She dipped her pen in the ink bottle and requested double the usual amount of molasses.

She was a great believer in the benefit of molasses for the morning meal and, although she continued to view her new employer with distain, she was sure he would agree with her choice of nourishment to maintain the health of the paupers.

By early October, Anne Caroline decided to leave the chill of the countryside and travel up to Glasgow.

Busy with her own chores, Cooper watched from the corner of her eye as wardrobes were emptied, trunks filled, bottles of beauty potions safely packed among straw in baskets and shoes were stuffed with rags and placed in pairs. Both Mr and Mrs Owen were planning to spend the winter in the city although, she was told, Mr Owen would be returning on his own, frequently, for short visits after the baby was born.

Following baby Daniel's death in the house, Cooper was still agonising over any part she might have played in the tragedy. No amount of praying or unburdening her conscience to the minister would relieve her of the deeply seated conviction that she was somehow to blame due to her own selfish wishes for the infant to be silent.

Any mention of the expected new baby brought a sharp stab of remorse. Alone in bed, she replayed the scene time and again of waking to Daniel's cries in the middle of the night and, aching with tiredness, muttering, 'Damn that child. Please God, let him cease so I might sleep.'

That memory of self-absorption haunted her from the moment she heard Mrs Owen's screams of distress.

It was therefore a relief for Cooper to see the trunks being carried out of the house with the knowledge that she would not have to face the object of her guilt, Mrs Owen, for several months.

When Rosie learned from her husband of the Owens' plans to leave the village, she immediately scurried along the street to tell Fiona. Together, on a small sheet of specially purchased paper, they composed a note to Sarah.

Dearest Sister, we trust this reaches your hands and hope you and your family enjoy good health and happiness. We are all well here and have good news of Sam. We beg you to send a reply with an address so we may write. Your loving sisters Rose and Fiona.

The next morning, Fiona chose her moment carefully, watching surreptitiously from the school room windows on the second floor in Mill Four. It was a cold day and the higher panes of glass in the windows were already misted from the rising warmth generated by hundreds of small bodies crammed into the long room. Fiona moved between her pupils, helping here and there, wiping slates and replacing chalks until Owen's carriage appeared beside the owner's house.

Pleading the excuse of urgently requiring leave to visit the privvy, which could hardly be refused given her obvious pregnancy, she hurried up the hill in search of Mrs Owen's lady's maid.

'Staun clear o' the horses!' Murdoch shouted to her as she approached. 'They're gie agitated wi' all the bangin' frae yon buildin'site.'

Fiona gave him a wide, beaming smile, 'Ah jist need tae ha'e a word wi' Mrs MacKintosh.'

'Yer frae the schoolroom, aren't ye?' He often noticed this lovely girl while accompanying his master and although Fiona was some years his senior, her memorable dark-lashed eyes and heart-shaped face made her stand out from the rest of the workers.

'Aye. An' dinnae fash yersel' aboot the horses, Ah ken tae keep well awa frae baith ends!'

Senga and Alice appeared, dragging a heavy basket between them and Murdoch went to their aid, hauling it up onto the roof with one enormous heave to show off his strength.

The maids giggled, glancing at Fiona in curiosity before returning to the house as Toshie came rustling out with a large hat box.

'Excuse me, ma'am,' Fiona bobbed a curtsey, bowing her neatly bonneted head. 'Ah wid be eternally gratefu' if ye wid pass this tae ma sister in law?' She proffered the carefully folded and tucked note. 'Ah gather she does werk fae Mrs Owen noo an' we din nae ken her address tae send it by the mail.'

Toshie took the letter, noting the name on one side and on turning it over, that it was not sealed. 'Mrs Sarah Rafferty? I do not believe we know of this woman.'

'Yer mistress telt ma man that she sews fer her?'

Toshie handed the letter back. 'I know of no Mrs Rafferty and Mrs Owen makes use of a great many seamstresses so I would not be able to agree to deliver this to the right person.'

'Bu' Toshie ...' Fiona blurted out.

'I beg your pardon! How dare ye be so familiar!'

'Och forgive me, Ah heard Sarah ca' ye that sae mony times that it jist slipped oot. She werked fer Mr Dale, here in this hoose, ye wid mind her if ye saw her,' Fiona was pushing the note forward, urging the older woman to take it, 'that's why Mrs Owen knew her, ye could ask her?'

'I will not! Bother Mrs Owen with the likes of this? a free postal service for a mill girl?' Fiona had succeeded in placing it in her hand again and she was about to reject it when she caught a touching look of hopeful anticipation. 'Well,' she turned the slim square of paper in her fingers, lips pursed. 'All I'll say is that I will pass it on if I come across Mrs Rafferty, but I'm no' promising, mind?'

Fiona was full of gratitude and hastily took her leave before the lady's maid could change her mind.

'Weel, Ah've gi'en the letter tae Mrs Owen's maid,' Fiona told her family that evening. 'But Ah can nae say if she'll no' jist throw it in the fire.'

'Ye can dae nae mair,' Cal said kindly.

'An' it wid tak Sean tae read it tae her ...' Joe's brow puckered. 'Ah hope he dis nae play silly buggars an' refuse tae read it or summat stupit.'

Fiona caressed her husband's hair, 'Surely no'.'

Cal blew his nose noisily, ending with several large sniffs. 'Ah can nae mak up ma mind whither it wid be better if she's no wi' that man, or if she is.'

'At least we ken she's alive an' in werk.' Fiona smiled, turning to Joe. 'Has Tam asked Mr Ewing fer his permission tae walk oot wi' wee Mel?'

'No yit! He telt me he's scared o' being thrown oot o' the yaird if Ewing dis nae agree.' Joe was laughing but then a serious note crept into his voice. 'The whole business up there, the paper werk and the lists o' figures he keeps ... an' being wi' me fer a blether ... he's fair made up wi' it. Ah can see why he dis nae want tae chance his luck. Wi'oot it, Tam's got nuthin'.'

'He's got his Ma,' Cal put in, 'an' it's no' as if he needs Ewing fer a roof o'er his heid?'

'It's mair than that,' Joe looked at his brother steadily. 'Ah reckon he wid be lost wi'oot Mel and his werk. They've gi'en him a whole new life, he wis sae doon afore. It wis in his heid as much as his useless arm. Ah pray it will be all richt. If only he did nae have these feelin's fer the lass, he wid jist be contented.'

'It's those feelin's that make life, Joe.' Fiona said softly.

Cal took a swig from his bottle of ale. 'Wimen! Ah'll no' be caught wi' sich fancies. Ma life's jist fine as it is ... an' Tam's wid be, an a'! Babbies an' noise ... an' yer time's no' yer ane. Och, Ah can nae be daen wi' it.'

Fiona pulled a face and grinned at him. 'My, that's us telt!'

'Nae body's askin' ye tae tak a wife, Cal.' Joe laughed.

'Naw, but it's all Ah've bin hearin' doon at the forge efter Kyle announced he's tae wed yon lassie frae the top o' Braxfield Row. '

'Kyle Macinnes is tae wed?' Joe was surprised.

'Aye, in a month or sae.'

'That'll be a gie disappointment tae the ither lassies in the toon.' Fiona cried, winking at Joe. 'An' a relief fer a' the men, Ah din nae doot!'

'Ah wish him well,' Joe gave a quirky smile and batted his eyelids innocently at Fiona's exaggerated expression of disbelief. 'Honest, Ah dae., lass! He's no' a bad man an' he can nae ha'e the bonniest lass in Scotland, fer Ah found ye first! Guid luck tae him and his lass.'

Fiona blew him a kiss and gathered up the remnants of their meal, making a mental note to find out the identity of Kyle's intended bride and, purely out of curiosity, see what she was like.

***

Robert and Anne Caroline both enjoyed visiting the City of Glasgow but in very different ways.

For Anne Caroline it embodied her happy childhood memories and gave her the companionship of her sisters and friends. While her advanced state of pregnancy ruled out attending dinners and theatre outings, Rosemary Pemberley, Mary MacIntosh and Margaret Tennant came to call and her aunt was often in the house to give friendly advice. The latest fashion accessories, who was courting who and all the gossip of Glasgow's high society was discussed at length while the ladies sipped weak, sugary China tea in Charlotte Street's drawing room.

It also gave her precious time to spend with her beloved father, praying with him and discussing aspects of the Bible and, of course, worshipping in his Church.

Owen revelled in the opportunities for business while living so close to the hub of the Merchant City. Leaving the house early, he would often ride towards the Clyde, watching the cargo ships being loaded with Scottish materials or disgorging their wares into wagons to be distributed throughout the land. His own warehouses were close to the docks and he would talk with the managers, bringing his keen eye for business to resolve problems and speed dispatch.

New Lanark Mills required a huge amount of raw material to keep the thousands of spindles running and the orders filled. The mighty sailing ships rocking gently at anchor in the Clyde brought cotton across the Atlantic from plantations near New Orleans and Georgia, Trinidad and Granada. Mill One alone could spin over 14,000lbs of yarn in one month, hence the need for constant relays of wagons to convey the bales overland from the docks to the village.

As well as overseeing the import of the raw material, he sought new sales outlets. Contracts were often settled by shaking hands in the convivial, smoky atmosphere of the Tontine Rooms with Scottish manufacturers from Aberdeen and Kirkcaldy or, just as readily, with agents negotiating for overseas customers in Trieste and St Petersberg.

Having the 'ear of David Dale' brought interested parties to seek him out but it was Owen's own charisma and sound practice which sealed the deals.

In the cramped back room of the Glasgow branch of the Royal Bank he became such a regular visitor that Scott Moncrieff would barely look up from his accounts when he entered, merely enquiring if he wished a refreshment to be brought before including him in the matters of the day.

Despite his stated intention to retire from business, David Dale continued to be invited to every occasion of consequence in the city and enjoyed taking his son in law to openings at galleries, merchants' dinners or discussions on the effects of the war on trade.

On one especially sunny morning with frost glistening on the roofs, they walked together to view the ongoing construction of Hutcheson's magnificent new Hospital in Ingram Street. The architect, David Hamilton, was well known to Dale but it was its proposed duel use as a place of refuge and support for the city's infirm elderly citizens and as a school for poor boys which the two men found so commendable.

A buyer for Spinningdale was in the offing and they debated the terms of the sale, making slow progress towards the Merchant City due to Dale's many rests along the route. Leaning on his cane or making use of a handy low wall to pause and take the weight off his legs, the older man would push back his tricorn hat and chuckle over reminiscences, pointing out shops and alleyways, each with an accompanying tale.

'Ye see over there,' Dale waved his stick to indicate, 'where the shadows hold the ice on the cobbles? On a snowy day some years back, I took a tumble there ...' Dale started to shake with mirth. 'I landed on ma backside! And when I met my colleagues they saw the snow on me and asked if lads were pelting me with snowballs? No, I told them, I fell all my length on the ice! Well, one says, 'thank the Lord ye didn't fall all your *width!*'

Owen laughed spontaneously, delighting in his company.

'I have a mind to travel to Wales and see my parents in the Spring,' he told Anne Caroline one afternoon while they were changing for dinner. 'My father is the same age as yours, my mother a little older, and I feel I should visit them before any more time has elapsed.'

'Perhaps I could come with you, dear?'

'It is a long journey and certainly not one for a small infant,' he smiled at her as she sat at the dressing table letting Toshie make the finishing touches to her hair. 'I will combine it with meetings in Manchester and be home before you know it.'

After several weeks of enjoying Glasgow hospitality, Anne Caroline went into labour in the early hours of the ninth of November.

Not wishing to make a fuss and wake the entire household, she insisted that only Toshie should be summoned. This was no easy task for on pulling the bell cord in their bedroom, it was Breen who appeared, candle in hand, wide-eyed and anxious.

Within minutes she came back with Toshie, before disappearing again and returning with two maids to assist with stripping the bed. Owen was ushered through to the guest bedroom but preferred to try and pass the time by working. His writing case was in the library so, partially dressed, he ventured quietly down the grand staircase only to find side lamps burning and Renwick pacing the hallway.

A footman was already running through the night streets to summon Mr Palmer and the butler was holding himself in readiness for answering the door before the bell rang.

With so many of the servants whispering and padding about their quarters, Cook was roused from her sleep and saw the wavering glow of passing candlelight beneath her door. She pushed back her covers, rubbed her sleepy eyes and reached for the tinderbox to light her own lamp: the baby was on the way.

And so it was that in the darkest hours of the winter night all the Dale servants were awake and congregated around the kitchen table, with the exception of Toshie who was upstairs with her mistress.

Owen was just wondering if he should return to the soft mattress in the guest room when he heard footsteps crossing the hallway and Renwick opened the door for Mr Palmer.

'All is well,' the physician reported in a loud, theatrical whisper. 'You have a fine and healthy son!'

Owen jumped to his feet and seized the man's hand, 'So quickly? Good gracious! Thank you, thank you, splendid news ... and my wife is well?'

'A very calm and strong young lady! Yes, she has done exceedingly well.'

'I may see her now?'

'In a little while, Sir, she has only just delivered the infant, but your wife implored me to tell you straight away.' He turned on his heel, 'if you will excuse me?'

'Of course!' Owen's joy spread to Renwick.

The butler bowed his head respectfully, allowing himself a wide smile. 'May I offer my congratulations, Sir, and that of all the servants!'

'Ah, thank you!' Owen clasped his hands together, turning this way and that, seized with an exhilaration which made him want to burst out laughing and cry at the same moment. 'When can we expect Mr Dale to rise?' he asked hopefully, desperate to share his news.

'It is barely past six o'clock and being still dark, I would not expect the Master for a while yet ...'

153

'And would ye not?' came Dale's booming tones. 'I met Mr Palmer on the upper landing! Congratulations me dear boy!' He reached for Owen's hand, slapping him heartily on the shoulder. 'Congratulations! Praise the Lord for keeping our dearest Anne Caroline safe and giving us a new life. We are blessed indeed!'

The men's enthusiastic exchange in the echoing hallway woke Jean and the other girls who were eager to join the celebrations. Donning flimsy night robes, Jean's head adorned with curling rags, they scampered barefoot down the cold stone stairs. Owen gave no thought to his unshaven cheeks or seeing his distinguished father in law in a full length, billowing night gown and slippers. This was an extraordinary night and neither he nor his sisters-in-law felt in any way self-conscious to give and receive hugs in their night attire.

'Oh dear,' Anne Caroline cried. 'And I thought I was keeping admirably quiet and giving little disruption to the house! It seems that everyone has been inconvenienced!'

'Not at all,' Owen sat on the edge of the bed, cradling her in his arms and admiring their new son. 'There is not one person who is in the least complaining, everyone is very happy, delighted! It is a wonderful event for the whole family.'

They lapsed into silence.

The scene around them was the same as it had been after Daniel's birth twelve months before and the striking similarity was not lost on either of them. Anne Caroline turned her head to glance at Robert and saw her own turmoil of emotions reflected in his eyes.

He said nothing, understanding exactly how she felt but not trusting himself to speak. Instead, he tightened his grip around her shoulder and gently squeezed it.

For a moment she thought she would burst with sadness for her first son; tears welling up, her lips trembling. The last time she held a child of her own it was limp, lifeless but now she felt the warm, moving weight of her second born in her arms: healthy, breathing, alive.

This is not Daniel, she told herself, but I can love this child with all my heart, love it for itself, yet it will never diminish the memory of my first little boy.

'How strange,' she murmured, swallowing hard. 'as soon as one feels intense love, it is accompanied immediately with the dread of loss. I should be filled with joy but my mind is overwhelmed with the horror of losing our precious child.'

Robert felt her shoulders moving with silent sobs, 'You have been through a great ordeal, my dearest. You are exhausted and need to sleep. Our boy is strong and healthy, see how deeply he breathes and how rosy his cheeks are? When you are rested you will feel more peaceful.' He kissed her softly and laid his cheek against her head. 'Your sisters and father are eager to see you but perhaps I should suggest they leave you to rest, eh?'

'No,' Anne Caroline said firmly. 'No, please, I would like to see them all and let them meet Robert Dale Owen,' she said their chosen name with wonderment. 'Perhaps, in a few minutes? I shall compose myself.'

Below stairs, the servants were in very high spirits. This was only partly due to the good news of the safe arrival of the new baby and mainly because Renwick ordered a cask of ale to be opened to 'toast the baby's head'.

After organising a selection of sliced cold meats, cheeses and fruit to be laid out in the dining room for the family, Renwick gathered his staff together in the kitchen and made a solemn, heartfelt speech. Then, stifling a yawn, he retired to his room to shave and change out of the clothes he threw on in haste during the night. Breen and Toshie also took the opportunity for a short rest in their rooms. It had been an eventful night and as it was still not yet eight o'clock in the morning there was a full day's work ahead.

Chapter Seven

"Why should we build our happiness on the opinons of
others, when we can find it in our own hearts?"
— *Jean-Jacques Rousseau*

Much to the villagers' dismay, Humphreys proclaimed he
would not give permission to set alight the large bonfire they
were building to celebrate Hogmanay.

Big Lachie was outraged. They always marked the passing of
the old year into the next with a ceilidh around the flames. Even
since Mr Dale sold up, the tradition had continued.

'There was too much drinking and debauchery last year,' he
was told. 'A bonfire in such close proximity to the dwellings is
a risk to life, especially when it is attended by an intoxicated
mob.' These declarations did not fool the Highlanders. They
believed the real reason behind forbidding the fire was to
appease the Christians who looked on the event as a pagan
festival.

Kyle asked to make a plea directly to Mr Owen. He knew the
hostility Owen was encountering due to his own religious
beliefs, or rather lack of belief, and felt he could put a good
case forward to allow the celebrations to take place.

Rosie was full of the story.

It was trying to snow when she left the mills, tiny white balls
scattering around the frozen ground, floating away from her
swishing hem at every step. By the time she reached the Scotts'
room her face was a pink beacon, her shawl glistening with
melting droplets.

'My it's cauld oot there,' she cried, picking up Robbie to take
his seat, before pulling him back onto her lap. The whole family

156

were home for the night; Fiona helping the children to eat at the table and Cal and Joe seated by the glowing hearth. 'An' me sae hot frae the jennie that Ah'll be steamin'! Wait til Ah tell ye whit went oan the ither eve. Ma Gerry heard it all!'

Having caught everyone's attention, except baby Sionaidh, Rosie launched into her tale.

'Yon Kyle Macinnes demands tae see Mr Owen aboot the ceilidh and that toff frae the sooth, Humphreys, telt him he couldnae. Flat oot, jist 'Naw!'.Weel, that wis a blaw, an' then Kyle asks, all polite like, if he wid reconsider? It's jist a party, an' a' the folk want a party tae see in the year. Humphreys tells him agin he'll no' have sich a dangerous fire in the village. An' whit aboot the ceilidh? Wi'oot a fire? Naw, Humphreys is deid set agin it. Sae Kyle bows his heid an' says he's gie disappointed but he'll tell his faither the bad news.

'Jist as he's turnin' tae the door he turns bak an' says he hopes he will be allowed a wee ceilidh fer his wedding? Oh aye, says Humphreys, a wee pairty fer his weddin' is agreeable. But if it's cauld, says the Highlander, an' ma guests are shiverin' an' we licht a fire, wid ye be efter tellin' me tae douse it?'

Rosie glanced around her audience, putting on a gruff, English accent. 'Not if it was small and constantly attended.' Donnie and Davey giggled. 'Ah'm mighty relieved tae hear ye say that, Kyle telt him. He then bid him a guid nicht, patted his hat back on his heid an' walked oot!'

'Sae? ' Fiona screwed up her face, 'Kyle can ha'e his nuptials but we still cannae ha'e a Hogmanay ceilidh.'

'Ah,' Rosie smirked, 'when the Highlander left, Humphreys telt ma Gerry tae find oot when the Macinnes wedding wis tae happen. Gerry ran efter Kyle an' catched him by the lade where Big Lachie an' a crowd o' ithers were waitin'. When's yer marriage tae tak place? he calls. 'Thursday!' Kyle shouts back, an' Gerry hurries tae the office ...'

Her words were lost under the eruption of laughter.

'Thursday's Hogmanay!' Joe explained to his sons, 'Ah weel, ye ha'e tae credit the man wi' sumat, I suppose.'

Fiona grinned at him impishly, 'Who wid ha'e thocht we wid be dancin' at Macinnes' wedding pairty?'

'Mibbec we'll no' be dancin'?' He nodded to Fiona's belly, 'That babbie might be on its way?'

'Ye could be richt, Ah fancy Ah've got muddled wi' when it's tae arrive. Ah telt Bessie it wisnae until end o' January ... but it's kickin' like the De'il an' Ah'm awfy big already.'

Rosie stood up, tired and suddenly uncomfortable. No longer the centre of attention, she wanted to leave her brother's brood of noisy children and return to her quiet, tidy home.

Bracing herself, she stepped out into the silent street where only the hundreds of footprints in the snow told of other human beings. The windows were shuttered in the grey walls of the tenements, a bleak, whining wind pressing her skirts against her legs.

As she entered her own street door, her mind was already on plans to hasten the romance between Gerry's youngest sister and the lad from the store room. Soon, if everything went smoothly, both of his sisters would be married and away and they would have their place to themselves.

Rosie liked that thought.

It was what all her neighbours craved and, between them, she and Gerry earned enough to make this happen. With this satisfying thought, she carefully shook the snow from her clothes, stamped hard on the landing floorboards to free any stuck to the soles of her clogs and entered her clean comfortable room.

***

'Whit d'ye ken tae her?' Rosie nudged Fiona, eyebrows raised quizzically.

'Weel, she's ... a bonnie lass ... different tae whit Ah expected, Ah'll admit.'

'She's a ghostie! Ah swear Ah could pit ma haun clean through her when she passed!'

'Dinnae be unkind,' Fiona chided her. 'She's jist sae pale, *bàn.*'

'Whitiver ye cry her, yon Freya's hair is like snaw!'

The Scotts were part of a deep circle of onlookers standing in the night air to witness Kyle and Freya's marriage vows. Many of the revellers were eager for the hand-fasting to be finished so the Hogmanay ceilidh could start in earnest. It was a noisy, lively affair up until the appearance of the bride but now a hush fell, all eyes on the ethereal figure taking her place beside Kyle.

Fiona was intrigued by the new Mrs Mcinnes, ashamed for having wondered if Kyle's chosen lass would resemble herself in appearance. Clearly, she did not. Dainty and slender, Freya was as fair as Fiona was dark, her oval face dominated by large, round blue eyes. She appeared fairy-like, a pale yellow cloak floating around her body, tied loosely at her throat with shining white satin ribbons; strands of ivy encircled her head, holding back a curtain of almost white blond hair.

'*Brèagha ... neònach ...*'

'Eh?' Rosie glanced at Fiona. 'Ye a'richt?'

'Ah wis thinking she's a beauty but ... awfy *strange* looking.'

Their promises declared to each other, Kyle and Freya held hands and leapt over the broom, where they were greeted by Freya's older married sister, ushering them beyond the crowd. Cheered on by clapping and whistling, they walked proudly around the outside of their well-wishers before re-entering the group as man and wife. Immediately, the fiddles burst into tune, close friends running to be the first to embrace the couple.

'Ah preferred oor wedding, lass.' Joe mused later, walking back to the Row, arm in arm, their children around them.

'Aye, oors wis special fer Mr Dale joined us.'

'Kyle's did nae seem like a proper marriage,' Joe added. 'Ah thocht they'd need a clergyman tae dae the job.'

'Cal telt me they were up at the Church porch this mornin' fer the Lord's blessing an' tae sign the register.'

Fiona stopped at their tenement door, her grasp tightening on Joe's arm, seized by a familiar gripping pain.

'D'ye think the babbie will be born this year?' she laughed.

'It'll ha'e tae be mighty quick, there's only twa oors left.' Suddenly he realised the importance of her words. 'Ye mean yer startin?'

The contraction receded and she released a long breath. 'Aye. Bessie's jist up in Lanark tae see in the Bells, can ye fetch her?'

Ailsa Scott was born in the early hours of the new year.

Beyond her mewing cries, fiddle music and singing could still be heard wafting in the dark night air of New Lanark.

A hopeful United Kingdom celebrated the arrival of 1802.

Although many people felt Pitt should be re-instated, Addington was still holding the position of Prime Minister.

Since the preceding autumn, neither protracted negotiations between the Foreign Secretary, Lord Hawkesbury, nor extensive diplomacy by his agent, Anthony Merry, in Paris, were successful in securing peace.

Whenever they felt agreement was reached, Napoleon changed his mind, despite signing papers of intent. Eventually, the very experienced Charles Cornwallis, previously Governor General in India, was dispatched to France. Having agreed an end to hostilities following several decisive British victories, especially the Siege of Alexandria, he was confident of signing a treaty to formally bring about peace.

'About time too,' Gilbert Hamilton grunted, 'we've been nigh on ten years at war with the Revolutionaries, perhaps now we can regain our markets in Europe and get on with business.'

It was a dreary February afternoon but in Dale's book lined octagonal study the two friends were mulling over the day's events beside a glowing coal fire. They were relaxing after a meeting at the Glasgow Chamber of Commerce, weary from dealing with the woes of an increasing number of failing and closing businesses.

'In many cases these casualties are purely the choice of trade,' Dale said, thoughtfully. 'We have just heard of five bankruptcies in this week alone, meaning hundreds of folk will be thrown into the ranks of the unemployed. Yet Scott Moncrieff and I have written business for the Sugar and Cotton merchants which exceed all postulated growth.'

'Ye haven't thought of retiring from the Royal Bank then?'

'Oh, I have thought of it ... and perhaps I should. William Simpson, over in Edinburgh, has brought in a new man, John More. He is becoming acquainted with the Glasgow office, but there is still much to interest me, I'm not ready to drop the reins yet awhile. These are such hard times for many in the city that I feel I can still offer a helping hand here and there.'

'Perhaps, if the country is relieved of the burden of paying for the war, we will be on a firmer footing.'

'Addington has already started to disarm, has he not?' Dale gave a wry smile. 'How does that affect your order books at the Carron Iron Works?'

'Ah, not as seriously as you would expect.' Hamilton, long time Glasgow representative of the iron works, leaned forward to knock the contents from his pipe into the hearth, digging into his pocket for his tobacco pouch to refill it. 'Our business is diverse, everything, ye know, from baths to pots and pans! I personally would be happier if we did not have the contract for armaments, either at home or for Russia and the Americas.'

'Your brother-in -law will be keeping the furnaces going as well. Everywhere, I hear there is demand for Watt's steam engine. My son-in-law, Owen, was telling me all about its wondrous power when he used it to great effect in Manchester.'

'It is a grand invention and producing the iron parts keeps a lot of men in work. Frames and water wheels are also in demand. When you think of it ...' He poked a taper into the fire and lit his pipe, damping it down again and relighting it in a habit Dale knew from old and waited patiently for the procedure to be completed before the conversation continued.

'When you think of it,' Hamilton said again, waving ineffectually at the cloud of blue smoke. 'Water is the main component in each method.'

A spattering of rain sounded on the windows and they both laughed.

'Aye,' said Dale, 'which is a blessing for us in Scotland seeing as God has seen fit to give us a plentiful supply.'

There was a sudden burst of piano music and girls' voices singing a spirited ballad, before being cut off by the sound of a door closing.

Dale smiled, 'The lassies are enjoying having their elder sister here.'

'And how are you enjoying your grand child?'

'Young Robert is a pleasure. I shall be sorry to see them leave when the spring arrives. I pray to the Lord to keep him safe and healthy, may Our God be merciful.'

'I was speaking with Owen a week past, he has many plans for the mills and, more so, for the children and schooling.'

'He is keen to do the best for them, although I believe his partners are more concerned with the profits he returns, rather than the education he affords his workers.'

'I gather the mills are still attracting visitors, as they were in your day. '

'They come and see the clean workrooms and well fed pauper apprentices as if it is some show put on for their entertainment. The frustration I, and now young Owen, feel for this attitude is hard to bear. Yet, we still read these scandalous reports of high infant mortality and brutality meted out to hundreds, nay, thousands of wretched souls being worked to death. Many more continue to fall prey to the fever created by filthy, badly managed factories.'

'At least Peel's Bill for the betterment of factory conditions is in Parliament, we can only hope it will be passed.'

'Dr Percival and my colleagues in Manchester at the Board of Health have provided scores of reports and expert advice but I fear it will be watered down.' Dale rubbed at his eyes, anxious. 'I have discussed this subject endlessly with Owen, ye know. He and his partners have long been involved in factory reform.'

'These massive factories are relatively new, David. It is only recently that the extent of the depravity and harm caused by the claustrophobic conditions is being recognised.'

'Pah! Arkwright knew it straight away and rectified it as much as he could in those days, back in the '80s. Good Lord, Gilbert, even my good self! I could see the starved, exhausted faces of the poor and knew I must supply not only employment but food and a decent place to sleep. It is the right and Christian thing to do. Cleanliness! Proper ventilation! Lack of disease! I am no genius yet I saw it immediately, so why do these abominations still exist today? Fifteen ... nearly twenty years later?'

'The usual culprit, my friend. We have met him before: Greed.'

'Aye, even as I ask, I know the answer. Owen is convinced the making of money and responsible care for the work force are mutually compatible. He is striving to create even better conditions at his mills, as I did in my time, with fewer deaths, less disease yet consistently high profits.'

'But is he succeeding?'

'In part. Slowly. He is impeded by his senior partners in Manchester who seem to be slaves to avarice.'

'You see! My point, exactly.'

'It is a vicious circle. May Our Lord give him the strength to stay the course and not be worn down by those who would have him fail in order to justify their own selfishness. He also has plans for improving the schooling.'

'Education is paramount.' Hamilton crossed his bony stockinged legs, the buckles on his shoes flashing in the firelight. 'I still instruct occasionally at Hutcheson's, and with Watt's close ties with the University, I like to keep abreast of things. Owen was telling me of Bell and Lancaster's work in England and there is much being done on the Continent. Very interesting.'

'We live in Enlightened times, Gilbert. Why even Napoleon and the revolutionaries across the Channel are raising awareness of the need to spread knowledge through education, science and the arts. I earnestly hope for the day when all men, no matter how poor, can have the opportunity to learn to read and be free to rejoice in the Lord's word.'

Clocks throughout the mansion rang out the hour and Hamilton suddenly realised how late and dark it was growing.

'These wretched short days of winter,' he muttered. 'I must be leaving if I am to reach home before the horses fail to see the road ahead of them.'

Dale accompanied his guest down to the hall, their presence spurring Renwick to retrieve Hamilton's cloak and hat. When they reached the foot of the stairs, Dale paused beside the oil painting of his late wife and son.

'Ye know,' he gestured to the portrait where Carolina and William were forever happy in the sunshine. 'They've christened the boy Robert Dale Owen.'

Hamilton was moved.

He stood silently beside his friend, remembering the times they shared when William played with his own son, Archibald.

Despite being much older, Archie humoured the inquisitive little boy, often letting him ride on his back around the nursery. And sweet, devoted Carolina, a close friend of his own wife, brought her gentle humour and understated fine breeding to the drawing room when she accompanied Dale for dinners at their house.

Happy memories.

'After losing William, I didn't think my name would carry on from my own blood,' Dale said, quietly. 'Of course, James has offspring, but, as ye know, we did not share the same mother. My brother Hugh's boy, David, seemed the only possibility but it's not quite the same ... then poor little Daniel passed away. Let us pray my new grandson remains hale and hearty.'

Composed again, Hamilton moved on down the steps into the hall, saying cheerily, 'I am sure your spirit and blood is in all the girls, have no fear for posterity, my old friend. When the days start to draw out, ' he paused to allow Renwick to help him into his heavy winter garments, 'you must come and spend some time with us, bring all the girls. Katharine and I would enjoy the company. We have the plans for our new house! We must put aside time, away from the Chambers and other business so I might show you the drawings.'

'So, you were successful in purchasing the land you were after?'

'Indeed we were. At Bowling. The ink is barely dry on the contract but the views south over the Clyde are spectacular, worth every penny. You built this fine mansion, perhaps you could guide me in a few matters? '

'I would be delighted,' Dale nodded, looking up at the taller man with affection. 'You must call on me at Cambuslang and see how Rosebank's coming along.'

'Did I mention to you that my grandfather used to be the minister at Cambuslang?'

Dale gave a great bellowing laugh, 'On several occasions! But I never tire of hearing it!'

'Age, eh?' Hamilton smiled, winking. 'At least it comes upon us all at the same rate.'

When Hamilton's carriage pulled away, Dale stood in the doorway until the gates of Charlotte Street clanged shut and the clatter of hoof beats and metal wheels were lost in the loud pattering of rain on the cobbled street. The chilled air wafted into the house, carrying aromas of coal smoke and dank gutters.

'Papa!' Anne Caroline called from the hall. 'Will you join us? Margaret has mastered the difficult passage of the sonata! Please come and hear her play?'

'I would welcome it,' Dale said amiably. 'I am sure the whole household and even Renwick, will be glad to know it has been tamed.'

His daughter gave a conspiratorial laugh, 'I believe we have all heard it, or at least parts of it, enough times to have it haunt our dreams, but now it is complete.' She linked her arm in his, kissing him lightly on the cheek. 'Our Margaret is a very determined young lady, but now that she has the piece in her repertoire I believe she will be as relieved as the rest of us to forego the incessant practice.'

Indeed, the music was performed without hesitation, if also lacking in feeling, but her family clapped and congratulated her on her achievement, before urging her to play other, lighter compositions so they might join her in song.

Anne Caroline had missed these hours spent together singing and taking turns to play the accompaniment.

As they sang, they would catch each other's eye, smiling through their words. Dale's deep timbred voice brought a richness to the harmony and sometimes he would gaze into the embers as he sang, lost in the meaning of the words, bringing such emotion to the lyrics that his daughters would fall quiet, giving him their complete attention.

Jean favoured more contemporary tunes and gave a spirited rendition of several popular songs compiled by Robert Burns.

'Now Jean has attained the age of sixteen, Papa,' Anne Caroline whispered, as they listened to her sister play. 'I have spoken with both Mrs Pemberley and Mrs Mackintosh and they wish to invite her to recitals and luncheons so she may become acquainted with others of her age in society. If you are agreeable?'

'Your aunt suggested the same,' he murmured. 'I cannot stop the passing of time, wish that I could, for you are all growing up too fast.'

Anne Caroline reached for his hand and patted it. 'We may be growing older but we are also growing closer, I believe. I appreciate and love my sisters as friends now, not just as siblings.'

'Bless you, my dear girl,' he smiled. 'And may God always allow it to be so.'

'Families are so important. I cannot imagine what it must be like to be alone in the world or parted from those you love.'

***

In the gathering dusk of that same evening, hundreds of miles away from the music and laughter in Dale's drawing room, the full rigged heavy frigate, Egyptienne, docked at Woolwich on England's south coast.

Finally making port was a relief to all aboard. After sailing safely all the way from Egypt, the ship narrowly missed disaster in the English Channel by colliding with the Marquise Wellesley, an East India Company ship. Fortunately, little damage was sustained to either and they were able to continue on their way.

Gratified to make land in one piece, Captain Stephenson gave the order to drop the gang planks and then poured himself a stiff glass of whisky.

The 40 gun Egyptienne was one of three ships seized from the French after the fall of Alexandria and immediately taken into service by the British to bring back hundreds of wounded troops. The Captain had also been charged with the onerous task of ensuring the safe passage of Colonel Hilgrove Turner and a curious engraved stone, captured from the French and believed to be of huge archaeological importance.

There was much to be done but Stephenson downed the last dregs of whisky and allowed himself a few moments of reflection. Taking his seat in the shadowy cabin he looked around at the panelled walls, maps and crammed bookcases; all horribly familiar to him after four months at sea. His mission was complete. Whatever happened to the rabble of men disembarking, or the ancient stone, boxed and strapped into the rear hold, was no longer his responsibility.

'Captain?'

Stephenson peered through the gloom to find the Chief Medical Officer silhouetted in the doorway.

'Well, Dr Young, I take it this is where we say goodbye.' he waved a hand to the decanter. 'Take a dram afore ye go?'

166

They lit a lamp and raised their glasses to His Majesty.

Over the course of the journey the two Scotsmen spent hours playing back gammon or cards, sharing jokes and, in the most difficult weeks, raising each other's spirits.

Fourteen men died during the crossing and it had fallen to the Captain, the Chaplain and Dr Young to oversee the burials at sea. Many more of the soldiers on board were suffering from infection to their wounds, disease and malnourishment and some were almost blind with an affliction to their eyes.

'Ah cursed ye at the stairt,' the Captain said bluntly. 'Ah didnae care fer takin' sae many half deid men on board wi' a surgeon.'

'I just wish I could have saved more of them.'

'There's many a man walkin' doon that plank this nicht who wid be wi' his maker if it were no' fer ye.'

Thomas Young handed him a sheaf of papers. 'Here's my report on those who perished on the voyage.'

Stephenson glanced at it, each name carrying a cloud of tragic memories.

'All too young tae die,' he said softly. 'As a Scot, I feel particular pain fer those young Cameronians.'

The doctor stood up. 'Aye, God rest their souls. I have passed the death certificates to their most senior officer on board, Leiutenant Samuel Scott.'

'At least he recovered.'

'Aye, he's a tough one, that. Well, Captain, I'll take my leave, I'm meeting Colonel Hilgrove Turner on the quay, he is eager to personally oversee the unloading of the stone from Rosetta and transport it to the British Museum without delay.'

'God speed! I hope that lump of granite is worthy of your efforts.'

Exhausted though he was, Dr Young's eyes glittered with excitement, 'Oh, have no fear on that account, it is priceless.'

***

'I'm no' looking forward tae leaving again,' Toshie confided in Breen, taking tea in the housekeeper's office at Charlotte Street.

'We'll miss you, that's for sure'

The date for the Owens' return to New Lanark was fast approaching.

'I can't help fearing the same might happen again,' Toshie's face contorted with anxiety, '... tae Master Robert ... like his wee brother.'

'Now, now, there's no point in fretting.' Breen comforted. 'That bairn upstairs has a fierce hold on life.'

'And there's Cooper tae contend with, her long face and dour ways can be very wearing. Young Murdoch lets her nippy words wash o'er him, but I wis struggling tae bite ma tongue.'

Breen sympathised. 'Aye, well, maybe it'll not be long afore you'll come and visit us down at Rosebank.'

'Mrs Owen was saying the very same thing this morning. She disnae want tae be too long apart from her sisters. It's been a tonic for her tae be with them an' she's full of plans for Miss Jean. They are all having fittings today for lighter dresses in preparation for the spring. Miss Jean is so tall now that none of my mistress's old gowns will reach the floor on her.'

'Miss Mary's already wearing that pink lace gown the late Mrs Dale chose, all those years ago.'

'Those fuller skirts were bonnie, d'ye no' agree? Nowadays there's barely a width of material, an' sich simple sleeves. Mrs Dale, God rest her soul, wore the most beautiful cla'es. Satin and taffeta ball gowns wi' yards an' yards o' lace.'

'Ye weren't sae fond of them at the time,' Breen laughed. 'All that pressing and re-stitching when you washed the petticoats! I mind seeing you with tears tripping ye, late into the night working with the irons.'

They reminisced on times gone by until a bell jangled in the corridor. Renwick swept out of his room, past the housekeeper's doorway and up the servants' stairs to answer the front door.

'That'll be Holroyds. Well, I had better get about ma business. Sitting blethering won't prepare the mistress's trunks.' Toshie suddenly put her hand to her mouth. 'Oh! I near forgot, an' I only jist minded it agin last nicht,' she reached into the pocket of her white apron, drawing out Fiona's note. 'I said I would try and hand this on.'

Breen looked at the name. 'Sarah Rafferty? Who's she when she's at home?'

168

'A woman at the mills said she's her sister and that she used tae werk in Mr Dale's hoose in the village. She wis adamant that this Rafferty woman is up here in the city, sewing fer Mrs Owen.'

'D'ye mind her?'

Toshie shook her head, looking at the letter in her hand. 'Naw, I cannae picture her but I'll away upstairs an' see whit I can dae.'

The hall was busy with two elegantly attired ladies being shown into the drawing room and several young boys in smart livery carrying rolls of material, heavy satchels and boxes. Having presented the dressmakers to Mrs Owen, Renwick returned to oversee the materials being carried in to the house.

He saw Toshie standing expectantly at the head of the servants' staircase.

'Can I help you?' he asked, keeping an eye on the proceedings.

'I'm not sure. D'ye ken if one of the women in the drawing room is a Mrs Rafferty?'

'Neither gave that name, we have a Mrs Holroyd and a Mrs Hendry.'

'Oh dear, the person I'm after used tae be a maid at New Lanark.'

Renwick's eyebrows raised. Toshie quickly related her mission and the butler decided the best thing to do would be to give the note to one of the page-boys.

'You shouldn't be wasting your time with errands from mill workers,' he chastised, taking the slip of paper. 'Here, you, lad!'

The youngest of the little boys stopped in his tracks. Immaculately dressed in an uncomfortable turquoise blue jacket with matching breeches, white stockings and shining buckled shoes, he was new to the job and only knew to fetch and carry as directed.

'Give this to Sarah Rafferty.'

'Ah dinnae ken the wummin.'

'Then give it to someone who does! Now, get on with you!'

The child turned on his heel and ran out the front door, quickly tucking the letter into his jacket while dodging a swipe from the driver's hand for being slow.

It was not until the end of the day, while the Holroyd carriage was rattling its way through the city streets back to the store room, that the letter surfaced again.

Sitting on one side of the coach were the two ladies and on the other seat, facing them, almost hidden under their burdens, were the three pages holding boxes of trimmings and rolls of the most expensive fabrics. The bulk of the material was stored on the roof.

Seeing the smallest boy taking something from inside his coat, Mrs Holroyd demanded ,'Thomas! What d'ye have there?'

The child handed over the letter, shrinking back into his seat where he was crammed into the corner.

Mrs Holroyd was outraged. 'Why do you have a letter addressed to a Sarah Rafferty?'

Sarah almost fainted.

Hearing her name, her real name, came as such a shock that she was glad to be sitting down.

'Speak child!' Mrs Holroyd cried, shaking the letter at him.

'The man gie it tae me.'

'Which *man*?'

'The man a' the hoose, wi'the black jaikit an' yon timepiece.'

'The butler? The butler to such a distinguished gentleman as Mr Dale, gave you ... *you* ... a letter? What lies! I should never have taken you on!'

For the rest of the journey Mrs Holroyd gave vent to her fury at being so betrayed in return for her generosity of giving employment to an orphan.

Sarah listened in horror as the whimpering boy was told he would be returned to the City Hospital that very evening for his thieving, deceitful nature.

'Ma'am' Sarah ventured, feigning a sudden recollection. 'I beg tae tell ye, there's bin a misunderstaundin'.' Rapid explanations sparked in her mind. 'Ah ken this Mrs Rafferty ... an' yin o' her family are in the employ o' Mr Dale. Perhaps this wis meant fer me? Tae tak tae her?' She smiled sympathetically at the poor child, imploring him to follow her lead. 'Thomas, did the man sae tae gie it tae me?'

The little boy nodded, tears streaming down his blotchy cheeks.

'Oh, may the Lord grant me patience!' Mrs Holroyd thrust the crumpled piece of paper at Sarah. 'Take it! And tell your friend that you will not be used as a means for correspondence again, and certainly not through your duties with me!'

'Thank ye, Ma'am, Ah'll be sure tae tell her.'

Mrs Holroyd's eyes fell on the page boy. She was not an unkind woman and felt it her Christian duty to take back her angry words.

'Thieving is a terrible sin, Thomas. Rest assured that if you should ever be found to be in possession of any item which is not yours, I shall have no hesitation in dismissing you and placing you at the mercy of the Courts. Do you understand?'

Thomas nodded, now so shrunk into his corner that his jacket collar was up around his ears. He stole a glance at the woman he knew as Mrs Hendry. She appeared to be watching him yet when he smiled his thanks, she made no response.

Sarah was not looking at Thomas, she was not looking at anything. Her thoughts were flying through ideas of what the contents of the note might contain. Something terrible must have happened to her family? Why would they write to her unless it was of an urgent matter? How did they even know where she was?

Gripped with fear, she tucked the precious letter into her bodice and attempted to maintain a normal conversation with her employer.

Hours later, trudging home in the darkness, another obstacle reared its ugly head. Sean was away and none of her neighbours, or at least those she knew well enough to ask, could read or write.

'D'ye ken ony yin who can read?' she asked the woman who kept an eye on Cathy and Stephen while she worked.

'Naw, hen. Whit aboot at yer werk?'

Sarah grimaced, 'Ah din nae like tae ask.'

'Ask the meenister?'

'Perhaps... ta, Aggie, Ah'll ha'e tae think on it.'

Attending the Church was not a regular activity for Sarah and she fought with her conscience for several days. Eventually, early one frosty morning, her footsteps lead her into the little stone church she passed everyday on her way into the city.

Amidst the candlelit gloom of its stark interior a young man was standing beside the pulpit. He was surprised by her presence and, raising the lantern in his hand, approached with a look of concern on his face. His congregation were mainly the poor unfortunates of the area; this young woman was dressed in a stylish hat and warm wool cape.

However, when she spoke, her broad lowland Scots pronunciation and timid behaviour showed her to be of the working class. He listened to her request, surprised to hear she could not read yet, clearly, possessed the means to purchase fine clothes. His first thought was that she must be the mistress of a wealthy merchant, her troubled luminous blue eyes and pretty face could certainly make that a possibility. However, when they talked, he learned of her occupation and soon he was drawing out the story behind her predicament.

He guided her to a settle beside the window where he carefully unfolded Fiona's letter in a streak of dawn light and read it out. His voice was soft, intimate, directing the words to Sarah in reverent tones.

'They're weel!' Sarah whispered, catching her breath for fear of crying out. 'An' ma big brither Sam.'

The minister smiled, captivated by her obvious delight.

'Thank ye kindly, Reverend. Ah can nae tell ye whit a joy it is tae ken they're all richt.'

'Have you not seen them for a while?'

'Years, it's bin years.'

He watched a shadow fall across her face, feeling her withdrawing from him, suddenly nervously biting her lip, eyes flicking around the church.

'You are frightened of something.' he said simply. 'What frightens you?'

Her lips parted in a parody of a smile, 'Ah'm no' feart! Whit ha'e Ah tae be scared aboot?'

The minister remained silent, seeing through her bravado.

'Ah'd best be awa'.' Sarah put out her hand for the letter, keeping her lashes lowered. 'Ye've bin very obliging, sir. Ah must be aff tae werk noo.'

He folded up the well-worn sheet of paper, tucking in the ends and smoothing it between his fingers. 'God will hear your prayers. Pray to the Lord and unburden yourself of whatever is causing you pain.'

She took the letter without looking at him and turned away, rustling along the aisle towards the arched doorway.

'You are welcome here at any time!' he called after her. 'Let the Lord God save your soul. He knows of your woes and sins whether you speak of them to me or not. Pray to Him for your Salvation and deliverance from evil ... and He will strike the fear from your heart!'

Sarah kept walking. Where was God in the loneliest, most agonising times of her life when she pleaded for His help?

'He is here!' the minister's voice rang out. 'Open your heart and embrace His teachings!'

She stopped, placing a hand on the rough stone lintel, momentarily blinded by the brilliant scene outside: the sun was rising, showering the frozen lane with sparkling diamonds.

It was not the thought of praying which disconcerted her, it was the realisation that God, for whom she held respect if not faith, must know of all her lies. This dreadful insight dismayed her to the point of tears.

The note from New Lanark sparked recollections of a wholesome life, open and honest, surrounded by people she loved. Ever since leaving, it was complicated, dark with deception, existing in the shadows, surrounded by the stench of poverty in its harshest form.

How could she put it right?

Winding her way down to the bridge over St Enoch's burn, she was swept into jostling morning crowds. Carts drawn by ragged ponies rattled between pedestrians and hand carts, the air loud with curses hurled at the street hawkers, forcing them to jump out the way as they slogged along, weighed down with full baskets of wares.

Sarah fell into step behind a woman balancing a pole across her shoulders, strung with swinging dead rabbits.

Reaching the quieter side streets, still white with ice, she straightened her back and raised her chin defiantly against the turmoil churning in her stomach.

Perhaps she should attend church and confess all her sins to the earnest young clergyman? Tell him of her terror that her husband might be tracked down and taken from her, thrown into jail or worse? Of her dread if he was arrested and she could not provide for her children and they would all end up in the Poor House? Of pretending to be a different person, denying her own children their true identity?

Or, by committing all these transgressions, was God already punishing her?

Would confessing lift this heaviness from her heart?

She felt a rush of relief at this thought but it was quickly banished on realising that she could never break her promise to Sean and disclose the truth to a living soul.

***

'This is splendid news!' Dale declared to the table at large, raising his glass to the sea of cheerful faces. 'A toast, Gentlemen! To Peace!'

His words carried to the surrounding tables in the crowded Tontine Rooms and a crescendo of hearty cries resounded to the ceiling.

The long awaited Treaty with France was finally signed in Amiens: the war was over.

'I read it was Charles Cornwallis who drew the short straw and travelled to the Continent,' Archibald Paterson shouted above the din. 'Good man! He pulled the strings for the Union last year to bring the Irish into the fold when we all thought the Frenchies would invade them.'

'Aye,' Dale agreed, a mischievous glint in his eyes. 'I wouldn't have minded being in the room when he met Joseph Bonaparte and handed him the quill pen after all the trouble his brother Napoleon has caused!'

'It is in Napoleon's hands now,' mused Scott Moncrieff. 'A strange fish, that one! After all his military achievements I read he is wearing civilian clothing since taking up the title of First Consul.'

Among the gathering were Glasgow's most powerful men but to Dale these were not just his colleagues, these were his friends. Paterson, snowy haired and red cheeked, MacIntosh, his fringe of grey hair catching on his mobile bushy black eyebrows, gesticulating expansively, the brass buttons on his jacket straining to contain him, Robert Scott Moncrieff, usually anxious-eyed but now vivacious; all casting off their worries to share the moment.

Owen, who was sitting opposite his father-in-law, declared it to be a fine day and hoped Parliament would now have time to attend to home matters.

'Of course, that will be the other side of the coin,' Robert Carrick nodded. He was a fellow Director at the Chambers as well as a senior partner of the Ship Bank. 'We will have a flood of men returning to a country where the recession has bitten deeply into the bone. Unemployment is our curse already and they are simply not suited to the jobs in manufacturing. Anyway, where one man once laboured, a single machine does the work of ten!'

'On t'other hand,' said Dale,'we should see a rise in demand from markets previously prohibited. There are great opportunities out there to be grasped. May the Lord Our God grant a time of peace and prosperity after these harsh years.'

'Amen,' murmured John Brown, the oldest of the party. Now in his seventies, he was Carrick's banking partner, and his pale wrinkled features showed the strain of recent personal bereavements.

Dale felt a wave of compassion for the man. Brown's wife and all three of his daughters departed this life within the previous three years and it was obvious he was only throwing himself into business affairs as a distraction.

Just a week ago, he heard the sad news of the death of his friend James Muir. The poor man could not recover from the devastating injustice and loss of his son Thomas and was in the process of selling the family home of Huntershill when he passed away.

These were indeed harsh years, in more ways than one.

Owen listened to the discussion at the table, adding points and suggestions here and there but, as was his way, he took a quiet, reasoned view of the state of the economy. His mind was already on prospective customers and ways to feed the demand he believed would soon be available to tap.

A few days later, in early April, the Owens returned to New Lanark.

Winter's icy tentacles were finally releasing their hold on Scotland, allowing warmer air to breathe through budding trees, coaxing bees to venture among yellow primroses and cowslips emerging among fresh spring grass. It was not only the change in weather which caused Anne Caroline to leave for the country, it was the increasing number of smallpox cases in the city.

Her friend, Rosemary, was fanatical about who she would entertain in her home for fear of contamination, even dismissing a housemaid when she heard the girl had never taken the pox. The sudden spread of the disease became the talk of drawing rooms and having suffered so severely in the past, the Dale household prepared to leave for Rosebank shortly after bidding farewell to the Owens.

Cooper received baby Robert Dale Owen into the house with all the trepidation of taking sole charge of the baby Jesus.

She considered the little house in New Lanark to be her own domain and took immense satisfaction from running her servants with the utmost efficiency. Every inch of the house was scrubbed, aired and polished to perfection. Ena and Senga were even instructed to clean between every floorboard with a pin to ensure there were no ill humours lurking to strike down the infant Owen.

Cooper's own religious fervour now ensured the day started with prayers for all the servants around the kitchen table before beginning the daily chores. It was how it had been done in her first employment and she congratulated herself for reviving this important spiritual ritual.

This new routine did not go down well with Alice and the under maids, having to drag themselves from their beds in the attic a full fifteen minutes earlier than normal. Murdoch knew of it from his visits with his master, choosing to ignore it while reassuring the housekeeper that he chose his own time for worship.

On their arrival this Spring, Toshie was non-plussed by Cooper's earnest, and quite arrogant, insistence on her attending morning prayers.

At Charlotte Street, Renwick presided over the servants' devotions and gave a few well chosen words before they all took their seats for the first meal of the day. However, in New Lanark's small household, with the pious Mrs Cooper officiating, Toshie politely declined the invitation to join them.

While the servants bustled upstairs and down, settling the family into their summer home, Owen disappeared to the manager's office and Anne Caroline sought the comfort of her chair by the fire in the parlour.

Easing off her kid-skin ankle boots, she plumped a cushion up behind her and lay back to gaze into the flames. Various thoughts were sliding through her mind: did Toshie remember to pack her favourite nightgown? when would Robert need feeding again? was Cooper ill? she looked even thinner than last autumn. There was also the pressing need to visit her Aunt Marion up in Lanark, lest she be thought unfriendly.

Yet, behind these wonderings she was recognising the familiar aromas and sounds of the mill village and shying away from the memories they evoked.

In a few days it would be the anniversary of Daniel's death, a milestone she dreaded. Life goes on, she was told, and she understood this more clearly every day. She thanked God for little Robert and her loving husband, fully aware of her privileged position and determined to support her family in any way the Lord prescribed.

She closed her eyes and swallowed back a rising feeling of nausea. Another responsibility was being thrust upon her: she was with child once again.

Chapter Eight

*"Adopt measures of fair equity and justice and you will
readily acquire the full and complete confidence of the lower
orders."* Robert Owen

Nursery Buildings were complete and habitable. Owen stood
outside on the steps and gave a short speech to an assemblage
of his managers and a swarm of children, all dressed alike, the
girls in grey tunics, the boys in blue, before he thrust open the
main door to let them stream past him. Laughing and
whispering, their arms full of bedding, they poured into their
new quarters while he looked on, glowing with satisfaction.

Joe was also proud of the structure, narrowing his eyes and
assessing it critically every time it came into view when he
walked along the Row.

However, it meant he must now find new jobs and this was
proving harder than expected. Ewing passed on small
commissions, hired him for short contracts and still allowed
him to use the yard and workshop but the work was limited and
keeping a steady income coming into the family was barely
achievable.

'Ah should be bringing in mair mony.' he confided in Tam
one evening, packing away his tools and starting to lock up the
workshop. 'Ah'm qualified noo, but Ah cannae get the joabs.
Look at Ewing, he's no' here late intae the eve, he's awa' tae
the toon fer a meeting ... an' a grand dinner! Me? Ah'm deid
on ma feet an' Ah've five bairns an' a wife waiting fer me in a
crampit wee room at the mills.'

Tam watched his friend's downcast expression, 'Ye've ne'er
bin this doon afore, Joe? Whit's wrang?'

Joe picked up a stray nail on the floor and threw it onto the
work bench. 'Tell me straight, am Ah stupit?'

178

'Ye daft eejit!' Tam slapped him on the back, 'Aye, yer stupit tae ask sich a question!'

'Ye dae the books fae Ewing, can Ah ask hoo much he quoted fer tha' last joab he did fer the Provost?'

'Forty pounds. The monies only jist bin paid.'

'Forty! Ah telt him Ah wid dae it fer thirty. How can Ewing ask sich big sums an' git the joab?'

'Forty wis a guid price,' Tam rubbed at his nose, wondering how to broach the next question. 'If ye'd bin gi'en the joab, an' bin paid yer thirty pounds, whit wid ye ha'e made fer yersel?'

Joe kept all his figures in his head and answered readily, 'Twa pounds and six shillings.'

'An' how lang wid it ha'e taken ye?'

'Weel,' Joe thought for a moment. 'Ah wis gaun tae tak on three lads ... aboot twa weeks?'

'An' that twa pounds wid pay fer yer rent an' food an' all yer family needs fer those twa weeks?'

'Aye ... jist ...' his pace slowed as the meaning dawned on him. 'Ah'm no' pricing ma werk richt, am Ah?'

Tam shrugged, an odd, awkward movement with only one arm. 'Mibbe naw,' if it's too cheap an' they din nae ken ye, they might take ye fer a tinker. Ye also need tae tell folk aboot ye? tender fer werk, seek it oot, like?'

'How?'

'Ah din nae ken.'

Fiona was aware of Joe's discontent but with the new baby and her own tediously long days in the school room, as well as helping to settle the orphans into their new dormitories, her precious hours alone with Joe were usually spent sleeping.

One night, in the thickly silent hours before dawn, she woke to feel him moving restlessly beside her. Dazed with sleep, she reached for his hand and he grasped it lovingly, raising it to his lips. Her eyes flickered open, adjusting to the weak moonlight to find him looking at her intently, his lashes and cheeks glistening with tears.

'Ye all richt?' she whispered.

He didn't answer, instead, kissing her hand again.

'Whit's wrang?' she tried again.

'Nuthin' darlin'... gae tae sleep, ye need yer rest.'

Wide awake with concern, she raised herself on her elbow to kiss his salty lips.

'Tell me?' she asked sweetly.

For a long time they lay in silence while he sought for words to describe his feelings of frustration and inadequacy as a provider for his family.

Eventually, he said softly, 'Ah jist want mair fer ye, fer us. Ye should nae be werking sae haird, we should nae be here, all packed in here.'

'Din nae fret, we're all richt as we are. Ah love ye Joe, an' it breaks ma hairt tae see ye sae distressed.'

He turned to face her, pulling her into a comforting embrace on the rustling mattress.

'Whit would Ah dae wi' oot ye? Eh?'

She nestled against him.

Their present life might be adequate for her but tonight, on witnessing his genuine anguish, it suddenly became clear to her that he needed more. She was ignoring his wishes, his own ambitions.

This revelation came as a shock.

Long after her husband's steady breathing told of his slumber, Fiona lay awake berating herself for her selfishness and searching for ways to support him.

She was no nearer a solution when the first bird calls heralded dawn and her exhausted thoughts melted into sleep.

***

The lengthening days of spring brought Clydesdale alive. All down the valley, Nature spread rainbows of colour through its woodland, pasture and orchards. Wildflowers and blossom trees were buzzing with bees, vivid crimson and blue dragonflies darted above waterways, joined by swirling sand martins, among the first of the summer arrivals. Bobbing dippers and sandpipers vied for the best riverside perches beside flashing, turquoise and orange kingfishers. The sepia landscape of winter transformed into a vibrant, colourful spectacle.

The New Lanark villagers welcomed the coming of warmer, longer days. Putting behind them the misery of bracing themselves against the cold, living in the gloom of coal smoke and lamplight, they now streamed into the mills with a lighter step. At the end of the fourteen hours of incarceration, daylight would greet them again with the possibility of mingling with their neighbours and letting children play in the streets.

Even the dreaded room inspections became less irksome when washing could be done in gossiping groups by the river and then strung up outside to dry.

Owen walked around his village taking note of repairs and improvements to be made, pleased with the obvious progress of his new regime. It was also abundantly clear to him that he was still very unpopular.

The main reason for both the enhancement of conditions and the contempt they showed towards him was his hard stance on drunkenness.

Under his instructions, the same as he applied to stealing, anyone found to be intoxicated or causing a nuisance due to the influence of alcohol was given a warning and fined. After two warnings they were told in no uncertain terms that they would be dismissed if it happened again

Owen firmly believed that if their antisocial deeds were explained to them, they should be given the chance to reform their character and not reoffend.

He argued his case well with his partners to allow the use of funds to police the community. Atkinson and Barton could see the benefits of curbing pilfering and, in making the work force sober, they were losing fewer days' labour from illness and inability to work.

Unfortunately, they were not so understanding about Owen's other petitions to divert income, which would normally be paid to them in profits. He wished to fit out the vacant rooms in Mill Four as further school rooms.

After receiving a boldly worded letter from Mr Atkinson questioning his plans and querying bills for new bedding and clothing for the orphans in Nursery Buildings, Owen decided to travel to Manchester.

'I can persuade them of my motives much more easily if I am face to face with all the partners,' he told Anne Caroline on one of their evening strolls. 'They know my views. Why, they are the same ones I presented a paper on years ago in the Philosophical Society which Dr Percival and many others applauded. If it is the right course of action and shows care and compassion for these poor children, it is not enough to nod their heads at the theory and then baulk at taking the action!'

'I am sure they will agree with you.' Anne Caroline caressed his arm. 'Will you be away long?'

'A few weeks, I expect. Perhaps I should take advantage of being closer to Wales and visit my parents at Newtown.'

'I would dearly love to meet your mother and father, but I fear I should not travel so far with the new baby on the way.'

He smiled at her, affectionately, 'Of course not. They will understand. It would also be difficult to take Robert on such an arduous expedition. Best you stay here, my dear, or would you prefer to be at Rosebank?'

For a moment, she hesitated then laughed at herself. 'Had you asked me that question last year I would have answered Rosebank in an instant, however, honestly, I would rather be here these days.'

'I am glad. This is our home, I wish you to be happy here.'

Her long silence drew his attention but on seeing she was deep in thought he remained quiet.

They walked companionably among the birdsong for several minutes before she spoke again, pausing to turn and face him.

'Everyday, I pray to God for our happiness in this place. Naively, I believed it would all be so easy. You would run the mills and I would entertain in our little home, we would have a family and,' she looked out across the river, 'we would be happy. Of course, we bear the scars of loss after Daniel passed away but there is also an *awkwardness* among the villagers, a hostility towards you which is difficult to pinpoint but I feel it. Do you not?'

'Ah, yes, I am aware of their attitude but it will pass.'

'You say that with great certainty.'

'I say that because I know I have their best interests at heart and when they come to understand these changes are for their own good, which they will, they will be happier.'

'We have that word again, happy, that ideal.'

'Surely that is what everyone is striving for? We all wish to be happy.'

'It is an elusive condition.'

'Indeed, but it is quite attainable if hardship, ignorance and obstacles are removed.'

Her expression showed her scepticism. 'You have set yourself a difficult task, dear husband. The workers were 'happier', if we are using this subject, when my father owned the mills because they worked fewer hours upon the factory floor.'

'At present I have no choice but to run the machines for these extended hours but I intend to reduce them as soon as I can. Apart from that, you must confess the state of the houses is greatly improved and the lives of the younger children.'

She nodded, a wistful look shadowing her eyes, 'I suppose the underlying reason for their furtive behaviour in your presence is your stance on the Church.'

For a moment she wondered if he would take offence.

'I have no quarrel with my employees attending their chosen Church.' Owen was not at all offended. 'I respect their personal choice to believe whatever they wish. I regularly impress on my managers to promote a message to everyone here to respect the rights of their neighbours and work colleagues to follow the religious teachings of their choice. Perhaps they will come to allow me to believe whatever I wish?'

Standing beside him while he gazed on the never ending ripples in the water below, she observed him objectively: his smooth boyish face, animated and earnest. Robert was an intelligent, well-read man, highly organised and proficient in his work but she wondered if he truly understood how much prejudice there was against him regarding his non-religious views.

She shivered.

'Come,' he placed his arm around her waist, 'it is growing dark and Cooper will be most perturbed if we are late to the table.' He sensed his wife's serious mood and strove to brighten the conversation. 'Let us achieve at least one person's happiness today by arriving at our dining table at the exact time prescribed by our housekeeper. We might even contrive to raise a smile of satisfaction from the good lady?'

'An ambitious goal,' Anne Caroline relaxed, her lips curving as she caught his eye. 'Although I did happen upon her in the nursery when Toshie was supervising the maid bathing Robert and I am sure I caught a hint of a smile.'

Owen threw back his head and laughed, 'Aha, our son has achieved a miracle already! Let us build on his good work and raise Cooper's spirits still further!'

Anne Caroline chuckled, feeling a rush of warmth towards this enigmatic and lovable man she was so proud to call her husband.

***

In a clearing surrounded by beech saplings on the hillside above New Lanark, lay a small cemetery. Crudely carved stones and wooden crosses jutted out above the turf marking the final resting places of deceased villagers. Among them, taller and beautifully engraved, stood the headstone Joe made for his little sister, Meg.

It was beside this grave that Sam Scott threw himself down to lie in the long grass.

His mind was cluttered with memories, distant and recent, jumbling and jostling, bringing snatches of words, scenes and stabs of the emotion. Throughout his absence many powerful experiences had aged him: physically and mentally.

He was now a recipient of a gold medal from Sultan Selim 3rd for the Cameronian's part in the Siege of Alexandria. As a soldier he was proud of the medal and also for the honour granted to his regiment to include a Sphinx on its colours, but the harrowing campaign left many dead and crippled, on both sides, steeping the fleeting glory of battle in blood.

He knew his family would be shocked by his appearance, just skin and bones, causing deep lines on his face, his eyes sunken. It was not just the lack of nourishing food or exercise throughout the campaign and months onboard the Egyptienne, he was particularly conscious of the scars down his back and arms.

He had no recollection of the explosion he detonated to destroy the armoury in Alexandria, only vague flashes of being blown off his feet, dragging himself up and running with his troops to escape the carnage.

Heat, smoke, screams, horses squealing ... dead and mutilated bodies lying awkwardly in dusty alleyways. Then nothing.

Five fragments of shrapnel were embedded in his head and back, narrowly missing vital arteries but causing no initial pain to his adrenalin fuelled body. The surgeon extracted the metal pieces while he was unconscious, for which he would be eternally grateful, but the large wounds became infected, leaving angry raised scars. His head was shaved for the surgery, his long golden locks, bloody and matted, discarded amongst the sand and debris of the hospital tent.

Like many soldiers in the regiments camped around Alexandria, scores of Cameronians fell victim to ophthalmia. Barely able to see, their bloodshot eyes streaming, companies took up the practice of marching in lines, a hand on the shoulder of the man in front, placing a sighted soldier in the lead position.

Sam suffered the excruciating eye condition while lying face down in a swelteringly hot tent. Shut behind his blindness, surrounded by the groans and stench of his fellow wounded, he gritted his teeth and, fearing he would be driven insane by the tedium and pain, focused his mind away from the horrors of war.

Scotland became his sanctuary.

In his mind's eye he roamed across moors and waded streams, the heather blooming purple to every horizon. Imprisoned in heat, he recalled drenching rain splashing over windswept ash and birch trees, their roots gripping onto the crags of steep glens. Torrents of icy water springing from hillsides, filling lochans, trickling into burns, cascading down cliffs in white waterfalls: crystal clear, refreshing.

This was where he travelled to in his thoughts: his homeland and, many times, to the hill above the mills and Meg's grave.

He took strength from remembering how his baby sister lived for years locked away from the everyday things of life. If she could endure it, he could endure it. Sam carried a heavy burden of guilt on his shoulders.

On leaving the ship in Woolwich, the regiment took stock of their situation. For scores of Cameronians, their duties were over, their designated terms of service complete and they chose to return to civilian life. Others were forced by disability to resign their positions, leaving only a handful of officers and a couple of hundred soldiers.

Recruitment was the order of the day so, drawing a poor response from England, the regiment marched slowly north. It was a dispiriting exercise because now the war with France was over few could be persuaded to sign up, especially with summer labour available in fields and orchards.

The gentle rustling leaves above his head soothed Sam. It was as peaceful as the scenes he recalled in his wild imaginings, the fresh air sweeter in reality than the conjured up notions he created under the Arabian sun.

Occasionally, a flurry of raised voices, clattering wheels and iron shod hooves from higher up the hill, told of another wagon descending or hauling a load up the steep incline. He dozed, waiting for the mill bell to alert him to the end of the day when his family would return to their homes and they could be reunited.

It was Donnie who saw him first.

'Mam, see yon soldier? Is it Uncle Sam? Aye! It's Uncle Sam!' he tore away, vanishing into the crowds of workers, jinking and ducking towards the red coated officer standing on the corner of the Row.

Fiona scarcely recognised Sam. Quickly assuming a welcoming smile to cover her consternation, she took a firm grasp of her two younger boys and ushered them through the throng.

'My it's grand tae see ye back!' she called over the noise. 'Come away up!' she gestured along the street. 'Donnie, fetch yer auntie.'

With Davey bouncing along beside him firing questions, Sam accompanied Fiona and the children to their doorway. The passing villagers ogled his uniform, some apprehensive, others admiring. He was unused to everyday domestic routines and stood awkwardly in the dingy stairwell. A gaggle of open mouthed children soon surrounded him while Fiona collected her daughters from Mrs Young.

'Ye have anither bairn?' he said, astonished to see Ailsa.

'A fine wee lassie,' Fiona hoisted Sionaidh onto her hip, reaching for the handles of the straw basket where Ailsa lay sleeping.

Sam stepped forward, seizing the basket from her. 'Let me tak ma newest wee niece!'

When Donnie returned with Rosie, Cal was already home from work and the crowded little room resounded with delighted cries. One of the first topics was their news of Sarah, knowledge that she was well and a seamstress was carefully relayed, stressing they still didn't know where she lived.

Fiona went about her chores, occasionally chipping into the chatter while dealing with the children and preparing food for everyone.

She was exhausted.

Pleased though she was to see her brother-in-law alive, if ravaged by the war, all she wanted to do was lie down and close her eyes.

Joe's arrival led to another commotion, exciting the children even further. None of them could be persuaded or scolded into the big bed they shared and Davey and Robert soon became bad tempered, snivelling and fighting, adding to the general racket.

The men were oblivious, but Rosie noticed Fiona's tearful exasperation.

'Ma Gerry wid be fair pleased if ye wid come up tae oors the morra?' she patted Sam lovingly on the shoulder, yawning. 'Efter werk? Ah'm that tired, ye ken, ma eyes are closin' sae Ah'll awa' the noo but it's braw tae see ye, brither.'

Sam left shortly after Rosie, promising to return the next evening.

'Weel,' Joe closed the door behind him. 'Sam's hame agin. Grand.'

'He's hame,' Cal sighed, 'but he's in a bad way. His face is all crampit, Ah din nae mind him like tha' afore. Ye see his heid wi'oot his hat?'

'That's the war ...' Joe muttered. 'Tam'll no' talk aboot it ither, an' ye ken how Sam kindae skirts aroond sayin' much aboot the fightin'? Lord help them all.'

'The war's o'er.' Cal said, helping Fiona hustle the boys into bed and relieved to see Sionaidh already asleep. 'Whit'll he dae noo, d'ye ken?'

'We can ask him t'morra,' Joe mounded the ash over the glowing coals in the grate. 'Ah'm jist gie happy he's alive.

Whit a surprise tae find him here when Ah came through yon door! Eh, Fiona?'

Fiona was climbing into their bed, baby Ailsa in her arms.

'Aye, but noo, Joe, Ah'm fer ma bed.'

She lay back and put her baby to her breast, closing her eyes. Yes, she was tired, her feet ached and a dull headache throbbed behind her eyes, but the uncomfortable, rattled feeling came from somewhere deeper.

She had a brother of her own, but he would never suddenly appear at their table or dangle her children on his knee. He didn't even know where she was or if she was alive. It was years since the thought last occurred to her but, having sparked memories, she struggled to remain composed.

'Och, Ah'm jist sae weary,' she told herself, cuddling the baby. 'It disnae dae ony guid tae fret. Ma babbies are weel an' ma man's weel ... Ah can nae ask fer mair.'

***

The summer rolled on, ripening corn, drying hay and turning hard berries and apples into soft, yielding fruit.

Sam stayed in Lanark for a few weeks, visiting his family as often as possible and always bearing gifts of food or luxuries like soap, passing them over in an offhand manner. He took up Cal's offer to join him fishing, called by Ewing's yard at the end of the day to persuade Joe to 'take a drink' with him and surprised Rosie and Fiona with trinkets and ribbons from the market.

'We ha'e new orders,' he told Joe one evening while they sat on the wall outside the Tavern in the dusk. 'We're aff tae the coast an' then doon tae Stranraer where we'll sail fer Ireland. Wi' the days closing in the harvests will soon be gathered an' we may ha'e mair chance o' recruitin' as the pennies dry up.'

Joe took a swig of ale before asking, 'When d'ye leave?'

'Efter the Sabbath ... four days awa'. There's plenty tae be done sae I'll no' be doon tae the mills sae much.'

They sat in silence, bats diving and fluttering around them.

'Ye lead a fine, exciting life, brither,' Joe said quietly. 'Ah've ne'er bin past ten mile frae here in a' ma days. Ye've seen countries tha' Ah din nae e'en ken exist.'

188

'That's as mibbee, but Scotland's as guid as ony, better than most.'

Joe had already confided in Sam about his worries for making a livelihood from his work and now he sighed. 'Weel, Ah doot ye'll find ony change in the Scotts' hoose when ye next call by ... excepting mair weans.'

'Din nae say it wi' sich a sigh.' Sam gave his brother a hefty shove. 'Ye have riches I wid want, an' *do* want in the future. Yer wife's the bonniest lass in the county an' she's true tae ye. An' yer bairns are a credit tae ye baith. There are many who wid want yer life, Joe. An' there'll be mair work now the war's o'er. Jist yesterday I heard aboot the new buildings planned fer up by Hietoun.'

'Whit buildings?'

'T'was in the paper? An' there's a notice beside the Court House, up Hope Street.'

'Ah cannae read, Sam. Ah jist see bits o' paper stuck up on boards.'

Sam swirled the dregs of his ale around the tankard. 'Yer lad can read? Donnie?'

'Aye, Ah ha'e Mr Dale tae thank fer tha'. An' Fiona has her letters, an' Rosie an' Cal.' Joe gave a bitter laugh. 'Ah'm the dullard!'

'Naw, yer no'. Ye had tae werk tae keep them. New Lanark has bin guid fer ye all in that way ... in mony ways.'

Joe returned to the subject. 'If Ah din nae hear aboot a joab an' Ah can nae read yon notices, Ah'm stuck.'

'Och no! You an' yer pride Joe! ye have yer woman an' Tam, as well as ither friends who can read an' ye can ask them tae keep an eye oot.' He gave him a nudge. 'I bet ye have nae used ony o' that mony I left ye?'

Joe shook his head, pulling a rueful expression. 'A wee bit, an' Ah gave some tae Rosie, like ye said.'

'Och,' Sam rolled his eyes. 'Onyway, tak wee Donnie wi' ye? He can tell ye whit's being written.'

'He's at the school wi' his Ma an' next year he can gae tae the mills.'

'D'ye want him in the mills?' Sam was incredulous.

189

'Oh Aye!' Joe's head jerked up in anger. 'As much as Ah want ma richt haun cut aff! Whit d'ye ken Ah want fer ma lads?'

'Tell me?' Sam snapped back.

'Ah want them tae be better aff than me ... no' tae fear where the next meal comes frae, earn a living sae they din nae ha'e tae be burdened wi' this haun tae mooth, day tae day carry oan. It wears ye doon, Sam. Ah can nae tak Donnie wi' me tae werk fer we need him tae earn fer the family. Ah can nae pay him.'

'When does he start at the mills?'

'Next year, when he reaches ten years.'

'An' does he ha'e tae be in the school room every day?'

'Naw... he's bin up at the farm, helping wi' the hay.'

'Then stop being sich a cussed auld de'il an' tak him oot wi' ye... see how it gaes? get a cart, be seen oot an' aboot... write yer name on it ...' Sam held up his hands. 'All richt ... get some one who can write tae dae it,' he was smiling. 'Ye din nae have tae dae it all yersel. *Use* the money.'

'Ye ken?'

'Aye, I dae. If ye'll nae dae it fer yersel', dae it fer yer woman an' the weans. An' if I come back again an' find ye have nae...'

'Ah ken! Ye telt me afore! ye'll be 'mighty angry'!'

'An' so I should have been! I've a few mair years tae serve an' then I'm thinkin' I'll try an' find a lass an' settle doon. If truth be told, I envy ye, Joe.'

'Away! Ye've none o' the responsibilities... mak the maist o' it!'

Sam stood up, spat on his hand and held it out. 'I will, if you do! Until we see each ither again!'

They shook hands, ending with a fierce, brotherly hug before quickly, almost self-consciously, parting.

***

Owen's visit to Manchester, and then to see his elderly parents in Wales, passed uneventfully and rather unsatisfactorily.

He enjoyed the days he spent with his family and it was pleasant to familiarise himself with his hometown of Newtown, meet old friends and take sentimental walks by the river.

He saw a change in his father; he was slowing up, mentally and physically, his broad shoulders now stooped, his big knuckled hands less steady. Robert Owen Snr was still holding the position of Postmaster and enjoyed a major role in the management of the Parish but he was taking a backseat from his saddlery and ironmongery business. The store was still trading and Owen was pleased to see it was in good hands, bustling with customers when he called in to pass a few words with the manager, Mr Davis and his cheerful young wife.

Pleased to have made the effort to see his parents and reassure himself that they were comfortable, he boarded the coach to Manchester. Unfortunately, the meetings with his business partners proved frustrating.

He returned to Scotland still bound by the constrictions of the Board's over-riding desire for increased profits. Mr Barton declared Owen's requests for a larger budget to be allocated for the orphans' welfare as 'irrelevant' to the running of the mills. Mr Atkinson, while agreeing with the principle of furthering the infants' education, would not be drawn into arguing in favour of extra expenditure.

Irrespective of his senior partners' wishes, and a consistently awkward number of his own villagers, Owen forged on with his plans. The Misses Edmonstone of Corehouse were still prevaricating about giving permission for the proposed dam across the river, but, intent on ensuring a constant head of water, Owen continued to discuss compromises and press for their signatures.

In direct contrast to the barriers and negativity he battled with every day, visitors were still arriving daily to view the mills and their comments left him in no doubt that he was doing the right thing.

'I have just waved farewell to Mr Svedenstierna from Sweden,' he told Anne Caroline one afternoon. 'A most intelligent man. He informed me, in excellent English, that he is a Metallurgist and has been travelling around Britain looking at iron working methods here. He was visiting the iron works at Wilsontown and on hearing about our mills thought he would take a look around. He was extremely interested in every aspect, questioning me in detail over production. Although Mill Three is currently undergoing an overhaul, he told me how very pleased he was to see such an efficient and clean factory.'

'Gratifying for you, my dear.' his wife smiled.

'Foreigners see things with such an objective eye, it is a pleasure to hear their comments. I can say without a shadow of doubt that everyone who comes here is amazed by the place.'

'Then your work has not been in vain.'

'It is not for their flattering remarks that I embark on this course, it is with the hope that they will emulate the system.'

'And were all the workers at their stations today?' Anne Caroline knew her husband was concerned by the absence of many due to the local harvest gathering.

'Enough to keep the jennies to full production, but only because we reassigned those usually at work in Mill Three, whilst it is closed. By next week, Tuesday at the latest, the repairs and whitewashing will be complete, happily coinciding with the fields being cleared!'

Since the early years at New Lanark, Cal Scott was one of the villagers who regularly helped with the harvest. He did not shirk his daily duties at the Forge but, spurred on by his natural interest in the countryside, as soon as Big Lachie called the end of the day he hurried up the hill to Bankhead Farm. His few hours of raking and stooking earned some extra pennies yet nowadays he took on the task for the sheer enjoyment of being in the fresh air and learning about the crops.

He would stand on the stubble and listen to skylarks singing far above, feel the breeze on his face and look to far horizons. Living deep within the gorge where the steep hillsides crowded in, blocking out the sun long before sunset, this sudden feeling of space always brought a smile to his lips.

This year Donnie was with him. The chatty little boy scuttled around gleaning dropped ears of wheat into a basket and carefully pouring its contents into one of the barrels tied to the back of a cart.

Scotland's erratic weather meant there was always an atmosphere of urgency to bringing in the harvest. To have two or three dry days together was unusual enough, to ask for more was foolhardy. A sudden storm could flatten a pasture, making scything nigh on impossible. When hay or barley stalks were cut and left to lie they were in danger of a soaking and going mouldy unless turned and re-turned in the sun before stacking.

Under colourful scarves or large straw hats, old folk moved among the children doing the lighter chores while men wielded scythes and the women raked and gathered. Working rhythmically in lines, sweeps of land turned from waving golden corn to flat, trampled fields, neatly dotted with stooks ready for collecting to go to the thresher or raised into haystacks.

It was a massive communal effort, followed by a ceilidh.

A Storyteller was in Lanark and word soon spread that he would be Telling at the gathering-in celebrations.

Even before the heavy horses pulled the wagons away, piled high with the last of the sheaves, men were digging a shallow pit to lay a fire. The women folk disappeared to their homes, returning laden with baskets of food and flagons containing all manner of alcoholic brews.

Long evening shadows spread across Clydesdale, the sun's last rays catching at the bonfire's plume of drifting smoke and sparkling on newly formed dew, bringing alive the sweet aroma of fresh straw and damp earth.

The Teller did not disappoint. Dressed in a hooded cloak, embroidered with gold and green leaves entwined with exotic animals, he held his audience captive with tales from far and near. Donnie was entranced, hanging on every word, his eyes round with wonder.

There were songs, laments, laughter and drama and when this dramatic figure raised his arms, like wings, bid them all good fortune and strode away into the darkness, the assembled crowd whooped and cheered.

'It were the best day o' ma life!' Donnie declared to his parents when he burst through the door.

Calum looked just as exhilarated and Joe and Fiona caught each other's eye, smiling a shared happiness between them.

They had spent the evening discussing Sam's suggestion of Donnie going out with Joe when he was working away from the yard. Fiona understood the benefit of Joe having someone with him who could read, but impressed on him how their son was not yet a fluent reader and must still attend lessons regularly.

The purchase of a handcart was mulled over at length; it was a major expense. Joe admitted to Sam's generous gift, wisely leaving out the fact that the money had been lying in the village Savings Bank for over a year.

'If it's bin the best day o' yer life, son,' Joe said, seriously, winking at Fiona,'then we'll wait till t'morra tae tell ye some ither guid news.'

'Aw Da', ye can nae dae that!' Donnie begged. 'Whit guid news?'

'Yer comin' wi' me tae the yaird t'morra.'

Donnie threw his arms around his father's neck, speechless.

When all the children were in bed behind their closed curtain, Cal asked, 'Whit made ye think on takin' the lad wi' ye tae werk?'

Joe explained, finishing; 'It's only 'til he's auld enough tae gae in tae yon mill or ... or Ah mak enough money tae keep him on wi' a wage.'

Cal shook his head with a look of disgust. 'Ah can nae bear the thocht o' the wee lad in the mills. I wish ye tae dae weel, Ah alis have, Joe, but noo Ah pray fer the bairn's sake that ye mak a proper business o' it.'

Behind the thick curtain, Donnie heard his uncle's vehement words.

He didn't know what happened inside the great rumbling mills but the children he saw in the streets everyday looked all right. Yet, there was a terrible note of dread in Cal's voice.

For a moment Donnie felt a knot of doubt in the pit of his stomach. Then, discarding it with the naivety of the very young, he snuggled into his blanket, wriggling his legs away from Robbie who was lying beside him and being careful not to kick Davey at the other end of the mattress.

There was nothing to worry about because his Da' would soon make his fortune.

Joe was also struck by the intensity of Cal's words.

He tossed and turned all night, remembering Cal as a child when they arrived in New Lanark and how desperately he hated working in the factory.

Joe could not change Cal's childhood, but he could try to make his own sons' lives better.

He set off up the hill to Lanark the next morning with a purposeful step, Donnie running along by his side. Their first stop was to order a hand-cart from the joiner at the top of Hietoun. Then down the hill beside Pudding Burn, past the new St Nicolas Church and into the market place where they slipped through a vennel to the sign-writer's house and asked about the cost of a bright blue name plate.

With Sam's money he could afford the purchase and, fuelled by his demented, sleepless night, he took the decision to plough on with his plan.

'Aye, Ah'll tak the sign. Big blue letters. Dark blue.'

The sign writer stroked his beard and squinted up at him with a quizzical smile. 'Weel are ye no' gaunae tell me whit ye want me tae write? Or am Ah jist tae mak it up?'

Joe opened his mouth to speak, feeling suddenly nervous. How often he hoped this day would come and now, on this damp morning, it was here.

He cleared his throat.

'Stonemason. Joseph Scott ... and Sons.'

It sounded like a proper business.

It was a proper business.

He just had to make it work.

Chapter Nine

" ... the worst formed disposition, short of incurable
insanity, will not long resist a firm, determined, well
directed, persevering kindness. " Robert Owen

Autumn's glorious colours were cut short by violent gales
whipping down from the north, stripping away golden leaves,
toppling chimneys and felling trees. Scudding across the skies,
leaden clouds unleashed waves of sleet to slither down window
panes and gather in slippery drifts.

The Clyde gushed through the gorge above New Lanark,
tearing off overhanging branches and tumbling huge tree trunks
into its swollen waters. Its immense power throbbed through
the earth and could be heard for miles around, sending a mist of
spray high above the waterfalls.

Cooper and her staff worked furiously to keep the house
warm, shuttering windows earlier in the day and drawing the
curtains closed against whistling draughts. All the fires were
stoked and re-stoked, lamps kept burning at their brightest and
the kitchen clattered with activity to present hot, comforting
dishes to the dining table.

To ward off the cold, both the Owens and their servants
resorted to wearing layer upon layer of clothing, producing
mounds of washing. Together with daily piles of soiled baby
linen, Senga and Ena's hands were raw from taking it in turns
to pound the dolly stick or heat water, threading clothes through
the mangle and struggling to dry and press them in the chilly
conditions. Leaving the maids to the cramped steamy scullery,
Toshie dealt with her mistress's finer garments in the kitchen,
much to Cooper's disapproval.

It was constant, back breaking work.

Therefore, it came as a relief to the housekeeper when Anne Caroline declared it was time to return to Glasgow for the winter.

Murdoch, Peggy, the new nursery maid, and Toshie spent the journey sharing the warmth of the coach with their employers: baby Robert lying in his Moses basket between their feet.

Toshie was as delighted by their change in residence as Cooper. She reached Charlotte Street with all the eagerness of a child returning to the bosom of its family after an enforced separation.

Only young Peggy struggled with the upheaval.

On taking up her position, she was issued with strict instructions on how to behave towards the infant in her charge. It was Mr Owen who laid down the rules: no displays of anger or upset, no shaking or smacking, he must be dealt with in a firm and kind manner at all times. This was far from easy because Master Robert was a boisterous baby, grabbing at her cap or hair, pulling his mother's glittering necklaces into his mouth and, when restrained, screaming with rising frustration and gusto!

Anne Caroline found his behaviour as difficult and distressing as the maids but, encouraged by Owen, they persevered. At times the baby's cries could be heard beyond the house's thick stone walls but, as instructed, they placed him safely on the nursery floor, propped up by pillows, and paid him no heed until, exhausted or bored, he grew peaceful again.

As the months passed, Robert became more contented. Peggy adored her job and found the Owens' little house luxurious but on arriving in Glasgow, she was completely overwhelmed by David Dale's vast mansion.

The immensity of the building terrified her. There were so many rooms and corridors, store cupboards and pantries, it made her head spin; not to mention meeting all the footmen and maids and the key-jangling housekeeper and butler. For the first few days she could barely eat for nerves and only slept from sheer tiredness, but slowly, she began to find her place in the household and started to relax.

In early December, Anne Caroline gave birth to another little boy.

197

Their choice of name, should it be a son, was already decided but they waited until Dale came to visit his new grandson before telling anyone.

Owen ushered his father in law upstairs, full of relief and nervous excitement at the momentous event, but, on reaching the bedroom door, allowed the older man to visit his daughter alone.

Dale entered the softly lit bedroom beaming with expectation and happiness. It was less than an hour since the delivery and Anne Caroline was lying against a mound of pillows, her hair brushed back to show her radiant face, cradling her new baby.

Perching his considerable backside on the bed, Dale gazed at them both in wonder, murmuring a prayer of gratitude.

'He is a fine boy,' he said, gruff with emotion. 'The Lord has truly blessed us.'

'We are going to call him William. William Dale Owen.' she said simply.

Her father's eyes instantly flooded with tears and she grasped his hand in hers.

'My dearest brother can never be replaced,' she whispered, imploringly, 'that is not our intention, not at all, but one day I will tell our little William about his namesake, the uncle he never knew, my little brother, may the Lord protect him and keep him forever safe.'

Dale nodded, his chin crumpling, blinking to clear his vision.

'Amen. William Dale,' he leaned across and tenderly stroked the baby's downy head. 'My father, your grandfather, was a William as well. A grand choice of name.'

'And Robert's grandfather also. It is a fine name. Pray with me, Papa? Here, in this peace after the storm of his arrival.'

'Of course, lass,'

She closed her eyes, listening to his comforting words and sensing a quiet satisfaction and tranquillity she once feared she would never feel again after Daniel's death.

It was a scene she was to hold dear throughout her entire life, as strongly etched in her mind as his rousing speech on the evening of the great mill fire.

***

Nowadays, Jean Dale was taking a more active role in the running of the house, encouraged by her father and Aunt Margaret. Her engaging intelligence and appealing good looks ensured she was much in demand at recitals and balls, often escorted by her cousin David. If she was not preparing for a social occasion, Jean would join Mary and the younger girls at Anne Caroline's bedside, reading and sewing companionably. When the new mother was sufficiently recovered to join them in the drawing room, the sisters kept each other amused through the dark, midwinter days.

Owen thoroughly enjoyed being in Glasgow, conducting business all day and spending time with his father in law. The newly passed Health and Morals of Apprentices Act was debated at length.

'Goodness knows how our mutual friend Dr Percival must feel about this outcome after all his hard work to improve the children's working conditions. This avaricious mind-set is endemic in mill-owners, I fear, with only a few exceptions.' Owen stated. 'Now that Peel's Bill has been passed into Law, they believe themselves safe to economise on the needs of their workforce and proceed with inhumane conditions.'

Being possibly the largest employer of mill workers in the land but too occupied with Parliamentary business to regulate his works himself, it was Peel's own wish to pass the new measures into law. They gave clear guidelines to managers for restricted working hours, basic provision of education and cleanliness but lacked any form of proper control or inspection. It was a simple matter for any wealthy, immoral mill owner to bribe the local Justice of the Peace to file a 'good' report because many were their own blood relations or shareholders in the very factory they inspected.

'A terrible wasted opportunity,' Dale proclaimed. 'After so much effort and heartfelt good intentions, the Act has no teeth.'

'I have been invited to speak at a meeting of merchants in the city regarding these new amendments,' Owen sighed. 'I hope I can do justice to the subject for we both know a new system is sorely needed.'

'I am sure you will acquit yourself excellently,' Dale encouraged him. 'They should listen to you for you do not speak idly. I pray daily for others to see the errors of their way and treat these vulnerable young people with Christian kindness.'

Owen's speech was greeted favourably but, he wondered, shaking hands with fellow merchants, many red cheeked and full of claret by the end of the evening, would they actually put the required new regime into practice?

Owen returned frequently to the mills and Cooper enjoyed his visits. They provided a focal point for her efforts, however, she was also pleased to see him leave again after a few days.

When her employer was in Glasgow, with Alice, Senga and little Ena to carry out her instructions, Cooper found she could delegate nearly all her own work to them. This gave her hours of time to herself in her attic bedroom: praying and reading the Bible.

The Sabbath assumed inordinate importance, permitting her to attend both the morning and the afternoon services conducted in the village on the Lord's Day. Regardless of the weather, her thin, black garbed figure emerged from the house and scuttled through the village; bonneted head bent low, her Bible clasped against her waist in both gloved hands.

After the harsh weather in the closing months of the year, the spring came early. Joe was managing to keep up a steady flow of work, enjoying having Donnie by his side for at least four days of the week. On the days he was without his son, Joe missed his company as much as the reassurance of knowing he would not be caught out by being unable to read a note or write instructions.

'Could ye learn me ma letters, lad?' he asked his son one morning while they waited for a delivery of materials.

'Aye ...' Donnie screwed up his face and scowled from under his thick thatch of yellow hair. 'But then ye'd no' be needin' me.'

'Ye've proved yersel' as a guid werker!' Joe laughed. 'An' havin' ye here maks the joab easier an' quicker, sae, if Ah said ye could stiy wi' me an' no' gae intae the mills *if* we can mak enough money, how aboot ye teach yer auld Da' tae read?'

'We'll mak enogh money! That'd be jist grand!'

'Dinnae tell yer Ma, mind. No' until Ah can surprise her.'

Lampooning the traders he saw in the market, Donnie spat on his hand and held it out, stating in a jaunty fashion, 'Ye ha'e a deal!'

Tam was also encouraging Joe to do well, keeping his ear to the ground for potential new customers for his friend. He was now officially Ewing's clerk, with daily access to upcoming business in the area and when he knew his employer was not interested in a contract he immediately passed the details to Joe.

At Melanie's gentle suggestion, Tam now dressed smartly in a dark frock coat with a selection of three different waistcoats, one daringly flamboyant, matched with cream or black breeches and fashionable tasselled boots. Even his wiry shock of hair was regularly cut and tamed to present a very respectable image.

'Ye look a proper gent!' Melanie declared one day, dimpling sweetly.

'Apart frae me airm?' he quipped.

'Och, it jist adds character tae ye! Every yin has twa airms, ye can be prood tae be different.'

Tam liked that. He thought about her shining eyes and the generous smile on her soft pink lips and hoped her father would also begin to see him as a 'proper gent': a worthy suitor for his daughter.

In the meantime, he redoubled his efforts to impress Ewing by working diligently and for much longer hours than necessary.

The months rolled on and the Owens returned to New Lanark, Joe moved precariously from one job to the next and Dale and his daughters left the city to enjoy clear country air at Rosebank.

In Europe the storm clouds were gathering.

After only a year of peace, Napoleon Bonaparte, First Consul of France, was galvanising his armies to stamp his domination on Europe. Great Britain was a thorn in his side and by May the two countries were once again at war.

Still reeling from the recession caused by the Revolutionary wars, the Treasury in Britain immediately felt the effects of Bonaparte's plans. Newspapers brought the bad news of his invasions into Italy and Switzerland and told of 'worse to come' with rumours of a plan to invade England.

Dale read the accounts of the French victories and spent hours discussing their ramifications on commerce. Whether around the gentile dining tables of wealthy burghers, in the loud smoky Tontine Rooms or with customers at the bank, the topic wrought grave concern. Far from being retired from business matters at the Royal Bank, he found himself embroiled in meetings with desperate men pleading him to grant essential loans.

Throughout the land, banks were in trouble, rising to a great panic when it was alleged that there was not enough gold left in the United Kingdom to cover the paper notes now being liberally issued. As businesses collapsed and once strong merchants fell victim to the hard times, Robert Scott Moncrieff took the plights of his clients to heart.

Dale knew his partner wished to retire but no suitable candidate could be found. The flamboyant John More, who was supposed to be taking over from Dale, was not capable of running the Glasgow branch alone so the old partners, now both in their sixties, carried on with their duties.

An ill wind was blowing over the land.

Small pox and typhus fever stalked the streets, carrying off their victims with terrifying frequency. Talk of a new vaccination was on every ones lips but few knew how to obtain it or even if it would work.

On a humid day in June, Anne Caroline received a letter from her Uncle James Dale, suggesting she should not call on his wife the following day, as had been previously agreed.

'I fear little Martha may have a touch of the fever,' he wrote, 'and both Marion and I feel it would be wise, given that your sons are such a tender age, to postpone your visit until our daughter is recovered.'

Tragically, Martha Dale, the youngest of James' five children at not yet three years old, died a few days later.

Barely a week after this sad event, Owen received news that his mother was seriously ill.

Immediately, the battle for power in Europe and daily struggle to keep his order books filled were forced to take second place. With great urgency, allowing no opportunity for his wife to make arrangements to accompany him, he travelled to Wales by post chaise and arrived just in time to see her before she passed away.

Both John Thomas, the second eldest Owen son, who emigrated to Canada years before and Richard, the youngest son, who left home to work in England and rarely kept in contact with the family, were absent from their mother's death bed. So, to spare their father the ordeal, Robert shared the task of making arrangements for his mother's burial with his oldest brother, William, who rode up from London.

During the dozen or so years since last meeting, William married his employer's widow, taking on the established saddlery business in the city. Robert remembered his sister-in-law from the early years when he stayed with William in London as a child: his first time away from home. She was considerably older than William and, as she was not with him, he enquired after her and was told she was not keeping in good health and found travelling outside London beyond her now.

Noticing the resigned tone in his brother's voice, Robert wondered if William, a strongly built man of not yet forty years, found it difficult being wed to such a much older woman.

The question would neither be posed nor answered for their relationship was not one of close brotherly confidences. The paths of their lives and choices along the way were putting a distance between them.

As the eldest son. William would inherit his father's business and Robert was content to listen at the dinner table to the discussions of saddlery and retail costs for iron goods. At least, William's well informed suggestions for improving the shop diverted his father's attention from the tragic reason for the family gathering.

Their sister, Anne, bustled about the house, fussing around their father and covering her grief by sorting out the disposal of her mother's effects.

When Owen returned to New Lanark he was drawn and pale, suffering the pain of bereavement. Physically exhausted from the long journey, as well as two problematic meetings with the board of the New Lanark Twist Company en route, he retired to bed straight away.

Anne Caroline joined him, tenderly stroking his hair off his forehead, as she did with her sons.

This was no rapturous reunion of man and wife after weeks of separation, but it was as deep and loving as any act of love making. He put his arms around her and she lay with her head against his shoulder, listening as he quietly related anecdotes of his early child hood; memories of the beloved mother now laid in her final resting place.

The next morning it was business as usual and he found two good pieces of news waiting for him.

The sale of Spinningdale in Sutherland was complete and, at last, the papers were signed agreeing to the weir across the river Clyde. This last piece of good news meant a great deal to the performance of the mills. As soon as Humphreys walked through the door, Owen swung into action, dictating letters, instructing clerks and assessing the speed with which the engineers could complete the construction.

Neither their employer's bereavement nor his anxious plans to keep the mills running and therefore his workers paid throughout this financial crisis, made much impression on the Scotts.

Joe took Donnie up the hill to work with him, collected his tools and handcart from Ewing's barn and laboured for as long as the season would provide light. Every day, he was becoming more fluent in reading and, for now at least, he could afford to keep his eldest son out of the mills but Davey was pestering to be allowed to join them. Fiona remained adamant that he should stay in school, grateful for the opportunity to give her family an education while Mr Owen threw open his doors to the village children.

This decision caused early morning tantrums and tears in the Scotts' room before Davey resigned himself to his parents' wishes.

Far from the Scottish mills, in Paris, Napoleon's arrogance knew no bounds. Declaring himself Emperor and placing a crown upon his head with his own hands, all notions of the revolutionary cause left his mind. He held absolute power and looked on Britain with disdain, convinced that his *Grand Armée* could easily conquer the islands across the Channel.

Britain fought alone throughout the first years of this new conflict, successfully fending off attempted coups in India and Ireland. Under Addington, the government was ineffectual and relied heavily on the fact that while France might have the upper hand on the land, the British Navy ruled the seas. However, early in 1804, reliable intelligence was gained that the long rumoured plot by Napoleon to cross the Channel and overpower England was actually in preparation.

To the relief of thinking men up and down the country, William Pitt returned to his position as Prime Minister, immediately implementing huge and long overdue investment in the army and navy.

Newspapers and Towncriers called out to the country for volunteers to protect their homeland and set about building defences and lighting beacons to repel an attack along the south coast. Over half a million men came forward, fearing the imminent sight of enemy ships sailing over the horizon.

'There's not a damned thing we can do from here, hundreds of miles from London, but we can keep the home fires burning.' Archibald Paterson told Dale while travelling together to a meeting of the directors of the Glasgow Royal Infirmary. 'Thank the Lord we live on an island or we would already be speaking French!'

'Where are the Prussians? The Austrians?' Dale rolled his eyes, exasperated. 'It was all good and well to declare we have a new coalition to stand alongside us and put this self-important little General in his place, but I don't see them now! And Russia?'

Paterson clutched at the side of the carriage, the horses lurching to a walk over uneven cobbles.

'Pitt will sort it out.' he said firmly. 'He dealt a master stroke of political manoevering persuading Fox, so long his enemy and staunch ally of Addington's, to be persuaded to join forces with him.'

'Aye, in times of such adversity, personal friendships must not stand in the way of the good of the country. We must be thankful for Pitt's return to office.' Dale shook out a large handkerchief and gave his nose a trumpeting blow, followed by a wheezing cough. 'I'm looking forward to returning to Rosebank next month. This ague is hanging over me and the city smoke of winter makes it worse. I feel old these days, fatigued by the discomfort in my body and hearing the tales of those poor souls ruined, or worse, by the wickedness of war.'

'Ye have your faculties, my dear friend, that's the important thing. This rattle in your chest after a bout of influenza can be expected and will clear, I have no doubt. I read in The Glasgow Herald that our King is ill again. They say he ranted for several days without a break for sleep, unintelligible nonsense! His physicians have removed him from public duties once more.'

'It must be a terrible thing to lose your senses, I pray for His Majesty's recovery. The brilliant work of our surgeons in the Infirmary can help those with a bodily ill, although we must place our faith in God, in His infinite wisdom, to redeem the mental state of those who suffer such wild delusions.'

The carriage came to a swaying halt close to the hospital gates, the footman jumping down to lower the steps.

'There's Hamilton!' Paterson struggled from his seat, making an undignified exit onto the street behind Dale.

All the directors arrived at the same time and were alighting into the damp afternoon. Their immaculate knee length wool coats, silk cravats and tall hats were in stark contrast to the ragged townsfolk gathered outside the high iron fence enclosing the building.

'This Infirmary is a great asset to the city,' said Dale, passing the gate keeper and acknowledging the man's deferential bow. 'Just look at the great dome against the sky!'

His colleagues paused in their step to let him lead the party towards the door.

'A remarkable design,' Gilbert Hamilton agreed, his interest in architecture heightened after experiencing the intricate planning and creation of his own new mansion, Glenarbuck.

'But it is the work within its walls which proves its worth.' Dale continued. 'I understand the wards are filled to capacity and the surgeons work tirelessly every day. Gentlemen, we must ensure they continue to receive all the financial requirements they need. In these dreadful times when purse strings are tightened, it is the poor and stricken who must receive our help.'

'Well, we will have to see what our Treasurer reports, eh?' came a flippant comment from a member of the Board.

Dale turned and sought out the owner of the remark, fixing him with a glower.

'Look behind you, Sir. Those destitute citizens crouched beyond the fence rely on us to ensure the care of their loved ones. It is our duty, deferred on us by the City, to ensure the continuation of this institution. Let God be your judge if you cannot find a way of carrying out your responsibilities today and throughout the course of your service to the city!'

The group fell quiet, apprehensive.

David Dale was famous for his amiable character but equally admired for his strong sense of justice and obligation. Paterson noted the offender's mortified expression, pleased to see that despite his friend's admitted current ill health, he had lost none of his fiery determination.

Satisfied his point was made, Dale strode into the hospital to greet his friend, John Hamilton, the serving Lord Provost, with a hearty handshake.

***

In Ireland, inland from the bustling port of Dublin and the lakes lying among the Wicklow Mountains, a blustery wind drove sheets of rain across a wide expanse of moorland. Buffeting and pulling at any loose flaps of canvas, it whined among hundreds of tents laid out in symmetrical rows. Flags clattered against their poles denoting the dividing lines between eight different regiments and hurried figures scurried up and down the narrow, muddy tracks between the guy ropes.

In the middle of the massive barracks the 26th Rifle Regiment, the Cameronians, were settling down for the night.

This flat piece of land was capable of holding up to fifty thousand men and had been used by the military for centuries. A mere half dozen years ago, where His Majesty's army now camped, thousands of patriotic men mustered to support the doomed United Irishmen Rebellion against British rule. It was little wonder that the soldiers were scarcely welcomed in the area.

As an officer, Sam Scott enjoyed the privilege of a comfortably equipped tent of his own. On that wet June evening, the ranks were dismissed for the night and with the light failing fast, he turned up the wick on his oil lamp and removed his boots.

It was too wet to venture to the local inn tonight and, besides, he was still suffering the effects of a heavy drinking session the previous evening. So, he decided, the time was upon him to stop prevaricating.

Dipping his quill in the ink bottle, he took some time positioning a small square of paper to best catch the pool of light before beginning to write.

'My dear family,

I hope this finds you all well. I seem to have walked or sat astride my horse every day since leaving you. Recruitment was hard on our first expedition to Ireland and we returned to Port Patrick with only a score of new men. Since then I have been in the north, at Fort George, beside the sea. The outbreak of war has changed our fortunes, raising our numbers to over 1,000 in the ranks.

I am once again in Ireland. I am writing to you from the Curragh of Kildare which is a fine place on a sunny day. Pray to God for an early end to this conflict for it rains here more than even in Clydesdale. You are in my thoughts, with greatest affection always, your obedient servant and brother. Samuel'

He read and re-read the letter, idly flicking the plume of his pen across his chin.

It was a short note, a simple message conveying his love and reassuring them that he was alive. So few words, inadequate perhaps, but it served to capture this period in his life because little really happened: marching, striking camp, more marching, cleaning rifles, firing practice and drilling. Hundreds, he grunted at the thought, more probably thousands of miles of road were traversed, steadily, one step after another. Up through the glens, past deep lochs lying like giant mirrors to reflect the grandeur of their surrounding mountains and then over moorland and bog, through forest trails and along coastal cliff tops.

The swell in the numbers joining the Cameronians and the other regiments had little to do with the French and all to do with Pitt's new system of obliging all men to serve their country when called upon to do so.

If a man was called to service but did not wish to join the militia, a new amendment allowed him to find a substitute and pass his service on to this recruit. In effect, it firmly placed the burden on individuals who, desperate to evade their obligation, were willing to pay another to take their place. The end result was the same: for every man ordered to serve, a man filled the position.

The trampled turf of Curragh Camp was home to thousands. Like a village, it held families, wives following their menfolk, bringing children and babies as well as pack horses and carts.

Long canvas awnings covered rows of trestles for serving food; dozens of cauldrons and hot braziers flared into action twice a day, their supplies piled up in yet more makeshift tents. Tethered along rails on the north perimeter were the regiment's horses, both the officers' well bred animals and the shaggy-legged work horses, accompanied by saddlers and blacksmiths with all their paraphernalia.

From the first sound of the bugle at dawn to the closing notes at sunset, the camp ran in strictly organised sessions. As one of the thirty five officers in charge of the 26th, Sam was rarely idle through the day and having been in camp for several months, they were all used to the routine. Time and conditions were on their side, a comforting thought after the rigors of disease and lack of supplies on the Egyptian campaign.

Sam folded up the letter and secured it with his personal red sealing wax and stamp, a purchase made on a whim from a booth in Dublin a few months earlier. He thought of Fiona opening it, for it would surely be Fiona who would read the letter to his brothers and the children.

Sitting alone in his tent with the tapping of raindrops, rattling gusts of wind and the muffled, distant rasp of a fox barking, he suddenly yearned to be with them. He could imagine them clustered around the little table beside the fire, the shutters closed, the babies squabbling. Cal was probably yawning, Joe and Fiona catching each other's eye with those half smiles they passed, saying nothing yet meaning everything.

He wished he could find a woman to share his life, a decent lass, healthy and light-hearted, who would care for him and satisfy his needs; soft and tender after a heavy day.

He stretched, unbuttoning his jacket, but who would want to wed a scarred old soldier: here today, gone tomorrow?

Unless, he settled down.

More and more the notion was creeping over him to leave the army when this term of duty was over.

The flap of the tent lifted and a sudden rush of fresh air heralded his batman, asking if he required anything further that night.

'Naw, ye can turn in.' Sam handed him the letter. 'Make sure this goes tomorrow, first thing.'

The young private saluted and backed out the tent, causing Sam to smile at the absurdity of having a servant.

With his batman to fetch and carry and Roisin, the obliging daughter of a local tradesman, providing an attractive diversion every few evenings, he was comfortable enough to see through the war.

He caught himself sharply, not wishing to tempt Fate, *if* he was spared by the good Lord to live to the end of the war.

***

'This came fer ye!' Mrs Young gave Fiona Sam's letter when she collected her youngest children after work.

Fiona strained to hear her words over the noisy pandemonium in the street. Great piles of straw bedding lay in heaps beside the doorways. Delivered that afternoon, they were already diminished by housewives and old folk leaving the returning workers to fight for the best of the rest.

'A letter?' Fiona seized it, not recognising the writing nor the official-looking scarlet seal. Perhaps it was news of Sarah? She hurried upstairs, her anxiety so great that on finding it contained a pleasant note from her brother in law, she breathed a great sigh of relief.

'Ah wis that feart it wis frae the magistrate aboot oor Sarah or her man, that Ah wis shakin' an' ma hairt wis banging!' she told Rosie later.

Fiona was pregnant again, with only a month or so to go before the birth so they arranged, weeks before, to help each other with refilling the mattresses when the bedding arrived.

Rosie grinned, delighted to hear from her brother but she also had some news of her own.

''Tis grand tae hear Sam's weel,' she read the letter again, making a show of savouring his words before blurting out, 'Ma

Gerry's been promoted! Yon Mr Owen telt him this very efternoon! "Office Manager" they'll cry 'im!'

'Away! Manager! Jeezo, a manager! Tha's splendid fer ye baithe!'

'Ye ken Mr Owen disnae say much aboot bein' pleased wi' onything?' Fiona nodded, she never heard a word of praise from the mill owner. 'Weel, he telt Gerry whit a 'good job' he did wi' the reports and knew he could rely on him to keep the books in order.'

'Why the noo? Gerry's bin a' tha' joab fer years.'

'Aye, but there wis all the carry on wi' the bills fer the new weir an' Ma Gerry wis the yin in charge o' sortin' it oot. Ah'm fair chuffed tae pieces!'

'Will it pay mair?'

'A wee bit, but Gerry's like a dog wi' twa tails an' a' fired up tae tak o'er frae auld baldy Humphreys noo!'

Both girls laughed, knowing the English manager would never be replaced. It was common knowledge that he and Owen were colleagues long before they came to Scotland.

Cal came home in time to help with the removal of the old bedding, a heavy mixture of heather and chaff. They were all glad to see the back of it for no amount of shaking or pummelling could make it comfortable.

'Ireland.' Cal held Sam's letter and looked dreamily out of the window at the forested hill rising steeply on the far bank of the river. 'Ah dinnae ken where Ireland is but Ah thocht it were the Frenchies we were fightin'?'

'It is.' Rosie straightened the blankets on the children's bed, giving a final sharp tweak to smooth the top creases. 'Ye should read yon newspapers, Cal, Ah dae. Gerry brings them hame when he shuts the offices of a nicht.'

'An' where am Ah tae git them?' Cal demanded.

'Ah'll pass them on tae ye, if ye ha'e a fancy tae see 'em?'

'Din nae bother,' Cal laid the letter on the table again. 'Ah doot Ah could nae understaun them anyhoo. Yon letter's hard enough!'

'Ye ha'e tae keep up wi' yer readin',' Fiona told him, 'Ah can help ye? Like Ah dae wi' those sheets Donnie brings doon the hill.'

'Ah'm no' a bairn! Whit dae Ah need tae be able tae read fer? Waste o' time!'

Fiona saw the bleak, withdrawn expression close over Cal's face. There was no point in arguing, she had other things to fill her mind and evenings.

A few weeks later, Cal regretted rejecting her offer.

Two of Owen's under managers came to the forge with papers, asking if anyone wanted to move to new positions in the village. Listening to their conversation with Kyle Mcinnes, Cal became intrigued. Men were being hired to keep the grounds and prepare areas of land for growing vegetables. Too shy to join their discussion, Cal waited until they left before cautiously reaching for one of the written sheets placed on the bench.

Some of the words made sense, but the longer ones, running together, were unintelligible.

Kyle was watching him from under his lashes. He could see the strain on the young man's face.

'Tak it awa' wi' ye an' read it at your leisure,' he called across the workshop.

Jim, a knife thin man with a sharp tongue, sniggered. 'He cannae mak heid nor tail o' it, the dolt!'

Another man glanced their way, joining in. 'Hey Cal, ye could nae lift a spade let alane dig a hole!'

'Leave him be,' Kyle said, dismissively. ''Course he can read it, he went tae classes afore you lot came tae the mills, sae jist shut yer mouth Jim. There's werk tae be done here sae if ony o' ye cares tae tak a sheet an' see whit these new joabs are aboot, then read them in yer hame, no' while the forge is working!'

Grateful for Kyle's words, Cal tucked the paper into his jacket pocket and carried on with the task of rubbing oil into a pair of cracked leather reins.

'Do ye fancy changing yer joab?' Joe asked him that evening when they all pored over the description of the new position.

'It's oot in the fresh air, working wi' the land, aye, it sounds grand.'

'The money's no' sae bad, an a'.' Fiona ran her finger along the letters. 'Apply immediately. Whit d'ye say, Cal?'

'Whit if it's gie heavy werk an' Ah'm nae strang enough? Then Ah'll ha'e lost ma place wi' Big Lachie?'

'It's up tae yersel',' Joe told him, keeping his voice neutral. If it was physical strength they were looking for then Cal had no chance.

Throughout the night, Cal wrestled with the problem and by the time the mill bell was ringing for morning duties, his mind was made up.

He would stay where he was, cleaning tack, grooming and handling the horses for visitors and carrying out the simple tasks he was confident in completing. To his family, he nonchalantly shrugged the matter off, saying he was quite content in his work and being a grounds' man was not what he wanted.

Inside, he was bitterly disappointed.

Disappointed in his weak body, fear of ridicule and most of all, his complete lack of self-confidence.

***

His cloak billowing around him, Owen stood on the riverbank and surveyed the new weir. He was upstream of the entrance to the long tunnel leading under the hillside to the mill lade, watching the water being corralled and diverted.

'Only time will tell if this will make the hoped for difference to our production.' He shouted to Humphreys above the strong wind, rustling leaves and whirring in their ears. 'Goodness knows, it has taken long enough to reach this point.'

The river was running low, 'showing its bones' as one of the engineers called it. Wide sand and gravel beaches bordered the current, rippling over jutting rocks and being forced to pool behind the newly built obstruction before swirling slowly towards the gaping hole of Dale's original tunnel.

Water still trickled over two lower sections, close to the Corehouse bank, splashing on down through the rock strewn gorge towards Dundaff Linn and the village lying a thousand yards downstream.

As the Misses Edmonstone warned, it invited trespassers to cross the natural boundary by walking along the weir. Owen's assurances of good behaviour from his employees were well intentioned but difficult to guarantee.

Despite his confidence, his instructions to the villagers, passed on by the managers and supervisors, forbidding them to cross the river or trespass on either Bonnington or Corehouse estate, were often being ignored.

The culprits were brought before a committee and after two fines the offender was threatened with dismissal. However, this was not usually the outcome because Owen allowed them yet another chance to redeem themselves which more often than not, brought about the necessary change of heart.

While Lady Elizabeth Lockart Ross in Bonnington House was content with the situation, the Edmonstones took issue with every incident.

'If this autumn is anything like last year's,' said Humphreys, 'no person with any sense will risk laying a foot into the torrent.'

They made their way back along the cliff top path to the village, bent into the wind, holding on to their hats, heads down against the gusts.

'Which will be excellent for the water wheels,' Owen agreed. 'It is when the snow and ice cover the countryside and we have a great freeze, *that* is when we need to be vigilant. The ladies at Corehouse will be justifiably displeased if their apple store or firewood is pilfered. It will also put this weir to the test.'

'At least it is running well today, all four mills are up to speed when we would normally have been down to two or even just Mill One after such a dry spell.'

The men parted beside the bridge over the lade; Humphreys setting off up the hill towards Caithness Row and Owen walking on to Mill Four. He wanted to make a cursory tour of the kitchen and laundry on the ground floor before going up to the school rooms.

Pausing in the hallway to remove his cloak, he became aware of a deep man's voice: shouting. At first he thought it must be coming from one of the carpenters' workshops in the basement but on taking a few steps up the winding staircase, he realised that it became louder.

These were angry, raging words, punctuated with loud thwacks and then another roar of violent threats, the male voice cracking with venom.

214

Eventually, on the second floor, Owen opened the door to the classroom.

Within a second, the bellowing stopped.

Open mouthed and flushing an ugly purple above his full beard and side burns, the teacher at the head of the room let his arms fall to his side, a heavy text book clutched in one hand. He stared in dismay at Owen standing in the doorway.

Slowly, Fiona and the other assistants followed his gaze and in turn all the children sitting on the floor, nearly a hundred of them, swung round to see the mill owner.

'Mr Crosslaw,' Owen said quietly, his terse words audible throughout the room. 'A word, sir.'

The teacher made his way stiffly to the doorway and followed Owen down the stairs to a small office.

'Please explain to me, Mr Crosslaw, what caused you to raise your voice and thump your book so alarmingly in front of the children?'

'Two of the older boys were playing with marbles during the lesson.'

'And did you ask them to refrain?'

'I was reading the Lord's word, Mr Owen. They are instructed to listen and repeat the words. It is blasphemous to enter into a game ... a game with coloured beads while we recite the Scriptures. The lack of respect! They showed no humility when I reprimanded them, indeed one was smiling. They must be taught a lesson!'

'It is true that they should have been attending their lessons but I have expressly asked for the children to be treated with civility and care at all times. I fear, Mr Crosslaw, from the stream of degrading insults and threats I heard coming from your own mouth, the only thing you have taught those infants is how to shout and create fear and oppression. That is not a desirable lesson, I am sure you would agree?'

Tugging at the white shirt cuffs around his wrists in an agitated manner, the teacher cleared his throat, 'I have to control the children or they would run amock! Some of these are devious, wicked boys and girls, they try my patience daily with their cunning ways and idle complacency towards the Lord's teachings!'

Owen observed the man for a while, before giving a brief nod.

'I can see you have found it a trying experience. The pupils upstairs are among our youngest and most impressionable in the village. All are under ten years old, many are mere babies.' His eyes flicked over the teacher's face, seeing the belligerent countenance of a man who believes himself to be right. 'Perhaps, it would be better for you and the children under my care if you were to take a position elsewhere.'

'Are you dismissing me? For raising my voice against ignorant paupers who would disrupt the class and play vulgar games ... there are many who would have whipped those lads and been praised for bringing order!'

'Indeed. Unfortunately, you are quite right, corporal punishment and verbal abuse are routinely used in school rooms throughout the land. And look at the results ... our society? No ... not here. Not in New Lanark. This was clearly stated to you when you took up the appointment.' Owen turned on his heel, his voice still reasoned and steady. 'You will not be required in the school room again, Mr Crosslaw. Please call at the office tomorrow, before you leave, and the clerk will see that you receive your wages up to today.'

Sitting quietly by their fireside later that day, Owen recounted the incident to his wife.

Anne Caroline was in the last weeks of carrying their fourth child. It being summer and having great respect for Mr McGibbon, the New Lanark physician, she was content to remain in the country for this confinement.

'How dreadful!' she cried, on hearing of Mr Crosslaw's tirade. 'Do you think he has long been in the habit of berating the pupils?'

'I fear he may. He is of the opinion that it is an acceptable method and if he were teaching in the majority of schools across the United Kingdom and many other countries, I am sure he would also be given to using the cane without restraint.'

'It is a horrible thought that our sons might one day fall prey to such a man.'

Owen looked up sharply, 'I will do everything in my power to ensure they don't, you can be assured of that, Caroline.'

'Did you suffer at the hands of such a tutor?' she asked, stitching away at the gift she was making for her sister Mary's birthday; a motif of colourful flowers decorating a dainty, lace edged pincushion.

'I was fortunate to enjoy the instructions of a benign schoolmaster, what was his name? Ah, yes, a Mr Thickness. He taught very rudimentary lessons in apartments at The Old Hall, a mansion house just beside Newtown. It was a beautiful old house, only recently used as a school having been the home of Sir John Powell Pryce until he fell on hard times. I was only there a few years and learnt so quickly that the last two years I was taken on as an usher, helping the other children with their work.'

'You have always had a bright and interested mind, my dear!'

Owen was deep in reminiscing, 'You asked if I ever suffered at the hands of a tutor and, to be truthful, I am happy to say I did not. While Mr Thickness supplied a basic knowledge of reading, writing and the four rules of arithmetic, I had the run of libraries throughout Newtown. The clergyman, the physician, the lawyer, they all threw open their doors to me because, through my father, I was well known in the town. I read voraciously! As I believe we discussed on our first private meeting, my dear Caroline,' he smiled at her, 'it was our love of books and reading which occupied our conversation.'

'I remember it well.' She returned the smile, holding his eyes for several tender moments before returning to her needlework.

'I was, however, whipped.'

She was shocked and glanced up anxiously.

'By my father and, I hasten to add, only on one occasion. I refused a request by my mother due to a misunderstanding. Unfortunately, the matter grew out of all proportion and father was called to make me yield. He whipped me until I said firmly that he 'could kill me' but I would not comply. That ended the matter and he never raised the whip or a hand to me again.'

'And what age were you?'

'Six or seven years old, no older. From my own feelings, which I well remember as a child, I am convinced that very often punishment is not only useless but very pernicious and injurious to the punisher and the punished.'

'Well, our boys will not have to endure such an incident.'

'Certainly not! Children suffer a great deal from being misunderstood. Had my parents taken the time to talk to me, we would easily have discovered the misunderstanding. One has to make the relationship between child and adult an open one, which allows the child to unburden themselves of their worries without fear of being ridiculed or beaten.' Owen gave a brief laugh. 'My brother used to beat me, at night. To allow me peace my mother gave me a separate bedroom.'

'Gracious! Why ever did he beat you?'

'You may not believe this, but it was for keeping him awake by saying my prayers so earnestly.'

'You? Praying? To Our Lord?'

'I have told you that I was an avid follower of Christianity when a child. Yes, I prayed every night and I even composed sermons. They called me the 'Little Pastor'.

Anne Caroline laid aside her sewing, looking at her husband in amazement.

'My father is a Deist,' he continued, 'but we knew three maiden ladies who were ardent Methodists and keen to introduce me to their peculiar faith. They gave me many books but as I was also reading works on Jews, Mahomedans, Chinese and those we call Pagan and Infidels, I became surprised by the opposition between the sects. They all held a deadly hatred towards each other and I thought at length and deeply on the subject. Even at ten years old, I came to the opinion that there must be something fundamentally wrong with all these religions.'

Anne Caroline remained silent. She wished with all her heart that he would change his mind and have faith in the word of the Lord and believe Christ to be the son of God, which she so fervently believed herself.

'Did I tell you of my letter to Mr Pitt?'

She shook her head, brown curls bouncing.

'I expressed my hope that the Government would adopt some measures to enforce a better observance of the Sabbath.'

'Goodness, my dear! That is hard to reconcile with the Robert I know!'

Owen gave a wide, rueful smile, 'That was when I was in Stamford and around twelve years old. Ah yes, I am one and the same. I studied and studied ... religious writings of every

218

creed, finding them all to believe, implicitly, that theirs was the one true religion.' He sighed. 'Who is to say which is right? If any?'

A knock at the parlour door ended their discussion. Cooper presented a letter on the salver and Owen opened it immediately.

It was his sister's handwriting and she rarely put pen to paper unless for a serious communication.

Anne Caroline saw his face blanche: this was bad news.

'Thank you, Cooper, you may go,' she muttered, moving to her husband's side.

'My father is dead,' he said in a whisper.

She cradled him in her arms, murmuring a prayer beneath her breath despite the knowledge that neither her husband nor the late Robert Owen was a Christian.

Once again, Owen made the long journey to mid Wales on his own to attend the burial of a loved parent. His brother William took over the responsibilities of winding up their father's affairs and mentioned to Robert that he was in no hurry to sell the family business in such a depressed market.

'My wife is very unwell,' he confided on Owen's last evening in Newtown. 'My first concern must be in looking after her. I have a mind to sell up in London and take these Welsh premises on myself but, as you know, the business was started by her late husband and she is adamant that we remain in the city.'

'Maybe when she is recovered?' Robert suggested. 'A change from the smog and crowding of the capital may appeal more.'

'She will not recover. The medics have been blunt with me, well, with both of us. She does not have long left and I do not intend to cause her any further distress by taking her away from all she has known for the last sixty years.'

'It must be a very difficult time for you,' Robert sympathised. 'I am sure you will do what is right.'

William nodded, gazing into the fire's embers thoughtfully.

'One can only do what is right at the time, eh?' he mused. 'In the meantime, I shall keep Mr Davis on to manage the business here. His wife is also very efficient so I am sure it will continue smoothly.' He glanced up at his younger brother, meeting the same blue and gold flecked eyes he saw in the mirror each day. 'I hope your life is good, Robert?'

'I am happy to say that, yes, it is good. You must try and come up and visit us at New Lanark. Meet Caroline and see my mills.'

'We'll see,' William looked doubtful. 'I am not sure where my life will turn in the coming months and years but I wish you well with your endeavours.'

Within weeks of one Owen leaving this world, another was born.

Robert was barely home before his daughter arrived. They named her after her mother, and her late grandmother: Anne Caroline.

On the same overcast summer day, a few hundred yards from where the Owens rejoiced in the safe arrival of a little girl, Fiona presented Joe with a baby boy.

Each thought they were the happiest, proudest parents alive and marvelled at the miracle of nature.

***

Robert Humphreys' wish came true for heavy rain in the autumn, subsequently the weir was not put to the test until early the following spring.

For weeks on end, the Clydesdale landscape lay encased in shimmering frost and ice. The low winter sun could not reach into the gorge and even on the high pastures, where hares crouched and redwing and grouse pecked hopefully, the weak rays barely melted the crystals before they were frozen again by plummeting temperatures after sunset.

The Clyde dwindled to a stream. Corra Linn's colossal shelves of rock dripped with ever increasing icicles as brilliant aquamarine water ran beneath the glassy surface to create an astonishing white display which dazzled even the weariest onlooker. In the village, the cobbles became so slippery they were impassable for horse or human and teams of men were set to the task of throwing sand and steaming manure-soiled straw on the roads.

To the enormous enjoyment of many, impromptu curling rinks were created during the first days of the freeze and remained playable for weeks. Joe and Donnie initiated Davey to the game and although the little boys were not yet strong enough to handle the stones, they soon made themselves useful on the side lines.

Yet, throughout this prolonged dry period all the mills remained in operation. Owen patrolled his noisy, productive workrooms, satisfied that the expensive project to build a weir was finally paying off.

Dale and his household remained in Charlotte Street late into April that year and Anne Caroline chose to stay with them in the comfort of the mansion.

Toshie was more than happy with their extended stay in the city.

'It's sae cramped in the nursery noo,' she told Breen and Giggs at the kitchen table, 'and with Peggy and the wee maid, Ena, tripping over one another and yon scare crow of a housekeeper poking her neb into everyone's duties, sniffin' her disapproval, it's a rare tonic to know I can be here through the winter.'

Cook dried her hands and took her seat, reaching for the tea pot.

'The Master was telling Renwick to prepare to leave for Rosebank next week. I've made most of the lists already and have the smoked meat on order, but perhaps Mrs Owen would like to add some items before Tam runs for the final messages?'

'I'll ask her,' Toshie cupped her hands around the warm tea. 'We've been here a full month longer this time. By, I'll miss these blethers by the range.'

'Perhaps you'll be coming over to Rosebank?'

'Ah doubt it. There's the three bairns noo and Ah have a feeling there's another on the way, so ye ken how Mrs Owen takes in the early months. She won't be wanting to travel.'

'Mr Owen often visits on his own. He's been with Mr Dale a great deal these past years'

'I gather the gentlemen were waiting for news from the War Office, but as nothing seems to be happening on that front, Mr Dale's eager to be in the country.'

'He's a grand man,' Toshie said, affectionately. 'He should be taking it easy, not up in town at the Chambers.'

'How do y'ken he's at the Chambers?' Cook asked.

'Mrs Owen mentioned it. She's concerned he's doing too much. I heard her talking with Mr Owen about how badly Mr Dale feels aboot the black slaves and the big ships taking them tae America. She said he was near to tears with it and was fair worried for him becoming too het up.'

'There are terrible things in this world,' Breen murmured, 'the likes of which we don't even know. Great men like our Master have to know these things and they can act and make the right decisions. It's a mighty price to pay, though. I thank God everyday that my only concerns are for having clean linen and keeping the house in candles.'

The clock struck eleven, sending Giggs hurrying up to the bedrooms to help Jean and Mary prepare for a visit to a friend's house for the afternoon.

Toshie sipped her tea, making the most of the comfortable scents and routines of the mansion.

Her prediction of another baby for her mistress was quite correct but although Anne Caroline endured a miserable few weeks of nausea it soon passed. When an invitation arrived for all the family to spend the month of August at Rosebank, it was happily accepted.

Not only were the Owens invited but also Anne Caroline's cousins from her mother's side, the Campbells, and James Dale's parent's in-law, the Haddows. The holiday was arranged to start with celebrations for Margaret's seventeenth birthday, which fell on the same day as Anne Caroline's twenty-seventh: the fourth of August.

Throughout Margaret's life, while living at home, Anne Caroline always demurred to her little sister, making a fuss of her on her birthday, taking up the maternal role left vacant by their mother's early death. When she grew older, Margaret came to understand this sacrifice and after discussions with Giggs, Breen and finally her father, she declared she wanted her elder sister to share the special day equally.

The day dawned with clear blue skies, enticing family and visitors to wander among the beautiful flower filled terraces and shady beech avenues surrounding Rosebank. Children ran around the lawns with hoops and balls, their hapless nursery maids trying to keep them in order while the ladies sat in groups chatting beneath lacy parasols. Gentlemen strolled down to the riverbank, some indulging in a little fishing, others carrying rugs and bottles of wine to settle beneath the trees and enjoy discussions.

Owen knew everybody present and moved from group to group before joining the Campbells around a table set beneath a spreading chestnut tree. Crystal glasses and plates of tidbits fought for space between pipes, tinderboxes and newspapers as the men debated the subjects of the day.

Dale was in his element.

All his family were around him, his half-brother James and his four eldest children were even staying on for a few days. Marion sent her apologies but with their newest baby only weeks old and little James still in frocks, she was unable to join them.

Rosebank's bowling green was the gardener's pride and joy, the grass whipped with canes to a fine, even sward, as smooth as velvet. Ever since it was first created and sufficiently established to allow play to commence, all the Dale girls enjoyed perfecting their game through the summers.

Dangling Robert Dale Owen on his knee, Dale watched his daughters taking part in a bowling match with four of their male cousins.

How had time passed so fast?

His little girls were fashionable, vivacious young ladies in wafting muslins, their hair swept up into neat bonnets, ear-rings dangling and swinging against slim necks. Even Julia, his baby, would be sixteen years old in the autumn.

When the setting sun cast long shadows across the dewy gardens, the house party moved inside. Lamps were lit, evening gowns and tail-coats donned and soon the adults appeared again on the terrace, jewels glittering, perfume and colognes mixing with the sweet scent of jasmine and honeysuckle on the night air. A string quartet played melodiously in the hallway.

Anne Caroline kissed her children goodnight and rustled along the corridors from the nursery wing. She was wearing her favourite dress, a deep forest-green taffeta adorned with sequins, its high waist and richly embroidered bodice designed to detract from the obvious bump beneath.

'Are you ready to go downstairs?'

She looked up to see Robert standing on the landing.

223

'Yes, the children are settling down. I believe they have been exhausted with all the fun and fresh air today.'

He reached for her hand, 'You are looking very beautiful, Caroline.'

The unexpected compliment caught her off guard, 'Thank you. I am feeling ... happy.'

'It shows.'

She dipped her head, embarrassed. 'It is good to be able to say that and mean it. I *am* happy, Robert.'

They descended the stairs to find the hall filled with family and friends waiting for them. Immediately, they burst into singing 'Happy Birthday', laughing and clapping at the end.

'You knew they were waiting!' Anne Caroline whispered in Robert's ear.

His eyes lit up playfully, 'Happy birthday, my dearest.'

Chapter Ten

*"Any general character, from the best to the worst, from
the most ignorant to the most enlightened, may be given to
any community, even to the world at large, by the
application of proper means." Robert Owen*

'Come in! Come away up!' Dale called from the top of the
grand staircase in Charlotte Street.

George MacIntosh strode across the flag-stoned hallway and
grasped the banisters to speed his ascent.

'You've heard the guid news then?' he called breathlessly,
lumbering up the stairs.

'Aye! Renwick's opened a fine brandy for us to celebrate.'

They shook hands and patted each other on the back, beaming
with relief.

'So,' MacIntosh dropped into his usual seat by the fire. 'The
great Emperor Napoleon has had to turn tail and run!'

'So they say. Damned shame about Nelson though, God rest
his soul.'

'His actions have saved thousands, ye know. Thank you,' he
took the proffered glass of amber liquid, swirling it and
breathing in the aroma. 'To Nelson! And an end to the threat of
invasion.'

Dale raised his glass and drank. 'The reports say there were
two hundred thousand men gathered and ready to cross from
Boulogne. Vast flotillas of barges to float them across the
water! Can you imagine? If Villeneuve had managed to shake
off Nelson's fleet and given protection for that army to cross ...
doesn't bear thinking of!'

'We would have fought them every step of the way, much as
the Swiss must be doing now, poor beggars. The Glasgow

Herald reported that there's not a French soldier left at the coast, Napoleon's moved the whole army east.'

'Well, we've won the battle of Trafalgar but the war is still raging.' Dale gazed at the red coals hissing in the grate. 'France is landlocked now, ye realise. What good is that to us for trade? And the Americans are still trading with them! Pitt needs to make them cut off supplies.'

Downstairs in the kitchen, Renwick and the servants were also celebrating.

Two footmen and a groom had gone to the war and although no-one knew what they were doing or where they were, it made the household feel personally involved. Throughout the country in inns and parlours, everyone felt a great weight lift from their shoulders.

In Ireland, Sam received the news with mixed feelings.

The regiment had been geared up and ready for action for so long that taking away the opposition left a vacuum, but this was quickly filled.

The Cameronians were to strike camp and sail to Hanover to support the Russians and Austrians.

Sam heard the orders at the morning briefing and dutifully passed them on to his men. Throughout the frantic, busy day of coping and juggling tricky situations after the monotonous years of waiting for action, he focused on the job in hand. It was after the ranks were dismissed and the camp grew quiet for the night that he let his own thoughts enter his head.

He could leave now.

His term of service was complete and he could lay down his arms and honourably retire from the regiment. Or, he could sign on for the next tour of duty and risk life and limb in Europe. He sat with his head in hands, rubbing at his skull in an effort to relieve the pressure of conflicting plans and hopes.

Leaving Kildare meant leaving Roisin and he was growing unexpectedly fond of her. Recently, she was particularly attentive and caring, how could he just walk away from her?

What to do?

It came to him during the night and early the next morning, before parade, he hurried to the white washed house on the edge of the town where Roisin lived with her parents. It was still dark but one of the windows glowed with lamplight.

He rapped at the door.

'Mr O'Reilly!' he pulled off his black shiko, tucking it under his arm. 'Good morning to you, I need to speak with you, urgently.'

'If it's not Lieutenant Scott! This is a fine early hour to call at a man's door.' The older man's face was half shaved, the other side white with soap.

'May I come in, sir?'

'No, my wife is not dressed for callers. What's your hurry?'

'I am about to leave, the regiment has orders to move out.' Sam clenched his fists at his sides, 'Sir, I have been seeing your daughter, Roisin.'

'Yes, I have noticed the two of you together.'

'I care very much for her and,' Sam took a deep breath. 'I am asking for her hand in marriage and your permission, sir, that, if Roisin is agreeable, she leaves with me and travels with the regiment.'

Mr O'Reilly's eyes bulged, his mouth opened, then closed, gaped again and then snapped shut.

Sam fidgeted from foot to foot, as awkward as a schoolboy. 'I have to know today. Please, Mr O'Reilly?'

After several moments of chewing his gums, the old Irishman said quietly. 'Come back later.'

Sam nodded encouragingly, 'Yes, yes, sir, how much later? Midday?'

'Sundown.'

'Thank ye! Thank ye, sir!' Sam backed away, hastily jamming his shiko on his head and running to the parade ground before the drummers started.

The day swept past, caught up in the momentum of packing up and moving the troops after such a long, established stay in one place.

He was resigned to the fact that if Roisin agreed to come with him, he would stay in the army. If she refused to join the other wives and families accompanying the regiment, then he would sign the papers for his release and take the opportunity to retire from duty.

Just after sunset, he made his way to the O'Reilly's, bracing himself for the outcome of the next few minutes.

To his surprise, Roisin was sitting on the white-washed wall in front of the house. She raised a hand and ran towards him, her black hair streaming around her shoulders.

'Sam!' she cried, when they embraced. 'O' course I'll come with ye! How did ye know?'

'Know whit?'

'Hush! Don't let Mammy hear ye!. That I'm carrying yer baby? Now we can be married and no-one will be any the wiser o' my sins.'

'A baby?'

'Shush! I thought that was why ye asked Da' for my hand?'

'I'm leaving here ... he explained to you? Are you *sure* ye want to come wi' me?'

'Why else would I have lain with you?' she smiled up at him. 'Yes, I want to leave here... I will marry you!'

He hugged her close, smelling the familiar musky perfume of rosemary water from her hair, aware of a nasty, unsettling sensation caused by her eagerness to leave Kildare.

There was a look in her deep blue eyes, a teasing smile playing around her lips.

A dreadful panic seized him. A baby. He thought of the hardships, the camps, the sea voyage. Other men took their women and children with them, he knew of three newborns currently in the camp, but his own child?

Had this been her plan all along? To tempt him to be her lover and then, on falling with child, as would surely happen, trap him into marriage to live the life of an officer's wife?

He cast his suspicions aside, formally offered her his arm and escorted her up to her father's front door.

His future was decided, he was going to Hanover.

***

News of the war took a long time to reach the ordinary, working people of New Lanark. There were many, like old Mrs Baxter across the landing from Rosie, who could not read and had little interest in anything beyond keeping food on the table. If they had no family members involved in the fighting, knowledge of Napoleon or any battles with the French simply never entered their minds.

The British naval victory at Trafalgar only became known to the Scotts due to Gerry's position in the office. Rosie readily passed it on, hurrying self-importantly along to Joe's with the newspaper report.

Without fully understanding the whole content of the article, the family were very relieved to read the concluding lines which stated 'the threat of invasion no longer terrorises our land.'

A few weeks later, while glancing over Owen's discarded paper, Gerry's eye caught the line '26th Rifles, Cameronian'.

Rapidly, he scanned down the report, the hairs on the back of his neck prickling, '...two of the three transport ships carrying the 26th Rifle Regiment have been wrecked off the coast of Germany the Maria went down with the loss of all hands... the Aurora also ran aground ... double tragedy ... over half the regiment drowned at sea.'

He gulped back the rising bile in his throat, hardly believing the words before his eyes. In clear typeset, a list of the numbers involved was laid out neatly in front of him; impersonal, carefully detailed.

Blinking hard, he read on, trying to impress on his brain that this must be a mistake, he could not be reading about Sam's regiment?

There was no mistake. Of the one thousand men, women and children who sailed to Hanover, nearly five hundred perished. Out of the original thirty two officers, fourteen officers drowned.

Fourteen officers drowned.

Gerry covered his face with his hands. How could he break this terrible news to Rosie?

At that moment, Humphreys came into the office, already speaking as he opened the door. On seeing his quiet, humble Office Manager in obvious distress, he closed the door briskly behind him, enquiring what was wrong.

Gerry turned the broadsheet around on the desk and indicated the bold typeface, 'Cameronians in catastrophic ship wrecks.'

'My wife's brother is an officer with the Cameronians,' Gerry said shakily. 'It is a local regiment. I fear this tragedy may affect others in the village.'

229

'My dear fellow ...' Humphreys murmured, reading the account. 'It says there were nearly one hundred women and children aboard the two stricken vessels. Did your brother in law have his family with him?'

'No, no, Sam, Lieutenant Scott, was not married.'

'Take heart, man. Although half were drowned, half survived! Perhaps Lieutenant Scott made the crossing on the third transport? and is safe and well, eh?'

'That's not how ma wife will tak this news.' Gerry's woeful face contorted as he realised the pain this would cause the whole family. 'What am I tae tell her?'

Humphreys gave the matter some thought, finally venturing, 'May I enquire a personal question? Can your wife read?'

'Aye, she can. She attended Mr Dale's classrooms as a bairn.'

'In that case, perhaps you could take the newspaper home with you. Prepare Mrs MacAllister by saying that it contains a report of an event involving her brother's regiment. However, before she reads it, impress on her that there is a high chance that her brother has survived.'

Gerry thanked him for his kind suggestion, knowing, even as he spoke, that he was not capable of calmly asking Rosie to read such a devastating report.

He left the office that afternoon weighed down by the looming prospect of inevitably provoking distress, whichever way he broke the news.

Walking slowly along the Row in misty rain, he looked over at the four huge mills, their lines of symmetrical windows glowing through the darkness. Rosie would be in Mill Three for another two hours. He stopped in his tracks, struggling with permutations of how to tell her. Right now she was happy. In the morning, as she tied her bonnet ribbons and kissed him on the cheek, she was happy...

'Hey, Gerry!' A man's hand slapped him on the back. 'Whit ye daen staundin' oot here in the rain?'

'Joe ...'

'Aye ... ye look mighty odd?' Joe peered at his brother in law in the dusk. Gerry always looked thin, but his jutting cheek bones and long nose were accentuated by the starched cravat wrapped high around his neck and the tall top hat. 'Are ye sick?'

Gerry became aware of Donnie and Davey standing in the shadows beside their father, caps at a jaunty angle, bemused smiles on their faces.

'Ah need tae talk wi' ye, Joe.' He nodded towards the boys. 'Alane, if ye please?'

'Awa' tae Mrs Young's hoose ...' Joe waved a hand at them. 'tell her Ah'll be alang. Noo, whit's this aboot? Is Rosie a'richt?'

Gerry drew a breath, snapping out of the confusion which haunted him since reading the paper. Of course, Joe would deal with this. Joe always knew how to cope with a crisis in the family and as Sam was Joe's brother, it was only right he should be told first.

'We cannae talk in the street,' Gerry caught hold of Joe's arm, so relieved to have found someone to pass the responsibility on to that he almost pulled Joe with him. 'Come up tae ma hoose.'

Gerry lit a lamp and the two men sat on either side of the table in the immaculately tidy room.

After using the short preamble suggested by Humphreys, Gerry read out the report.

Joe listened in silence.

'There's as much chance Sam's alive as otherwise,' Gerry comforted, again using the manager's words. 'Half o' the regiment survived, he may no' e'en ha'e bin on yon stricken boats.'

'Ah pray tae God he wisnae.' Joe tilted his head right back and stared up at the ceiling. He was numb, shocked.

After a long period of silence, Gerry asked, 'Whit shall we tell the lassies? Rosie's gonnae be fair grieved.'

'We tell her whit's written there. We tell Cal an a' the family. Sam's a soldier, he faces death a' the time. Whither he's deid or no', he chose the way he leads his life.' Joe stood up abruptly, picking up his chair and placing it deliberately back into position close to the table. 'Until we hear one way or the ither, we should remain hopeful.'

He left Gerry and ran down the gloomily lit stairwell, throwing open the outer door and plunging out into the dripping evening. Swinging away from home, he struck off towards the end of the street until he could go no further. Lying beyond the boundary fence lay the steep wooded slopes of Braxfield Estate, falling away in a jumble of blackness to the riverbed far below.

He wanted to scream and lash out, do something, anything, to release the hurt and desperate loss bursting in his heart.

His business was barely making enough to keep the family going. Every time he thought he was making a little to put money aside or buy more equipment, something came along to use it up: blankets for winter, more clothes for Donnie and the others, boots, his own boots needing resoling ... another mouth to feed. He loved his children fiercely but having six to provide for, let alone the months when Fiona could not earn after they were born, was a weary struggle.

And now this. Was Sam alive or dead? How many times did this question prey on his mind in the past? Sarah sprang to mind, giving another pang of anxiety.

The mill bell suddenly peeled out across the valley and he realised he was soaked through. How long had he been standing there?

Fiona would be coming back from the school room with Robbie. He hurried back into the village, relieved the rain would cover his angry tears of frustration. By the time he turned in at his tenement door he was composed, the frown wiped from his brow and prepared for the ordeal ahead.

***

Early on the 29th of December, a pale dawn sky reflected on the snow-dusted spires and roofs across Glasgow. The city was beginning to stir. Rekindled fires sent smoke drifting into the freezing air, shrouding pigeons huddled for warmth beside chimney stacks. Dim lamp light showed at windows, spreading through the houses, in bedrooms, then parlours and stable yards. A few pedestrians became many, the empty streets began to ring with rumbling cart wheels, horses hooves and the shouts of market traders setting up for the day.

Just before the sun crested the horizon, Anne Caroline welcomed her second daughter into the world.

Jane Dale Owen was baptised by her grandfather at home in the drawing room during the first week of the New Year.

Unlike her brothers and sister before her, she distinguished herself by crying lustily throughout the ceremony.

Dale rejoiced in spending time with his grandchildren, insisting on having them brought to him after their evening meal so he could bestow blessings on them and wish them good night. He was not alone in enjoying having small children in the house. His daughters doted upon their little nephews and nieces, spoiling Robert and William with treats and visiting the nursery on the slightest of excuses to coo over Anne and tiny, pink Jane.

The garden at the back of Charlotte Street once again became a play ground. Dale would stand at his study window and chuckle at the sight of his little grandsons playing hide and seek or shooting rubber ended arrows into the shrubbery. It seemed a blink of an eye since his own son bounded around the lawns, often laying out canes across the paths to jump over them on his imaginary pony.

William would have been twenty-one years old now, had he lived. Although he, his three little sisters and their mother all died many years ago, they remained alive in Dale's prayers and memories, forever loved.

Every Sunday, the girls and the senior servants walked up to the Old Scotch Independents church and filled the front pew to listen to Dale preaching. On those Sabbaths following Jane's birth when Anne Caroline was not able to attend, Dale repeated his sermon to her, privately, later in the day.

Owen was pleased to see his wife content and made no comment on the hours she spent engrossed in the Scriptures. He was busily engaged with business matters, every day being packed with meeting merchants, cotton brokers, machine-part suppliers or riding up and down to the mills.

Stanley Mills were taking up a great deal of his attention because Craig, the manager, proved inept at reporting and organising much needed repairs to the machinery. Two mill wrights from New Lanark were up in Perthshire to aid with the problem but it fell to Owen to oversee the work.

John Campbell of Jura was staying in Glasgow throughout the winter months and took up the practice of calling regularly at Charlotte Street to spend time with Dale, bringing him all the latest gossip from the Tontine.

In the early weeks of the year the country was dealt a severe blow: William Pitt, the Prime Minister, died. This opened the floor to Lord Grenville to form a ministry, a topic which the three gentlemen chewed over with Cook's pastries and good claret, or in Owen's case, sweet tea.

Owen was glad to have the opportunity to spend time with Campbell again. Although of very different social backgrounds and generations, the two men developed a friendship at Rosebank the previous summer and Campbell was interested in Owen's plans for extending the facilities for educating the pauper children at New Lanark.

One afternoon, Owen received a letter from George MacIntosh bearing the sad news of the sudden death of Lord David Methven. Recalling the generous hospitality they received at Methven Castle on their Highland tour, Owen immediately composed a letter of condolence to his young widow, Lady Euphemia.

He was at this task in the library, kindly laid at his disposal by Dale, when Campbell's reedy figure appeared in the doorway.

'Mr Owen!' He cried, bushy white eyebrows raised enquiringly. 'I thought I might find you here. Your father in law has retired for his nap and I would welcome a chance to put a proposal to you.'

The elderly gentleman arranged himself in a chair by the fire and gestured to Owen to sit opposite.

Intrigued and flattered to be sought out, Owen immediately complied. The meeting only lasted a few minutes but when Campbell took his leave, tapping the side of his nose in a knowing manner, he passed Owen a cheque for several thousand pounds.

The money was entrusted to Owen to invest in the New Lanark mills with the condition that he did not want 'a song and dance' about it, 'strictly between us' he stated. Presuming this eminently wealthy man did not wish his generosity advertised around the city, which might open the flood gates to a plague of requests, Owen accepted the terms.

Dale rarely left the house on business these days, preferring to invite colleagues to dine or take refreshments with him in the comfort of his home. However, he made an exception of taking up the request to give a speech in honour of his long time close friend and business associate, Gilbert Hamilton.

The Glasgow Chamber of Commerce, which both he and Hamilton were founding directors, was holding the formal dinner in a private room at the Tontine, to which Owen was also invited.

'Papa, you look magnificent,' Jean exclaimed, admiring him descend the stairs, dressed for the occasion.

Hearing the exchange in the hallway, Margaret and Mary left the fireside and tripped through to add their compliments.

Dale pulled at the sleeves of the black tail coat, his double chins resting against the smartly knotted cravat.

'I fear this jacket and waistcoat must have shrunk in the laundry for they are a little too tight! Happens a lot!' he chuckled, 'but it looks well enough, I believe.'

Margaret smiled lovingly at him. 'It looks much more than 'well enough', dear Papa.'

For all that her father was short in stature and rotund in build, there was something indefinably pleasing about his appearance. He no longer wore powdered wigs but in this formal outfit, this was how she remembered him from childhood, with black knee breeches, buckles flashing, his stocky legs encased in thick woollen hose and highly polished shoes.

His daughters crowded around the door beside Renwick to watch him climb into his carriage with Owen's assistance.

The lamps inside the cabin were lit against the gloom of the winter's day and the girls laughed and waved to the two men, pretending to misunderstand their gestures bidding them to go back inside to the warmth.

Dale gave a lively speech to his fellow directors of the Chambers. They were gathered around a table in an oak panelled room, set aside from the open Tontine rooms. Heated and lit by the flames of an open fire at one end and several well tended candelabra standing tall above the dishes, it was a welcoming, opulent scene. Silver cutlery and crystal glasses sparkled between lavish arrangements of hothouse flowers and trailing greenery.

Most of the men, like Dale and Owen, wore black and white, but among some of the younger members, like the dashing Kirkman Finlay, there were waistcoats and cravats of brilliant scarlet, canary yellow and startling blue, some with white lace ruffles frothing at their cuffs and necks.

Speaking without notes, Dale judged the fine line between revealing humorous anecdotes about Hamilton as a friend and lauding praise on him for his many achievements in his continuing role as their first and most diligent Secretary.

The rich meal was demolished, claret flowed, toasts were made and the evening ended with rousing cheers and much thumping on the tables before retiring to their carriages.

The dinner took its toll on Dale who rested until late the following morning, blaming his over indulgence for a severe attack of indigestion during the night. For several days afterwards he often retired to his room to lie down, rather than snooze in his chair. Until one morning, dressing with Duncan's help, he began to feel very unwell, his legs buckling unexpectedly.

'I believe I may have contracted influenza,' he told Duncan, returning to bed to lie back against the pillows. 'My chest is tight and feels as if a great weight is bearing down upon me.'

His loyal valet was alarmed to hear his master's rasping breath.

'Permit me to call for the doctor, sir?'

Dale nodded, closing his eyes, labouring over each breath.

After dispatching their fastest footman to bring the physician, Breen went straight to the drawing room and informed Anne Caroline and her sisters of their father's sudden illness.

The girls were aghast, each wanting to visit their father but unsure of how to help.

Anne Caroline quietly took charge.

'Breen and Duncan both tell us he is resting and we must not over burden him by fussing. I shall go up until the doctor arrives, after which, I am sure we will all be welcome at his bedside.'

She tiptoed into his room to find the curtains drawn closed against the daylight, an oil lamp set upon the dresser to aid the fire's feeble glow. Duncan was standing attentively by the bed.

'Is he sleeping?' she whispered.

'Aye, Madame.'

They stood in silence, listening to the wheeze of his breathing, watching the uneven rise and fall of the bedcovers over his chest. She had never seen him so unwell and longed to take his hand in hers and press it to her cheek; refraining in case he was disturbed.

Alerted to the passing of time by the little ormolu clock on the mantelpiece chiming the quarter hour, she dragged herself away to return to her sisters.

'He is sleeping,' she told them, 'we must not sit here and worry, come, we will pray for his safe recovery.'

'What is wrong with Papa?' Julie asked quietly. 'Is he sick? Is he fevered?'

'I saw no fever, perhaps this malady has been caused by a tainted dish while dining in the city last week.' Anne Caroline dropped her eyes, pretending to look around for her Bible. She could not lie to her sisters but neither could she bear to tell them of the uneasiness she felt the moment she looked upon his face.

Renwick was in a state of silent agitation, pacing up and down the hall, glancing anxiously at the grandfather clock every few minutes. Eventually, the familiar clang of the street's gate and hooves scraping on the cobbles ended his wait and he hastened to meet the physician and usher him upstairs.

Once the doctor was ensconced with his patient, Renwick and Breen hovered on the upstairs landing, ready to bring anything which might be required. All the servants were upset and Peggy took Robert and William out for a walk on the Green to keep them amused, away from the anxious atmosphere pervading the house.

His examination complete, the doctor asked to speak with Mrs Owen, alone, in the library.

'Your esteemed father is, I am afraid, rather poorly.' he told her. 'I fear it is quite serious. Perhaps, if I might suggest ...' he sought for the kindest words he could employ, 'this is a time to set his affairs in order.'

Anne Caroline's eyes were wide with terror, shimmering with tears, but she bravely held back the threatened sobs.

'What is ailing my father?'

'His heart is failing.'

'Is he in pain?

'He has some discomfort, yes, but not pain. He is a little ... breathless and must not be excited or allowed to exert himself in any way. Complete rest is essential.'

Anne Caroline remained composed, thanking the doctor and watching him leave the room. She saw the door close, the waft of draft move the leaves on a houseplant, heard the hiss of the fire in the hearth and felt the stillness of the empty room.

For several seconds she was unable to gather her scattered thoughts, then, murmuring a fervent prayer, she reached for the bell pull.

Renwick appeared instantly.

'Send for the Rev Balfour ... ' she heard her voice saying. 'Also ... Mr Paterson next door, he will know who must be informed.'

'Very good, madam.'

'And my husband! Mr Owen is at the bank's office in Hopkirk Land this afternoon.'

Renwick marched away, his footsteps ringing out across the hall and disappearing through the green baize door.

Informing her sisters was a terrible task, but she performed the duty as if in a trance, her voice low and matter of fact. She knew she must remain strong as long as her father was still among them. This precious time could not be fettered with tears and hysteria.

The word soon travelled far and wide.

The great and much loved David Dale was seriously ill. Everyone who knew him, from stable lads to Honourable Members of Parliament, felt the shock of the news. Soon the house was besieged with callers but only Dale's closest friends and relatives were admitted.

Behind their counters, shopkeepers passed on their concerns to customers in hushed tones, merchants stopped each other in the street to enquire of any further news. Even thieves and fraudsters, recalling their appearance before Dale in the court room, knew him to be a just, sympathetic man and were saddened.

Robert Owen remained in Glasgow, staying close to Charlotte Street and cancelling or postponing appointments so he could support his wife and sisters in law. The servants were deeply distressed, none more so than Cook who had been in Dale's employ all her working life.

'This broth will cheer him,' she said, turning her face away from clouds of steam as she strained beef stock into a pot of chopped vegetables. 'An' I've made a bowl o' flummery to have with prunes, his favourite.'

'The young ladies are not eating, barely at all,' Breen told her. 'Miss Julia's eyes are black with shadows so I daresay she's no' sleeping either.'

'Poor lassies. Renwick says there's always one or other of them beside his bed. Mrs Owen had tae speak firmly wi' Duncan tae gae tae his room an' take some rest. For all that he keeps a calm way aboot him, the man's fair vexed.'

The kitchen table was groaning with sweet and savoury pastries, sliced cold meat, loaves and bowls of chutneys and pickles. Although the family may have lost their appetite, there was constant demand for platters of food to be offered to the flood of visitors.

Owen fell into the role of being responsible for hosting this flow of Dale's colleagues and relatives, quietly receiving their messages and assuring them all that their words would be passed on, or with especially close friends, escorting them up to the bedchamber.

One afternoon, while surrounded by his daughters, Dale mentioned rather wistfully that he would have liked to have seen Rosebank one more time.

'Then we shall travel down tomorrow,' Anne Caroline said, brightly.

'My dear girl, don't go to all that trouble.'

'It will not be the slightest trouble at all, Papa,' she handed her Bible to Jean to continue reading to their father and slipped from the room.

A message was immediately dispatched to Rosebank to prepare for their imminent arrival: if David Dale wished to see his country home again then everyone involved would do their utmost to make it happen. Cocooned among feather pillows and medication, Dale was kept blissfully unaware of the ensuing frenzy of activity throughout the house.

Between his valet and physician, he was kept as comfortable as possible throughout the journey and installed in his high four poster bed in his country residence, affording him views out towards the Clyde. Maids crept in and out, almost holding their breath as they tended the fire, brought water to the wash stand and surreptitiously polished surfaces and swept floor coverings.

239

They each felt proud to play their part in presenting their master's bedchamber to his visitors' inquisitive eyes.

'By, ye have a cosy lair here, Baillie Dale.' Paterson greeted him one morning. ''Tis a raw morning out on the roads.'

'Ye are a guid friend tae turn out on such a day.' Dale gave his customary chuckle, smiling up from under his nightcap. His chubby cheeks were now lined, sunken. 'I fear ye have a longer road to travel to see me than ye would prefer.'

'Aye, damned inconsiderate of ye!' Paterson dragged a chair to the bedside, knowing Dale would take the remark in jest. No matter how far he needed to travel, Paterson would have made the journey.

'We have shared some grand times,' Dale murmured. 'I was trying to recall, how many years have the two o' us been acquainted?'

'A fair few. Long before we established the yarn shop in the '60s.'

They spoke of friends long gone and the early years of breaking away from the main Church to form the Scotch Independents. Those ministers who were still alive from the start of the sect, had already called at Charlotte Street to pray with Dale and, he was gratified to find, also the newest preachers.

'Archie, please tell my brethren ... if I have ever caused any offence or hurt to the members of the Church ... it would have been out of ignorance and I beg their forgiveness and the Divine Forgiveness of Our Lord.'

Paterson clasped his hand over Dale's, 'A better man than ye has yet to walk the streets of Glasgow. Have no fear of your passing, my dearest old friend, you have followed the righteous path of the Lord, not merely in words or pretensions but in your every action.'

Paterson began to pray, speaking quietly, imbuing every word with meaning while observing Dale's eyes close, a half smile settling on his lips.

Two days later, on the 17th of March, David Dale died peacefully with his family around him.

Chapter Eleven

*"Possessed of a disposition kind, hospitable and
benevolent, of a heart generous, sincere and philanthropic,
his charities, public and private, were probably not
surpassed by any individual in Scotland."*
David Dale's obituary, Scot's Magazine 1806

Sarah looked up from her sewing, squeezing her eyes tight
shut to relieve the blurriness and strain. It was not yet midday,
yet the recurring headaches were plaguing her already.

She was seated by the window of Holroyds second floor
workrooms surrounded by a dozen other women bent over close
stitch-work or cutting out patterns from cloth at long tables set
down the middle of the room. There were several such rooms in
the building but this was exclusively for producing outer
garments for the most important clients.

'Whit's tha' a' aboot?' a girl called across the room.

'Whit?'

'Yon Bellman? Ah can hear his bells but no' whit he's
shoutin'.'

Sarah shrugged and looked out the window at the bright,
frosty morning.

'Din nae ken.'

A lad appeared on the street below, smartly attired in a dark
blue and gold footman's livery. He ran along the cobbles, a
sheet of paper flapping in his hand, then paused opposite
Holroyds, before pushing his hair back and walking directly
beneath Sarah's window.

Within moments he was out in the street again, retracing his
steps.

'Mrs Hendry!'

Sarah jumped.

'We have been given the honour of producing mourning wear for the ladies of Mr David Dale's house.' Mrs Holroyd's face was flushed beneath her stiffly curled fringe, eyes sparkling. 'I trust you have their measurements to hand? It must take top priority!' she swung round to address the room. 'We also have instructions for a suit for a five year old boy.' She thrust a paper towards Sarah. 'His details are here. A terrible misfortune has befallen the city ... a very great man has died. We must endeavour to show our respect by clothing his grieving family in the very best of warm cloth.'

Boys from the store room were already barging through the door with bolts of black taffeta and finely woven wool. The room was filled with busy bodies, tempers flaring when the new material was pushed on to the tables before Sarah and the other girls could gather up their current pieces.

'That'll be why yon bells are clangin',' said the woman beside Sarah. 'He must jist ha'e passed over.'

'Hurry up! Don't chatter now,' Mrs Holroyd cried, sweeping back into the room, frowning at her workforce. 'We have been greatly blessed to be chosen to provide this service to the Dale family. We must show our gratitude by producing the items requested within the next three days. To work!'

As soon as she left, the gossiping started.

'Och, she's sae fu' o' it this mornin'!' an older woman sneered. 'Whit does she care tha' a fine auld gentleman is lying deid. A' she can see is a muckle order fae new claes. An honour! Huh! She'll be through by tottin' up the punds she's gonnae be paid!'

'No' tha' ony o' us bodies will see it!'

'Nae chance, but Ah bet she'll mak us stiy late every day till it's a' feenished.'

Dale's death was no sudden shock to Sarah, like everyone else in Glasgow she had known he was ill. It came at a time when she was wrestling with personal demons.

The only part of her life which was normal was at Holroyds. Here, she was the head seamstress. Her own designs were being taken up by many of the great and good of Glasgow and she was often asked for personally, by name. Mrs Holroyd steadily increased her wages, wary that a competitor might lure her away.

It was at home that her problems lay. Sean, or John as she had to call him, took all the money she earned, leaving her with only enough for food and essentials for the little ones. At first she agreed for the money to be put aside due to his insistence that it was to save up for a better life.

The 'better life' was a long time coming.

It was at the turn of the year that he told her they were all moving to the United States of America. A new identity was being secured for them and they would be sailing within a few months.

The notion did not appeal to her at all but he slowly won her over, saying it would be a fresh start and with her skills she could even have her own dressmaking business! What he had not told her, until a few days ago, was the complicated sequence of actions they would have to complete to comply with the immigration laws of the New World.

Measuring and cutting, her mind went back to New Lanark and the time she spent in David Dale's smart little house.

If she had not met Sean, if she had not committed the sinful acts which lead to her dismissal from a good job, with a fine master ... Simply, *if* she had not *sinned*, how different her life would be.

'Weel, there's yin thing Ah can be sure o',' the woman beside her was saying, 'Mr Dale will be in Heaven noo.'

'Ah can nae say tha' aboot ma man!' came another voice. 'Sinfu' beggar! He'll be sent doon tae the bad fire, an' tha's a fact!'

Sarah made an attempt to join in the laughter, only managing a tight smile. Was that where she was heading? To eternal damnation and the burning flames of hell?

She felt suddenly sick and had to excuse herself from the room. Her head bursting with pain, she only just made it to the privy before vomiting.

She remembered a sermon in New Lanark, given by Dale. He told the congregation about choosing the right path to follow through life. The honest, God fearing path to salvation, and warned of the perils of being seduced by the Devil's ways.

It came to her as clearly as the sun shining on the frosted spider's web above the privy door.

She would not go along with Sean's plan, she would choose the Right path. Let him be damned to hell, for she would not be coerced into any further lies and deception or allow her children to be drawn into his schemes.

Sean was away and not due to return for several days so she would use that time to make her own plans; plans that could redeem her in the eyes of the Lord.

Feeling a little calmer, she returned to the workroom and threw herself into making the tiny black wool suit for Mr Dale's grandson.

***

'Master Robert, please stand still ...' Peggy wrestled with the buttons on the child's jacket.

'Are you ready?' Anne Caroline asked, hurrying into the nursery at Charlotte Street. 'Good, good ... everyone is gathered to proceed.'

Peggy mastered the last button and reached for a hair brush to smooth Robert's shoulder-length waves into place.

He was not the easiest little boy to handle and he was unsettled by the sudden commotion of moving back to the city, his mourning suit arriving and the hurried change of clothes.

'Come along.' His mother was in no mood for one of his outbursts and took him quickly along the landing and down the stairs. 'Now, do exactly as your father bids. This is an important day and you are very fortunate to be included.'

Owen was waiting in the hall. Severely dressed in a thick, knee length black coat, black cravat bound at his throat and his top hat already pressed into place; his sensitive face was pinched with emotion.

'Take my hand, Robert,' he said, giving his son a reassuring smile. 'There is nothing to fear, we are simply walking up to Ingram Street. It is not too far.'

Anne Caroline touched her husband's arm, squeezing it affectionately, her eyes expressing her gratitude and support. Her lips were trembling too much to speak.

She said her own farewell to her father the night before; praying beside his open coffin with her sisters, each kissing him on the cheek for the last time. Now, the undertakers had secured the casket lid and removed Dale's mortal remains to the hearse standing outside the front door.

As soon as Owen and his little boy joined the cortege beside James Dale and other close male members of the family, the coachman raised his whip to send the horses forward.

Four coal black carriage horses, their coats groomed to a sheen, manes flowing, clattered into a slow, steady walk.

The gates at the end of Charlotte Street were kept closed until that moment because of the throng of people which had been growing since early morning. On opening the gates, the gathering parted, silently standing back to allow the hearse to pass through towards the city.

All the shops in Glasgow were closed, market stalls covered or bare. Walking immediately behind the coffin, Owen was incredulous to see not only the main streets lined with mourners, but the eager, solemn figures of others crammed into side lanes and vennels, desperate to catch a glimpse of the coffin and pay their respects.

On and on they walked, the crowds falling into step behind them to form a river of black. With each stride, the horses' noble heads dipped, sending the high black plumes on their bridles fluttering against the air. The harness and flat, draped carriage creaked, accompanied only by rhythmic hoof beats and the tramping of thousands of shoes on the cobbles.

At Ingram Street the procession came to a halt beside St David's Church and a short hiatus occurred to remove the ornate mort cloth before the coffin was carried ceremoniously to the grave.

There was nothing pompous about Dale's final resting place. A simply engraved plaque in the cemetery's boundary wall stated 'Here lies David Dale, Merchant. 1780', being the date he bought the lair.

Owen thought how apt the inscription was, so humble, like the man himself. He felt Robert gripping his fingers more tightly when the coffin was lowered into the ground. He released his tiny hand to draw him closer, laying an arm comfortingly around his shoulders.

It was utterly quiet, only the minister's voice resounded to the furthest corner of the packed churchyard and out along the hushed, crowded streets of Glasgow. The wealthiest, most powerful merchants in the country stood perfectly still beside lawyers and physicians, shoulder to shoulder with clergymen, inn keepers, clerks, cobblers, tradesmen and brokers. Standing beside Dale's family and closest friends, were all the male servants from Rosebank and Charlotte Street, their stricken faces telling of their grief.

Archibald Paterson, George MacIntosh, Gilbert Hamilton, Claud Alexander and Robert Scott Moncrieff were among those closest to the casket, their cheeks glistening with unashamed tears.

When the minister's final words rang out, a whispering murmur rose from the mourners, each saying their personal prayers and goodbyes.

For a long time afterwards, as the grave diggers covered the coffin, the cemetary was filled with slow moving lines of sombrely dressed figures, patiently waiting their chance to lay a flower, add a handful of earth, say a prayer or murmur their chosen words of respect beside the freshly turned earth under which Dale was laid.

The City of Glasgow turned out to honour one of their greatest founding fathers. Other good men would make their mark on Scottish society but none would be more loved and revered than David Dale.

***

In New Lanark, Dale was also mourned.

Cooper heard of his passing from one of Humphreys' junior clerks.

'Mr Humphreys telt me tae tell ye that Mr Owen will nae be back until next week.'

Cooper already knew David Dale was ill, hence Mr Owen's continued absence from the village.

She looked the young man up and down, 'And does Mr Humphreys know if Mr Owen is *definitely* returning next week?'

'Aye, tha's whit he sed. Mr Owen will be back efter the funeral.'

'Funeral! Mr Dale has died?'

'Aye.'

'Why did you not tell me this important news straight way?'

'Ah am, the noo!'

Cooper took an exasperated breath but was too shocked to waste any more time with the clerk and abruptly shut the door in his face.

Many conflicting emotions seized her and the maids watched in dismay as she seemed to gasp and clutch at her bosom before rushing up the stairs. After hours of prayer and reflection, Cooper returned to the kitchen with a serene expression on her bony features.

'Are ye all richt, Mrs Cooper?' Alice asked, disconcerted.

'I am, thank you. As you may have heard, Mr David Dale, has passed away. We will remember him in our prayers this evening in the sure and certain knowledge that he is now with Our Lord God in Heaven.' Cooper picked up her hat and tied the ribbons in fast, efficient movements, before pulling on her gloves. 'I am going up to the church in Lanark. Keep the fires burning and eat anything you wish from the larder, except the eggs.'

With that, she was gone.

The majority of villagers remembered Dale well and looked back on the 'guid auld days' when he was their employer. The Highland families who he brought to the mills after they were shipwrecked held their own memorial service for him, sharing memories and telling the younger generation of his grand gesture which rescued them from destitution.

Joe and Fiona attended the Sunday service in the village that week, wishing to show their respect for the man who gave them shelter and employment.

'Mr Dale's Christian name wis David, tha's why we named ye David,' Fiona told her son as the family dressed in their best clothes. 'He wis a kind hearted gentleman an' owned the mills afore Mr Owen.'

'Whit did he die o'?' Donnie asked.

'Ah din nae ken, son.' Joe answered, looking at Fiona. 'Auld age?'

'Mibbe,' she pulled her hair back into a pony tail, wound it expertly into a bun and pushed long hair-pins into it until the thick bunch didn't move. 'He alis looked gie auld tae me but then Ah wis a bairn at the time an' thocht every yin wis auld if they were past thirty years, an' noo Ah'm passed that an' a'!'

Joe looked at her fondly. 'Weel, yer a gie bonny auld woman.'

She pulled a face at him, stepping over Tom who was playing on the rag rug.

'Noo,' she slipped her bonnet over her head, 'let me see ... Donnie, there's mud on yer knees ... here's a clae, spit oan it an' gie them a rub. Robbie, gie the comb tae Davey, an' Sionaidh ... Sionaidh! Get yer shoes on, Ah telt ye oors ago, ye ha'e tae wear shoes tae church.'

Joe pulled his daughter onto his knee, pushing her feet into the shoes.

Sionaidh was different from the other children, dreamy and slow. She rarely spoke but seemed to understand what was being said to her, even if she didn't comply. Often, they would notice her just gazing into space, but if annoyed or frustrated for not getting her own way, she lashed out and even bit whoever was nearest. Fiona decided the best way to deal with her was just to let her be and hoped she would grow out of these strange habits when she was older.

With only minutes to spare, the Scott family entered the large room in Mill Four where church services were held. The space was bursting with villagers, many of whom, like the Scotts, rarely went to church. Luckily, they managed to find a chair at the side where Fiona could sit with Tom on her knee while the others remained standing.

'Yer Da' an' I were wed here,' Fiona whispered to her children. 'It wis Mr Dale who declared us man and wife before God. Wheesht noo, the meenister will tel ye a' aboot him.'

On that cloudy Sunday afternoon in March, marriage was also the subject in Sarah and Sean's cottage.

'Ah'll no dae it!' Sarah shouted, her face crimson with rage. 'It's wrang! Ye can nae ask me tae dae it!'

She jumped up from the stool beside the fire and paced the cramped room.

Cathy and Stephen were huddled on the bed, a blanket over them for warmth, watching their parents. They were used to these loud, dramatic arguments but this time their mother was even more upset than usual.

Sean was sitting at the table, a sheaf of papers spread out in front of him. A lamp and two tallow candles made little impression on the gloomy interior and apart from its strong smoky aroma, the peat fire only added a dull glow beneath the kettle.

Angrily, Sean picked up one of the papers. 'In the name of heaven, it's no' as bad as ye are making out.'

Sarah clutched at her head, loose strands of hair escaping from the muslin bonnet.

'First ye say we're gaun tae the Americas. Then ye tell me we ha'e tae ha'e a new name ... anither new name! An' noo ye tell me that ye ha'e a piece o' paper saying that yer deid! Sean Rafferty's deid! An' Ah'm a widow!' she stared at him, biting nervously on her lip. 'Yer sitting there afore me, Sean Rafferty, yer no' deid!'

'This paper says I'm dead. That's all we need to stop the Guard coming after me. When they make enquiries, they'll find a gravestone.'

'A gravestone?' She was bewildered.

'Well, no' exactly a gravestone, he's bin put in a pauper's grave.'

'Who? Who's been pit in a pauper's grave?'

'Nathan Kydd. The man I'm taking the name of ... but he's been recorded in the register of deaths as being Sean Rafferty.'

Sarah spread her arms out towards him imploringly, 'How?'

'A colleague got wind of Kydd's death, we had been waiting for someone like him.' Sean did not mention the months his colleagues had spent watching the alcoholic, nor how they duped him into telling them all about his life on the pretext of offering him work. 'No family, around my age, no one to claim the body, so they took charge and called the constable to the scene, telling them it was Sean Rafferty.'

'Whit did he die o'? No' the pox?'

'What does it matter how he died! Sarah, the man's dead, what's the harm of me taking his name ... he's no needing it anymore! I can be free again! I can nae dig him up an' ask him if he minds, can I?'

'Mibbee he dis nae ken whit ye've done, but God does. God knows *everything* an' whit yer daen is wrong! Sinful!'

Sean shook his head in exasperation. 'It is a way for us to leave here, to be free ... I have spent years, *years* hiding and watching my back!'

'Ye should nae have said ye would be a soldier in the first place!'

'I can see that now, but I was locked in a cell with a dozen other men, rotting! You have no idea of the hell that was ...'

'Hell? Ah'll gie ye hell! if ye thocht the jail wis hell, ye stepped richt oot o' the cells and on tae the path tae eternal damnation when ye ran awa' frae the army. These years o' torment an' lying ...' Sarah's voice rose to a shriek, 'they bring their own kind o' hell ... an' me an' the bairns ha'e tae bear it alang side ye.'

'Well, it's over now!' Sean stood up, pounding his fist on the table. 'This death certificate shows you are a widow an' these papers,' he laid his hand firmly on Nathan Kydd's personal papers, 'show I'm Mr Kydd. All we need to do now is marry. As Mr and Mrs Kydd we can take the children and sail to the Americas and leave all this ... this poverty and struggle behind.'

'Naw! We were merrit in a church, in the eyes of the Lord! Naw, Sean, fer a' yer bits o' paper, Ah'm no' marrying a deid man!' Sarah snatched up her shawl, threw it around her shoulders and slammed her way out of the cottage.

Debris from the thatch spattered down onto the floor, the flames on the candles guttering wildly.

After a few minutes of tense silence, Stephen asked anxiously, 'Are we no' gaun tae America, then, Da?'

His father sat down again, rubbing his forehead and sighing. 'Yes, we are going. Your mammy's just upset, she'll agree soon enough.'

Sean arranged for the wedding to take place, for the banns to be posted and purchased tickets for the family to board a ship for New York. All the time, Sarah remained adamant that she would take no part in his schemes.

On the day when they were to be wed, she refused to get out of bed, causing such a scene that Sean resorted to playing his trump card.

'Ye'll have to see sense! In a few days the ship's sailing and ye cannot stay here.'

'Why no'? Ah've stayed here mony times wi' the bairns while yer awa' galavantin' wi' yer Irish brithers. It's ma wages that pay the rent, Sean!'

'The rent on what? I told the landlord we were leaving and paid the final rent up front. He already has a family waiting to move in here ... next week.'

She reared up, throwing back the blankets, her long dishevelled hair flying around her shoulders.

'Sae ye wid put yer wife and weans oot on the street, wid ye?'

'No! I want to take you all to a better life! Stop being so ... so *stupid*! Can you not see? This is the only chance we have of being happy, all together, as a family?'

'Pretending tae be someone yer not ... makin' me an' the bairns gae through a sham wedding ... in a church? Before God? It's a sin!'

Losing his temper, Sean grabbed her by the wrists and hauled her out of bed. 'Ye've lied before, many times! Put your clothes on!'

She wriggled free and leapt back under the blankets.

'An' I've seen the error of ma ways!'

Sean lifted his arm, blinded by rage; everything was ready for their voyage and now she was ruining it.

'Da' no!' Stephen flung himself across the room, catching at his father's jacket, 'Din nae hurt Mammy!'

Sean stopped, his arm still raised, the hand tightly balled into a fist.

What was he doing?

Breathless with emotion, he lowered his arm and pointed a finger at Sarah, saying quietly, 'Get yourself out in the street ... dressed for the church ... I'll wait outside with the children.'

Sarah lay under the blanket trembling. After a long time she heard the latch on the door and tensed, holding her breath.

'Mammy,' Cathy shook her mother's shoulder, with Stephen leaning over to lift the covers from her face. 'Da's gone awa'. He says he'll be bak in a day or two.'

Pulling herself up against the bolster, Sarah patted the bed beside her and cuddled them both under her arms.

'It'll be a'richt, ma wee darlin's. Dinnae fret. Da' will come hame an' it'll be a'richt.'

She was so exhausted from the trauma of the day that she did not even wonder how it could be all right. It seemed the thing to say at the time, to comfort her children and soothe herself.

When she returned from work a few days later, Sean was in the cottage, alone. After a tense greeting, he told her Stephen and Cathy were with the neighbour and asked her to sit down at the table.

'I have found a new place for you,' he said quietly, withdrawn and efficient. 'Beside the smithy on the low road. It's the first thatched cottage in the row and will be vacant in a couple of days, so I have paid up a month's rent. It is a Mrs Collins you need to ask for.'

Sarah was scanning his face, watching for any tell tale softening towards her but as he spoke and the meaning of the words filtered through, she cried out, 'Yer still gaun awa'? Wi'oot us?'

'I have no other choice, Sarah, I cannot even take my children for they bear your name.'

''Tis your name. We all bear *your* name.'

Her blue eyes were brimming with tears, dripping and splashing down her face. 'Ah didnae think ye'd leave us.'

'Sean is dead. I have to go.' His voice was cracking, the facade falling away. 'It is all over. You are a widow now. I have no hold over you.'

'Ah love ye, Sean. Ah can nae bear ye tae leave me ... no' like this ... saying yer deid and ... no' even owning me as yer wife.'

She reached towards him and he took her hand in his, kissing it and murmuring, 'It breaks ma heart but I have waited so long and this is my chance to live a free life.'

Suddenly, she was in his arms; they were embracing, kissing, demonstrating to each other the love they took for granted for years but which was now fiercely binding them together with the threat of separation.

Sarah was asleep when Sean climbed from the bed, dressing as quietly as he could. It would be better for both of them if he left before she woke.

Carefully tucking the blanket over her naked shoulders, he took a moment to feel her silky golden hair between his fingers.

Gazing at the line of her cheek, sweep of her lashes; a face he knew intimately yet never tired of seeing.

The ache of loss was unbearable but he had to leave.

'Take care, ma darlin'.' he whispered, 'I'll never find another you.'

Then he picked up his bag and quietly let himself out the door, not daring to look back.

***

Owen was a tremendous support to Anne Caroline and the family, handling the legalities as well as the practical matters arising from his father in law's death. Not being able to spend long periods away from the mills, he divided his time between Lanark and Glasgow throughout the spring.

When the sticky buds emerged on the old horse chestnut tree at the end of the garden, the household prepared to move to Rosebank for the first time without David Dale.

Anne Caroline stayed with her sisters until they were settled in the country for the summer; it was a bitter-sweet time.

In April, in an attempt to force the French and British to acknowledge its neutral stance in the European wars, the U S Congress decided to teach them a serious lesson and passed legislation to stop certain goods from Britain and France entering the United States. So, the spring of 1806 was a demanding period for thousands of merchants who relied on sales across the Atlantic to keep their companies afloat.

When Anne Caroline judged the time was right to leave her sisters alone, Owen was so embroiled with the difficult business of finding new overseas markets that he could not leave New Lanark. Eventually, he ordered his coachman to take the carriage up to Cambuslang without him.

On a misty morning in June, Anne Caroline hugged her sisters in the honeysuckle covered porch at Rosebank and climbed aboard with Toshie, Peggy and the children to make the long twisting, turning journey along the Clyde Valley. The sun's warmth burnt off the mist and the little party were enchanted by orchards of every hue, pink and white cherry blossom falling like snow as the horses rattled beneath arching boughs.

She was emotionally drained and found it a blessèd relief to look forward to the relatively simple life with only her own children to worry about.

Dale left his four younger daughters well provided for in his Will, allowing them to maintain both houses and continue to lead the lifestyle to which they were accustomed. Only Duncan, his valet, was sadly no longer required. Furnished with an excellent reference from Owen, and the acclaim of being Dale's manservant for so many years, he was soon assured of another appointment.

The transition between different houses took its toll on the servants. Still reeling after losing their master, Breen and Renwick rose to the responsibility of looking after the young Miss Dales while taking instructions from Mr and Mrs Owen and Miss Jean. For the Owens' servants, there was a third house to deal with and after nearly eight months away, this was not an easy task.

'This hoose has shrunk,' Peggy declared to Toshie, staggering down the narrow staircase, her arms embracing a pile of the children's washing.

'Ye've jist got used tae the Dales' grand mansions.' Toshie pulled a bunch of infants' smocks off the top, 'Mind yersel' lass! Ye must be sure ye can alis see where yer puttin' yer feet or ye'll land at the bottom afore he ken! It'd be an awfy nuisance fer us tae find anither nursery maid.'

They reached the kitchen laughing and almost colliding with Alice who was carrying a fish kettle full of boiling water.

'Och! ye nearly had that doon yer fronts!'

'Whit did Ah tell ye?' Peggy dumped the laundry into the wash tub. 'This hoose has shrunk!'

'There's too many o' us crowded aboot, tis all.'

Cooper was standing silently by the range melting gelatine for a posset. Her back was turned to the commotion but the noisy chatter of the five maids all talking at once made her head ache.

The little house in the centre of New Lanark was a very different place from the quiet days before Robert Owen took up residence. Anne Caroline received the ladies of the county calling on her to offer condolences in her recent bereavement, while Peggy looked after the children in the nursery. Senga and

Alice kept order in all the rooms, Mrs Cooper made lists and issued orders, as well as making the meals, and little Ena skivvied for everyone.

Every room was occupied, bustling with activity from the earliest streaks of dawn to late into the night. Even through the few dark hours of Scotland's summer nights, the house was often roused from slumber by babies' cries and the whispered, muffled movements in the nursery.

Toshie's position as the mistress's Lady's Maid, soon included supervising Robert and William to alleviate the strain on Peggy whose hands were full with the two little girls.

While his domestic arrangements changed and his responsibilities extended to include his sisters in law, Robert Owen never neglected his duties to the mills.

His expertise and importance as a merchant in the development of trade was acknowledged in the summer when he was made a Burgher of the city of Glasgow. The elite members of the usually politically conservative Merchants House were aware of the need for 'new blood' among their ranks and Owen was included in a younger, more progressive minded group of men honoured that year, including William Kelly and Kirkman Finlay.

Although the great victory over Napoleon at Trafalgar brought an end to the immediate danger of being overrun by the French, it did not end the war. Every week, newspapers spread the word of British losses and rising taxes to pay for the armies and armaments. Towncriers walked the streets telling of local businesses crumbling, food prices rising and the latest defeats against the French Emperor's domination of Europe.

Yet, while this depressing picture was shouted nationwide, Owen's dedication and sheer hard work kept the mills in full production. A steady supply of raw material rolled down the roads from his Glasgow warehouses to fulfil the orders he negotiated with customers both at home and abroad.

When he was in residence in the village, he often accompanied the teams of young lamp lighters through the silent, unmoving workrooms. He enjoyed this opportunity, before his employees arrived, to cast a critical eye on every aspect of the factory.

He demanded the spaces to be kept spotless. Presenting a good example, he personally made a point of snatching up even the smallest collection of fibres, wafted together by draughts behind a door or in a corner, reinforcing the concern that any build-up of cotton or debris was a fire hazard.

When the lamps were lit, the huge boilers in the basement, so brilliantly devised by Kelly, began spreading hot steamy heat throughout the spinning rooms.

The factory set for the day, Owen would return to his house for some food before the bell peeled, the gates opened and the working day began.

A recent addition to his plans for a smooth running, productive workforce, was the instigation of a method of monitoring good behaviour without the need for punishment. A similar approach was being used in Quaker establishments which strongly disapproved of physical abuse. It was also employed to good effect in school rooms by Joseph Lancaster, the enlightened teacher.

Owen approved of this idea and after due consideration of how to apply this to his workforce, he ordered the manufacture of 1600 coloured wooden blocks.

When the boxes of pristine new 'monitors' arrived, he called a meeting of his superintendents and mill managers.

'One of these will be suspended beside every work-station, in clear view of all who pass.' He held one up. 'We will call it a Silent Monitor. As you see, it is a simple block of wood, tapering to a point and this little wire hoop and ring at the top of the point will allow it to be attached easily to a hook. Each side of the block is painted a different colour.' He swung it round to allow his audience to view the effect. 'Each of these colours denotes the behaviour and performance of the person it is allocated to monitor.'

He took several from the box in front of him and passed them around the assembled men for examination.

Then he held up a report book. 'The superintendent of each department will decide the placing of these monitors and mark it down beside the employee's name. The black side, being numbered 4, meaning bad. The blue, number 3, indifferent. yellow, number 2 being good and the white side, number 1, being excellent.'

'Mr Owen,' asked a superintendent from Mill Two. 'Are you saying we require to do this with every operative ... every day?'

'Yes. You will assess the worker's performance of the previous day and turn the monitor to the appropriate colour. Then, you will make a note of the corresponding number in this book.' Owen glanced around the meeting. 'It will take only a few moments, gentlemen, and I am convinced it will improve morale and reduce the incidence of slovenly behaviour.'

'There'll be a gie lot o' black an' blue on ma flair at the minute. Mony o' them sneakin' aff tae harvest.'

'A perfect example!' Owen smiled. 'When the offender returns to his position, you place the monitor with the black side facing out and write a 4 beside his name in the report book. Perhaps the man beside him has a yellow, or even a white side emblazoned to passers-by, showing he has been diligently attending his work, and also showing in comparison, how the offender has not.'

'They'll no' like it!'

'If anyone does not agree with the colour which they are allocated and feel they have been unjustly judged, they have the right to complain to me, or in my absence, the matter must be referred to the master of the mill. This is an important point, a *very* important point. Where this system has been used before, the worker or pupil could not appeal the decision of his judge. By giving him the right, yes gentleman, the *right* to argue his point, he can learn from his behaviour and take responsibility for his actions. I believe the right to appeal is vital.

'Take your duties seriously, gentlemen, and strive for fairness in your assessments, they will respect you and the system all the more. Do not, I stress, do *not* write down their number until any complaint has been addressed. Once the number is recorded, it will not be blotted out and will lie there forever, denoting their behaviour.'

'How long are we to do this?'

'From now on.' Owen replied, enthusiastically. 'These report books will be marked up into columns for each employee's name and subsequent columns for days of the week, excluding the Sabbath.' He riffled the pages. 'Each book will last two months and be renewed six times a year. The completed registers, recording the character of each individual in the workforce, will be preserved.'

His managers left the meeting with resigned expressions: another innovation, more paperwork. The days were over of simply rapping out orders, running the spinning jennies and sending the finished yarn down to the waiting wagons. Owen insisted on counting everything, reporting everything and keeping a close eye on every man, woman and child in his mills.

Theft was still occurring but the random searches and spot checks at the end of the day were saving the company a useful amount of money. There were no longer tiny infants running under foot, misunderstanding instructions, squabbling and crying with exhaustion, or falling asleep in dangerous situations. All the children employed in the mills were over ten years old, even the youngest orphan in the Nursery Buildings was now above this age which made the day to day organisation much easier.

Beneath Nursery Buildings, the Village Shop was taking customers from most of the stalls and single traders who trailed down from Old Lanark to ply their wares. Owen's ambitious plans to purchase goods in large quantities, securing low prices and then passing the savings on to food, household items and clothes for the villagers, was finally taking shape.

'Ah see there's milk in yon shop noo,' Rosie told Fiona one evening while out scouring the hedgerows for fruit. The smaller children were at home with Donnie so the sisters-in-law were enjoying this rare chance for a bit of peace and quiet.

'Aye, an' the tatties are braw. Big an' smooth, wi' no green bits sprouting or black worms.'

'The milk's frae the broon an' white coos at the farm up the hill, an' ma Gerry telt me tha' Mr Owen has asked them tae send doon kale an' apples an' a' sorts, he'll tak it straight in tae the shop.'

'Whit a difference tae the rotten stuff they used tae sell.' Fiona lifted a drooping stem of raspberries, expertly pulling the ruby red berries and dropping them into her basket. 'The birds ha'e taken a' the easy pickings,' she wandered a few steps further, eyeing the straggling branches. 'Yon brambles will nae be lang in ripening.'

Pink clouds floated in the blue sky above them, their fluffy edges gilded by rays from the sinking sun. There was a nip in the air but it was a calm, scented evening, still light enough after finishing in the mills to tempt them out along the lanes for fruit and into pastures for mushrooms.

'Ah hear there wis trouble last nicht ... o'er the watter,' Rosie laid dock leaves over her raspberries, turning to pluck bunches of deep purple elderberries. 'Those MacCall lads frae the end o' yer Row were o'er at Corehoose. Gerry said the estate manager wis roarin' when he wis roond tae speak wi' Mr Owen. He says they crossed o'er the new weir an' cleared twa bushes o' plums!'

'Naw? D'ye ken they did?

'Och aye,' Rosie winked at Fiona, 'their uncle's stall at the market did a grand trade in plums this morn!'

'Wid ye tak a look a' these!' Fiona squatted down to peer at plate-sized toadstools, their fawn tops sprinkled with dark crinkly markings. 'We should ha'e Cal wi' us, he kens which tae eat an' a' that, frae that friend o' his doon at the forge.'

'Din nae touch 'em,' Rosie said, suspiciously. 'Ken a few years back when the whole o' Myra's family were struck doon efter eatin' summat like that?'

'But they look a'richt. Ah'll ask Cal tae come up t'morra.'

Dusk was suddenly descending, the skies busy with rooks taking their final noisy flight together before settling into their ancient rookery on Bonnington estate. Along with several other housewives, the women turned back towards the village, pausing for a few minutes to watch a spectacular display of swirling starlings, rising and falling, switching direction in perfect symmetry.

'Joe's gonnae be late bak this eve,' Fiona said when, with a last swoop, the starlings poured straight down to earth to roost among scrubby bushes near the riverbank. 'He wis asked tae gae alang wi' Mr Ewing tae a meetin'.'

'Whit aboot?'

'Dinnae ken. Ah pit oot his best claes afore werk this morn an' he's bin hame an' changed, sae ... nae doobt he'll tell me later.'

'How's it gaun?'

'His werk? Better. Aye, a bit better. Tam's bin awfy guid aboot daen the figures fer him an' the last joab paid weel. He can afford tae keep Donnie an' Davey wi' him, he says they're a help tae him, an' Donnie's a strong lad.'

'He's fair grown these past months.'

'He'll be like his Da',' Fiona said proudly, 'but Ah cannae see whit wee Davey does a' day, bless him. He sometimes comes tae the school room wi' me an' Sionaidh but he could be earnin' at the mills by noo.'

'Oor Cal wis only Davey's age when we came tae the mills, ye ken. Mind, he had bin werkin' in the mines at Douglas afore that ... since he could walk, it seems like.' Rosie's voice dropped to a whisper. 'It didnae dae him ony guid, paur lad's suffered e'er since. He hated the mines an' he hated the mills. He disnae seem tae want tae dae onything but soap harnesses and haud cuddies fer the gentry.'

'It wis mair from when he spent that time awa', wherever he was, an' wis sae ill. That knocked the stuffing oot him, an' no mistake. Och, if Davey wis in the mills, or when Robbie's time comes, it's no' sae bad these days.'

Through the falling darkness they sauntered slowly back down to the village. Heavy skirts swinging, bonneted heads nodding together, sharing family concerns, hopes and problems. Down among the shadows of the tenement buildings they picked their steps by the lamplight seeping from dozens of windows not yet shuttered against the evening. Coal smoke was rising in columns from every chimney, its sharp scent caught in the dew filled air, oyster catchers sending haunting calls along the river bed.

They parted outside the Scotts' tenement door with a 'cheerio' and Fiona smiled to herself all the way up the stairs.

Since the babies were born she could hardly remember a time when one of them was not demanding her attention or in her arms, unless she was at work. Although fruit picking with Rosie possibly only lasted an hour, it was a luxury. Much as she adored her family, those few minutes of just 'being herself' gave a warm feeling.

It reminded her of the early days at the Scotts' room, newly married, chattering and laughing with Sarah and Rosie.

Fiona opened the door to her room to find Cal and Donnie by the hearth, a pan of porridge hanging from the swee, Davey and Robbie flat on their stomachs engrossed with marbles, the younger ones playing on their set-in bed.

She laid her basket on the table and went to the window to close the shutters, seeing her smiling reflection in the glass panes. They were warm and comfortable, was Sarah settling down for the night with her family? Sam? Oh, how she hoped they were both all right.

Securing the bar across the shutters, it was on the tip of her tongue to utter her thoughts but instantly decided against it. Everyone was content, she would not disturb the harmony in the room.

'Ye hungry lads?' she asked instead, nodding towards the bubbling oats.

'Aye.' Cal gave her one of his quizzical looks. 'Whit did ye gather? rasps?'

She showed them the basket, picking out a white grub and throwing it towards the fire. 'Rasps, some currants and bonnie elderberries. Gie me a moment an' ye can ha'e em wi' yer porridge.'

She carefully chose a few of each of the best fruit, laying them aside in a wooden bowl for Joe and wondering what his meeting with Ewing was all about.

Much later, Joe came down the hill from Lanark with a bounce in his stride more usual in the morning than the end of a long day.

New Lanark was sleeping. Only the grey shapes of badgers moved on the green beside the mill lade, snuffling for worms, their bright black and white snouts occasionally lifting to sniff the air for danger.

The evening with Ewing had been one of the most incredible of his life. At first he was anxious, frightened of the unknown and nervous he would not acquit himself as the other men expected, but then he was swept up into the proceedings.

It was his initiation into the Masonic Lodge.

He had heard of this body of men, knew a little about it being a 'gentlemen's club', as Ewing first described it, but now he knew more. Over the last few months Ewing took an interest in Joe's new ability to read, staying to chat with him in the yard of an evening, passing him pamphlets and books, casually introducing him to local businessmen when they called by: all leading to an invitation to join the Brotherhood.

The memories of being entered into the meeting, given as a present to the Right Worshipful Master by Ewing, all seemed very unreal now that he was outside again, in the moonlight. They placed a linen bag over his head, a noose around his neck, parading him before the assembly, guiding him through a series of rehearsed questions and responses. On being uncovered, his eyes bleary, he found himself in a small hall, standing on a black and white tiled floor surrounded by men in ceremonial dress. The words spoken, the oaths, so seriously undertaken, lingered in his mind.

He recognised several of the faces, business men and merchants, professionals in their chosen trade: he was now a part of this elite band of brothers.

How many times did he walk past the little thatched building of St John's Lodge in Lanark? Had he ever given it another glance? Imagined he could be part of such company? He shook his head, a wide, incredulous grin on his face. Who would have thought Willie Logan or Matt Murray, both well respected men from New Lanark, were involved in the Masons?

They were good men, as were Ewing and Bob Lawson.

Joe ran quietly up the tenement stairs, exhilarated. The fact that Ewing considered him worthy of joining their ranks gave a huge and much needed boost to his confidence.

***

Scraping her nail up the ice on the inside of the bedroom window, Anne Caroline gave a resigned sigh.

'The winter is closing in on us earlier this year,' she told Toshie. 'I will write to my sisters and inform them that we will be joining them in Glasgow next week. On Monday?'

'Very good, Ma'am.' Toshie smothered a cry of delight.

It was so cold in New Lanark that she could barely feel the tips of her fingers which kept turning a numb, bloodless white to the first knuckles. Her feet were causing problems as well. Chilblains alternately ached and itched, driving her mad at night, even with bran poultices and thick bed socks. Time was not being kind to Toshie; a worrying reality as she reached the end of her fifth decade.

Cooper and the maids were also relieved to hear the Owens were leaving for the winter. Both the master and mistress were keen followers of the new practice of cleanliness, washing every day and, especially Mrs Owen, bathing at least once a week. As well as the children to keep similarly clean and the usual household laundry, Ena and Senga were eagerly looking forward to more leisurely months ahead.

However, as soon as the carriage drew away from the village, Cooper declared the entire house must be scrubbed out with scalding water and sand.

'We have perhaps a week, maybe less,' she told the maids, 'before Mr Owen returns. I want everything, every curtain, piece of bedding, carpet and fire-grate thoroughly refreshed.'

'Why?' Ena blurted out.

The housekeeper's eyes narrowed to slits, 'It is our duty to keep our employer's property in perfect condition. Just because the family are not here does not mean we can be idle!'

The next few days saw a hive of activity around the Owens' house. Lines of washing flapped in the bitter wind, rugs were beaten, windows washed, even the heavy horsehair mattress from the main bedroom was dragged outside to be aired.

Alice wielded the bent-cane beater, while Ena and Senga propped the stiff mattress between them, bracing themselves with every whack.

'It's fine fer that auld bisom tae gie oot her orders,' Senga muttered, pulling her shawl tightly over her apron again and tying it after every few strikes. 'She's up in yon wee room o' hers, nae icy watter on *her* hauns ... naw! It's sae cauld oot here there cannae be a bug left alive.'

'Weel, there's no' much left in the hoose tae tak a scrubbing brush tae, sae she'll ha'e tae let us be noo.'

Cooper had other ideas, declaring the brass, copper and silver all needed shining, the grates blacked, the candles trimmed and new, thick beeswax polish rubbed into all the furniture.

Satisfied the maids were fully occupied, Cooper made good use of the hours available to her while the Owens were away. These were her times. Hour upon hour she read the bible, her knees calloused from kneeling on the floorboards infront of the simple wooden cross hanging above her bed.

More than anything, Cooper wanted to go to Heaven.

Her life on Earth was a silently borne struggle between depression and monotony but if she followed the path of the Lord, as David Dale had done, she would find redemption and everlasting Life in a glorious place.

When Owen and Murdoch returned, they found fires burning, filled lamps glowing and the pleasant aroma of beeswax filling the air.

'Will that be all for you this evening, sir?' Cooper enquired, hovering in the parlour doorway late on the evening of his arrival.

Owen was engrossed in a letter and glanced up, pulling his thoughts away from the contents.

'Yes, thank you, Cooper.' He turned back to the paper in his hand, adding, 'you have done a fine job on the brass fender, it shines like a beacon.'

'Thank you, sir,' the housekeeper dipped her head in acknowledgement and left the room.

She was surprised, not only that he noticed the difference in the hearth but that he mentioned it. She held a fierce loyalty for her mistress, the daughter of Mr Dale and a devout churchgoer, but she stoically suffered her master.

It was still beyond her understanding how Mrs Owen could have married such a man. For all that he was polite and pleasant enough: he was an Infidel. Sometimes, her feelings of outrage were so strong that they put her position in his house in jeopardy.

Yet, apart from his outrageous disregard of the Lord's word, which should have made him utterly repugnant, she could not help allowing him a grudging respect. He was a fair employer, she reasoned with herself, toiling up the two flights of stairs with her candle, she would pray for him and beg forgiveness of his ignorance from the Lord God in heaven.

The Silent Monitors were slowly showing an improved picture of the workforce in the mills.

'Look here,' Humphreys ran his finger down a column. 'Two months ago, mainly Threes and Fours, with the odd Two here and there.' He flicked to the end of the report book. 'Now, it's more Threes and Twos, with the odd Four.'

'Just as I expected!' Owen exclaimed, picking out the names of those he was particularly aware of as troublemakers. 'Aha! I see even David Cameron has been acquiring some Twos. I daresay the Blues and Yellows are winning throughout the work rooms? Are there any Whites?'

'We have several of the women who have the White side of the monitor turned outwards almost continuously. Rose MacAllister, our Office manager's wife and Netta Monteith are steady workers, they rarely miss a day.'

Owen was studying the pages. 'I see there is a trend, Mondays show more Blacks. Both men and women, but the children have little difference to their performance.' He sat back. 'I have it! This is another indication of the harmful effect of over imbibing alcohol.'

He seized the book again. 'Yes, I recognise these names, recurrent bingers. Let me see the record for the beginning of the month. Again, the days after they receive their wages, they are either absent or have Blacks.'

'How can you stop them drinking?'

'That, Humphreys, is a question my late father in law used to ponder and countless others, I am sure. When I took over, the drunkards were in the street almost every night, yet these last couple of years the problem seems much less.'

'Old Timpson and Andy Bogle caused a lot of those problems and since they were dismissed ...'

'I gave them several chances to reform.'

'Indeed you did, but, as I was saying, since they were dismissed and, of course, the stall selling grog left the village after the new shop opened, the incidence of fighting and outright drunkenness is greatly improved. There is still an element within the village who will steal anything that might raise a few pennies up the hill.'

'I heard a scuffle last night,' Owen said. 'It was very late but there were bursts of shouting.'

'Perhaps that was when the coal bunker was emptied.'

'Coal bunker?'

'These past weeks have been very cold, there's a ready market for coal, cheap coal. We've had several bunkers emptied under cover of darkness. I was going to speak to you about it.'

'In general the village is much more orderly, this is annoying.' Owen wandered around the office; thinking. 'We will employ inspectors to patrol the streets through the winter evenings. It will discourage the thieves and identify the drunkards. Unless someone has good cause to be out after dark, all law abiding citizens should be within their homes.'

'That will be about as popular as the house inspectors!'

Owen gave him a frank look, 'I am not trying to be popular. I am making this community safe so it is a better place to live, raise children and therefore, to work.

'Mill work carries a terrible stigma, perpetuated by many owners caring only for profits. I look at the mill as a whole. If a man takes a position in my mills, his family will have good housing, access to wholesome food, safe streets for their women and children and schooling.'

He gestured out the window towards the mills. 'If you had these benefits, wouldn't you take more care to retain your job? Surely, it is preferable to sleep at night knowing there are no criminals in the street outside? Many men drink their wages before their wives can clothe and feed their children, this mentality and conduct is rife across the land. As is stealing. In New Lanark, I am doing something about this wayward behaviour and, as I am sure you can agree, Humphreys, there has already been a marked improvement? Inspectors on the streets during the dark winter months will be a useful improvement.'

It was decided to recruit two men as Street Inspectors and within the week the new system was up and running. They were instructed to pay attention to the places where goods could be pilfered and to patrol the areas where access could be gained to the village from woodland paths, as well as the main road. It was also their job to take down the details of anyone found drunk and disorderly and write a report for Owen so he could deal with the matter.

In mid December, late on a cloudy, starless evening, the inspectors saw a group of figures descending the steep flight of steps from Lanark. The people were moving slowly and kept stopping, until they appeared to huddle down on the hillside.

The wardens, holding their lanterns high, approached them.
'Whit ye daen up there? Are ye comin' doon? make yerselves known!'

A child's voice replied. 'Mam's in a bad way! Please help us?'

The men hurried up the steps, taking them two at a time.

A woman was laid on her side in the grass, her cloak and skirts fanned out around her, half covering a large bag.

'Does she ha'e the pox?' an inspector asked gruffly. The poor wretch was clearly suffering but the village was blessedly free of disease this winter.

One of the children, a boy with a cap clamped on his long, lank hair, cried out, 'No, she's havin' a babbie.'

'She's havin' a bairn noo?' there was alarm in the man's voice.

The woman pushed herself up, breathing heavily. 'Dinnae fash yersel', Ah'm noo ready yit, the bairn will stiy where it is a while longer. Ah jist couldnae walk anither step an' needit a rest.'

'Yer no frae the village, are ye?

'Why a' the questions? Can a woman no' tak a rest ... Jist gie me a meenit ... '

The younger inspector looked over his shoulder, down to the mills. This seemed a mighty queer thing? A heavily pregnant woman out in the countryside with her two young children at this time of night? He wondered if they were trying it on, creating a diversion to allow thieves to nip into the store rooms behind their backs.

Nothing moved among the grey, indistinct buildings, only the dappled silver ribbon of the mill lade disturbed the complete stillness.

'Richt then,' the men pushed back their capes to lean over, bracing themselves on either side of the woman to grip her under the arms, pulling her to her feet. 'We'll gie ye a haun doon the hill. Ye can nae lie here a' nicht, yer soakin'.'

'Ah can manage noo, leave us be!' she pushed the men's hands away, staggering slightly. The girl ran to her side to support her, the little boy trying unsuccessfully to pick up their bag of belongings and dragging it, one step at a time down the hill.

267

The inspectors walked behind, still suspicious, their eyes scanning the shadows.

Fiona was mending a rip in Ailsa'a smock when they heard a commotion in the stairwell.

'In the name o' the wee man,' she murmured under her breath. 'The bairns are sleepin' can they no' keep the noise doon.'

Joe was dozing in the chair opposite, Cal was already asleep.

Suddenly, two sharp bangs on the door brought them wide awake.

Joe sprang to his feet and opened the door to find one of the new street inspectors.

'Joe Scott? There's a wuman sayin' she's yer sister doon in the street ... wi' twa bairns.'

'Whit?'

'Sarah Rafferty she ca's hersel''

'Sarah!' Joe pushed past the man and tore down the stairs, Cal struggling into his breeches to race after him.

'Why's she in the street? Why didnae she come hersel'?' Fiona demanded, pushing her feet into clogs: the men had gone barefoot.

'Ye ken this Mrs Rafferty?'

'Aye, she's ma sister in law, richt enough.'

'She's no' weel, can nae walk mair than a few yairds.'

Praying for forgiveness for her selfishness, Fiona recoiled from taking anyone into their home who was ill, even Sarah.

The inspector saw the panic in her eyes, 'They say it's no' the pox, an' she didnae look tae have a fever. Jist tired an' heavy wi' child.'

'Wi child?'

Then Joe came striding into the room carrying his sister, Cal behind him with the carpet bag, Cathy and Stephen at his heels. The older Scott children were craning to see what was happening, hair standing on end, knuckling their eyes.

There was no space to move.

Fiona rushed to pull back the blanket of her own bed so Joe could lay his sister down.

'Naw, naw, a seat is guid enough!' Sarah implored, 'Ma legs are tha' tired an' sore they will nae haud me.' She sank onto the chair beside the fire.

Joe knelt down in front of her, cupping her face in his hands. 'Sarah! Sarah ... it's grand tae see ye again,' he took her in his arms in a tight, heartfelt embrace..

His sister's face was thin, almost skull-like, the skin stretched over sharp cheekbones, her sunken cheeks accentuating the jutting lines of her wide mouth and jaw. Whatever happened to bring her home was clearly not good.

He sat back on his heels, 'We thocht ye were sewing fer Mrs Owen, did ye git oor letter?'

'Aye, Ah got it.' Sarah rubbed at her running nose, tears wet on her lashes. 'Ah din nae ken where tae stairt tae tell ye whit a fool Ah've bin.' The tears trickled freely, 'Thank God ye are here, Joe. Dearest, dearest Joe. Ye can nae imagine how glad Ah am tae be here wi' ye.'

He held her for a long time while she sobbed and Fiona and Cal, exchanging questioning glances, turned their attention to the two children clinging nervously to each other beside their mother's chair.

'Weel,' Fiona clasped her hands and forced a friendly smile to stretch her lips. 'Do ye remember us? Ye were nae mair than babes in airms when ye left here, but this is yer Uncle Cal an' Ah'm yer Auntie Fiona.' Seeing no reaction, she gave another smile, making eye contact with them, noticing a softening in their tense expressions. 'Let's git some hot food intae ye baith an' then sleep. Ye can tell us a' aboot yersels t'morra.'

Somehow, they all managed to find a place to lie down for the night. Although, Cal soon discovered that having Robbie and Sionaidh beside him meant his sleep was frequently disturbed by kicks and restless tossing and turning.

Sarah slept with her children in the big set in bed usually occupied by her youngest nieces and nephews. They fell asleep the moment the curtain was drawn and were still silent when the Scotts woke and left the room for the day.

Throughout the day, Joe's mind was filled with questions. His sister was obviously very distressed and from the state of her and the children, whatever dire situation they were in, it must have been going on for some time.

By four o'clock it was too dark to work on his current job, a new gable end wall and chimney for one of the estate houses near Jerviswood. Sending the boys back to the yard with the cart, he took the opportunity to call in at the office in New Lanark to tell Gerry of Sarah's return.

'Sae, can ye tell Rosie?' he finished, 'can she ca' roond anytime efter she comes in frae werk.'

'Aye, she'll be keen tae see her.' Gerry sat comfortably behind the desk in the outer office. This was his domain and his quiet, hesitant character changed among the cupboards and shelves of neatly filed documents, piles of paper, bottles of ink and blotters. Here, he was firm, accurate and, unlike in his domestic life, in charge.

'Bye the bye,' Joe asked, 'if Sarah's staying fer a while, she'll need a place o' her own. We can nae manage tae breathe fer bodies in oor room noo. There wis twelve o' us last nicht! D'ye think there's a place she can ha'e in the village?'

'Will she be werkin' in the mills?'

Joe rubbed his chin, 'Ah can nae say, but fer now she will nae. She can nae, she's carrying anither bairn an' by the looks o' her it'll be here afore the new year.'

'Whit aboot her children? Are they old enough tae enter the mills?' Gerry was pulling out a plan of the village, each tenement divided into squares with the tenant's name written over it.

Joe's brow creased with concentration. 'Tae tell ye the truth, Ah can nae mind how auld her weans are, mibbee Cathy's ten years noo?'

'If one of the family, even Cathy, the dottir, wis an employee, we could try an' find a room. It's winter an' there's mair folk seeking work tae get a roof than we ha'e joabs fer them .'

The office door opened and Owen came in, his cloak carrying the chill night air.

Joe caught the door before it closed, making to leave and nodding politely at Owen.

'We can see whit her plans are,' he said quickly to Gerry, 'if she has any. Until later!'

'Mr Scott!' Owen called to his retreating figure. 'May I detain you for a moment? It is opportune that you are here, for you are a stonemason, yes? You worked on the Nursery Buildings?'

'Yes, sir.' Joe closed the door against the draught and followed Owen into the main office.

'I require some building work undertaken at the end of Nursery Buildings, perhaps two storeys high, no more. This will extend the storerooms for the Village Shop and I have plans that they should also accommodate an abbatoir to provide fresh meat. Would you be in a position to carry this out?'

'Ah wid, Sir. With pleasure. When wid ye be wishin' tae have yon werk completed?'

'As soon as possible,' Owen's dark blue eyes were lively with the vision of the new premises. 'Certainly before the Spring. I understand the weather can create unforeseen delays but, yes, before the end of March, shall we say?'

'Aye, end of March, if Ah can meet wi' ye soon, sharp like, on the site an' ye show me whit ye want. Shall Ah mak oot an estimate fer ye?'

'I was recommended to make contact with you by one of my managers, Mr Logan. He told me you were a sound man and your ability has already been demonstrated in the village. I shall require an estimate, yes, but only to put before my partners for I shall approach no-one else. You have the contract.'

'Weel, thank ye kindly, Sir. When can we meet in the daylight to see the grun ?'

'Humphreys will show you, I am leaving for the city soon. Can you call by the office,' he consulted a diary, 'on Friday morning? Eleven o'clock?'

Once out on the street, Joe marvelled at what just happened. Was Logan's recommendation a pure coincidence, or was it because he was a fellow Freemason?

Although he was bursting to tell Fiona the good news, his thoughts returned to Sarah on his short walk home.

His sister was sitting by the fire stirring a pot of barley and leek broth. Her hair lay loose around her shoulders in long golden waves and the way her body was turned, with the shawl draped over her arms, she looked exactly as he remembered her from many years before.

It was when she turned to greet him that he was brought shockingly into present time. Her haggard face and the swelling of the new baby were starkly illuminated by the firelight, causing him a sting of sadness.

271

'Ah thocht Ah'd git the dinner oan,' she said, making an effort to sound bright. 'It'll be an oor or mair afore it's ready. Ye have a grand big pail o' coal up here an' Ah wis fair surprised by the water pumps in the street.'

Cathy and Stephen were seated at the bench beside the table, legs dangling, baleful eyes watching Joe.

'Ah'm sure yer cousins wid nae mind ye playin' wi' their marbles,' Joe took a box down from the dresser. 'See, many colours.'

Stephen held his cupped hands out for them, turning each one to catch the light.

'Here,' Joe knelt down on the floorboards and briefly explained how to play with them, then he took a seat beside Sarah.

'Sae lass, are ye here fer a visit or tae stay?'

'Ah've nowhere else tae turn, Joe.'

'Ye ken ye alis ha'e a hame wi' me an' Fiona, whenever ye need it. Ah telt ye tha' afore ye left, an' Ah mean it.'

'Ye did. Ah truly thocht Ah wid be alricht, that everything wid work oot wi' Sean.'

'Where is he?'

Sarah looked away, 'He's gone awa' tae the Americas.'

'An' left ye?' Joe exploded, 'an' his bairns! In this state!'

'Naw, he wanted tae tak us wi' him, but I wid nae gae wi' him.' She squared her shoulders, 'Ah've made a terrible mistake, Joe. Ah've ruined ma life ... an' lost ma man. It's a lang story an' the worst bit fae me is that Ah'm suffering frae ma ane doing.'

Trying to calm the rage he felt against Sean, Joe gritted his teeth and listened while she poured out her tale.

'Fer all those years,' she finished, 'Ah managed no' tae fall wi' a bairn but when Sean was leaving, the last time Ah saw him ... oor parting wis sae unexpected, sae passionate ... an' noo the babbie's due. Holroyds wouldn't employ me efter Ah missed sae many days feeling like death an' greetin' a' the time. E'en dragging mesel' oot a bed wis too much effort. Cathy wis sich a help, she's a wee stoater, so she is. Then it stairtit tae get cauld an' we were running oot o' mony fer the rent. Sae ... here we are.' She gave a wavering smile, 'Och, Joe, Ah've bin nuchin but trouble fer ye.'

272

'Ye have no'. Yer ma sister, ye stood by me an' helped me wi' Ma an' Meg. Ye jist seem tae lose all sense wi' yon man Sean Rafferty, or whitever he cries hisself noo.'

'Joe, please din nae tell ony one else aboot that. Jist say Sean's deid, fer that's whit he is, deid an' buried.' Suddenly, her face lit up, 'Sam! Ye sed in yer letter there wis guid news aboot Sam! Tell me!'

This time it was Joe who had the tale to tell and by the time Cal and, a little later, Fiona and Rosie arrived, Sarah knew all the family's business. Including the unsavoury matter of Sam's orders to track down deserters and the news of the dreadful losses suffered by the Cameronians the previous winter.

'We must pray Sam is alive and well,' she said, sincerely. 'He has his joab tae dae, whether it's finding Sean or fighting the French.'

Rosie thoughtfully brought a pile of oatcakes with her and some ginger parleys, a treat from a neighbour, to add to the meal. She laid them beside the big bowl of broth and settled in to hear Sarah's story of the last seven years. It soon became clear to her that her sister would be staying in New Lanark for the foreseeable future. So, when the evening drew to a close with sleepy children being hustled into bed and Joe yawning in the big chair by the dying embers, she stood up and looked around the little room.

'Gerry an' I have a whole place tae oorselves. There's nae point in ye all being crushed in here, pick up yer things an' come up tae mine. Ye can stiy wi' us until ye find a room.'

'Can we?' Sarah's body seemed to droop with relief. 'Och Rosie, that'd be awfy guid o' ye. Ah've bin feelin' bad aboot takin' o'er the weans bed here an' budgin' ye all up. Are ye sure yer man won't mind?'

'Naw, away! Come wi' me noo an' we'll get the bairns doon fer the nicht.'

Joe caught Fiona's eye: Gerry would have little to say about it if Rosie wanted her sister to stay.

Fiona gave Sarah a hug, rubbing her back and holding her close.

'Ah ken it's no' whit ye wid ha'e wished, but it's guid tae have ye hame, Sarah. Ah'll send Bessie a wee note an' see if she can come up an' be wi' ye fer the babbie.'

Sarah gave her an extra squeeze before releasing her, 'Thank ye, thank ye fer bein' sae kind tae me an' the bairns.'

Later, cuddled sleepily behind their curtain, Joe whispered to Fiona about Owen's new building work. 'Och yer sum man, Joe ...' she whispered back, pressing a tender kiss on his lips. 'Whit a fine man Ah'm merrit tae! Ah'm that proud o' ye, ma darling.'

'Let's see if Ah can pull a team t'gether an' build the thing afore ye say that.'

'Ye'll be fine, it'll be the first big joab o' many.' She snuggled into him, yawning. 'Joseph Scott and Sons. Oh my.'

Chapter Twelve

"To preserve permanent good health, the state of mind must
be taken into consideration."
Robert Owen

The clocks rang out through the lofty rooms of the Charlotte
Street mansion: it was five o'clock on a dull March afternoon.

Upstairs, coal fires and lamplight warmed the bed chambers
where Anne Caroline and her sisters were putting the finishing
touches to their evening wear. Maids fussed around them
securing clasps on necklaces, fixing jewelled hairpins deep into
their fashionably styled hair and making final adjustments to
recalcitrant curls with heated tongs.

A year had passed since David Dale died and his daughters
were moving out of the sombre colours and plain styles of
mourning. Julia and Margaret both preferred their formal
dresses to be of patterned material, trimmed with deep frills of
cream lace, while Mary chose a pale turquoise blue shot-silk
taffeta. Jean's peach silk gown was the least adorned yet
showed off her small, neat figure to stunning effect. She suited
any design, a fact of life her sisters acknowledged without
jealousy and of which Jean seemed oblivious.

Crystal perfume bottles sprayed their fine mists onto wrists
and collar bones. Perfectly ironed satin ribbons were tied
symmetrically, gathering the dresses into high waists beneath
the bust and leaving long straight skirts to fall until they
touched the toe of satin pumps.

It was an evening ritual, becoming later each week as the
spring brought longer days, however today more care than
usual was being paid to their appearance; the family were
entertaining.

Downstairs, Cook spooned red currant jelly and ground black pepper into the gravy to be served with roasted haunch of venison. This generous piece of meat was a present from George Dempster who was staying with them for a few days.

This evening's dinner was to honour his last day as a guest at Charlotte Street and three other couples were invited to celebrate the occasion.

Rosemary Pemberly and her husband arrived first, barely a minute after the requested time which was considered by Renwick to be a little too early for good manners. When, seven minutes later, the carriage drew up with both Margaret and Charles Tennant and the MacIntosh's, the butler received them with a more gracious air of welcome.

Dempster's larger than life personality reigned over the proceedings, often verging on being uncouth but never in the presence of the younger ladies in the household. He was known to enjoy a flirtatious conversation with any female and was in his element with the four attractive Dale daughters, not to mention the three young married ladies in their choicest gowns.

Immediately on entering the dining room, Anne Caroline noticed the place setting at the head of the table. This position, which had always been her father's for as long as she could remember, had not been occupied since he died. When arrangements for the evening were being discussed with Breen, Jean proposed the chair should be used again, graciously suggesting her brother-in-law should take it when he was residing in the house.

From beneath her lashes, Anne Caroline watched her husband pause for a moment, no more than a heartbeat, before taking the seat. His hands lingered on the chair's polished arms, his fingers gripping them, taking time to notice the sensation of the wood. He looked up directly into her eyes, wanting to share the action with her, confirm her agreement. She gave the briefest nod, a warm understanding passing between them, invisible to the others.

Then the seconds were past: a final taboo conquered.

Anne Caroline, as she was accustomed, said Grace, conversation broke out and the party settled down to eat.

After Cook's elaborate dishes were consumed, the ladies left the men to their pipes and made themselves comfortable in the drawing room, relaxing after the rich and filling meal. Jean and Mary took turns at the piano and from time to time others in the party sang accompaniment. The Dale girls had newly acquired a little dog, a Cavalier King Charles spaniel, and Julia rang for Renwick, requesting the animal be brought to them. It was enthusiastically greeted by the ladies but soon decided the warmth of the hearth rug was preferable to being petted and lay down, out of their reach, in front of the fire.

'It is so good having you here in the city, dear Anne Caroline,' Rosemary sighed, arranging her evening gown into more flattering folds to mask how stout she was becoming. 'I fear, though, you will soon be telling me you are leaving for the country.'

'It is very comfortable here and the children are happy in their large nursery but we will probably return to New Lanark in a week or so.' Anne Caroline brought her sisters into the conversation. 'Perhaps I should arrange to leave when you are going to Rosebank? Like we did last year?'

Jean agreed and Mary MacIntosh reminded them of the wonderful hot summer's day they all spent celebrating Margaret and Anne Caroline's birthdays. Suddenly, they were reminiscing about the party and the grounds of the mansion on the banks of the river Clyde.

'It was truly idyllic!' Margaret Tennant cried. 'Charles and I are striving to make the gardens around our new home as beautiful. We purchased a sundial and planted around it with roses and lavender after seeing the one at Rosebank.' She laughed. 'Whenever I think of that place, I am sure I catch the heady scent of those blooms!'

The partnership between MacIntosh and Tennant was proving to be extremely successful and, fortunately, they were both still firm friends. They and their other two business partners were now wealthy men and their fortunes were increasing every day. Similarly, their families were growing and the size of their homes, carriages and household servants expanding to keep pace.

The ladies talked of flowers, children, clothes and problems with domestic staff while, across the hall, among the candlelight and pipe smock in the dining room, the topics had turned to the serious subjects of war, politics and the latest news from Parliament: the Act for the Abolition of the Slave Trade had been passed.

'After all these years of campaigning!' cheered Dempster.

'Twenty years! Wilberforce must be jubilant!'

'It is such a shame Mr Dale did not live to see this day,' Owen declared. 'He was heavily involved in supporting the abolitionists and would talk to me at length about the Saints, the alliance Wilberforce lead.'

'It was a massive majority, only sixteen against! I wonder who they were?'

'They have no decency and no conscience, that is for sure.'

'That criteria hardly narrows the field!' Tennant quipped.

Dempster guffawed, causing the candelabra to flicker and smoke.

'It is a first step,' Tennant continued, 'man's inhumanity to man knows no bounds. As I understand the new law, it only prohibits the making of new slaves, not the end of slavery as it stands today.'

'Alas,' Owen said solemnly. 'I believe that is the case. Let us hope we are not like Napoleon and banish the curse of slavery when we are caught on a wave of Enlightenment, only to reinstate it a few years later because it no longer suits our aims.'

'Napoleon's barbaric actions in the Caribbean may have actually done the cause a favour,' MacIntosh put in. 'For surely Britain would not want to be seen to stoop as low as the Emperor.'

'We can be an example,' Pemberly said, vehemently. 'We can lead the so-called civilised world in persuading Sweden, Holland, Spain and America to banish this abhorrent practice. They say Wilberforce and Clarkson were so sickened by what they researched that both suffered physically just from being party to the reports. May God bless their perserverance!'

'Unfortunately,' Tennant cleared his throat, glancing at Owen, 'there are cases in the factories and mills across Britain where our own people, white skinned and born in our country, are treated as little more than slaves.'

'I absolutely believe this to be the case,' Owen said firmly, 'It is outrageous that the cruelty and degradation meted out to those employed by unscrupulous mill owners is allowed to continue unchecked. The conditions in the factories are appalling, fever rages through the infants and there are far too many children, tiny children, running from stifling, thick air among the unending noise of machinery to be thrown out at the end of their shift into thin, freezing air.'

'You are passionate about it, Mr Owen?' Tennant asked.

'Indeed I am, sir. I have argued, debated and written papers on the very subject for many years and will continue to do so. Moreover, my mills in New Lanark will show, indeed *are* showing, that the correct way forward in manufacturing is by looking after the needs and health of the workforce, not working them to death like slaves.'

Dempster had heard Owen's views on the subject many times and, his manners reduced by alcohol, he cut into the conversation abruptly.

'We must discuss this further another day, I applaud your fine work at the mills ... but I hear the merry sound of music, let us join the ladies!'

Tennant gave his host an apologetic smile. 'Let us accompany Honest George to the drawing room but please, I would like to hear your thoughts on the sham Poor Law we were lumbered with, it is a subject I am keen to explore. I hope we can continue this conversation in the near future.'

Owen stood up, brushing crumbs from his waistcoat, a good humoured curve to his lips, 'I shall look forward to it.'

Jean and Mary were playing ballads by Robert Burns when Dempster appeared at the doorway, glass in hand, persuading them to allow him to join them.

'Burns was a fine fellow,' Dempster said in a loud whisper while the girls entertained them. 'He had a social conscience and managed to get away with it by wrapping his revolutionary ideals up in pretty words. Oh, he could charm the birds from the trees, hold a roomful of Edinburgh Establishment bods in the palm of his hand, ministers of the Kirk, an' all. Then, slice into the Church or Government's hypocrisy with a cunning turn of phrase! Clever man, died far too young!'

'I confess, a great deal of what he wrote is quite indecipherable to me,' Owen said apologetically, 'but my wife and her sisters enjoy his lighter work.'

'Aye,' Dempster gave Owen a meaningful nudge, 'although there's a lot that should not be seen by the fair sex.' he grinned broadly, remembering some of the more outrageously bawdy verses. 'He immortalised me, ye know?'

'Gracious ...' Rosemary raised an eyebrow.

'Oh nothing indiscreet! Some believe it was in jest, who knows? It was at the height of my political career, so I was fair game. "A title Dempster merits it, A Garter gie tae Willie Pitt'. And now poor old Pitt is dead. Fox too." He took a sip of his brandy. 'It is good to be in this house again, but damned strange without my old friend.'

From where she was sitting near the piano with Julia and Mary MacIntosh, Anne Caroline caught his words.

It was strange not to have her father in their midst, yet the intervening months had dulled the raw pain of loss to permit his family to continue their lives and feel at peace with his passing. She prayed daily for his soul, knowing he would wish them all to be happy. He was in Heaven with her mother and departed brother and sisters, of this she was certain and that certainty brought a reassuring calm.

Now, she concentrated on the living; on her children, her sisters and, of course, on her dear husband.

Her gaze roved over the assembled friends and family and she wondered if her father could see them.

If he could, she hoped he would approve.

Sadly, just a few weeks later, Glasgow lost another of its venerable citizens when Dale's friend, Owen's Highland companion, George MacIntosh, passed away.

***

Rosie's original intention of giving Sarah a safe haven soon began to turn sour.

The first few days saw cosy talks by the fire, hugs before bedtime and treats for the children. Then, on the last day of the year, the new baby arrived.

From experience, Rosie knew the hustle and bustle attached to giving birth. She was prepared for Bessie taking charge, the unpleasant mess and smells and the noisy early days of a newborn. These, she coped with. Even Gerry, who had never been in a family situation, bore the turmoil in his home with patience. Then, as the days grew into weeks and no room became available within the village, half forgotten frictions reared up again between the sisters.

Cathy went to work in the mills, accepting her duties with a quiet grace because she was the only one capable of bringing in any money. The little girl had never been subjected to any sort of routine or authority in her life. She found the long hours daunting, returning home exhausted and quite incapable of attending evening lessons.

On hearing he could not join his sister as a wage earner, but was to go to Day School with Fiona instead, Stephen refused to comply. No amount of coaxing or scolding would persuade him and eventually Sarah picked up a shoe, threw him over her knee and delivered several hard smacks on his backside.

His dramatic screaming could be heard all down the Row but he still would not go to school.

Gerry removed himself from the house as much as possible and Rosie's long hours on the factory floor meant their room was mainly occupied by Sarah.

'Ye jist din nae unnerstaun,' Rosie said in annoyance. 'Ah'm the inspector fer this stairwell an' ma hoose is an example. It's alis clean an' tidy, an' ma washing's done, the closet's emptied.' She waved her hands at the clutter around the room. 'Hoo can ye mak sich a mess wi' yin wee bairn?'

'It jist happens, Rosie.' Sarah murmured, her attention on feeding baby Lily. 'Ah'll see tae it t'morra.'

Rosie glared at her. 'T'morra? ye telt me tha' yesterday! An' a week past! Naw!' Rosie swept her hand across the table sending vegetable peelings and soiled clothes flying on to the floor. 'Dae it noo!'

Shaking with anger, Rosie ran over to Joe's and recounted the latest argument.

'An' the boy's as bad.' Rosie added.

'Whit dae ye mean?' asked Fiona, growing tired of hearing about the squabbles in the MacAllister room.

'Only the guid Lord kens whit he gits up tae! He's oot a' day, or so Sarah says. Up in Old Lanark, he telt me when Ah asked. He says he jist walks aboot an' helps folk at the market, running errands but he had pennies on him the ither nicht, an' Ah dread tae think hoo he came by them.'

Fiona shook her head, tut-tutting, 'He's a wild yin. An' there's still nae word o' a room coming free fer them all tae move oot an' gie ye peace?'

'An' d'ye think Ah'd be sittin here moanin' if there wis?'

Joe listened to the conversation from the fireside, his eyes closed, feigning sleep. He was working on a possibility to change the fraught situation.

Throughout the winter months he had successfully run the construction site beside the village shop, labouring on the building as well as organising all the other trades necessary to complete the store rooms. As his first major project, it was a huge undertaking, much more than he anticipated but with the help and advice of Ewing, Tam and a new friend from the Lodge, he orchestrated the sub contractors, the supply of materials and man power to bring the job in on time.

Robert Owen was satisfied with the result and with only a couple of minor points to sort out in the morning, it would be finished.

The terms agreed with the New Lanark Twist Company meant that the final payment due to him should be handed over straight away.

Sure enough, after a thorough inspection of the new building with Humphreys and another manager, Owen invited Joe into his office and wrote out the cheque.

'Thank you, Mr Scott.' Owen held out his hand, shaking Joe's with a firm grip. 'The stores will be an excellent addition to the village.'

Joe thanked him, doffed his cap and marched straight out, across the road and into the Counting House. In these unusual curved offices attached to the end of Caithness Row, clerks sat at desks behind a counter, filling endless ledgers, weighing coins and counting money. It was here that the wages were handed out, money paid in to personal Savings Accounts and cheques exchanged.

If anyone required an advance on their wages, it was usually received in the form of foreign coins, over-stamped with the New Lanark stamp. This arrangement worked well for both the mills and the employees, especially as the wages were only paid monthly and families often ran short by the fourth week.

At dinner break, Fiona was surprised to find Joe waiting for her outside Mill Four.

'Tis like when we were courting!' she laughed, slipping her hand in his. 'An' ma hairt still sings when Ah look upon ye, ma sweethairt.'

He squeezed her fingers, 'Can ye leave the bairns wi' Mrs Young an' come wi' me. Ah'll ha'e ye bak here afore the bell rings.'

'Bells!' Fiona threw back her head, smiling happily. 'Is oor life alis tae be ruled by bells? O' course, ma darlin', Ah'll come wi' ye.'

Her curiosity grew when, on leaving the younger children with their neighbour, Joe lead her up the steps to Lanark.

'Where are Davey an' Donnie,' she gasped, unused to the steep climb.

'At the yaird, wi' Tam. They'll be makin' theirsel's useful, they'r guid lads.'

'Where are ye takin' me, Joe? Why can ye no' tell me?'

'Anither wee bit, ye'll see soon enough.'

They were high above the village on the road to Lanark.

'There!' Joe stopped and placed his arm around her waist. 'Whit d'ye see?'

'The farm road, bonnie primroses peeping oot under the beech trees?'

'Ahead o' ye.'

'The toon. The road tae the Wellgate an' broon, ploughed fields ...' She glanced up at him, perplexed.

'Naw, in front o' ye, efter the track tae Bankheid Farm.'

'Hooses, three wee white hooses wi' thatched roofs?'

'Aye! ye see the yin at the far end, wi' the fence beside it an' a bit o' land running up the hill?'

'Aye.'

'Ah've a mind tae rent it. Fer us an' the bairns.'

'A whole hoose? Jist fer us?' Fiona's eyes grew wide with astonishment. 'There's twa wee windaes in the roof! Joe, Joe, it's the brawest wee hoose Ah've e'er seen!'

'It's empty, tak a closer look! There's four big rooms, twa up an' twa doon, an iron range wi' an oven an' a shed at the back which wid be grand fer ma werk.'

Catching up her skirts to run from window to window, hurrying all round the building, Fiona's breathless exclamations made him smile.

'Ye like it?' he called. 'Fer sure?'

In answer, she threw herself into his arms, kissing him through their laughter.

'Ah'll tell them we'll tak it then?'

'Oh aye ... Ah'm sae excited Ah'm a' of a jitter!'

'Weel, that's settled then.' He took a folded piece of paper out of his satchel and held it out to her.

She opened it, 'Whit's this?'

'The letter tae agree tae the terms o' the tenancy.'

Her eyes scanned down the strong handwriting, taking in the amount they were to pay and confirming the right to use the outhouse and pasture land and then she saw the signature.

'Joe! Oh dear Lord, Joe, *you* wrote this? You *wrote* this!'

'Does it read all richt?' He half smiled, embarrassed and proud. 'Donnie started teaching me tae read an' all, years back. Then Tam an' Mel ha'e been guid tae me.'

'An' ye ne'er telt me!' There was hurt in her eyes: she thought she knew everything about him.

'Ah wanted tae surprise ye, lass. Ah wanted tae tell ye on a day when Ah could gi'e ye a present ... a special day.'

The feeling of upset remained but Joe's bashful, earnest expression forced her to push it aside.

'Ah'm fair prood o' ye, darlin'! Ah'm lost fer words.' She covered her conflicting emotions by hugging him and burying her head against his chest.

'Come oan, we hid better git ye bak tae the mills.' He tucked her arm in his and they turned to retrace their steps. 'It's no' far tae walk fer yer werk, an' ye can still esk Mrs Young tae keep an eye on the bairns. Ye ken Ah've been wantin' us tae ha'e oor ane hame fer years an' it's taken a muckle lang time an' sweat tae git it, but noo we can.'

'It's grand, Joe!'

'Ah've bin thinkin' on this fer months, an' if we move up here, Sarah can move in tae oor room wi' Cal.'

Fiona's radiant smile faded slightly, 'But Cal's no' earnin' enough tae pay the whole rent, an' ye ken whit it's like when his chest is bad an' he can nae werk.'

'Cathy's in the picking rooms an' that wee brat o' a brither o' hers will soon be auld enough fer the mills.'

'But he's no' ten yit an' Sarah has Lily tae care fer.'

'Ah've thocht o' that. Ah can gie em enough each month sae they git by until Sarah's back on her feet.'

Fiona stopped and swung round to face him, looking searchingly into his eyes. 'Ye have a new way aboot ye,' she said, quietly. 'These last few months ye ha'e bin, och, Ah can nae think whit tae ca' it. Stronger ... no, ye've alis bin strong, an' kind.'

'Mibbee Ah'm jist aulder an' wiser?' he suggested, enjoying being alone with his wife, holding her close, causing her to smile at him in her own unique, appealing way.

'Yer werk's gaun weel, an' ye ha'e friends, businessmen.' She kissed him again, seeing the dancing lights in his piercing blue eyes. 'An' Ah'm still dizzy wi' the memory o' yon fine letter ye wrote! Ye can mak all the money in the world but Ah doubt ye'll ever mak me happier than Ah am richt noo.'

He gently pushed her ahead of him down the hill, 'Ah can try! Hurry up noo, or ye'll be late.'

'When can we tell the ithers?'

'Tonight? Ah want tae speak wi' Cal first, afore ma sisters. Din nae say a word fer noo.'

He watched her hurrying away through the crowds of workers funnelling back into the mills. It would be strange not to live in the village: he hoped he was doing the right thing.

No, he corrected himself, he *knew* he was doing the right thing. Ever since becoming a Freemason, although he was only in the First Stage, he was aware of the difference it was making to him.

His wife could feel it; he could feel it.

He was no longer alone, without support. Not having a father, or at least a father he could turn to in times of need, had left an empty, insecure hole inside him. Now, he was part of a brotherhood which was broadening his horizons, teaching him aspects of life and how to live it which he had not even imagined. He wanted to better himself and the lives of those around him and who better to start with than his own family.

The mill bell swung in its tower above Mill One, pealing out across the village. Joe chuckled to himself. They would still be

285

living near enough to the mills to hear the bells, some things would not change.

***

When the great day came for the Scotts to move up to their new home, Sarah and Cal both watched their departure with mixed feelings. Neither of them really wanted to live with the other but nor could they see any alternative.

Sarah was still withdrawn and depressed, often lost in thoughts of regret. She yearned to turn back the clock, cast her religious principles to the wind and be with Sean again. Then, Lily would cry or something else would happen to force her into the day to day reality of being back in New Lanark without the man she loved.

Only Joe knew the truth, everyone else believed her to be a grieving widow and she hid behind this convenient excuse to explain her tears and melancholy.

At first, Rosie saw her brother's sudden move out of the village as the answer to her prayers: she could have her room back. Within hours of her sister moving out to be with Cal, the place was spick and span. A pot of barley stew simmered on the range to welcome her husband back into the quiet home they had been denied for months. However, this contentment was tinged with a niggling envy for the space and facilities of Joe and Fiona's new home.

She chided herself for being selfish, prayed to ask forgiveness for her jealous feelings but nevertheless, a chill of resentment remained.

Fiona was aware of Rosie's feelings and also of the imposed alteration to Cal's life but her loyalties lay with Joe and their children and she felt no guilt in enjoying this new chapter of their lives.

***

On a hot summer afternoon, after spending hours closeted in the office attending to paperwork, Owen glanced at the clock and decided to go over to see the dancing class.

286

He always maintained that dancing was an important part of the school day and was a keen and proficient dancer as a child. It provided exercise as well as giving the children an opportunity to interact with one another instead of sitting in rows. When showing off the mills to visitors he tried to engineer his guided tours so they would arrive in Mill Four when the children were practicing Scottish reels.

'Carry on!' he called to the teacher when he entered, closing the door behind him and taking up a stance at the side, arms folded.

The infants continued with their performance, giggling and swinging their arms while they learned new steps and formations. All the windows were open, allowing a cool breeze to catch at their smocks as they jumped and hopped, barefoot, on the floorboards, smiling at one another spontaneously whenever they clasped hands.

Around the room, standing out the way beside the walls, the teacher and his assistants clapped their hands in time to the fiddler's tune, encouraging the pupils with cheery grins and pointed instructions.

After half an hour, the class was dismissed and all the infants sat down to hear the teacher launch into a long reading from the Bible.

Within a few minutes, the lively, bright-eyed children became heavy lidded, yawning or gazing out the window.

Owen watched with interest.

A row of larger boys, around seven or eight years old, began to fidget, whispering between themselves and being immediately corrected by a nearby assistant.

Owen waited until a natural break in the reading and then asked the teacher if he could speak with him outside.

'It is a beautiful, sunny day today and I am sure the children would far prefer to be outside than sitting indoors. Please take them for a walk, a ramble perhaps? let them see the flowers and trees, and feel the grass beneath their feet.'

The teacher was taken aback but agreed it was a fine day and, given that Scotland saw too few of such days, he would assemble them in pairs and walk them up on to the hill behind Caithness Row.

'As soon as it was announced that the class was going out for a walk,' Owen told his wife that evening, 'the dozy, bored expressions quite disappeared and were immediately replaced with excitement.'

'We have seen the same with our sons,' Anne Caroline agreed. 'Robert can be slumped in his chair one moment, saying he is too tired to practice writing, and yet, when he is free of lessons, he is romping in the garden with all the energy of a puppy.'

'I recall the same from my own childhood. Nature holds a deep fascination for children, they should be encouraged to explore the countryside and learn the wonders of plants and animals.'

'I noticed the children returning from their walk and they certainly seemed to be in very high spirits!'

'All of them were smiling, even the class assistants! Children are far too often overlooked, in both the working class and upper society. We forget they will grow up to take our places and we should have prepared them properly for the task ahead.'

'Well, happily, you and my dear Papa shared the same views and have always supplied education to children within your factories.'

'The bare essentials only. Many leave to enter the mills with only a minimal knowledge of mathematics. I fear their understanding of reading is also very basic.'

'Do they need more?' Anne Caroline asked, innocently.

Owen gave her a puzzled look, 'Who is to say how much they need? A child will learn as much as it is taught and can explore for itself. I have been reading Joseph Lancaster's recent pamphlet, Improvements in Education. His theories have always interested me, so much so that I invested in his school many years ago.'

'How did his theories interest you, my dear?'

'He wished to make his lessons open to everyone, without charge. Free! A laudable aim but, of course, he soon found he could not afford teachers. So, being an enthusiastic young man, he discovered a solution to his lack of funds by following the principles of the Scots army chaplain, Andrew Bell, in which you teach a subject to the brighter, older pupils and they then teach the younger ones. He calls it the Monitorial System and I can see how it would work when you wish to teach a large number of students without the cost of paying wages to a lot of teachers.'

'I heard Papa speak of Dr Bell.' She tilted her head on one side, enjoying the conversation. 'He was a priest in the Episcopalian Church, was he not?'

'Yes, and later ordained as a Deacon in the Church of England.' Owen frowned, 'Having invested in the Quaker, Mr Lancaster, I also offered Dr Bell a sum of money to invest in his school but I attached the condition that if, like Lancaster, he threw his doors open to all students, regardless of their religious beliefs, I would invest the whole amount. If he maintained his position of accepting only those of the Church of England, then I would invest half the sum.'

'And what happened?'

'We agreed on the smaller sum because Dr Bell's schools are closed to all but followers of the Established Church.'

Anne Caroline gave a resigned sigh, 'I am sure they are acting in good faith, Robert.'

He did not respond, turning his attention to his pocket watch. 'It is still a fine day, why don't we take the boys for a stroll by the river before I have to attend a managers' meeting?'

Anne Caroline immediately hurried upstairs to collect the children from the nursery, relieved to drop the contentious subject of religious involvement in education.

'Will ye be wantin' me tae come wi' ye, Madam?' Peggy asked, buckling William's shoes.

'Yes.' Anne Caroline took Robert's hand, waiting for her youngest son to finish dressing. 'Where is Toshie?'

'Weel, Ah thocht we wid jist be in the nursery until tea time sae she went fer a nap.'

'Oh dear. Then there is no-one on hand to care for the babies?'

'Naw.' Peggy stood up and looked blankly at her employer.

'Is Toshie unwell?' Anne Caroline asked, concerned.

'Oh no, Ma'am, but she wis helpin' me through the nicht wi' Miss Jane who's awfy troubled wi' her teeth.'

Peggy desperately wanted another maid to assist her with the children but was scared to broach the subject.

289

'Perhaps you could fetch Toshie from her room then, and she can take a rest in here. The girls are both sleeping anyway.'

Peggy bobbed a curtsey and ran up the attic stairs to wake the Lady's Maid.

Toshie was not pleased.

'Madam,' she said, as soon as she hurried into the nursery, still grappling with tying the sash of her long white apron. 'Ah must beg o' ye tae take on anither maid. Ah'm too auld tae walk the flair wi' cryin' babbies a' nicht an' care for your needs during the day as my position demands.'

Anne Caroline looked on her faithful maid with new eyes. In front of her was a rattled older woman, wisps of grey hair escaping her starched bonnet, her eyes ringed with shadows.

'Dear me, Toshie, I have been very remiss. The nursery is so well ordered that I mistook the situation, believing it to be under control. If further help is required, then we will immediately engage a new maid.' She turned to Peggy. 'Why did you not say anything?'

'Ah wis feart tae, Ma'am.'

Giving her kindest smile, Anne Caroline reassured her that she was not an unreasonable employer and could always be approached on matters relating to the running of the nursery and the welfare of her children.

She raised the topic during the walk with her husband. 'I do believe I saw genuine fear in the girl's eyes. I never believed I could create such a response.'

'These servants are often subjected to terrible ordeals in other houses. I know of places in Manchester, and I daresay there are as many in Clydesdale, where beatings and punishments are regular occurrences.'

'May the Lord protect them. There shall be no such ill treatment here.'

They sauntered on, arm in arm, crossing the little bridge on the road to Bonnington. It was their usual route, taking them close to the river just above the new weir, where another stream joined the Clyde.

'Shall I instruct Cooper to send out word for a new nursery maid?' Anne Caroline asked.

'Certainly, although this raises another question. Our little home is bursting at the seams already. The servants' rooms are packed and we cannot request Cooper to share with a maid, yet, a nursery maid would have to live within the home to carry out her duties.'

They paused as the road turned a corner to reveal the Mid Lodge of Bonnington estate. It was their habit to end the walk at this point and retrace their steps, which they did, still mulling over the dilemma of accommodating everyone in the New Lanark house.

Peggy walked ahead, trying to hear what was being said while gathering long seed heads of grass with the little boys.

'An' whit wis decided?' Toshie asked, as soon as Peggy returned.

'Aye, they're hiring a new maid.'

'Thank the Lord fer tha'.'

'They're jist wonderin' hoo tae sleep us all.'

'Noo, there's a thing! Mibbee snooty Mrs Cooper will ha'e tae share her bed wi' yin o' us!'

'Weel, Ah'm fer the streets then, if it's me. She's gie weird tha' yin. Mad as a chookie hen, if ye esk me.'

There was a creak on the landing floorboards outside the door: Cooper was making her way up the stairs.

She closed her bedroom door, blinded by tears.

What was worse? the horrid things they said about her or their shared fit of unsuccessfully suppressed laughter when they realised their words were overheard?

Behind her bolted door, Cooper fell to her knees beside the bed and prayed for strength and guidance.

When she reappeared downstairs to finish the meal preparations, her drawn face and bloodshot eyes caused Toshie a stab of guilt. She waited until they were alone in the kitchen before opening the conversation by asking if the housekeeper was unwell.

'Why do you ask, Mrs Mackintosh? Perhaps if you looked into your own conscience you might find the answer.'

Toshie looked down at her hands, picking nervously at her fingernails.

'I suppose ye heard Peggy's comments earlier. Ah'm ashamed tae say Ah did nae scold her. Ah ask fer yer forgiveness an' can only tell ye that Ah wis sae tired Ah lost all judgement.'

'Only the Lord can forgive your sins. Anyway, it is of no consequence to me now. I will be leaving this house as soon as I can find alternative employment.'

'Leaving! Och noo, Mrs Cooper, din nae be rash. This is a good hoose with a fine employer. Joabs in this kind o' household are as hard tae find as hens' teeth.'

The analogy was lost on Cooper. She reached for her notebook, making no attempt to open the ink bottle or take up her pen, instead turning it and lining it up to lie square with the edge of the table.

'My mind is made up. I was engaged for this position by Mr Dale, God rest his soul. There is now a new employer and the duties have changed considerably. I am a cook by profession, I shall seek a new position as a cook.'

'Weel ...' Toshie was speechless. 'Ah'm fair grieved if this has come aboot because o' me an' ma rudeness.'

'There are numerous reasons. I trust that you will keep this conversation confidential.'

'If ye wish. Aye.'

Without another word, Cooper picked up her book and swept from the room.

Toshie put the kettle on the range, opening the fire door and rattling the coals into life to coax a long enough burst of heat to boil some water. She was shocked by Cooper's intentions but, at the same time thought how much nicer their summers in New Lanark would be without Cooper's long face and snippy orders. She just hoped the next housekeeper would be an improvement and looked forward to chatting with Breen and Cook about this surprising turn of events.

***

Opening the door to a work room in Mill One, the clatter and whirr of the great machines hit Owen in a wall of sound. He paused to adjust to the noise, opening his note book to a new page before walking up and down the rows of women in the Carding Room.

Their long skirts hanging above dusty bare feet, all the workers wore their hair held back in bonnets or plaited and pinned at the nape of their neck, well out of the way. They were feeding rolls of rough cotton through slots in the metal guards to be caught up onto belts of bristling metal brushes.

There was no point in speaking in this work room, the human voice could not compete with the monstrous roar of the latest technology. The girls communicated with each other through hand signals which new recruits quickly became familiar with to join the camaraderie.

Owen was satisfied with the new machinery whose sturdy wrought iron wheels and gears were proving reliable. Even the heavy coils of leather belt, studded with bristles, did not need replacing as often as had been feared. They were a sound investment, raising production from this part of the process and yet requiring fewer employees.

At each work station he noted the Silent Monitor relating to the woman toiling beside it. These were now mainly blue, indifferent, or yellow, good. When he came to those with the black side facing out, he would observe the offender for fractionally longer than the others but did not berate them, merely showing them that their behaviour had been noted. Similarly, when he saw a white monitor, he might smile as he passed, nothing more.

The Overseers, three bearded men in loose shirts and knee breeches, watched his progress, aware that they too had Silent Monitors to tell him, at a glance, how well they performed their duties. Owen was known for remembering who was a diligent employee and who was not, but they heard neither praise nor displeasure from him.

He expected them to do their job properly, that was why he paid them at the end of each month. It therefore did not seem appropriate to heap praise on those with white monitors because, after all, they were only doing what they were supposed to do.

Once outside in the stairwell again, his ears still ringing, he made some notes in his little book and set off down the steps to check the progress in Level Two.

So far, his overhaul of the machinery, the expensive construction of the weir and the strict controls on wastage and thieving were achieving good results.

Out-with Owen's control was the raging war with Europe which was soon to impinge on the smooth running of his business.

For years, the Americans, lead by their president, Jefferson, were becoming increasingly infuriated by the war between France and Britain. Britain's powerful sea force endeavoured to cut off trade to Europe, aiming to put pressure on Napoleon. They blocked French ports and forced American merchant ships to dock at a British port, not permitting them to leave until they paid taxes on the goods bound for France, Spain or other countries under the Emperor's control.

Both France and Britain looked upon American ships as pawns, still disregarding the pleas of neutrality from Thomas Jefferson and his Congress. Worse, the seamen of both warring nations would frequently board American merchantmen and seize their cargo as contraband. The British navy, being a far greater force, became especially despised by the Americans because it would not only take the cargo but also press the crews into serving on British warships.

This came to a head in December, causing outrage and panic among the merchants in the Tontine Rooms.

'Jefferson's passed his Embargo Act!' Kirkman Finlay shouted towards Owen when he entered the cacophony. 'He won't allow Americans to trade with either us or France!'

Owen took the seat offered to him, taking off his hat and squeezing in beside a group of agitated businessmen.

He was already aware of the news but allowed the others to announce it to him again in excited, horrified terms.

'Well,' he said when there was a chance to break the flow. 'Last spring he failed in his efforts to stop his own ships trading with any foreign markets, I can only see him facing the same result.'

'Och, he's cutting aff his nose tae spite his face,' a plump, bald colleague cried, crumbs from his meat pastie gathering in the brocade folds of his waistcoat. 'He'll nae be popular!'

'At least he hasn't declared war on us! After the Chesapeke, Leopard affair in the summer, I thought that was on the cards!'

'We have managed without the American markets since he forbade our imports.'

'But now we will not have access to the cotton plantations or tobacco fields.'

'I am sure there will be a way around this problem. America is not the only country in the world.'

Owen listened to the debate. His warehouse stock was low, waiting for the imminent arrival of the next shipment of raw cotton. Now, when these merchant vessels docked, they would not be allowed to discharge their cargo.

His quick brain analysed the situation while coffee was served. Other suppliers had to be found straight away but obviously every man at the table, especially Finlay who owned Catrine and his newly acquired mills at Deanston, would be in the same situation.

'We have the Asian markets,' Finlay was saying confidently. Apart from the cotton mills, his company was almost as powerful as the East India Company in trade with Asia.

For the rest of the morning, Owen moved from table to table in the Tontine, speaking with brokers, fellow merchants, agents, gathering information. There were supplies of raw cotton already in store in Britain but the brokers were keen to make as much as possible from this scarce commodity. It was clear that its value was growing with every quote and soon Owen realised the figures already being banded about would be double by the time he confirmed agreement to buy from his partners.

'It's a cold day in all respects,' Kirkman Finlay murmured to Owen when they left the warmth of the Tontine.

Owen closed the clasp on his cloak and pulled on his thick leather gloves. Snowflakes spiralled slowly down in front of where they stood beneath the magnificent sculpted stone arch covering the main entrance.

'Even the price of cotton today would make it unviable to process.' Owen said quietly. The freezing air tingled his face and he wished he had ridden up from Charlotte Street rather than choosing to walk. 'Goodness knows what it will cost tomorrow ... or next week!'

'Aye, the next three or four months will see the end of the smaller mills, I fear.' Finlay tapped his hat into place, screwing up his eyes against the harsh white light of the winter street. He was younger than Owen by a couple of years and they found they often gravitated towards each other when in the company of the more elderly squires.

'My regards to Mrs Owen,' he said with a friendly smile. 'I trust she and the Miss Dales are well?'

'Very well, thank you. And Mrs Finlay? I understand you have a new son?'

'Alexander! He is thriving! Well remembered my friend!'

They parted cheerily despite the serious business of the day and, walking briskly through slippy snow, Owen remembered Dale's views on Finlay when he became a Dean of Guild a few years before. He found him a loud, self confident lad who liked the sound of his own voice but held firm principles and precocious entrepreneurial skills.

Snowflakes were catching on his lashes, covering the front of his dark blue wool cloak. He marched on, composing a letter to his partners to relay his proposals for surviving the coming crisis.

As soon as he arrived at Charlotte Street and Renwick relieved him of his soaked outer garments, he called for a bowl of soup to be brought to the library where he lost no time laying out his suggestion for coping with Jefferson's embargo. The seal was still molten when he handed it to a page boy with instructions to ensure it made the Mail Coach for Manchester.

Their response came within a few days. Although they had misgivings, there seemed no alternative and agreed to back his plans, finding them the lesser of two evils.

With their reply still in his hand, Owen sought out his wife in the drawing room.

'I must travel to New Lanark immediately,' he told her. 'I cannot delegate this news to Humphreys, it is too delicate.'

Anne Caroline understood but was very concerned for her husband's safety on the treacherous winter roads.

'We will take the carriage, it is more robust and I do not relish riding with this freezing Scottish ice blowing in my face.'

Cooper was taken unawares by her master's sudden return. He usually sent advance notice so that she could warm the rooms and prepare food, but suddenly, late in the evening, the front door opened and she heard Murdoch's deep voice in the hallway above. Only Alice was with her in the kitchen and she rushed to rouse the other maids.

It was the next morning, at a hastily convened meeting with all his managers and senior supervisors, that Owen revealed his intentions.

'Gentlemen, many of you will have heard about the difficulties we are having with the United States at present. These are very challenging times! We have European markets denied us due to the ongoing war and the trade restrictions with the Americas have caused more problems for our sales. We now have another major obstacle in our path, Jefferson has stopped all trade with Britain and as our raw cotton comes predominantly from the United States, we are now without the basic commodity for our factory.'

The men stared at him in silence: this was worse than they had imagined.

'Fear not! I have spent the last week pursuing other avenues. There is still cotton to be had, stock piles around the country which brokers are eager to sell.'

A sigh of relief whooshed round the room. Some men sat back in their chairs, opening the buttons on their jackets, crossing their legs and relaxing.

'Those warehouses of raw cotton are now reaching such high prices that if I bought it and worked it through our mills, I would not be able to sell it again without making massive losses. It cannot be done. I have looked at every alternative. No, gentlemen, we cannot buy the cotton which is currently in the country and we cannot buy the cotton from our usual suppliers in America. So, what are we to do?'

He looked around, not expecting an answer and none came.

'I will tell you. There are other places in the world growing cotton and I have already placed orders for quantities to be shipped to Glasgow marked with the New Lanark stamp. There is, however, a necessary delay of about three to four months to load the ships, sail the seas and dock here.'

'How much stock do we have?' someone called. 'Can we keep going until it arrives?'

'Unfortunately, no. The mills will have to close.'

Forty voices rose as one in a clamour of upset and alarm.

'But it's winter! How are we to live without the mills?'

Owen raised his arms, pleading for quiet.

297

'Let me tell you!' he shouted over the noise. 'There is no need for panic. Obviously, if there is no cotton we cannot process it but all my employees will be paid basic wages until the new stock arrives.'

The racket stopped and Owen looked at the astonished expressions and blinking eyes.

'Ye'll pay us, all o' us, e'en the bairns?'

'I have the agreement of the partners of the New Lanark Twist Company and that is what we intend to do.'

Owen waited for the next rumble of comments and cheers to subside before adding, 'I came from the city as fast as I could for I did not wish the bad news of the lack of cotton to arrive before me. Tell everyone! All my workers must know that their livelihood is safe after the last batch of cotton is brought to the mills next week. I do not know exactly how long the wheels will lie still, but they will run again ... the mills will run again ... your jobs are safe!'

The meeting began to disperse with many of the managers coming up to Owen and shaking his hand, thanking him for this unusual generosity

The last to leave was an older man, walking with a cane, who Owen knew to be the excellent manager of Mill Two.

'It is a grand thing ye ha'e done, Mr Owen, sir. I am proud tae werk fer ye. There's mony who wid shut the doors an' turn the villagers awa' tae fend fer their selves.' His craggy face twisted into a grimace of deep emotion. 'It puts me in mind of the late Mr Dale, may the Lord show him everlasting mercy, the nicht the first mill burnt doon. Ah wis a young man then, wi' weans an' a wife bearin' ma youngest daughter at the time. Ah wis in despair but that great man gathered us together and telt us no' tae fear! He wid still pay us ... an' the mill wid be rebuilt. He wis as guid as his word an' Ah ha'e nae doubt ye will be as weel.'

Owen gripped the man's hand. 'Your trust is safe with me, Mr Yarrow,' he said, resolutely. 'We will all see this through together.'

Chapter Thirteen

*"Were all men trained to be rational, the art of war would be rendered useless. " **Robert Owen***

All four New Lanark Mills sat idle through the darkest months of the year. The great iron water wheels turned for a few minutes once a week for maintenance but otherwise hung in their mountings gathering snow and wind blown leaves.

It was a drastic step to take but Owen's decision to stop production paid off in more ways than he could ever have imagined.

Cotton prices soared, bearing out his original theory and proving he was right to sit tight, keep expenses to a minimum and wait for the new, affordable cotton to arrive.

The male workers were found as many other tasks as he and his managers could conceive, white washing and scrubbing the workrooms and carrying out manual work on the grounds. Keeping the women occupied was more difficult although many felt duty bound to tackle often neglected household chores to gain recognition in the weekly inspection reports. For the hundreds of children, including the orphans in Nursery Buildings, the solution was simple: they went to school.

One major development which arose from this dramatic event was the change in the villagers' attitude towards their employer.

When he walked around the streets he saw smiling faces, children ran up to him, men doffed their caps of their own accord, sometimes calling out to him with a cheery greeting. Housewives who had long borne a grudge against his 'meddling' in their domestic lives, bobbed curtseys when he passed while they swept their stairwells or washed windows.

He was no longer 'the Englishman', he was their Master, their high heid yin, respectfully referred to by Big Lachie and the

Highlanders as their *ceannard*: chief. They acknowledged that he was looking after them with such unexpected compassion that even the most bigoted employee could not fault his actions.

It was spring before the new shipments of cotton arrived and normal production resumed.

Having struggled through an entire year with Joe and Cal's help, Sarah pulled herself out of her lethargy long enough to apply for work on the factory floor. She dreaded it. This was where she started, it was as if the years with Sean and working for Holroyds did not exist. The stylish, competent seamstress, designing gowns for the wives of Glasgow's wealthiest merchants, was another person, a strange, vaguely remembered ghost.

After enjoying the relative freedom of the mill closure, her daughter, Cathy, went back to the factory floor with good grace, but Stephen, eligible to work now that he was just into his tenth year of age, refused to join her. At least, since being forced to attend the school room with his cousins and sister through the winter, he reluctantly relented to spend his days under Fiona's watchful eye in Mill Four.

Sarah was at her wits end with him, asking Fiona, Rosie and friends in the village for advice to deal with her wayward son. Beating was suggested and although she resorted to it on occasions, Fiona, an enthusiastic follower of Mr Owen's kinder, more reasoned doctrines, persuaded her to refrain.

Every day was a struggle with the wilful, rude little boy, another reason for Sarah's lack of sleep and appetite.

A week after the mills resumed, she waited until Cal left for work, asked Mrs Young to care for Lily and presented herself at the office.

'Weel? Hoo d'ye get oan?' Mrs Young asked.

'Ah got the joab,' she said in a flat tone, closing the door to keep the heat in. 'Ta fer minding the wean.'

The room was full of children, Fiona's youngest ones mingling with the Young's brood. Lily was fast asleep, laid under a shawl on the hearth rug beside a baby boy. Only a few months old, he was lying on his back, holding his feet and rolling contentedly from side to side, gurgling. Little Molly Young was playing with her brother as if he was a doll but

Sionaidh, the same age, sat at the side, rocking and sucking her thumb.

'Tak a seat if ye can find yin! Ah'm aboot done wi' this mending an' a ha'e a nice piece o' currant loaf that Mrs Stark haunded in efter Ah helped her wi' her poorly bairn.'

Sarah moved a mound of darned blankets and sat down.

'Ah'm tae be shown how tae werk yon big jennies fer twisting the thread. Ah telt him it wis mony years since Ah'd bin in the mills but Ah wis a quick learner.' She sniffed, 'Ah hope Ah can mind whit Ah'm telt.'

'Och, ye'll dae fine.'

There was a sharp rap on the door.

'Who the de'ils tha'? Come away in!'

A man stuck his head around the door, 'Pardon the intrusion. Can ye tell me if Mr and Mrs Scott are still livin' up the stairs?'

Mrs Young regarded him suspiciously, 'Which Mr Scott?'

'Mr Joseph Scott.'

'Naw, they're awa' noo. Whit d'ye want tae ken fer?'

The man came further into the room, revealing the scarlet and braid jacket of an officer, his large black bicorn hat under his arm. 'We met the last time I wis here visitin'. If I mind richt, ye'r Mistress Young?' he saluted. 'Lieutenant Scott.'

With a cry, Sarah jumped to her feet, her hands flying to her face, 'Sam? Is it you ... Sam?'

'Sarah? It cannae be ... Sarah!'

She flew into his arms, hugging him with all her might, tears of joy and relief flowing down her cheeks. He was alive! His broad shoulders and smiling face showed a health and vigour she had not imagined after Cal's descriptions of him as a war ravaged veteran.

'Och, dinnae greet!' he laughed, taken aback by her violently emotional welcome.

'Din nae mind her, son,' Mrs Young grinned at him. 'She greets at everything! Dis nae matter whit it is, happy or sad, yon lass will ha'e a wet face.'

At the neighbour's suggestion, they left Lily in her care and went up to Sarah's room. It was cold and untidy, a very different place from the one Sam remembered under Fiona's tenancy. His sister seemed oblivious to her surroundings, staring at him, her eyes devouring the sight of him while she chattered continuously about how worried they had all been for him and the news of Joe moving out of the village.

He quickly laid a fire and swung the kettle over its meagre flames; it would be a long time before it produced any heat.

'I wrote tae ye? Did Joe no' get ma letter?'

'Aye!' Sarah indicated the folded paper bearing his red seal, still proudly displayed on the mantelshelf. 'Ye were in Ireland.'

'No, I wrote frae Hanover tae tell ye I wis a'richt. Efter the ships sank an' sae many drowned.'

Sarah shook her head, pulling her shawl tighter around her bony shoulders.

'We ne'er got tha' yin.'

Sam swore at the bad luck of his carefully composed letter being lost.

'I saw it gae in tae the mail bag! Damnation! Sae ye'd all be thinking I was deid?'

'Efter the shock an' all, we thocht it best tae believe ye alive. Unless we heard fer sure. Och Sam, Ah can nae believe yer really here! Whit happened when the boat sank?'

He sat back in the chair Joe once used, crossing his arms and tucking his cold hands under his armpits.

'I'll tell ye about a' that later, when the ithers are there. So, lass, whit's bin happening wi' ye? Ye were in Glesgie the last I heard.'

Sarah poured out her story, changing parts about her wayward husband to show him in a better light.

'Then Sean died,' she did not need to act the sadness in her voice, 'an' Ah found Ah wis wi' child an'... things got awfy hard sae Ah came back tae Joe.'

'Joe's bin a grand brither.' Sam said with feeling.

'That he has. When will ye gae up an' see him?'

'When it gets dark. I thocht he would be hame then. I jist wanted tae make sure they were still here afore ... afore Ah surprised them.'

'Shall Ah tell Rosie an' Cal an' join ye up at Joe's then?' A sudden shining smile spread over Sarah's face: it was a long time since the warmth of happiness smoothed her features and lit her eyes. 'Och Sam, we'll all be t'gither again!'

When the mills closed, Sarah was waiting at Mrs Young's when Fiona collected the children.

'Ye look gie pleased wi' yersel!' Fiona said, surprised at the obvious change in Sarah. 'They gave ye the joab, then?'

'Joab? Oh aye, Ah have the joab but ... brace yersel'? Sam's hame! He wis here an' he's gaun tae come tae yer hoose this eve.'

Chivvying her children up the hill in the darkness, Fiona praised whatever Almighty Power might be looking down on them, ordaining their fate and allowing her brother-in-law's safe return. She was fond of Sam, but her gratitude and relief were for the pleasure this would give Joe.

She knew Joe would already be at home with the older boys and lifted the latch wondering if she could hold her news as a secret but as soon as she stepped inside she couldn't keep it contained.

'Sam's back! Joe, yer brither's back an' he's all richt!'

Donnie jumped up, 'Frae the war, the soldier ? Ah mind him frae years back. Is he here?'

'He will be soon, son. He telt yer Auntie Sarah he wid be calling on us this very eve.'

'Away!' Donnie started to tell his younger siblings all about the brave army officer with dreadful scars and medals.

'How is he?' Joe asked his wife over the hubbub around them: staggered by her news

'Sarah says he's lookin' braw.' Fiona was hastily setting the room straight and filling a large saucepan with water and cupfuls of oats. 'Ah'm fair starvin' ... Sarah's bringing her tea up the hill wi' the ithers as soon as they're hame.'

She hung the children's jackets on hooks by the door, threw her own cloak over them and looked around the room. How would Joe see it? To her eyes, it was comfortable and welcoming. She was pleased with all aspects of the flag-stoned floor, white washed plaster walls and ceiling, showing three large oak beams, and the crowning glory, the cast iron grate and oven set into the chimney. When they moved in, Cal kept the old rag rug, table and chairs and the smaller of the kists, which were all from Douglas, leaving Joe to find new furniture.

Over the four seasons of living here, he gathered two settles, a wide seated bent wood chair, which had belonged to Ewing and was given as a present at Hogmanay, and a long, boarded table with benches on either side.

Her pride and joy was the new rag-rug, brightly coloured and soft under their feet, which lay before the hearth.

'Donnie, Davey! Licht the twa lamps an' stoke the fire. Robbie, awa' an' fetch in mair sticks fer a blaze. We can nae ha'e Sam feelin' the cauld.'

'There's a lantern comin' doon the road frae toon!' Ailsa shouted. She was perched on the large kist set under the window. 'It's comin' this way!'

Joe eagerly opened the door.

'Sam!' he cried, then burst out laughing, 'Ah din nae ken whit ma eyes are seeing!'

Sam was carrying an infant and beside him, holding his arm, was a young woman, peeping up from under her bonnet with a nervous smile.

Ushering them into the warmth, Joe waited until the child was set on its wobbly legs before embracing his brother.

'This is ma wife!' Sam said proudly. 'Roisin. And our wee son, Connor.'

After a few minutes of awkwardness, Ailsa took charge of Connor, entranced by his black hair and sweet, heart-shaped face. She led him over to where Tom was playing and the adults launched into a barrage of questions and stories. When Cal, Sarah and Rosie arrived, bringing Cathy and Stephen, there was barely room to move.

Joe and Cal arranged the benches on either side of the hearth, pushing the table back against the wall to make room for all the children to sit or sprawl on the floor.

Roisin hardly spoke but her dark lashed eyes were taking everything in, hovering especially on Fiona's animated face. The other women in the room were her sisters-in-law, posing no threat, however the vivacious Highland girl with her lilting voice and generous smile, caused a stab of jealousy.

Sam told them of his adventures, brushing quickly over the disaster at sea when they were travelling to Europe and concentrating on the homeward journey, the long time spent in Deal at the barracks and the arrival of his son.

'As Ah telt Sarah, Ah wrote tae ye from Germany. Ah thocht ye wid be worried and wanted tae let ye know I was alive.'

'It was all in the newspapers,' Rosie cried, 'ma Gerry saw it first an' we were fair upset.'

Sam leaned over and ran the back of his finger gently down her cheek, 'Aw, lass, an' that's exactly whit Ah didnae want tae have happen. God alane knows whit must ha'e happened between there an' here.'

While they talked and supped on bowls of porridge and salted mashed potato, contributed by Sarah, the fire burned low and seeing his sons were nearly asleep, Joe picked up the log basket.

Sam stood up, following him to the door. 'Ah'll gie ye a haun.'

'Roisin is a fine looking lass, sich raven black hair, like a Highlander,' Joe commented, hooking the lantern against the covered log pile. 'Ah hope ye are as happy as Ah am wi' Fiona.'

'She's a guid lass but we ha'e oor troubles. I should nae have taken her to Europe. The ither women shunned her, she wis nae one of the lassies married tae a regular soldier and the officers' wives were worse! Cruel, snooty lot, wi' their demeaning remarks an' niver accepting her intae their circle. The conditions were appalling. I tell ye, Joe, if there is a hell on earth, that's the closest I've come tae finding it.'

'Ye were makin' light o' the ship sinking an' Ah can understaun if ye din nae care tae tell me, but whit happened?'

'We never speak of it, Roisin an' I. She can't bear to have it mentioned.' He took a deep breath, slowly exhaling into the night air. 'We were on the Aurora, clustered t'gether below deck. Then there was this jolt an' this squeaking, creaking of the timbers under us. Scraping on something, grinding an' then splintering. Every one started whimpering, crying out and then the ship began tae rock an' suddenly we were all sliding sideways, on top of one anither.'

Sam ran his hands back through his hair, his eyes moving rapidly as he recalled the horror. No longer with Joe in Scotland, he was trapped between decks amongst the freezing waves.

'The watter wis icy cauld, bitter, ma legs were aching within seconds but I wis feart fer Roisin being crushed sae somehow, to this day I know not how, but I dragged her oot from under bodies who were all writhin an'screaming ... made it up the ladder to the open deck.

'A boat wis bein' lowered, all uneven like, people toppling oot intae the sea. I grabbed the ropes alang wi' a dozen or sae ither men an' we made it straight. God help me, I tried tae save ithers on the sloping deck. The masts were touching the waves an' Major Davidson ordered us tae jump an' row away like the devil ...' He stopped, caught up in the scene.

'The Major wis drowned, hundreds were lost. When a ship sinks it drags ye doon wi' it, but when we looked back, it wis still stuck there, low in the watter on its side. I have visions o' people hanging on tae the masts ... the folk in ma boat telt me I wis seein' things ... but it plagues me.' He cleared his throat. 'We were picked up by a merchantman, thank God. I found oot later we hit the Goodwin Sands an' were still close tae Deal, the port we left that morning.'

'Did ye gae back tae Deal then?'

'I wish we had. When we rowed awa' we headed east, out onto deep water. The Captain of the rescue vessel would nae gae near the Sands an' maintained his course east.'

Joe carried on filling the log basket. 'Ye've bin through some gie bad things in yer life, brither.'

'We all ha'e bad times. I put in fer a transfer from the 1st Battalion tae come north wi' the 2nd. We've bin in Scotland some time noo, recruiting in Dumfrieshire but I sought leave tae see ye all afore we get oor next marching orders.

'The 1st battalion is in Ireland and I'm takin' Roisin to her family o'er there and leaving her with them. If I'm killed, weel, fair enough, that's ma job, but when I saw paur wee Roisin suffering ... an' noo there's Connor tae think aboot. Naw, I'm leaving ma wife an' wean on dry land under her faither's roof.'

'Yer a braver man than me!'

Sam clapped him on the back and swung around to see the shed and hillside behind him. Their eyes were accustomed to the darkness and Sam insisted on walking the length of the pasture and looking back down the hill.

'This is a grand place. I tak it yer business is doing weel?'

'Weel enough tae repay ye.'

'Och mon! It wis a gift! But if ye insist, then ... when I next come back, eh? For then I plan tae leave the army and retire.' He gave a hearty chuckle, 'unless the Lord has ither plans fer me!'

Chapter Fourteen

"While Europe's eye is fix'd on mighty things,
The fate of empires and the fall of kings;
While quacks of State must each produce his plan,
And even children lisp the Rights of Man;
Amid this mighty fuss just let me mention,
The Rights of Woman merit some attention."

The Rights of Woman, Robert Burns (1792)

Jefferson's regulations to penalize Britain and France by outlawing trade with the United States quickly backfired.

Merchants and powerfully wealthy plantation owners across the States felt the loss far more keenly than the warring nations in Europe. His electorate were up in arms, baying for the restrictions to be removed, some of the States even convening meetings to seriously discuss leaving the Union.

The hiatus soon passed at New Lanark and Owen was able to view his order books with confidence. He was comfortable that the contracts were in place for consistent supplies from new countries, allowing him to deliver the finished goods as a competitive price.

Another challenge awaited him, this time on the domestic front.

Early in the year, Anne Caroline confirmed a new member of their brood was on the way. Cooper was unsuccessful in her efforts to find a trustworthy nursery maid to assist Peggy, but when this request was passed to Breen, in Glasgow, it bore fruit.

Dora Bell, an eager,cheery lass who was distantly related to Cook, was already learning her duties under Giggs' experienced eye and would be returning to New Lanark with the family for the summer. With four children in the family and now eight servants to squeeze into the little house, Owen set himself the task to find larger accommodation.

It was not only the amount of bodies under his roof which forced the issue; the reasons were mounting.

Since her father's death, Anne Caroline felt responsible for her younger sisters and wished they could stay with them in New Lanark. This not being possible, she tended to stay in Glasgow for longer in the winter and also visit Rosebank for weeks at a time through the summer months.

Owen wished to have his family around him and his wife at his side for entertaining. He was becoming well known in the area, recently accepting the honour of becoming a Dean of Guild in Lanark and he required to return hospitality to local Lords and Ladies, magistrates and Members of Parliament. The cramped little dining room in the village house was not an ideal venue.

When David Dale proposed to build New Lanark, he bought the piece of steep hillside for his mills from Mr McQueen: the eminent Judge, Lord Justice Braxfield.

Braxfield died in 1799, a few months before Owen travelled north to reside in New Lanark, and the extensive estate adjacent to the mills had been sitting virtually empty ever since.

Owen made enquiries of the current Lord Braxfield who sent an agent down from the city to give him a tour of the magnificent country house, stable yard and surrounding lawns and woodland. Clothed in dust sheets, many of the windows shuttered against the elements, it was a grand establishment and, anticipating his wife's appreciation of the architectural details and spacious interior, he offered to rent the whole estate.

Discussions took place and he eventually shook hands on the deal the day before leaving for Rosebank to collect his family for the summer.

Rumours spread like wild fire through the village, reaching Cooper's ears when she entered the Village Shop.

For the last few years, since the New Lanark Twist Company equipped and stocked the shop with good quality groceries and merchandise, the house keeper visited it regularly

'Guid day tae ye, Mrs Cooper,' Mr Niven, the aproned store keeper, smiled, 'We hope an' pray ye will still purchase supplies frae oor humble shelves when ye move up the brae tae the Big Hoose.'

Cooper looked askance. 'Whatever do you mean?'

Did they know she was seeking a new position and had heard of someone requiring her services?

'When yer up at Braxfield Hoose? Wi' Mr and Mrs Owen?'

'Braxfield House? The Judge's old house? What do you mean?'

'He's rented the big hoose! Did ye not know? It was yisterday he signed the papers, or so we've heard tell. Did he not say?'

'If this is indeed true,' Cooper raised her chin defiantly, 'Mr Owen will tell me in his own good time.'

Mr Niven's moon face beamed, his cheeks standing out like rosy apples. 'He's bin tha' guid tae us and is alis coming in tae see how the shop is running, making wee suggestions aboot stock and having yon big store rooms built.' He drew breath before winking cheerily, 'My, but ye'll have yer hauns full runnin' tha' muckle hoose!'

Cooper often found his exuberant, over familiar manner difficult but managed a tight smile, 'Half a pound of butter, if you please, and four ounces of saleratus.'

Mr Niven prattled on about his memories of the late, despised Judge Braxfield, all the while weighing out a large pat of butter and wrapping it carefully in greased brown paper.

'The wife's brither wis a footman up by, aw, the stories he wid tell! Years ago, mind,' he laid a new sheet of paper on the scales, corrected the weights and then poured white baking soda up to four ounces before neatly twisting the paper into a packet. 'His Lordship wid tak a glass o' spirits as soon as he awoke in the morn and wis hardly e'er sober. A man of fiery temper!'

Cooper made no comment, paid for her articles, dropped them in her basket and hurried away, politely murmuring her thanks.

To be the housekeeper of a prestigious country house like Braxfield would elevate her position considerably. However, it also held enormous responsibilities and the prospect of at least double the number of servants to organise. Was she capable of commanding such a household? The maids already viewed her with contempt and regardless of how hard she tried, or how fervently she prayed for guidance, she remained on the outside: friendless, ridiculed and lonely.

Since starting her search, she soon found there was a dearth of alternative positions open to her, which she blamed on being the wrong side of forty and also that few people sought to expand their households while the country was afflicted by the uncertainties and financial depression of the war. Yet, no matter how improbable it might be in reality, Cooper comforted herself throughout the winter with the thought of this escape route from her unhappy life.

A few days later, Anne Caroline arrived in New Lanark filled with excited anticipation. As soon as she was refreshed after the journey from Rosebank, Owen took her to see their new home.

'I have passed this Lodge a hundred times and wondered where the driveway led,' she cried, sitting forward in the carriage to see as much as possible of the unfolding avenue. 'We are so close to the mills!'

'I walked up to the house when I met the agent here and it takes no time at all. I hope you will approve. It meets our every requirement for space. The location is perfect and look! Tell me what you think of your first impression?'

'Oh, goodness, my dear,' glimpses of white rendered walls rising to crow-step gables appeared tantalisingly through the over-hanging boughs of budding beech trees. 'It is very large ... imposing!'

After the last corner, Braxfield House sat boldly before them, its smooth exterior displaying two symmetrical lines of tall, stone framed windows and an ornately carved portico above the front door. Additional wings ran off to merge with a stable yard in the back ground.

They were met by one of the present Lord Braxfield's servants who welcomed them into the lofty hall, suggesting they take a tour of the rooms at their leisure. At every turn, Anne Caroline was delighted by the accommodation, noting the elaborate plaster cornices, large fireplaces, tall, low-silled sash windows and plenty of well appointed bedrooms for their expanding family, as well as guest rooms for her sisters.

The original house was over two hundred years old but within the last century it had been extended in every direction and fitted out with the latest conveniences, including the provision of dressing rooms beside the master bedroom.

They stood by the window in the room which would be the nursery and looked down on the lawns at the side of the house, surrounded by mature oak and beech trees.

'It is charming.' Anne Caroline squeezed her husband's arm. 'I cannot see how you could have found us a better home! It is wonderfully fortunate that it is available to rent for there are no other houses of this size and comfort close to the mills.'

'I hardly dared hope myself! We can take possession of the keys within the month but Lord Braxfield has only offered us the outside staff and two footmen within the rent so we will require to hire senior servants which may take longer.'

'We will attend to that at once! Oh, there is so much to plan and arrange but, oh Robert! I am very content with this beautiful home to raise our children.'

Before leaving, they descended the back stairs and glanced briefly into the servants' hall, seeing the butler's pantry, housekeeper's sitting room and beyond them, the kitchen. Through a long, narrow window set high in the wall, late afternoon sun threw streaks of light onto a massive black range and showed the ceiling to be hanging with empty hooks where hams, pheasants and bunches of herbs once hung.

'The servants' sleeping quarters are in the wings to the rear,' Owen told her, his voice echoing around empty stone walls. 'Lord Braxfield ran a large household so I am sure we will all fit in here with ease.'

It was cold in these lower apartments, the north and west facing windows much smaller, many of them barred. Bare walled corridors held lines of doors opening off into the scullery, boot rooms, storerooms and laundry.

Seeing his wife shiver, Owen guided her up stairs again.

'You must be fatigued after the drive from Cambuslang, my dearest,' he said with concern, aware of the extra strain on her due to being halfway through her pregnancy. 'Perhaps it was too much to ask to bring you here straight away but I was so looking forward to showing you everything.'

'I do not regret it for a moment!'

They stepped out into the high, light filled hall, their footsteps and words muffled by wall hangings, rugs and sumptuous curtains.

'I will write to Lady Mary Honyman for this was her childhood home, as she has told me several times.'

Now out on the gravel in the fresh air, Owen helped her into the carriage, taking an appraising look back at the house.

'Ah yes! A judge's daughter became a judge's wife! However, from my brief knowledge of Honyman, Lord Armadale, he is a benign and good man, unlike her father.'

'You should not speak ill of the dead.' Anne Caroline quietly chastised, 'may Lord Braxfield be granted redemption for his sins by Our Lord God.'

The coachman glanced down to watch Owen climb safely aboard, noticing his master did not comment on his wife's admonishment.

He was glad: Braxfield was generally loathed by the ordinary or fair minded people of Clydesdale. He flicked the reins, sending the horses on their way. Privately, he hoped the great, uncouth bear of a man was suffering eternal damnation in the flames of Hell for cruelly sending men to the gallows or to the ends of the earth away from their families for even the slightest crime.

It was the next morning before Cooper was called to the parlour by her mistress.

'Cooper,' Anne Caroline smiled at the nervous housekeeper. 'As you may be aware, Mr Owen has arranged for us to stay at Braxfield House. This does not mean we will be abandoning our home here, not at all, Mr Owen will be requiring it to be maintained for his occasional use and is keen for us all, as a family, to return to the centre of the village from time to time.'

Cooper narrowed her troubled, dark shadowed eyes: two houses to supervise?

'I understand that recently you have been finding your duties here burdensome?' Anne Caroline continued, giving a little laugh. 'Our family continues to grow and I can completely understand if you still wish to leave, you are assured of an excellent reference, but I hope you will consider staying on and keeping this house in good order?'

Incensed by Toshie's obvious betrayal, Cooper tried to remain calm, digging her finger nails into her clasped hands.

'That is very generous of you, Madam. Do you require to know immediately?'

'Oh no, by the end of the week would be sufficient. I will be engaging new servants for Braxfield, it requires a much larger household and with the comings and goings and the children becoming ever more active and boisterous, I realise it would not suit you at all.' Anne Caroline handed her some letters. 'Please see these are dispatched directly. Thank you, Cooper.'

The last words were said firmly, dismissively.

Toshie was in the kitchen, folding baby clothes into a neat pile.

'What did you say to the Mistress?' Cooper hissed, rustling into the kitchen, her mouth pinched into a lipless line. 'I asked you not to mention anything of my thoughts of leaving this position!'

The outburst was not unexpected and Toshie was prepared.

'Mrs Owen was talking aboot ye moving tae the big hoose wi' them an' Ah might ha'e mentioned something aboot ye saying how ye wanted tae gae back tae being a cook ...'

'You might have mentioned? I think you must have said a good deal more than that!' Smarting with rage, her hands trembling, Cooper paced around the kitchen. 'So, you are all off up the hill and I will be left here.'

'Ye said ye were leaving the joab! Din nae blame me fer yer ane choice!'

'You don't understand ...' an unstoppable urge to burst into tears was rising inside her. 'I asked you to keep that confidential and now ... now!' she caught at her skirts and rushed for the stairs.

Toshie shrugged, picking up one of Master Robert's night shirts and giving it a good shake. True, she should not have broken a confidence but on finding Cooper was still at New Lanark and her mistress planned to install her in the new mansion, she felt she must speak out. None of the servants liked her and most thought her 'touched'. Having her as head of the household in Braxfield was a dreadful prospect but one easily avoided by divulging a few facts to her employer.

Behind her bolted door, Cooper knelt by her bed and prayed. She was overwhelmed by memories of how low and depressed she used to feel throughout the long months when Mr Dale lived in Glasgow: the silent house, days of not speaking to another human being. Was this going to be repeated? While Alice, Senga and Ena enjoyed the chatter of the servants' hall, was she to be cast aside and left here, alone?

Pent up tears trickled down her cheeks and it was a long time before she gained enough control to realise there was no option.

Loneliness in comfort or no roof over her head with the spectre of the Poor House looming in her future?

There was only one path to choose.

***

Two weeks before the family moved up to Braxfield House, Owen confirmed the appointment of a butler, William Sheddon, a smart, respectful man in his early forties, and the new housekeeper, Miss Wilson. These senior members of the household came with personal recommendations and trustworthy testimonials and took up residence straight away. Having never met before, they set about their task of making all the necessary arrangements to prepare for the Owen family's arrival.

'Our first night under this roof! Oh, it has been such an adventure. I think I will sleep from the moment I lay my head upon the pillow!' Anne Caroline laughed, sitting at the dressing table while Toshie brushed her hair.

It was a warm evening, a slight breeze wafting the curtains drawn closed over the windows, letting the cool air in and keeping the moths and midges out. Anne Caroline was wearing her favourite yellow silk night gown, its thin straps leaving her arms bare and allowing the generously cut fabric to hang loosely over the growing baby.

'Aye, an' Master Robert and Master William too! They must have run aroond the gardens a' efternoon!' Toshie agreed, watching her mistress's happy face reflected in the mirror.

'Have you ever seen the children so excited? I do believe even little Anne understands this is her new home.'

314

Toshie laid down the brush, running her hand down her mistress's long waves of silken brown hair.

'Is that everything fer you this eve, Ma'am?'

'Thank you, yes,' Anne Caroline picked up her silver covered bible and turned it in her hand, smoothing a finger over her initials which were engraved on the front plate. 'I pray we will be happy here, all of us, the servants as well. You and I have been together in many new places, have we not, Toshie?'

'Aye, Ma'am, we have.'

'You remember the house in Manchester? Greenheyes? It was pleasant enough, but I was so far away from Papa,' she looked up, 'I believe Papa would approve of this house. Certainly the gardens! Oh how he enjoyed his garden at Rosebank!'

'He did that.'

Although bone tired, Toshie listened to Anne Caroline while noticing little gestures, the turn of her head, intonations in her speech, the way she slightly frowned when emphasising a point. It could have been her late mother, Carolina, rising from the tapestry covered stool, bible in hand, mulling over her thoughts before climbing into bed.

The memories and similarities were poignantly strong; twenty years on.

'One last thing, Toshie. You hear what the servants and villagers are saying? Am I being naive or is there a different, warmer attitude towards my husband these days?'

'Ye'r quite correct. E'er since the winter an' the closures an' the like, Ah've seen it mesel'. They've taken Mr Owen in tae their hairts.'

Anne Caroline smiled, resting back into the mound of freshly laundered eider duck down pillows.

'At last, after all these years. Bless you, Toshie, good night.'

Owen was delighted with Braxfield House. Within a few weeks, family and servants were so settled within the estate that it was hard to imagine how they managed in the village house.

His domestic affairs running smoothly and the mills back in full operation, he turned his attention to new projects. Uppermost in his mind were improvements to the school and he spent hours pacing out areas in the village, looking for pieces of land suitable to construct a building large enough to hold the village pupils.

'I have it!' he told Humphreys and Logan one day. 'There are two places where it would be possiblc to level the ground sufficiently. Come! I will show you.'

Grey clouds threatened rain and the men reluctantly left the office fireside and donned their hats and jackets. Owen's enthusiasm was contagious and soon they were walking back and forth viewing the proposed building sites, trying to grasp Owen's imaginings.

'Sae yin building is here, on the riverside, beside Mill Four,' Logan stood at the top of the steep bank, kicking a pebble over the edge to watch it bounce and roll down to the wagon track below.

'Exactly!' Owen cried. 'It would be constructed in the same manner and style as the rest of the village, its basement being cut into the hillside and its entrance opening onto this road leading to the Mechanics' workshop.' Owen waved his arms expansively. 'There's plenty of room and it would also have kitchens and dining halls for the whole village.'

Humphreys nodded, thoughtfully, eyeing the space between the mill lade and the edge of the drop to the river.

'And over on this side ...' Owen marched smartly across the footbridge to the grassy bank beneath Caithness Row. 'Here, there is ample room for an institution to progress the formation of character of the children.'

Logan wandered around the hillside. 'It would take a devil of a lot of earth tae be dug oot frae here.'

'I daresay it would, but Gentlemen, look around you at the magnificent buildings already rising from this difficult plot of land. This is no harder task.'

'Sae which site dae ye favour, Mr Owen?' Logan asked.

'Both! The more I consider the matter, the clearer the plans become. I have wished to do this since taking charge and now, with the problem of cotton supply on an even keel, our order books are full and the mills are running to full production. Now is the time!'

Invigorated, Owen penned a long letter to his senior partners, seeking their approval for the costs of the new buildings.

'Oh, it is too bad!' he declared to his wife some days later, hot with frustration on reading their reply.

'Are they refusing outright?' she asked.

316

'Not in so many words, but they are definitely not agreeing to allow the project to continue until they have seen first-hand what I have already explained, perfectly adequately, on paper.'

'Well then, when you show them how it will enhance and benefit the village, you will gain their support.'

'They tell me that they do not plan to travel to Scotland until next year! It really is too bad!'

One of the most endearing facets of Owen's character was his lack of moodiness. He was invariably even-tempered and pleasant and although he could speak passionately on a subject or vent a sudden burst of irritation, he did not carry bad feeling or anger with him or inflict it on those around him.

Anne Caroline murmured some comforting words and returned to the letter she was writing to her sisters, inviting them to stay at Braxfield House.

***

Every Sunday, Sarah dressed herself and her children in their best clothes and joined the procession of villagers on the path to Lanark to attend church.

After a bitter battle of wills, Stephen was now working in the mills but was still surly and loutish, especially to his mother. A routine became established whereby Sarah called in at Joe's after church and Cal would meet her there to join the family for a meal.

Fiona enjoyed these occasions, ensuring there was meat on the table and a sufficient quantity of vegetables to allow everyone to eat their fill. She was sure they existed solely on bowls of oats or barley stew from one week to the next and took it upon herself to supplement their meagre diet by providing wholesome food without appearing to flaunt her own growing prosperity.

Joe was rarely short of work these days and now employed Donnie formally as his apprentice. Davey laboured beside them but he wanted to be a joiner and enquiries were being made to apprentice him to a trustworthy woodworker. Surprisingly, on turning ten years old in the spring, their third son, Robert, chose to go into the mills having made friends in the schoolroom with the son of a weaver.

317

'Ah ken it's rough tae stairt wi',' he told Joe and Fiona solemnly, 'but it pays weel in the end an' Ah want tae earn fer the hoose.'

The Scotts soon found themselves in the fortunate position of being able to buy a horse and cart. After weeks of spending every spare moment hard at work with his elder sons, the shed at the back of the house was repaired and extended to become a stable and workshop.

Joe enlisted Cal's help in buying a suitable beast and they inspected several local horses. Most were either too flighty or too aged until they returned one blustery evening with Rusty, a shaggy-legged Highland pony.

Rusty's owner had died and she was being sold by the widow as a job lot with a small wagon and all the harness. This made her more expensive than Joe would have wished but her biddable nature and Cal's confident decision that she was right for the job, sealed the deal. The strong, dark eyed pony was immediately adored by all the children who clamoured to pat her, feed her and plead with Cal to show them how to groom her golden coat and black mane and tail.

Even Sionaidh, who rarely joined in with her brothers and sisters, tentatively stroked Rusty's soft muzzle, a contented smile on her lips.

The first Sunday after Rusty arrived, Joe looked out at promising blue sky and suggested they take a drive 'doon the valley'. With cries of delight at this novelty, everyone scrambled to dress and with Joe and Fiona on the driving seat and the children crowded into the wagon behind them, they set off.

'We could ca' by the wee shop in Kirkfieldbank fer some parleys,' Fiona suggested, 'it's no' tha' far wi' a horse?'

The sun warmed their faces and dried the ripening crops on either side of the road from Castlebank towards Kirkfieldbank, where they would cross the river at Clydesholm bridge. The children burst into song, waving to passers by and giggling at the unaccustomed speed of the hedgerows whisking past.

'Whit a grand pony!' Joe shouted over the clattering hooves, rolling metal wheels and his childrens' lively singing.

Fiona grinned, gripping the seat and bouncing happily beside her husband. She was enjoying the views, squinting against the sudden flashes of brilliant sunshine as they rushed along under an avenue of trees.

'Da! Stoap!' Donnie's screams cut through the laughter. 'Stoap! Mam! There's summat wrang wi' Sionaidh!'

Joe hauled on the reins, shouting to the pony to 'whoa' as Fiona twisted round to see Sionaidh lying in the middle of the wagon, the others clustered over her.

Her body was writhing and twisting, jerking this way and that, suddenly arching up and then shaking violently.

'Whit's the matter wi' her?' Davey cried. 'She let oot a great cry and then jist toppled o'er!'

Donnie ran to take hold of Rusty, alarmed by the sight.

'Git aff the wagon,'Fiona told the others. 'Gie us space!'

Together, Joe and Fiona knelt on either side of their daughter, trying to hold her down, keep her from banging her head and hitting herself, or them, with her thrashing limbs.

After several agonising minutes, she began to relax, her head lolling, dribbling, until she lay still, floppy in their arms.

No one spoke.

Aware of their children watching them intently, the terrified parents held back their own anguish, breathing heavily, staring down at the child between them.

'We ha'e tae gae hame.' Fiona whispered, giving Joe a meaningful look. 'She's wet hersel'...'

Sionaidh moaned, curling up on her side and covering her head with her hands.

'It's alricht, ma wee angel,' Fiona murmured, drawing her into her arms in the corner of the wagon. 'Yer alricht noo.'

The older boys chose to walk, deeply shocked and worried for their sister. Ailsa sat up beside her father with a protective arm around little Thomas. She was stunned, mimicking her mother's reassuring tones to calm her little brother.

It was a subdued and frightened family who wound their way slowly back to their cottage. Suddenly, the scents of honeysuckle, cows snuffling over gate posts and the striking views of Clydesdale, all so appealing minutes before, became worthless, irrelevant.

Fiona gazed on Sionaidh's peaceful sleeping face. It stirred memories of a winter's eve in her childhood, a girl writhing on the floor, spittle foaming from her mouth, her head rapidly striking the mud floor. Thud, thud, thud, she kept recalling the rapid sound.

Who was it? Her cousin? Her aunt? The mental images floated in and out of focus. It was Jinty! What happened to her cousin Jinty? She wasn't with them on the trek to Glasgow. Fiona concentrated hard then choked back a sob: Jinty wasn't with them because she died before the soldiers cleared them off the land.

Fiona was adamant that she did not want Joe to fetch the New Lanark doctor. He had never seen such terror in her eyes before and did not press her for an explanation until they were alone.

She told him about Jinty, becoming tearful with the memories, then reached for his hand.

'Joe, Ah minded whit they said aboot Jinty, an' we can nae ha'e that wi' oor wee lass. They said she was possessed by the De'il, that her shakin' could be passed tae ithers an' she should be put awa' frae the village, cast oot! Ma mither an' aunt wid ha'e none of it, but they had tae keep the paur chiel hidden.' Fiona's eyes rippled with tears,'some called her a *buidseach,* a witch.'

He put his arm around her and hugged her close.

'No body's gaun tae tak oor lass awa', din nae fret, ma darling. She's sleepin' an' quiet noo an' mibbee it'll ne'er happen agin.'

Sniffing, Fiona tried to pull herself together. 'We ken there's summat wrang wi' her. We all ken she's different frae the ithers, no' bletherin' or playing wi' the ithers ... but she's ne'er bin ill afore.'

'Aye, she's a healthy chiel and let's pray this is the first an' last time she takes sich a fit.'

They held each other for some time, drawing strength from sharing their fears and knowing the other was there to give comfort.

By the next morning, Sionaidh appeared to be back to normal and Fiona decided she could take her to the school room as usual.

'Mind now,' Fiona told Ailsa before they reached the foot of the steps into the village. 'Din nae say a word aboot Sionaidh takin' a turn. Not a word!'

'Even tae Mrs Young?'

'Not tae ony yin! Unnerstaun?'

Ailsa nodded, 'Sionaidh's alricht noo.'

'Aye, she's alricht, sae, no' a word!'

***

Anne Caroline thoroughly enjoyed having her sisters to stay. They were enthusiastic in their admiration of Braxfield House and equally complimentary regarding the clean streets and perfectly ordered mill buildings in the village. Local gentry were invited to dinner parties which resulted in reciprocal invitations, taking the four eligible Miss Dales into a new social circle. Too quickly, the visit came to an end but Anne Caroline waved them away knowing they would all soon be reunited at Charlotte Street. This was a bittersweet thought because it reminded her of how quickly her next confinement was approaching.

One morning, Owen was surprised to receive a letter from his brother, William.

'Well, would you believe it!' he cried, handing the letter to his wife. 'William has returned to Wales and married again!'

'I thought he was already married?' Anne Caroline quickly read the contents. 'Goodness! He writes of his first wife's death and his new bride in the same letter.' She looked up, puzzled. 'It is a shame that you and your brother do not keep in closer contact for I see here that his late wife actually died three years ago, so, it is perfectly respectful for him to have taken a second wife.'

'I have met this lady, Dinah Davis,' Owen said thoughtfully, recalling the manager of his father's ironmongery store and his attractive young wife. 'As he says, she is a widow with two young children. Her husband was my father's shop manager, not much older than I am myself, how sad. He seemed to be a genuinely nice fellow.'

Anne Caroline finished reading the letter, saying, 'Well, from all you have told me about the little market town of Newtown, it is much like Lanark so I daresay he will find it very different living there after London.'

'If you note his last lines, he does not sound settled after selling up and making the move north. I wish him well, whatever he plans to do.'

Owen went straight to his study and replied to William, congratulating him on his marriage but his mind was caught up with the mills.

Issues were, once again, erupting between the company and the Miss Edmonstones at Corehouse regarding the weir.

Legal advice was sought and he spent several tiresome meetings with his lawyer trying to resolve the matter. The weir was proving vital to maintain a continuous flow for the water-wheels but there was ongoing trespass on Corehouse estate and the blame was being laid on the villagers. Unfortunately, several ugly scenes ensued, with some of his employees pelting Corehouse workers with stones and even threatening to open the dam and drown them.

Owen called a meeting of his managers and reiterated his orders to instruct the villagers to abide by the law.

'In all, the community is far more moral and respectful than when I took over,' he said to Humphreys one afternoon in the office. 'Yet, there is still a number who are so ingrained with bad habits, taught to them, no doubt, by their parents and older siblings, that they continue to disregard the law.'

Humphreys reached for the record book of misdemeanours.

'There's a steady decrease in stealing from the work place, although it is by no means stamped out.' He licked his fingers and turned pages. 'Drunkenness is slowly being reformed and swearing or causing disturbance is greatly reduced, although it still appears here almost every week.'

'Compared to when the records began? It is greatly improved.' Owen sighed, watching the clouds scudding across the sky beyond the window. Autumn leaves drifted in the air, the wind droning in the chimney. 'I am returning to Glasgow on Friday and expect to stay there for at least a week. Please ensure the Street Inspectors keep their eyes open and make sure they patrol the furthest reaches of the village. We cannot afford to have the Corehouse estate manager knocking on our door again while we deal with this delicate issue.'

After coping with the frustrations of the Edmonstones and his Manchester partners, Owen was looking forward to spending time with progressive thinking gentlemen in the city.

Anne Caroline was pleased to be in the care of her usual physician in Glasgow when she went into labour. It took away a little of the fear of child birth but none of the pain.

Breen sent out for Mr Palmer early in the morning, even before the fires were lit and the household spent the day holding their breath and waiting for news. It was late afternoon, with the shutters closed and chandeliers glowing, before they could rejoice at the first bleating cries reported from the upper landing.

The new baby was a boy and when Owen announced the name, David Dale Owen, it brought tears of joy to servants and family alike.

'What other name could possibly be chosen?' Owen hugged his wife in the privacy of their own bedchamber. 'Your father will always be remembered for himself. His strong character and good hearted philanthropy will live forever in the hearts of the Scottish people. Our son will be his own man, however, he can bear the name with pride.'

After a visit from her sisters, with baby David lying asleep in her arms, Anne Caroline closed her eyes, replaying the scene following Jane's birth, three years before.

It was as clear as if it happened that evening.

She looked again on her father's beloved face, felt the pressure of his hand around hers and heard his deep, rolling Ayrshire voice praying at her bedside. Their quiet time together ended with them both reciting the Lord's Prayer and she murmured the words softly to her son adding a whispered, 'God bless you, my dearest Papa.'

Chapter Fifteen

"I prefer liberty with danger to peace with slavery."
Jean Jacques Rousseau

In the furthest north-west tip of Spain, the Cameronians were among the outnumbered, cornered British soldiers fleeing for their lives.

From their positions in Elvina, a tiny village above Corunna, Sam and his rifle regiment were desperately trying to hold the French at bay. Behind them, on the coast, wounded and dying men and scores of the regiments' terrified wives and children were frantically embarking onto transport ships. The line of red-coats had to be maintained while the evacuation took place.

Swirling snowstorms blanketed the mountains, sending a bitterly cold wind whining through the village streets. Rations were long since finished, disease and injuries plagued the forces on both sides but the battle continued. The French were winning under the brilliant strategist Marshall Soult, there was no doubt of that. All that remained was for the British, nearly thirty thousand of them, to retreat to their ships with as few losses as possible.

Acting as the rear guard, the Cameronians lined up beside the Perthshire 90th Light Infantry under Sir Thomas Graham. Their fast firing and accurate marksmanship keeping the enemy pinned down in the foothills.

After a vicious exchange, Sam signalled to his men to take refuge in the lee of a barn, throwing themselves down into the banks of icy snow, rapidly adjusting straps with frozen fingers, checking gunpowder and reloading.

'They can nae move the canon through the snow drifts!' he shouted above the deafening sound of gunfire.

'Mibbee naw ... but they're too damn near a'ready!'

'Anither half hour an' it'll be dark ...'

A trumpet sounded for the next attack and they scrambled to their feet, sliding and slipping, hearts pounding, the stench of sulphur in their nostrils.

Flashes of fire exploded from the enemy lines, sending canon balls raining down just yards infront of them.

Suddenly, there was a commotion to Sam's left: Sir John Moore, the army commander, was being carried away from the front line accompanied by the heavy, older figure of Colonel Graham stumbling and running at his side.

'Moore's been hit!' someone yelled.

'All the mair reason tae fight on!' Sam bellowed down the lines. 'Follow his last orders ... hold the line! Load, aim, fire! Load, aim, fire!' Sam's voice was hoarse and rasping.

A further frenzied hour ensued until it was no longer possible to tell friend from foe, all light having disappeared behind the dense snow clouds smothering the sky. Under cover of this natural darkness, Sam gathered with the rest of the regiment to receive their orders, their breath rising in a cloud in the freezing air.

They were to march to Corunna immediately and board any vessel with space.

'Sir,' Sam asked, 'Permission to ask the condition of the Commander?'

Colonel Graham's chin jutted forward, snow catching on his stubbly chin.

'God rest his soul! Sir John Moore succumbed to his wounds. A great man and a terrible loss to our country. Take heart!' The older man's eyes glistened with emotion as he gazed over the assembled soldiers, ragged and exhausted, soaked in the falling snow. 'He knew you held off the French! He knew the enemies' guns fell silent before ours! Well done all! Now! To the ships and we will finish this fight another day!'

***

As often happened in Scotland, an early, mild spring suddenly gave way to freezing temperatures and a bitter blast of snow from the north. Anne Caroline and her children did not return to Braxfield until April, frustrated at being denied the pleasure of their new country house for much longer than intended.

'Are ye all right, Toshie?' Miss Wilson asked with concern. The lady's maid was hunched in her chair at Braxfield's kitchen table, rubbing her hands together as if she was cold. She raised her bowed head, a perplexed expression deepening the lines around her mouth.

'Ah'd be fibbing if Ah telt ye Ah wis,' she gave a long sigh. 'Ah've no' bin feeling sae weel an' noo ma hauns are aching like the blazes. Ah'm jist auld an' done.'

Miss Wilson, with not yet forty years behind her, laid a comforting hand on the older woman's shoulder.

'Shall I ask the physician to call. Perhaps a tonic and maybe some ointment for your hands?' She placed the kettle on the range. 'We will share a pot of tea. It is earlier than usual and Cook is still having her afternoon rest but, why not, eh?'

Miss Wilson and Sheddon, the butler, were genial, well-organized and very experienced in their responsibilities. They demanded no more from the servants under their command than could be expected in any efficiently managed house, although neither of them suffered fools or malingerers.

Consequently, the Owen servants took smoothly to the new regime at Braxfield, finding Miss Wilson's cordial nature a welcome relief after Cooper.

'Tea wid be very nice, thank ye, Miss Wilson. Ye see, Ah'd bin ready tae tell the mistress that Ah thocht it wis time fer me tae leave. Ah'm findin' it awfy hard these days, an' all the stairs here an' in Glesgie, up an' doon, up an' doon.'

'These are unforgiving steps,' Miss Wilson sympathised. 'I feel it in my knees myself.'

'Weel, wi' wee Master David thriving, Ah pulled ma wits aroond me tae say something an' then she finds herself wi' anither bairn on the way.'

'Oh dear,' Miss Wilson murmured, understandingly. The pregnancy was still in the early stages and few knew of the mistress's delicate condition.

'How can Ah leave her noo?' Toshie cried. 'Ah've attended her fer every delivery an' her mother, the dear Mrs Dale, afore her. God rest her soul.'

The housekeeper slipped into the larder and returned with a plate of shortbread.

'I think this is the best time to broach the subject,' she said slowly, laying cups on the table. 'The baby is due in about six months, is it not?'

'So we believe.'

'Why not have a word with the mistress now and suggest you leave after the baby is born?'

Toshie rubbed at her shiny, swollen knuckles, 'Ah may dae tha'. Aye. It wid nae be sae sudden fer her.'

'And can you manage for another few months?'

'Oh, aye. Ah dread the day Ah have tae leave but if Ah can nae dae ma joab, weel ...'

'I do not wish to pry and you need not disclose your private affairs to me, but I am assuming you will be awarded a stipend.'

'That's richt. Ah'm indebted tae the late Mr Dale for having already made arrangements fer me. Ah've a younger sister in Ayr an' plan tae live oot ma days o'er there, by the sea.' she gave a little laugh. 'Ye ken, Ah made yon plans mony years ago, never expectin' the time wid come.' She glanced up to meet Miss Wilson's gentle gaze. 'It seems the time is nearly here.'

'Well, when the time comes, I'm sure you will be sorely missed by us all.'

'Ye're very kind. Ah'm glad ye're here tae care fer ma lady, she's as dear tae me as if she were ma ane bairn.'

Miss Wilson's caring nature was also appreciated by the Owen children for the homely comforts she provided especially for them.

Their father prescribed their meals, instructing them to be kept simple and nourishing, just as he preferred for himself. However, Miss Wilson persuaded her employers to allow her to invite the children to a tea party on a Sunday afternoon, to be taken in her parlour.

The housekeeper's sitting room was below stairs beside the servants' hall and every week she made much of welcoming Robert, William and Ann into her private domain and settling them around a little table. Then, with an almost conspiratorial air, she would present toast, little cups of sweet tea and sugared biscuits.

Robert was a spirited boy, always up to some adventure, imagined or otherwise and, along with William, explored every inch of Braxfield's expansive estate. Tutors visited the house for daily lessons and Anne Caroline insisted on them attending morning and evening prayers, with Sunday devoted entirely to religious studies. However, the boys took full advantage of every moment when they were not under these restrictions.

'I see the boys have a new game!' Owen said, standing at the drawing room window and watching his sons playing on the lawn.

'Yes,' Anne Caroline went to stand beside him. 'I understand our nice postman brought them clay pipes the other day as a present and they have spent hours perfecting the mixture of soap and water to blow the best bubbles.'

'Such innocent pleasures,' Owen murmured, smiling. 'See how delighted they are amusing themselves. Children will find fascination in everything.'

'The boys seem to be almost constantly outside! And when it is very wet they play hide and seek and read books up in the attics. They love the countryside, even from when they were infants at Rosebank they liked to be in the garden.'

'Ah, Rosebank, that reminds me. I have been making enquiries of friends who own houses in London,' Owen gazed out of the window while he spoke. 'Do you remember we discussed the possibility of your sisters going down to London for the Season?'

'Why, yes, I do ... but the season is nearly over now.'

'For this year, yes, but I felt it would be easier for them to travel so far from the family if they made their host's acquaintance over the winter in Glasgow. Do you not agree?'

Anne Caroline slipped her hand into his, kissing his cheek. 'How do you find time to think of these things? Dear Robert, you are such a good brother to them.'

'I am sure your father would have made the same arrangements.'

'Oh, I doubt if the London Season would have been acceptable!' she spoke lightly, teasing. 'You know how much he wished I would marry a Scot. The thought of English, or, gracious me, *foreign* gentlemen partnering his daughters at a ball may not have been approved!'

'The people I know are very reputable, they would take the greatest care of the girls.'

'Then it is an excellent idea! I shall write to them this evening and we will have much to discuss throughout the winter months, ready for their Spring adventure,' she gave him another peck on the cheek.

Owen returned her affectionate gesture by kissing the curls of her carefully styled fringe, his eyes twinkling.

Early one morning, a few days later, Owen sat at his desk in the study writing to Dr Donne of Oswestry, a friend since childhood. Ever since the carefree days of their country rambles in Wales, Owen enjoyed their regular correspondence, especially in relaying sightings of new plants or wild birds at his Scottish home. The solid country mansion was peaceful, the silence only disturbed by the occasional distant clink from where Senga and a footman were laying fires and replenishing log baskets.

Suddenly, there were hurried footsteps crossing the hall and a sharp knock at his door.

'Sir,' Sheddon appeared, striving to control his alarm. 'There has been an incident. Master Robert, sir.'

Owen jumped to his feet, 'Robert! Is he all right? What has happened?'

'Master Robert is quite unharmed. It is Miss Wilson who has been injured, sir, it appears that Master Robert hit her on the head with a broom.'

'Good grief! Is Miss Wilson badly hurt? Where are they?'

'In the shoe hole in the courtyard.'

Together, the men rushed to the scene, hearing Robert's screams long before they saw him. Peggy was guiding the hysterical child across the yard, unable to make any sense of the matter.

Miss Wilson, her white lace cap scarlet with blood, recovered enough to be helped to her room where Toshie took charge.

Everyone was aghast, why would Master Robert attack sweet little Miss Wilson? And what were they both doing in the shoe hole at all, never mind so early in the morning?

Anne Caroline could not believe the news and burst into tears from the upset and distress that a child of hers could be so wicked.

Eventually, the story came out.

Sandy, the boot boy, deliberately broke Robert's prize clay pipe, given to him by Mr Dunn, the post man, for making soap bubbles. It appeared Sandy was known to be a nasty piece of work, bullying the Owen boys and ridiculing Dunn because he only had one arm following an accident in the mills.

The breaking of the pipe proved to be the last straw for little Robert and he sought revenge by stealing down to the shoe hole, where Sandy was supposed to arrive to work. There, he lay in wait for him with the heavy broom.

Unfortunately, Sandy was late for his duties that day and it was Miss Wilson who opened the door and received the mighty blow to her head.

Robert was inconsolable. He loved Miss Wilson and was appalled by his actions.

More sorrowful than angry, Owen told him to be thankful it was not Sandy who received the blow, for it would probably have killed the boy.

'Are you sorry for what you have done, Robert?' he asked.

'I am very *very* sorry I have hurt Miss Wilson!' the child sobbed, 'Please let me tell her so.'

'I am going to take you to ask her pardon. But it's of no use to be sorry unless you do better. Remember this! I have never struck you. You must never strike anybody.'

Owen took his bereft son to the housekeeper's room where they found her sitting in her armchair with a bandage around her head.

Robert flung himself into her arms, pleading forgiveness with such fervour that Owen asked if he should take the child away.

'No, no ... please,' Miss Wilson hugged him against her. 'Leave him be. We will be just fine here, sir'

When Owen returned to the library, Anne Caroline looked up nervously from her chair by the window, the harsh white daylight accentuating her red eyes.

'Where is Robert?'

'He is making peace with the poor woman. She has a good heart and has readily forgiven him. I hope he has learned his lesson.'

About a month later, Sandy was quietly dismissed.

***

'The foundations can easily be accommodated here!' Owen declared, enthusiasm bubbling in his words.

The senior partners of the New Lanark Twist Company strode around the open ground below Nursery Buildings, beside the mill lade. After much prevarication, they had finally arrived to make an inspection of Owen's latest plans.

'So, let me see if I understand you' Mr Barton enquired, 'you would arrive at the New Lanark Mills and find ... a school?'

'It would be much more than a school, it would be an Institution for the formation of the character, open to all the villagers.'

'I thought your plans were for a school, Mr Owen?' Mr Barton pressed. 'And I believe a public kitchen was mentioned in your last letter? And now you talk of an 'Institution'. I am bewildered! What say you, Mr Atkinson?'

Mr Atkinson stroked his beard and held his counsel.

Owen looked expectantly from one to the other, their clerk, standing to one side, looked down at his polished boots, now caked with mud.

'Gentlemen, this is one of the sites which I propose developing and over there,' he pointed to the space beyond Mill Four, 'is the second.'

The party trooped down the slope of slippery grass below Caithness Row and crossed the little bridge over the lade.

Taking up a stance with his back to the steep drop to the river bed, Owen spread his arms wide.

'This is where the school will be built. It will house sufficient space for kitchens and dining halls to feed all the employees! Think of the savings, gentlemen! In preparation time as well as the considerable discount we can demand for buying in bulk. I speak from experience for we can see this system works admirably well when we purchase products for the orphans in Nursery Buildings and also to retail through the Village Store.'

'Good Lord, man, we are cotton merchants!' exclaimed Barton, 'Why are we talking about schools and village shops?'

Owen noticed the colour rising on the older man's cheeks, a fierce glare hardening his expression.

'As I believe I explained in my letters, sir,' Owen dropped his voice to a reasonable, conversational tone, 'this is a community.' Knowing Barton's chief concern was the profit returned from the business, not the people on the factory floor, he continued, 'If we take care of our employees, educate them and feed them, they will produce more. Why? because they feel better, fitter, they can concentrate on the job in hand without worrying how to care for their children or where to find the next meal. Do you know how many hours are wasted by accidents and mistakes which stop the production line if a worker is unfit for work? That wasted time, is wasted money. We would not expect a machine to run properly if it was not cleaned and oiled regularly, would we?'

'I applaud your high ideals, Mr Owen,' Barton said, more calmly, 'but you already run an excellent school here and the orphan children apprenticed to the works receive more meat and oats than many tradesmen's children. I, for one, do not think any extensions to the mills are required.'

Mr Atkinson stepped forward, peering over the edge of the bank to the drop below.

'I too must congratulate you on the admirable work you are doing here,' he smiled at Owen. 'The ventilation and heating system is second to none and the high standard of engineering in these mills is astounding! Its orderliness and the demeanour of all the employees is gratifying.' He patted Owen on the back. 'Well done! When we asked you to come north and take charge, by Jove, ye did us proud.'

Owen was not swayed from his path.

'And the future projects? The schools. Will you grant me leave to take charge of them as well?'

Mr Barton turned away, 'Let us think on it, Mr Owen. Give us the figures for construction and fitting them out ... let us think on it.'

'I have the estimates in the office. Follow me, gentlemen,' he lead them towards his village house. 'Please make yourselves comfortable in the parlour and I will arrange for my housekeeper to bring you refreshments.'

Leaving his partners in Cooper's hands, he hurried next door to the office.

'Well?' asked Humphreys.

Gerry MacAllister looked up from his desk, noting Owen's quick movements and the square set to his jaw: his employer was not happy.

'I have sent them all these figures many times but now they wish to see them again! Why do they give lip service to bettering the working conditions in factories and yet,' he snatched up a scroll of papers tied with blue ribbon, 'when the opportunity is handed to them to put these changes into practise, while still assuring them of profits, as I *repeatedly* tell them ... they refuse to act!'

He left with the tails of his jacket flying, a determinedly bland expression smoothing his forehead.

'Ah dear,' Humphreys remarked. 'I hope they change their minds because Mr Owen has worked hard to draw up grand plans for the villagers and it would be satisfying to see them come to fruition.'

Clegg, the new young clerk, mumbled agreement and returned to tallying the house inspectors' reports.

Gerry also hoped Mr Owen would receive the backing of the Englishmen. Recently, due to the pressures of the war, more customers were defaulting on payment for their cotton, necessitating Owen to raise legal actions against them and, just that morning, another letter arrived from the lawyer with further complaints from the Edmonstones at Corehouse.

Gerry felt his employer could benefit from some good news for a change.

There was good news, but not in the form Owen expected.

After examining the extensive lists and calculations laid out in front of them regarding the new buildings, Barton and Atkinson were still of the opinion that it would be an expensive exercise with no direct bearing on the production of cotton.

They did, however, wish to honour his work as a diligent manager and co-partner by presenting him with a silver salver.

The exquisite piece of solid silver craftsmanship did nothing to alleviate Owen's profound disappointment but he accepted it with good grace.

'It is obvious,' he confided in Anne Caroline that evening, pacing up and down in front of the fire at Braxfield. 'My partners and I are trying to steer the same wagon in two different directions.'

'It was a generous gift, though, Robert. They must think very highly of you.'

'I am sure it was meant with the best of intentions but I fear the time has come to acknowledge our differences. There are many men in Glasgow who agree with my views, men who have not read the words of philosophers merely to pass the time and brag of their literacy at dinner tables.

'We say we are in Enlightened times! That the French revolution taught us the lesson of suppressing and cruelly ignoring the needs of our working classes, yet educated, apparently cultured men like Mr Barton, refuse to forego even five per cent of their profits for the good of their employees.'

'If you acknowledge your differences, as you say, what good will that do?'

'I want to create a proper school and expand the curriculum to include useful subjects, applicable in real life. I want to give the villagers an opportunity of bettering themselves while giving them gainful employment in the mills. My partners are only interested in making money.' He stopped and leaned against the marble mantelpiece. 'Those are the two different directions. So, Caroline, if I am to fulfil my plans, which I fully intend to do, I require new partners.'

Anne Caroline gasped, 'Gracious, my dear. Where ever will you find them?'

'I have several people in mind, wealthy and eager to support progressive ideas aimed at helping the poor.'

At that moment, Peggy knocked at the drawing room door and the children trooped in to say goodnight to their parents. Straight away, Owen's face lit up at the sight of them.

'Now then,' he said, with a tender note in his voice, taking a seat so that Jane, all curls and frills, could climb upon his knee, 'what excitements have you been up to today?'

***

Having made the decision to break away from his Manchester partners, Owen ploughed his energy into finding new ones.

Uppermost in his mind was the desire to carry on with his plans in New Lanark.

It would be a complete waste of ten years of improvements if he simply left the partnership and started up elsewhere. So, he had to ensure the capital was in place before declaring his position to Barton and Atkinson at which time he could offer a substantial sum to buy them out.

Within months, he secured the backing of three eminent Glasgow merchants. Two of whom were relatives of Anne Caroline, the sons in law of John Campbell of Jura: Robert Dennistoun and Alexander Campbell of Hallyards. These were the same gentlemen who first showed an interest in Owen's plans during conversations in Rosebank's garden during Dale's memorable summer house-party four years earlier.

The third wealthy business man, also a Campbell but no relation to Campbell of Jura, was well known in the city business community and professed an eagerness to be involved in the famous mills.

Owen's long time colleague and under manager, Robert Humphreys, also wished to remain at New Lanark and was willing to invest in a new partnership.

With this financial backing verbally agreed, Owen travelled to Manchester. After a brief discussion on the different futures they each envisaged for their Scottish mills, Owen formally offered to buy them out at a good and reasonable price. There was little hesitation on Barton's part, he agreed with the sum and wished Owen well. Although, he still believed it was unwise to mix business with philanthropy.

John Atkinson, however, surprised Owen by saying that while he accepted the price was fair and would settle for dissolving the current company on those terms, he also wished to invest in the new partnership.

The outcome could not have been better and the men adjourned to a nearby inn to enjoy a meal together and toast the amicable end to a successful ten year business venture.

It would take months of legal paperwork to wind up the New Lanark Twist Company and create the New Lanark Company. This did not deter Owen from immediately having the ground cleared to make way for the new schools.

'Ah've bin asked tae tender fer the building werk doon at Owen's mills,' Ewing told Joe while walking back from a meeting at St John's Lodge.

'Aye, Ah've been asked as weel. It's a muckle task, mair than Ah can handle.'

Both men were smartly dressed in black tail coats, sombre waistcoats, with white cravats and dark grey breeches into black boots: their usual attire for the Lodge. At first, Joe felt ill at ease, an imposter, when he buttoned himself into these formal clothes but now he changed into them for a meeting without a second thought. Permission had been granted for a Lodge to be opened in New Lanark and Joe was charged with the responsibility of seeking possible premises but his thoughts were absorbed with Owen's work on the horizon.

'That's whit Ah thocht.' Ewing nodded, rubbing his carefully trimmed grey beard. 'If we should pit oor heids together an' run twa teams, we could use Jocky Mackay's lads fer the heavy werk.'

'That wid dae the trick! Yon men Ah had wi' me fer the store rooms, they were guid ... reliable.'

'Winter's approachin', they'll turn up! There's barely a joab tae be had aroond here when the harvest's gathered sae Mr Owen's chosen a grand time tae stairt.'

'Ah've tae be at Orchard Quarry t'morra but shall Ah ca' roond tae the yaird the next morning?'

'Dae that.' Ewing stopped, they were at the fork in the road. 'Tam will mak a stairt on the figures. He's a bricht lad, shame aboot his airm. Ah fancy he hauds a candle fer ma dear Melanie.'

'She could dae worse than Tam Murdoch,' Joe said loyally.

'He's a sound and true friend. Yer dottir learned him his letters, helped him tae see life wis worth living when he came hame sae crippled efter his soldiering. He's mighty gratefu' tae her. '

Ewing gave Joe a shrewd, assessing look. 'Ye knew him afore the war?'

'Oh aye, we've bin pals fer mair than twenty year. We broke rocks t'gither fer the mills afore the great fire an' tae see him noo in his top hat an' dandy shirts!'

'Ma dottir has refused the hand of several men, beseechin' me tae look favourably on young Tam.'

'He's a hard werker an' Ah ken fer a fact he wid treat Miss Melanie as if she were a Princess o' the Realm!'

Ewing roared with laughter, clapping Joe on the shoulder and bidding him goodnight, still chortling as he walked off into the dusk.

The next day, Joe and his elder boys rose early and hitched Rusty up to their wagon. It was painted on both sides to proudly display a larger edition of the hand cart's name board: Joseph Scott & Sons, Stonemason.

Donnie, now sixteen years of age, was turning into a shorter, stockier version of his father. Even on a brief acquaintance the resemblance was striking, the same cropped flaxen hair and direct look from brilliant blue eyes. Davey favoured his mother's side of the family, a slim youth with a ready smile, choosing to let his dark hair grow long to fall around his shoulders, held off his face with a chequered kerchief bound in a band around his head.

All three Scotts drew admiring glances from the females of Clydesdale as they went about their work and were often plied with sweet biscuits or fruit from the girls in the valley.

At Orchard Quarry itself, several enterprising local families set up stalls selling soft fruit, potatoes, kale or blocks of comb honey in season.   Most popular was the weak ale which they kept deliciously cold in the summertime by storing the bottles in a nearby stream. This was where the gossip could be shared, word put out for employment and prices haggled over.

Joe selected his pieces of stone and left his sons to load the wagon while he chatted to folk gathered around the stall. He was letting it be known that he might be looking for men through the winter.

'Ah heard tell ye were efter an apprenticeship fer yer son wi' a Joiner?' Mr Selkirk, a respected fellow stonemason called to him. 'Ah ken a man who may be interested in takin' him oan.'

'D'ye rate him as a Joiner?' Joe asked.

'Aye, an' he's fair wi' his price. The boy wid live in an' eat wi' the family. They're a guid, God fearing family.'

'Well, thank ye, Mr Selkirk. Ah'll fetch Davey o'er tae speak wi' ye an' perhaps ye can arrange an introduction?'

'Nae bother,' Selkirk swallowed the last of his cool ale and slapped the tankard down on the stall's counter.

'How's yer apprentice comin' alang?' Joe asked, filling a bag with potatoes. 'The lad Donnie wis friendly wi' last summer, Robert Forrest?'

'Grand! He kens his craft richt enough, has a guid eye fer the inner lines o' the stanes but is alis carving yon we animals frae lumps o' rock!'

Joe laughed, 'Is he still at that? Ah mind a few years back he wis showing Donnie yin. It wis a bonnie piece o' handy-werk but who wants a lion ye can hauld in yer haun!'

Mr Selkirk glanced across at the Scotts' wagon where Rusty stood dozing lopsidedly between the shafts, resting a hind hoof.

'They're growin' at sich a rate!' his eyes followed the brothers bracing themselves to move the final stone. 'Yer lads were barely up tae yer knee when we first met!'

'Weel, ma ane flesh or blood or no', Ah'm glad Donnie's taken up the profession.'

Selkirk yawned, 'Come, if ye've paid fer yer tatties, let's tell young Davey about his joinery!'

***

Braxfield's high ceilings and large windows, so attractive in the summer months, became as cold as an open mouthed cave in winter. By early November, Anne Caroline and the children moved up to live with her sisters in the comparative warmth of Charlotte Street. Following in the tradition of other merchants with two residences, it made sense to close down their country mansions and move into their city dwellings. Provisions were more easily obtained and the dark days could be filled with theatres, recitals and dinner parties.

As usual, Owen divided his time, staying in the village house whenever he was in New Lanark.

Cooper was pleased with this distraction. She was coming to terms with the new arrangements, encouraged by one of the local ministers to whom she was forever going to for guidance. He suggested she should thank the Lord for giving her good health and a warm hearth, food on her table and service to others throughout the day. He was less vitriolic than Reverend McKenzie in his comments regarding her employer. Yet, while chastising her for uncharitable thoughts towards her fellow man, he would listen attentively to her dismay at Mr Owen's lack of religious belief, all the while surreptitiously fuelling her abhorrence at being under the roof of an Infidel.

If Owen knew of her aversion to him, he made no hint of the fact and treated her, as he treated everyone, with respect and consideration.

***

The rancorous legal battle with Corehouse Estate was finally settled in the summer, with Owen agreeing to pay a new, higher, annual water rate of two hundred pounds. When the freezing weather set in and the Clyde dwindled to a stream beneath thick sheets of ice, the weir proved itself invaluable.

Standing majestically under a coat of translucent crystals, the waterfalls in the gorge above the mills lay still: frozen in sparkling glory. The edges of their great rocky shelves dangled with icicles as broad as tree trunks, fifteen or twenty feet long to their sharp, clear points.

It was an incredible spectacle but the Lockhart-Rosses were not in residence and the spinster sisters in Corehouse considered it too dangerous for either themselves or their servants to dare to undertake a walk near the precipitous cliffs.

Only the woodland creatures inhabited this silent, white chasm of astounding natural beauty.

Red squirrels bounded among surrounding fir trees, shaking snow from boughs with every leap, sending nibbled cones tinkling through the branches to scatter on the forest floor. Roe deer pawed the edge of the river, breaking the thinner, glassy ice to drink. Badgers and foxes, hares and pine martens padded through dimpled snow drifts, leaving blue shadowed foot prints. Snow topped stone walls became lively with inquisitive little stoats darting around flushing out mice. Even if these startled rodents escaped their pursuer's jaws, they soon ended up as the unsuspecting prey of a hungry hawk or owl. Their fate clearly illustrated in intricate swirling patterns in the snow where a raptor once swooped.

Over the dark days of the winter solstice the sun's low arc never penetrated the deep ravine, giving barely enough hours of daylight to forage before it was time to seek shelter for the night. Eerie, prehistoric cries of peregrine falcons and barking foxes rang out clearly in the empty air, devoid of the river's customary roar.

Owen's plans to start construction before the new year were postponed. Not only was the ground rock-hard under the snow and impossible to dig, but the roads into the village were often impassably slippery or filled with new snow.

During this quiet, snow bound period, Big Lachie decided the forge should be re-arranged but his orders to undertake this heavy work were opposed by Kyle.

'*Chan eil mi a' tuigsinn!*' Kyle protested. '*I don't understand! Why is it necessary to move the two main work benches to the other side? It is madness! All that work ... for little benefit!*'

Cal listened to the fiery Gaelic exchange from his seat by the open door. He usually took up this position in the winter, with his bucket of soapy water by his side and the leather harnesses across his knees. He was close enough to the warmth of the fire yet gaining as much daylight as possible. Today, the brilliance reflecting off the white snow was dazzling.

By the raised voices and angry gestures, the argument was growing fiercer. Big Lachie was used to being obeyed. When he arrived at New Lanark he forced compliance by sheer physical strength. Now past his sixtieth year, he was no longer the giant of his younger days and it was his strong character which held command.

'*Bidh sàmhach* !' he growled at his son, '*and just help me move the bench!*'

'I will not be quiet!' **Kyle** flared, *'we have used the workshop like this for years ... it works well ...'*

The other men jumped forward to clear their tools from the work top before Big Lachie knocked them off.

He seized one end and wrenched it from the wall. It came away faster than he judged and he staggered backwards, catching the heel of his boot on a raised cobble and falling heavily against the open door jamb.

'Athair!' Kyle ran to his father's side. 'He's bleeding! Fetch the doctor!'

Cal ran as fast as he could through the thick snow, sliding and almost losing his footing on the hill up to New Buildings.

Hammering on the door in a panic, he fought for breath in the icy air, his lungs aching.

'What has happened?' the doctor demanded, taking Cal's chin in his hand and raising his head. 'Are you unable to breath?'

'Tis no' me ... tis Mr Macinnes ... doon at the forge ... accident ...'

McGibbon threw his cape around his shoulders, grabbed his bag and set off at a rapid pace with the aid of his cane to keep his balance on the icy road.

Big Lachie could not be roused to consciousness and by the time Cal returned to the forge, they were rolling him onto a makeshift sledge. There was little Cal could do to help but he followed the procession up to the Macinnes' door in Caithness Row.

Highlanders began appearing in the street, mainly womenfolk, the men being at work. They huddled under their shawls, hats drawn low, watching the tenement.

Then a window flew open on the second floor, banging shut instantly. There was a gasp from the assembled crowd and Cal saw them clutch at each other in grief, moaning and crying.

Then, within minutes, they turned as one and melted back into their homes.

'Whit's happened?' Cal asked a woman as she passed.

'He's deid, son. Big Lachie's deid.'

'How d'ye ken tha'?'

'They let his spirit oot the windae, did ye no' see?'

'Ah saw the windae open an' shut.'

'Aye, quick like! Ye ha'e tae let it oot, set it free an' mak damn sure ye slam the latch close agin afore it can git bak in!'

Cal wandered down to the empty forge and sat beside the fire. He looked at the splintered wood and disarray all around him and then stared out at the shining snow.

The fire hissed and rats rustled in the storeroom above.

Was that it? A man as alive and powerful as Big Lachie was gone from them ... just like that? In an instant?

Where had he gone?

***

The Hogmanay celebrations to herald the tenth year of the new century were less than a week away when Big Lachlan Macinnes died. Freya Macinnes, Kyle's wife, assisted the other women in the family to cleanse his body and wrap it in winding sheets before laying him in the coffin.

Throughout the Dead Days, the women and children guarded the body behind shuttered windows, mirrors turned to the wall, clocks stopped. Big Lachie's passing was mourned by many in the village as well as throughout Lanark and beyond. A stream of friends and colleagues made their way up the stairwell to pay their last respects. They brought presents for the bereaved family of peat or coal for the fire, simple parcels of food and ale or whisky.

The day before the funeral, Cal forced himself to walk along to Caithness Row and say farewell to the man who offered him a job when he was in deep despair. Had it not been for Big Lachie's compassion, Cal wondered whether he would have survived.

'*Ceud mile failte!*' Freya called, weaving her way through the crowded room. '*He's over there,*' she pointed to the open coffin laid along the seats of two rows of chairs, placed facing each other.

Cal was aghast!

Freya's eyes were glassy, half closed, a bemused, dreamy look relaxing her pale oval face. Released from the usual constraints of a bonnet or kerch, a mass of milky white locks snaked around her shoulders, falling to her waist. She looked beautiful, exotic ... wild; drunk!

342

In fact, everyone was in a state of intoxication, laughing, reciting poems and breaking into song while passing a flagon between them. A fiddler stood close to the fire, his bow producing snatches of melody to follow the singers. Cal couldn't understand the Gaelic but several around him spoke Scots and urged him to take a drink and make a toast to the departed.

The next thing he knew, someone was tapping him hard on the shoulder.

'Oi, Cal! Ye've tae git oot noo!'

Cal opened his eyes to see a hazy figure pulling at his arm.

It was still dark in the room but as he scrambled to his feet he saw white daylight showing in strips through the shutters. It was morning, the morning of the funeral.

As soon as the room was cleared of men, Freya and a group of Macinnes women clustered around the coffin. They kissed the corpse's brow for the last time then laid the lid on top and secured it into place. Their duty of keeping the devil away from the body of their loved one was nearly done.

Cal hovered on the stairwell, shivering, his head throbbing, but despite his discomfort he was fascinated by what he could see through the half open door.

The heavy coffin was lifted up and with unhurried movements two of the younger girls carefully turned the chairs upside down. Then, with all of them helping to take the weight, they carried Big Lachie, feet first, out of the house.

Cal ran quickly up to the next landing, hanging over the banisters to watch their slow, unsteady descent. Their hushed voices whispered around the stone walls, guiding each other to raise or lower the coffin, slow up, pause for a rest, take the next step down, until they emerged into the snowy street and passed it to the men.

His teeth chattering with cold, Cal did not join the sombre procession following the piper's mournful lament up the hill to the graveyard in Lanark. The forge was closed for the day, so he went back to his own room, pulled off his snow laden boots and climbed into bed. Sarah and the children were already in the mills and he lay in the peace and quiet, listening to his heart beating and swearing never to drink again. His stomach was churning, head aching and the clothes dangling from pulleys across the ceiling seemed to be moving on their own accord. His mind was buzzing with questions about the Highland funeral but, still dazed by whisky, he soon fell into a fitful sleep.

It was the next morning before he could face the world again. Hurrying down the stairs, wrapping his thick scarf tightly around his neck, cap jammed down, he bumped into his sister in law outside Mrs Young's door.

'Whit wis that all aboot wi' the chairs,' Cal asked Fiona, when he recounted the scene. 'Ah thocht it awfy odd tae bother fussing wi' the chairs when the ithers were haudin' sich a heavy burden.'

'Ye ha'e tae turn the chairs wi' their legs in the air in case the deid yin's ghost is sittin' upon them.'

'D'ye believe tha'?'

'Weel, it could be richt or it could be a load o' nonsense,' Fiona wrinkled her nose, walking beside him through the dark, freezing morning. ' But Ah widnae be wantin tae ha'e a ghostie in the hoose sae Ah wid jist turn the chairs an' be done wi' it.'

'Are ye gaun tae the ceilidh?' Cal asked.

'Aye, the bairns are fair lookin forward tae it,' she yawned, rubbing her eyes.

'It'll be odd no' tae ha'e Mr Macinnes whirling yon chains wi' balls o' fire aroond his heid an' biddin' us all a guid New Year.'

'Mibbee his family will nae gae, efter a' ... they've bin drinkin' an' carryin' oan fer days.'

'Naw. Kyle telt me that seein' as Mr Owen agreed tae the festivities an' is allowin' braziers tae be lit, every yin frae Caithness Row is minded tae dance a' nicht!'

Owen's unbiased views on allowing his employees to openly follow their chosen religion were being received with mixed feelings. Celebrations to mark the dawn of the New Year were one thing, but members of the Established Church, and in particular the Free Church, did not hold with the bawdy frenzy of reels accompanying the Highlanders' swirling pipes and blazing fiddles.

Cooper shuttered the windows early. She was sorry to hear of Lachlan Macinnes' accident but felt Mr Owen should not be encouraging this wanton, heathen behaviour. The Macinnes family, many of whom attended her church, should be ashamed of enjoying themselves when one of their senior members was barely cold in his grave.

When, two days into the new year, many workers were still too inebriated to do their jobs, Humphreys and his managers also wondered if their employer's decision to grant permission for the ceilidh was sensible.

As soon as the tha set in, construction began on the large building beside Mill Four. Ewing, Joe and two other senior stonemasons gathered together the best men in their trade to work on the structure, with teams arriving on site before day break and toiling until it was too dark to see.

It was a symbol of hope for the future against the depressing background of rampant unemployment, outbreaks of typhus in the cities, bankrupt companies and battles lost to Napoleon in Europe.

Chapter Sixteen

"Our wretched species is so made that those who walk on the well-trodden path always throw stones at those who are showing a new road."
Voltaire

On January 16th, Richard Dale Owen took his first breath. Adding to the emotion of the scene was the knowledge that this would be the last time Toshie would attend Anne Caroline during the intensely intimate and perilous event of child birth.

After briefly showing the squirming, meowing baby to its mother, Mr Palmer handed him to Toshie. She gently washed his smeared body, examining his tiny features and wrinkled fingers and toes as if he was the only newly born infant she had ever seen. Looking into his questioning blue eyes, she uttered a prayer of thanks, asking for God's mercy to let him survive and grow to be strong.

Owen was enchanted with his new son, kissing and hugging Anne Caroline with unbounded joy. He cared little whether it was a son or daughter so long as his dear wife and the baby were healthy.

When the frosts of March warmed to the soft showers of April, the days lengthened and plans were soon being finalised for Jean and Julia to travel south for the London Season. During the winter the girls were introduced to the families who would host them in the southern capital and enjoyed attending balls, theatre parties, recitals and luncheons together, so they were not at all nervous about their adventure.

Having met a very attentive young minister, James Haldane Stuart, Mary did not wish to go to London. She thought it a foolish idea to break off their friendship and possibly lose his affections, simply to travel hundreds of miles to be with strangers. Margaret elected to stay with her sister for a while longer in the city and then they both planned to go to Rosebank, a mere four miles away.

The Owens decided to return to New Lanark a few days before the girls set off for London, allowing them a little peace without the children to distract them.

While their employers took leisurely walks and drank tea with friends in the drawing room, below stairs, the house was in uproar. Packing up for both the Dales and Owens meant the servants were kept on their toes from dawn to dark.

On a dull, breezy afternoon all the Dale servants sat around the long table in Charlotte Street's kitchen. They were finishing their main meal of the day, chattering amongst themselves and reaching for the last slices of bread to mop up any residue of Cook's delicious fish broth.

Renwick dabbed his mouth methodically with his serviette, pushed back his chair and rose to his feet.

'Bring the tray I have prepared from the pantry,' he instructed a footman.

Everyone stopped talking and looked towards the butler.

'We reach a memorable day, a day which could be viewed as sad but which we must all consider to be merely the start of a new chapter. After nearly thirty years serving this family, Mrs Mackintosh is leaving us tomorrow.'

The servants looked suitably dejected, all eyes going to where Toshie was seated beside Breen. Opposite her was her replacement, Miss Ramsay, a demure young woman, half Toshie's age.

They were all aware of the Lady's Maid's departure but, on hearing Renwick's formal speech, realised this was their last meal together.

The footman walked around the table carrying a tray laden with small crystal glasses of sweet sherry which he distributed to everyone.

'Mrs Mackintosh, Toshie,' Renwick allowed himself the familiar name. 'We ask the Lord our God to take care of you and keep you safe and in good health to enjoy a long, comfortable retirement. Your presence will be sorely missed and I speak for us all when I say we will welcome you as a guest and friend whenever you wish to visit.' He raised his glass and indicated the company should stand, pausing to let the noise of scraping chairs recede. 'Join with me in a toast to this fine lady! To Toshie! God Bless you!'

'Thank ye, all o' ye. It's been a rare pleasure tae werk in this hoose an' Ah count ye all as ma friends.' Her lips began to tremble. 'Ah'll no say any mair fer fear o' embarrassing mesel'.' She tried to smile, finding her lips wouldn't curve upwards. 'Ah'll fair miss ye all. Thank ye all. God bless ye.'

With considerate timing, Renwick dismissed the gathering, hurrying the staff to their duties and engaging Breen and Giggs in a discussion about preparations for the Owen's departure for the country.

'Ah wis tha' gratefu' tae Renwick fer finishin' aff sae quick,' Toshie confided much later that evening whilst sharing a last pot of tea with her old friends. 'Ah confess, Ah slipped awa' fae a wee greet in ma room.'

'Mind an' come back an' see us,' Giggs told her with mock annoyance. 'Nae excuses!'

Breen and Cook chuckled.

'It'll not be long afore I will be going the same way,' Breen commented. 'Maybe I will join you on the Ayrshire coast? I have no family, alive, so you may not have seen the back of me yet.'

It was not long before they wished each other 'night night' and Toshie went through to her room.

She sat on the bed holding the present Anne Caroline gave her when she dressed her for dinner. It was a beautifully bound Bible with gold lettering on the spine and fantastical designs of coloured ink marbling on the inside of the covers.

On the title page, there was an inscription. 'To my dear Toshie, in earnest gratitude and with the greatest love and affection always, Anne Caroline Owen.'

Toshie hugged it to her bosom, listening to the familiar sounds of the house she had long considered her home: the wind rustling in the horse chestnut tree outside the window, the hum in the chimney of her little tiled fireplace, the heavy silence of thick walls and flag-stoned floors.

348

In the morning, the Owens were leaving for New Lanark and she would be taking the Mail Coach to Ayr. She heard the distant chimes of the kitchen clock: eleven. She would be at her sister's at this time tomorrow. Life goes on.

***

The prolonged war with Napoleon was impinging badly on Britain and there appeared to be no end in sight.

Spencer Perceval, the Prime Minister, put his trust in Major General Wellesley in the Iberian Peninsula. His intention behind freeing Portugal and sending soldiers to aid the Spanish in their fight against France was to tie up vast numbers of Napoleon's Grand Army in Spain.

It was working, for the time being.

In consequence of the battles both at sea and on land, French Prisoners of War were growing rapidly. Camps were set up for the rank and file but it soon became normal practice to release the officers, on licence, to be billeted to outlying towns where they worked in the community. Even the market town of Lanark became used to the sight of over two dozen stylish, colourful French officers walking the streets.

As well as the French problem, Perceval and his government faced many pressing issues at home. One of particular interest to Owen was being reported with growing frequency and caused significant concern to cotton manufacturers.

'Thank God we are north of the border!' Colin Campbell cried, while on a visit to New Lanark with Robert Dennistoun. 'The Luddites are showing their teeth again around Nottingham, they're threatening to break into mills and smash frames.'

'They believe the new machinery is taking away their jobs,' Owen said, reasonably. 'Where five skilled men were required, there is only need for one. They are angry, which is understandable.'

'Good Lord, man, how can ye say it's understandable? We have spinning jennies here which can handle with one operative what used to take ten or even a dozen! That does not mean it is understandable! If this General Ned Ludd sent us threatening

349

letters or sent his Army of Redressers storming over our walls to break our machines, I for one would not be 'understanding'!'

'Other work should be found for them,' Owen continued. 'If they were educated there would be other means open to them to gain a living. They are frightened and see their craft being done by machines so they are breaking the machines.'

The three gentlemen were taking refreshments in Owen's office before inspecting the ongoing building work.

'The order book is not as full as we would have hoped,' Dennistoun muttered, changing the subject. 'I fear the income may fall short of your projected figures.'

'These times will pass,' Owen said, reassuringly. 'It is the same for everyone and we are in the fortunate position of being large enough to cope with dips in the market.'

When the ale was supped and Cooper's savoury pastries devoured, they all donned jackets and hats to move outside.

'My! Now that I stand beside the brute, it is even bigger than I expected,' Campbell declared, shading his eyes and peering up at the massive stone exterior.

A low blanket of white cloud dampened the day but it was still bright above the roof tops.

'It will soon be complete and then we will start fitting it out.'

Campbell clasped his hands behind his back and rocked on his heels, pushing his top hat back to see better.

'And ye plan another building? As big as this?' he nodded across the mill-lade to the cleared space below Nursery Buildings..

'Indeed,' Owen kept the irritation out of his voice: his plans for the Institution were the subject of close inspection before the new partnership was agreed. He felt the start of a growing wariness and recalled his lawyer advising caution. The New Lanark Company's papers were still not signed and he urged Owen to put prudence before confidence.

Instead of heeding the warning, Owen was forging ahead.

Dennistoun was quiet, his lips pressed into a line as if wishing to speak but controlling the words from escaping.

Their reception to the simple but beautifully in-keeping architecture of the building was cool: worryingly cool.

A few days later he received a letter from Colin Campbell.

'Aha!' Owen called across to Humphreys, 'I thought as much! Mr Colin Campbell wishes to have a list of the full cost, itemised, of everything we need to complete the proposed buildings.'

'Ye told them it would be £3,000?'

'For the Institute, yes, and also an additional sum for the school and kitchens.'

'If he has been advised ... what's his game?'

Owen shook his head, 'From all accounts, his game is gambling at cards, or anything he's offered a challenge to wager upon! In this instance, he would be wise to play by the rules of business.'

'Tis true enough that next quarter's figures are not looking good. Do you think we will clear a profit this year?'

'Who can say? I will aim for a profit, but these are exceptional times.'

'The thing is,' Humphreys rose from his desk and pushed the door closed so the clerks in the outside office could not over hear. 'The thing is, Mr Owen, my wife has been finding it difficult living up here, away from her family in Derbyshire.'

'I am sorry to hear that but fail to see how I can alleviate Mrs Humphreys' distress.'

'She takes frequent journeys south, ye see, and I try and treat her to what she likes in the way of clothes an' ladies' fancy goods but it has been costing me quite a lot.' Humphreys shot him a direct look. 'At present, my income is sufficient, but if it were to drop or my share of the promised profits did not materialise ... I would be in trouble both financially and matrimonially.'

Owen looked at his colleague. They'd been together as young men, starting out, and shared the same enlightened views of treating the workers beneath them with respect, way back in their years under Drinkwater at Bank Top Mill.

'I cannot guarantee you a profit, you knew that when we first spoke of the terms of the partnership.'

'Yes, I knew and I understand. Unfortunately, these new figures are a worrying sight.'

Concealing a sudden panic, Owen sat back in his chair, steepling his fingers while alarming thoughts rushed through his mind.

Was Humphreys about to back out? Decide he could not risk his capital in the mills and withdraw from their agreement? If he were to be known to drop out, what message would that send to the Campbells and Dennistoun?

A knot of fear was cramping his stomach.

He needed their capital to keep the mills afloat and pay for the new buildings but if they withdrew their support before the contract was formally signed, he could lose everything.

With his characteristic quick thinking, he decided a show of confidence was required.

'The following quarter's orders are looking promising!' he cried, optimistically. 'Let me give you a proposal, eh? You are needing a higher income? Am I right? And you do not have great confidence in receiving a good return for your capital?'

Humphreys was nodding.

'Well, I am of the opinion that the returns will be healthy, therefore, what would you say if I raised your salary and, in return, you assigned your share of the year end profits to me?'

Humphreys looked like a dying man being offered the elixir of life.

'I would ask how much you would raise my salary, but I would be keen, very keen, to follow up the proposal!'

By the end of the afternoon they reached an agreed figure and drew up a short contract whereby Humphreys would receive a further £350 per year and pay his share of the profits over to Owen.

'This is between the two of us,' Owen said cheerfully, rolling the blotter over their signatures. 'There is no need to change any wording in the partnership because as soon as you perceive you would be more handsomely rewarded by taking your profit share, we can tear up this paper!'

Humphreys was more than satisfied and they shook hands on the deal.

With Campbell and Dennistoun's visit to the mills taking up most of the day and then the unexpected discussions with Humphreys, Owen found himself working in the office until late in the evening. He thought he was alone but on hearing a noise beyond his door, he went to investigate.

'Mr Clegg! It is long past your time to go home.'

The young man jumped to his feet.

'Sir! My apologies if I disturbed you. There were some reports which needed attending to ...'

'I have the same problem!' Owen saw the clerk was cleaning his quill. 'But I see you are finishing now, I believe I have another hour yet.'

'Mr Owen, sir, can I be of assistance? I have no pressing need to return home.'

'Perhaps you can.'

They worked together for the next hour and Owen found Clegg to be good company as well exceedingly efficient.

'Tell me,' Owen asked, when they were blowing out candles and turning down the lamp wicks. 'I see you are very capable so why did you fall behind with reports today? Are you being unreasonably burdened?'

'No sir, it was just an unusual set of circumstances which brought more work.'

'Has something happened of which I should be aware?'

'No, sir.' the young man flushed to his temples, fiddling nervously with the folds of his white cravat.

Owen watched him, perceptively. 'Were you asked to take on someone else's work?'

'That might have been the case, yes sir.'

'And might it have been Mr Humphreys' work which you were so diligently finishing for him?'

'It might have been, sir.'

'How often have you remained late to do Mr Humphreys' work?'

'Not often. I am willing to take it on.'

'You would not have told me this had I not enquired, which is commendable.'

They walked out the door together, Owen turning the key and pocketing it.

'Mr Clegg, as you saw this evening, I seem to be having more and more correspondence to deal with and require an assistant. Would you like the position?'

'To be your assistant? Oh yes, thank you, Mr Owen.'

'I shall see you tomorrow in the office then, as my assistant. Good night to you!' Owen put his hat on his head, pressed it firmly into place and struck off up Braxfield Road.

Clegg watched the slim, frock coated figure disappearing lithely into the gloom with the happy realisation that he was no longer the junior office clerk under Gerry MacAllister. He was Mr Owen's personal assistant. Nothing was said about wages but he didn't care, it was enough to have been chosen to work closely for such a respected businessman.

***

Anne Caroline watched from an upstairs window while Robert and William mounted their ponies and rode around the stable yard.

Their father was with them, standing in the shade beside the coal store talking with the groom. Swallows darted in and out of the coach house feeding their chicks, the strong afternoon sun throwing their speeding shadows across the ground.

Life was easy and comfortable in Braxfield House.

The family soon relaxed into country pursuits and now there were two spaniels and a collection of barn cats, newly with kittens, for the children to play with as well as the boys' ponies.

It was a perfect summer home. In the winter, she enjoyed residing in Glasgow because it gave her a chance to spend time with her sisters, friends like Rosemary and catch up with the social gossip. Inconveniently, she always seemed to be in a state of advanced pregnancy during these visits.

She missed her father palpably.

There were many evenings when she remained alone in the drawing room reading or sewing while her sisters went out to society gatherings. Owen was occupied with the Chamber of Commerce or Royal Bank business and was regularly invited to dine in the afternoons with important contacts eager for his views on new, emerging markets.

She changed her position, standing up straight and rubbing her back through the soft muslin gown.

She adored all her children but in just over ten years of marriage, her body was suffering from the trauma of bearing seven children and now there was another one on the way.

Sighing, her attention returned to the scene outside the window.

Owen's voice was drifting up, the words indistinct but the intonations so uniquely his own: a mix of midlands English and Welsh. She loved his voice, she loved his intense, soulful blue eyes, flecked with green and gold to sparkle when he looked at her lovingly. The intervening years since they first met were filled with exhilarating joy and the deepest of grief. Yet their love and mutual attraction remained as steadfast as the day they declared their feelings to one another: their children were living proof of this fact.

He was unlike any man she had ever met, before or since, and her friends would often comment on how 'different' her husband was to other husbands. Those habits they considered strange, she now took for granted, like his preference for very plain food, only taking one glass of wine or ale with a meal and never becoming awkward or unreasonable. A quality Rosemary Pemberly was frequently complimenting because her own husband, now appearing considerably older than her, was prone to difficult moods.

Owen was calm and considerate to others, often having a turn of phrase or expression which was quietly humorous and he always looked on the bright side of even the most disheartening matter. Whether it was her concern for the success of a dinner party she was arranging, the ease of travelling to a friend's house during stormy weather or simply seeing the qualities of a dull, rainy afternoon: 'excellent for playing chess beside the fire!'

However, she was not blind to her husband's faults.

If he became convinced of a course of action he could not be dissuaded, believing his own judgement to be utterly correct. His self confidence could, at times, appear over-bearing and in his accounts of the improvements he was making at the mills, he boardered on being boastful.

However, even his critics could not fault his sincerity and good heart, although sadly, there were those amongst them who would not forgive his lack of Christian beliefs.

Every day, she prayed for his salvation. Her dearest wish was for him to be convinced of the truth of the Lord's word and follow the path to everlasting life by embracing the Holy Scriptures.

355

Outside, the groom swung himself up into the saddle of a shining chestnut hunter, with Owen waving to his sons as the cavalcade clattered out of the stable yard and off down the driveway.

How grown up little Robert looked riding Donald, his dapple grey pony, rhythmically rising up and down with ease when they broke into a trot. William bounced along behind them on Dougie, an elderly, sweet natured Exmoor pony loaned to them by Lady Elizabeth at Bonnington.

'I am so fortunate,' Anne Caroline thought. 'Please Lord, forgive any selfish desire I may own to ask for more than I have now, for I am truly blessed with a fine husband, healthy children and a beautiful home, so help me, Almighty God.'

A few weeks later, when the first tints of autumn gilded the leaves of the surrounding beech woods, Anne Caroline fell ill.

At first she told her husband it was just a chill and a day or two in bed would find her well again. After three days, seeing no improvement and the worsening of a fever, the doctor was called and he advised more bed rest and frequent blood letting.

She protested over the painful treatment, finally succeeding in being left to recover with Ramsay administering nourishing bowls of chicken broth and suet dumplings.

'I have to travel to Glasgow tomorrow, my dear Caroline,' Owen told her one afternoon, sitting on the edge of the bed. 'I wish you could accompany me but McGibbon advises that you are not strong enough to endure the roads so close to your confinement.'

'He said the same to me,' she smiled, holding his hand. 'I feel a lot better these days but perhaps it is wiser for our new baby to begin life here. I am perfectly content, after all, Mr McGibbon was most dutiful when Anne was born.'

Owen looked at his young wife's pale face and wished he could postpone his business affairs in the city but, on this occasion, it was just not possible.

Three days later, on the fifth of October, he joined Alexander Campbell of Hallyards, Robert Dennistoun, and Colin Campbell in one of the private, wood panelled meeting rooms at the Tontine.

In the presence of his solicitor, Mr Macgregor, Owen added his name beneath those of his new partners, confirming and legally binding the formation of the New Lanark Company. He was relieved to have the contract signed and having reported more encouraging sales figures in the months since their disappointing discussions at the mills, the other gentlemen were in enthusiastic form.

'A platter of your finest meats and more claret!' Dennistoun shouted down the corridor to one of the waiters in the main dining hall. 'Let's raise a glass to the famous New Lanark cotton mills! May they continue to be bountiful under our ownership!'

Owen smiled at them over his glass, already looking forward to returning to his family at Braxfield and finally getting started with the construction of the Institute.

***

Joe sat shivering beside the range, feeding dry sticks into the fire. A ferocious gale was raging outside, wind whining in the window frames, sleet battering against the door.

It was not nature's winter blasts which chilled him to the core, it was the letter he found when he arrived home.

Believing it to be from Sam, he immediately sought out the tinderbox beside the mantelshelf and lit a lamp. In the growing glow of the golden flame it took a moment to make sense of the letters on the outside. It was addressed to Donald Scott. He turned it over and saw the King's Coat of Arms stamped on the reverse.

And then it dawned on him.

Donnie was being called up to fight in the war.

Every grown man in Great Britain was expected to join the army or navy if balloted. It had been the law now for several years due to heavy losses incurred against Napoleon and he knew of several local families whose sons were serving abroad. He also knew of those whose sons would never return.

It was a long time before he laid the letter to one side and set about raising a spark from the damped-down fire in the grate. Fiona would be distraught. For all his fears for Donnie's life and the dread of seeing him leave, Joe's over riding anxiety was the effect the news would have on his wife.

Fiona already agonised over Sionaidh who suffered from recurring, debilitating fits since first being struck down. He knew she also missed Davey since he took up the apprenticeship; more than she would say.

And now Donnie was to be taken from them.

Joe cursed loudly to the empty room, seizing the poker and rattling the embers in a fury before flinging it down to clatter against the stone floor.

Last week, he was rejoicing at the opening of the new Lodge in New Lanark and being given a date to start Mr Owen's ambitious new building. Now he felt sick to the stomach, with a terrible fizzing in his head of rage and loss and powerlessness. Someone else was taking his son from under his roof and sending him to face death in a foreign land!

With the noise of the storm and his own chaotic thoughts loud in his mind, he did not hear Rusty's hoof beats, nor the thump of the wagon being unhitched and the shed door slamming shut in the wind.

He jumped when the front door burst open.

'By, it's gie cauld the nicht!' Donnie shouted, deafened by the swirling blizzard behind him. He forced the door closed as quickly as he could manage with his arms full of logs. 'It's awfy dark in here ... are ye a'richt, Da'?'

Unable to find words, Joe handed him the letter. He saw the hopeful smile disappear, the brows converge, the pensive, puzzled expressions and then Donnie looked up with terror in his eyes.

'Ah ken whit it is, son.' Joe said, gruffly.

Donnie slumped onto a chair by the table, his legs suddenly weak. Melting sleet dripped from his hat onto his heavy, glistening jute cape and on down to the floor.

'Ah niver thocht Ah'd be ca'd up,' Donnie rubbed at his nose. 'Ither yins gae tae the war, no' me. Ah jist niver thocht it wid happen tae me.'

Joe made a conscious effort to stop staring at his son. He was not seeing the strong young man seated at the table, he saw the little boy he once was: bright eyed, cheeky faced, eager to help his father in any way he could, so proud to show off his reading skills and be part of their new business.

It broke Joe's heart to think of him as cannon fodder, for that was what he was to become.

When Fiona came home they waited to tell her until after the younger children were asleep upstairs. Her first gasps and tears of shock were replaced by a much deeper sadness which could not be released by physical displays; the pain was in her heart, in her soul.

It was a terrible, distressing night.

Joe slept fitfully with Fiona clinging to him, even in her exhausted sleep. It was pitch dark when he woke up, alert, aware of a sudden silence. The storm had passed.

His mind was reeling with the horror of the previous evening and of what was about to happen to his eldest son.

He must be strong for Fiona and the family and especially for Donnie. After his horrified disbelief, Donnie was bracing himself for what he viewed as inevitable and Joe admired his son's composure.

It was inconceivable to him that men would willingly enlist, but then Sam chose to be a soldier and many young men signed up of their own volition.

The letter stated Donnie was to report for duty within seven days. It was common knowledge that any man would be accepted as a recruit unless he failed the medical examination. Donnie was physically fit and in good health so he would easily qualify.

There was another way to avoid service and Joe struggled with this shred of hope until he heard the creak of footsteps descending the stairs.

Donnie and Robbie were heating porridge, talking in low voices beside the fire when he joined them.

'Ah've telt him,' Donnie whispered, nodding at his brother.

Robbie's face was smudged with ash and tears, trying to be brave about the news while making a bad job of brushing around the hearth.

They ate their oats in a solemn silence until Robbie pulled on his jacket, ready to leave for the mills.

'Din nae look sae feart!' Donnie muttered, giving his young brother's cap a playful tweak. 'Ah'll still be here when ye git hame!'

'Ye'd better be!' Robbie replied, attempting to sound cheerful. Then he scurried out into the darkness to join the other workers pouring down the hill to the calling mill bell.

'Donnie,' Joe whispered. 'Ah ken yer resigned tae yer fate, willin' tae fight fer yer King and country. It's a credit tae ye. Tell me straight, son, if there wis a way fer ye ta be rid o' these orders, wid ye tak it?'

'Aye, in a blink! Efter a' these years o' learnin' ma craft an' being wi' ye through the beginning' o' oor business. It's fair vexing tae leave noo, wi' the New Lanark werk jist aboot tae stairt! But Ah'm nae shirker ... an' if it's ma duty, weel, Ah'd better mak the best o' it.'

Donnie filled the kettle from the pitcher of water and swung the swee over the heat. It was a routine he performed every morning: the water would be hot when his mother came down with the little ones.

'Yer a grand lad,' Joe's voice broke and he turned it into a cough. 'Ah see the wind's died richt doon sae ye can feenish aff the werk ye stairted yesterday at Hietoun. Ah'll gie Rusty her mash an' oats the noo an' she'll be settled fer harnessing at day break.'

'Are ye no' comin' wi' me the day?'

'Later. Ye can manage the mornin'. Ah'll meet ye at Ewing's aroond noon.'

There was a lot to attend to before midday and Joe hurried through shaving and dressed in his best clothes, eager to be on his way.

Although he now attended the newly opened St David's Lodge in New Lanark, he knew he could call on any of the Brotherhood: they would help him, they would advise him on his plans. He strode around Lanark, knocking at doors, sitting by firesides, talking privately in offices and waiting beside the Grammar School for a break in the lessons to allow a few minutes' discussion with the Mathematics tutor, a fellow Mason.

When St Nicholas' Church bell struck twelve, Joe was pacing nervously around the muddy back yard of a slaughter house.

He was waiting to meet the man all his enquiries pointed to as being his best chance of a solution: the butcher, Mr Eugene Clark.

This strident, ill tempered brute of a man was famous in the town for two things: his tender, well cut, well hung meat and his violent, bullying character.

'Whit d'ye want?' Clark demanded, barging through the swing-doors of the killing shed, his apron soaked in blood, his muscled arms bulging at his sides.

Joe was primed with a great deal of advice on the best way to handle the man, but had his mission not been so vital he would have made an excuse and rushed from the yard.

'Mr Clark. Ma name is Joseph Scott and I am here tae mak ye an offer. Ye can tak it or leave it, Ah have nae the time tae waste wi' bargaining.'

'Whit ye gaun oan aboot? Offer fer whit?'

'Ah unnerstaun yer eldest son, Peter, is keen tae see the world an' fight the French, but Ah also understaun that ye can nae afford tae let the lad follow his path for ye wid be short of a slaughterman. Am Ah richt?'

'Ye unnerstaun a lot o' ma private business. And why dis it interest ye?'

'We are baithe businessmen, Mr Clark. Ye hav a butchery an' Ah'm a stonemason. We baithe ha'e sons who werk at oor sides. Ma ane lad has bin balloted in tae His Majesty's forces but he is ma apprentice an' keen tae follow ma trade. Peter wid gladly tak up arms but it's well kent he only stiys tae be a dutiful son tae ye.' Joe wondered at his own words, finding them ridiculous, for the only thing well known about this father and son was the regular beatings.

'Ma lad's aboot tae leave,' Joe imbued his voice with confidence, 'an' Ah will lose ma apprentice jist as Ah embark on the new building doon at the mills. Mr Clark, Ah want tae pay ye a sum o' money sae ye can hire a new slaughterman an' yer lad can tak ma son's place. Peter can follow his chosen career in the army an' Ah can keep ma apprentice.'

'An' whit are ye offering?'

Joe had done his homework. An experienced slaughter man could demand up to one hundred and fifty pounds a year, a good sum, but poor Peter earned nothing but beer money and the other man at Clark's took home no more than one hundred.

'One hundred pounds.'

'One hundred an' twenty.'

Joe felt a stab of excitement: Clark was taking the bait.

'One hundred an' ten,' Joe made a show of being firm.

'Naw, naw, one hundred an' fifteen, mair like. If ye mak it that, ye have a deal.'

Holding his breath for a moment, Joe allowed the pause to lengthen, as if pondering, calculating.

'Very well,' he said at last, as if reluctant. 'One hundred and fifteen pounds it is.'

Clark gave a sneering grin, 'Ye should nae try an' be cheap wi' me, Mr Scott. Ah alis git ma price!'

'Ah ken that noo.' Joe gave a slight bow of his head, pretending to show deference to the older man while hiding his relief. He was prepared to pay all his life savings, one hundred and sixty four pounds, but was warned to start low because Clark needed to feel he had the upper hand.

'Should we no' ask yer son, afore we shake on the deal?' Joe asked, nervous in case the bargain collapsed.

Clark spat on his hand, stained brown with blood, 'He'll dae whit he's telt! Ye have yer deal. Ma word's enough!'

Joe was revolted at the sight of the massive, slippery hand being proffered but followed suit, adding a convivial slap on the shoulder.

'Tae be paid tae ye when yer lad signs up.'

Clark's eyes narrowed. 'Half the money noo!'

'When yer lad signs up,' Joe feigned a confident smile and repeated Clark's words back to him. 'Ma word's enough! Guid day tae ye, Mr Clark.'

Shouldering his way along the Castlegate and through the crowded market place, Joe headed up onto the wide roads of Hietoun, astonished to find a sparkling scene all around him. Consumed with his problems since waking, he was seeing the day for the first time.

Washed by the storm, everything shone under a clear pale blue sky. He screwed up his eyes at the flickering puddles reflecting white sunshine, slate roofs glinting silver, golden thatch cleansed and gleaming. Pouring down the hill, Puddin'

Burn rushed with gurgling brown water, churning with fallen leaves. He breathed the fresh air and felt the sharp nip of a coming frost against his skin. He felt wonderfully alive.

It was a beautiful winter day and yet had anyone asked him his memories of the morning he would have told them it was dark, overcast.

On reaching Ewing's yard, he immediately told Donnie and Tam his morning's business. It was hard to see which was the more relieved for Tam had been appalled by the thought of Donnie, who he thought of as a nephew, facing the horrors of war.

'Are ye sure this lad, Peter Clark, wants tae join up?' Donnie asked. It was his only reservation to the plan.

'That's whit Ah heard frae every yin when Ah asked if they knew a man who wid be willing tae tak yer place. Clark's a cruel faither an' maister. There's word that he kill't his first wife in a drunken rage an' the second Mistress Clark is oft wi' a black eye or worse ... the bairns tae. Peter's tried tae run awa' mony a time as a wean, his last try wis tae the army but his faither dragged him hame.'

The men were still standing beside Rusty discussing this fortunate change in Donnie's future when a dishevelled figure came tearing into the yard.

'Mr Scott?' he shouted, 'Ah'm efter Mr Joseph Scott, the stonemason? Or Donald Scott?'

'Aye,' Joe and Donnie said together, eyeing the stocky smocked stranger expectantly.

'Ah'm Peter ... Peter Clark ... is it true?' he fought for breath having run all the way from town. 'Am Ah free tae leave ma faither's hoose?'

It was Donnie who answered. 'If ye truly want tae tak ma place an gae tae war, aye.'

'Ye have saved me! Ah've prayed fer this day. God has sent ye tae be ma salvation! Since Ah wis a bairn ... Ah've asked fer his mercy ... thank ye ... thank ye.'

Tam and the Scotts were staggered at the vehemence in the lad's voice.

'Ye ha'e tae leave within the week ...' Donnie started to explain.

'Ah ken that!' Peter lifted the heavy bag off his shoulder. 'Ah ha'e ma belonging's wi' me, here. Ah'm ne'er gaun bak tae yon auld buggar's hoose agin!'

'Weel,' Joe stepped forward and shook Peter's hand, 'if ye cannae gae hame then ye'll stiy wi' us this nicht, an' Donnie will gae with ye up tae the barracks at Hamilton t'morra.'

When Fiona walked through the door that evening her confusion at seeing a strange youth seated by her fire was turned to joy when they told her the turn of events.

'Ah cannae believe it!' Fiona hugged Donnie fiercely to her, barely releasing him before pulling him into her arms again and again.

'Wi' ye leave me be!' he laughed, good naturedly. 'Ah'll be awa' wi' Peter in the mornin', mak sure the papers are all signed an' that ... sae we thocht he should ha'e a braw meal afore we gae?' He pointed to a pot on the stove. 'Da' got a chicken an' Mel's already made a stew fer us a'.'

Fiona beamed around her family. 'Och it's the brawest day o' ma life!'

Later, while brushing her hair before climbing into bed beside Joe, Fiona said wistfully, 'Ye ken, Joe, it's a terrible thocht, which Ah've ne'er felt fer real until noo. All yon soldiers we hear aboot dyin' in the battles, all those names o' men listed in yon newspapers Rosie brings us... every yin o' them is some paur woman's son.'

'We are spared that. Come tae bed, ma lovely wife, an' pit the caunel oot, fer if Ah slept a wink last nicht Ah wid be surprised.'

Smoothing back her long, dark auburn tresses to cascade over one shoulder, away from the flame, she leaned forward to blow out the candle. He was watching her and she glanced up to see glints of desire in his eyes.

She returned the look; suddenly newly and acutely aware of each other's presence.

'Ye are sae bonnie, ma darlin',' he murmured, pushing back the blankets for her to join him on the mattress. 'Leave it lit fer a wee while longer.'

Chapter Seventeen

"Mankind are divided into sects, and individuals think very differently on religious subjects, from the purest motives; and that gracious common Parent, who loves all his children alike, beholds with approbation every one who worships him in sincerity."
Joseph Lancaster

Miss Wilson and Ramsay were becoming very good friends. In their positions as housekeeper and lady's maid they walked a fine line between having a close relationship with their employers yet also being part of the servants' hall.

When Anne Caroline went into labour the whole household held its breath but it was Miss Wilson's calm support which encouraged Ramsay to do her duties.

It was a difficult birth and Anne Caroline was more nervous than usual without Toshie.

'Is Mrs Owen any better today?' Miss Wilson enquired, sharing a quiet pot of tea in her sitting room with Ramsay.

'A little. She's too pale for my liking, the birth was far from easy and she was laid so low with her illness beforehand.'

'And baby Mary?

'Peggy said she'd a sleepless night with her last night but now she's as docile as you like!'

'That wee maid, Dora, is a laugh! Cheery smiles every time I meet her in the corridor. It's as if she *enjoys* washing the babbies' linen.'

'She has eight younger brothers and sisters so a new baby is no novelty to that one.' Ramsay sipped her tea, helping herself to a square of gingerbread.

'She was asking for permission to go down to the village to see the Hogmanay ceilidh this evening. I think it would be all right, don't you? Murdoch and two of the footmen are going. Sheddon has instructed them to return within half an hour of the bells and I was going to ask the men to chaperone the lassies.'

'I thought I might go myself,' Ramsay said, raising her eyebrows as if this was a very daring thought, 'but with the mistress still poorly, maybe I should forego it.'

'Shame, you will probably be in Glasgow next year. The family are rarely here through the winter.'

'Master Robert was pleading with his father to be allowed to go, but to no avail.'

'I daresay, Mr Owen would not wish his son to see the drinking which takes place. '

'And quite right,' Ramsay agreed, 'Although, I believe he is allowing him to join them at the dinner table from tomorrow.'

'So Mr Sheddon informed me. Master Robert can be a wee scally-wag sometimes but he is actually a sweet child!'

Ramsay laughed, having been told of the dramatic incident of Master Robert's misguided plan which unwittingly caused Miss Wilson serious injury.

Knowing their employer was just up the hill in Braxfield House made some of his employees more wary of over-indulging at the Hogmanay ceilidh. They wondered if he would attend and were grateful when, after a brief, cheerful chat with some of the women preparing food for the celebration, Mr Owen mounted his horse and left the village before the mill bell ended the day.

Unfortunately, their good intentions were thrown aside when the party swung into action and the next few days saw a rash of Black Silent Monitors.

Measles was making its insidious presence felt in Britain that winter. Fourteen New Lanark residents were diagnosed and successfully nursed back to health.

Disease, the great leveller, took its victims from every walk of life.

The King's favourite and youngest daughter, Princess Amelia, always a delicate, consumptive girl, contracted measles and her health declined steadily until she died.

Her father, already virtually blind, became overwhelmed by grief, wailing and sobbing or talking gibberish for weeks on end.

By the turn of the year, it was clear this was much more serious than his earlier bouts of insanity and King George's deranged state of mind was not going to recover normality. With the country in the midst of a violent war and financial recession, Perceval passed the Regency Act, permitting Prince George to act in his father's place.

Owen and his colleagues discussed the fate of the King who was now living in isolation at Windsor Castle. Tragic though this situation was, it did not interfere with the day to day running of the mills.

Their chief concern lay with the poor markets and rising costs, which, coupled with the ongoing problems of finding new suppliers, badly affected the mill's finances.

While New Lanark was finding it difficult to function profitably, Stanley Mills were struggling, dangerously. In May, after consultation with John More, Dale's replacement at the Royal Bank and a trustee of Dale's estate, Owen demanded the removal of the manager, declaring Mr Craig utterly incompetent and would 'ruin the richest man in the Kingdom' if he were connected to him.

It was decided that the mills should be let to a third party and the word was circulated among the Glasgow merchants. In the meantime, apart from sending Humphreys up to handle matters on a couple of occasions, Owen shouldered the majority of the management himself: an unsustainable workload.

Owen was not the only one in a difficult position.

In England, the Luddites, a rumbling nuisance to the cotton merchants at first, suddenly burst into action in Nottingham, setting fire to mills and destroying machinery. They would gather on the moors in the northern counties, arming themselves with whatever came to hand, picks, axes and rakes, then descend to cause havoc on the mill towns.

Throughout these challenging months, Owen remained focused on his plans for his own company.

The walls of the Institute were growing every day, the workers were more efficient and the problem of over-crowding in the tenements was being overcome: he was making progress.

Nursery Buildings were also gradually being altered to house families. The five hundred pauper apprentices he inherited from Dale were almost all grown up, many having even moved out of the village. The few remaining who were only four or five years old when Owen took over, could easily be accommodated in two large rooms: one for boys, one for girls.

With her husband engrossed in his work, Anne Caroline threw herself into running Braxfield House and caring for her children.

Since the dreadful day when her eldest son injured the housekeeper, she took it upon herself to make sure Robert and all her children were strictly guided by the word of the Bible. Chiding herself for not ensuring he was being raised with sound morals, she insisted on daily devotions and several hours a day being dedicated exclusively to reading the Holy Scriptures.

Robert Dale Owen took after his father in both looks and an enquiring, questioning mind which, now aged nine years, was beginning to be noticed.

One afternoon in the spring, after sharing the dinner table with his parents and a visiting Bishop from the Anglican Church, the little boy confidently entered into the adults' conversation.

Owen was telling his guest how he believed a bad man could be turned to be good if he learned the errors of his ways. He was only bad due to early experiences and bad examples in his formative life.

''Papa!' Robert piped up, 'I think you would find it a very difficult thing to make a bad heart a good one.'

The Bishop laughed and patted the boy's shoulder.

'You're right, my little fellow. God only can do that.'

Encouraged by this praise, Robert joined in more fully with the debate.

Owen indulged him, listening and replying with all the respect he would afford an adult. Anne Caroline was mortally embarrassed.

'You must know your place, Robert.' she scolded, when the Bishop left the house for a tour of the mills. 'It is not for you to question the words of your elders.'

Robert apologised, his dark blonde curls bobbing, but his intelligent eyes were regarding her curiously. He was filled with questions which his tutors could not answer and upon reading the Bible and reciting his catechisms, more queries arose than were resolved.

'Why does Papa state these things? And why does he not agree with the Bishop?'

Anne Caroline took a deep breath, choosing her words carefully.

'I must confess, my dearest, that I doubt whether your father believes that Christ is the Son of God.'

Her son's face became a mask of abject dismay, lips open, eyes round.

'But only wicked people do not believe in the Lord!' Robert swallowed hard, shocked by this appalling thought. 'You told me ... only the lowly and ignorant or wild natives in far away lands like New Zealand were not Christians! Is my father wicked?'

Seeing he was becoming distressed, Anne Caroline put her arm around him and guided him to sit beside her on the chaise longue.

'If he does not believe in God,' his lips were trembling, 'when he dies will he be punished by the Devil and his angels and burn forever in the fires of Hell like it says in the Bible?'

Taking her time, she assured him that his father was in no way wicked and the kind, pleasant demeanour he showed his family and all people, was entirely genuine.

'He is everything that is good and estimable,' she told him, watching the emotions flickering over his smooth, innocent features. 'Pray to God, my child, that He will turn your dear father's heart from the error of his way and make him pious like your grandfather.' She blinked away the tears blurring her vision. 'Oh, if he could only be converted he would be everything that my heart could desire; and when we die he would be in heaven with us all.'

Robert seemed more settled after their talk and soon it was time for his French lessons with Mr Lavasseur, one of the French prisoners of war currently living in Lanark.

Outwardly, Robert appeared to be content enough, however, he took his mother's words to heart and decided that he would convert his father to the word of God. Then his mother's

369

dearest wish would be granted and they could all be in heaven together, rewarded with everlasting life.

The opportunity arose a few days later. Owen often took a turn around the grounds with his eldest son, or a stroll to the mills together. They would talk as they admired and explored the natural wonders around them.

The little boy could not contain himself and launched straight in to his 'mission' as he called it to himself, to change his father's views on Christianity.

'Papa,' he asked, slightly nervously now the moment was upon him. 'What do you think about Jesus Christ?'

'You would do well to heed his teachings, especially those relating to charity and to our loving one another.'

'Do you not believe that Christ is the Son of God?'

Owen stopped in his tracks, surprised.

'Why,' he asked after a long pause, 'do you ask me that question, my son?'

'Because I am sure ...'

'That he *is* God's Son?'

'Yes, I am.'

'Did you ever hear of the Mohametans?' Owen asked, gently.

'I think so, they live in a far off land.'

'Do you know what their religion is?'

'No.'

'They believe that Christ is not the Son of God but that another person, called Mohamet, was God's chosen prophet.'

Robert was aghast. 'Do they not believe the Bible?'

'No. Mohamet wrote a book called the Koran and Mohametans believe it to be the word of God. That book tells them that God sent Mohamet to preach the gospel to them and to save their souls.'

Owen watched his son's reactions of puzzlement as they wandered further along the path towards the garden.

After several minutes, Robert asked, 'Are you *quite* sure this is true, Papa?'

'Yes, my dear, I am quite sure.'

'But ...' Robert said, earnestly, 'I suppose there are very few Mohametans, not near, *near* so many of them as of Christians?'

'Do you call Catholics Christians, Robert?'

'Oh no, Papa! The Pope is Antichrist.'

370

Owen smiled, 'Then by Christians you mean Protestants?'

'Yes.'

'Well, there are many more Mohametans than Protestants in the world. Almost a hundred and forty million Mohametans and less than a hundred million Protestants.'

'I thought almost everybody believed in Christ, as Mama does.'

They were in the dappled shade of the beech wood, birds calling among the bare, budding branches, foraging under the carpet of discarded leaves and dead grass.

Owen stopped and leaned against a tree, looking at his son with interest.

'There are probably twelve hundred million people in the world.' he said slowly. 'So out of every twelve persons, only one is a Protestant. Are you *quite* sure that the one is right and the eleven wrong?'

Robert fell silent and they continued their walk. His father had not directly answered the question but his reply certainly gave him a great deal to think about.

Owen was pleased to have spoken with his son about such a deep subject but he did not wish to tell him what he should, or should not, believe: that was up to him to decide for himself.

'Only teach children the facts', he told his teachers at New Lanark, 'only those things they can see for themselves or we know to be truths. Once they have this knowledge they can explore and form their own opinions on any matters which require faith'.

***

'Weel,' Sarah said, thoughtfully. 'If ye esk me, it maks the place look cluttered.'

'Away! It's a braw sicht! An' ma Gerry says Mr Owen has grand plans fer it.'

The sisters were doing their washing together in the street, discussing the newly built Institute. All around them other housewives were also taking advantage of the warm summer evening, sitting chatting while they darned, suckled babies or stamped the dirt out of clothes in wash tubs. Since Owen's arrival, the middens were emptied daily, with lads also employed to clear the streets of horse and dog dung making it altogether a more pleasant place to gather.

A light breeze carried snatches of conversation, fiddle music and singing, the indiscernible words adding to the squeals of children playing ball or rolling hoops.

'Ta fer helping me wi' this,' Sarah said, wiping the back of her hand across her forehead. 'Ah'm that tired. Yon muckle twisters are bisoms tae handle.'

Rosie gave a final twist to the smock she was wringing and shook it out.

'Aye, sae Ah heard frae Mina beside me on the jennies. She wis on the carding yins, wi' the big rolls o' brushes, an' telt me she wis moved frae yon machines efter her man telt Mr Humphreys she wis deaf.'

'Oh aye, Ah cannae hear nuthin' but the roaring in ma ears fer oors efter Ah'm hame. Ah pit in tae be moved, but when they showed me the ither joab Ah couldnae see tae dae it. Sae ...' Sarah gave a heavy sigh and climbed out of the wash tub, 'Ah'm stuck wi' the twister.'

'Ye could nae see?'

'Ma eyes are a' tae pot! Ah cannae see tae sew noo, even catchin' up a hem is hard.'

'Ye should git spectacles. Esk the doctor?'

'Silly metal things on ma neb?' Sarah screwed up her nose, 'Weel, ye jist tak them aff when ye din nae need them.'

'Ah'll think aboot it.'

On reflection, she wondered why she bothered about her appearance. Long ago, she decided not to take up with another man. There was only one man for her and he was living a new life without her now. The pain was still there. Regret, she decided, was the worst feeling in the world.

In the long hours of lying alone in her bed gazing at the ceiling in despair, she knew this wearying, drab life was all of her own making. Oh, how well she knew the line of the wall, the jaggy crack in the plaster above the window and frayed threads on the pulley rope. They were the constant background to all her thoughts and lost dreams, the stark reminder that she was living in a rented room in a cotton mill.

When the sun dipped behind the wooded hills of Corehouse Estate, the evening flights of swallows swooped, chattering, through the village streets. Dirty water was thrown into middens, children were called to their beds and increasing clouds of smoke drifted from hundreds of chimneys pots where fires were lit for late suppers and pots of tea.

Rosie wrapped her shawl around her and trotted back to her own room. Another day was over; the next would be the same. There was a visiting minister coming to the Kirk on Sunday and the family meal to look forward to at Joe's.

She still felt envious of her brother's house but there was little chance of Gerry earning enough money to change their own home.

'An' there's jist ye an' me in here,' Gerry comforted, 'peacefu' like. We din nae need a lot o' rooms tae bother with. Whit wid we dae wi' em? Yer brither has all those weans clamourin' aroond him. At the end o' the day, we hae mair privacy.'

However, the envy remained and Fiona was expecting another baby in the autumn. After the initial pang of wishing she and Gerry could have a child, Rosie prayed for forgiveness for her uncharitable thoughts.

She entered her tenement door and tripped up the stairs, glancing around with a practiced eye. Had Mrs Jamieson swept the landings? Was the wick replaced in the first floor stairwell lamp?

Up the hill in Braxfield, Owen was entertaining one of his partners, Colin Campbell. Being no relation to Anne Caroline, this gentlemen was an investor in the mills through his business and social connections with Alexander Campbell and Robert Dennistoun. All three men were members of the infamous Green Card Club, where, rumour had it, they spent every Tuesday evening, almost without exception, playing cards and drinking copious amounts of claret with other wealthy young city merchants.

Of all his new partners, Colin Campbell seemed to be the most interested in the day to day running of the mills. Owen explained every aspect of his management in a long, in-depth tour during the afternoon. Then, after a pleasant meal accompanied by Anne Caroline and young Robert, the two gentlemen took themselves off to relax by the fire in Owen's study.

'Ye live in grand style,' Campbell remarked, taking a glass of brandy from the tray offered by Sheddon.

'This house is rented,' Owen told him. 'We find it very agreeable but I would have no wish to place capital in a large estate. Money should be used to make a difference, where it gives employment or betters the lives of others.'

'Come come, Owen, ye hardly slum it! From your son's lively conversation at the table I gather you live the country life to the full!'

Owen sat back into his bent wood chair, one item of furniture which was his own, not loaned by Braxfield estate.

'Ah yes, Robert was hunting today, only his second time out with hounds and as you could hear, he obviously enjoyed the experience. I, myself, do not hunt, nor do I wish to shoot pheasants or crows, another pursuit which my son has been invited to try with a generous neighbour.'

'Did I hear you are a Dean of Guild in Clydesdale?'

'Yes, an interesting position through which I have met many influential local landowners and merchants. Although, I have to confess, the accepted level of alcohol consumption within the country houses far exceeds my capabilities! I had to jump from a window to escape the other week!'

Campbell roared with laughter. 'Tell me more!'

'The squire will remain nameless, however, suffice to say that following a very congenial dinner, the ladies left us alone in the dining room and before we knew it, my host instructed the butler to bring many bottles of wine to the room. Then, he locked the door!'

'Great heavens!'

Owen chuckled at the memory. 'He told us he would release us when his best bottles were empty! I can only manage a glass, perhaps two if I am persuaded, but it does not agree with me at all so I was of no use in helping the other poor guests in this predicament. So, seeing the window sills were low and the lawns just beyond, I threw the window open and made my escape!'

'Well, I never! What did your host have to say to that?'

'He was filled with a rage! I was followed by the other members of the party and we sought out the ladies to spend the evening in the drawing room. However, while we were still upon the lawns, we heard a great bellowing of oaths and then saw our host pushing the table onto its side ... all the glasses and bottles smashing on the floor!'

'Have you returned to his house?'

'No, I fear the incident has destroyed our relationship.'

'You do not sound too upset,' Campbell winked.

'Oh, not at all! There are many other fine people in Clydesdale who do not behave in this wild and uncouth manner, so my wife and I prefer to socialise with them.'

The rest of the evening passed with shared anecdotes and views on the current problems in the country, each man sounding out the other.

'The world seems to be at war wherever one looks nowadays.' Campbell yawned, revealing an array of gold teeth: it was getting late. 'A battle won today is countered by a battle lost tomorrow.'

'Battles and Laws are just coping with the symptoms of the flawed behaviour of Man. If a man steals, they lock him up or hang him, if he wages war, they raise armies to wage a counter war. We should be dealing with *why* the man steals or the leader of a country feels the need to invade his neighbour. Why? It is the foundation of our society which requires attention, not the superficial battles and punishments to suppress the bad behaviour. We should be dealing with the cause of the bad behaviour in the first place.'

'You may well be right, Mr Owen, but the world is the way it is, we cannot change it.'

'And why not? We made it the way it is, so why not make it better, instead of suffering with the results of our mistakes?'

Campbell stood up, 'I know you are something of a philosopher ... but I fear my brain is half asleep from your warming fireside and excellent table. It is too complex a subject for me to enter into a debate at this hour.' He smiled, smothering another yawn. 'I will bid you good night.'

'Good night to you, I trust you will be comfortable.'

Alone, Owen glanced at the carriage clock before opening the French doors and stepping out into the clear moonlit night.

A million stars were shimmering in the inky darkness above his head; the lawn heavy with dew. Leaving traces of his footsteps in the grass, he wandered towards the open garden area and paused, breathing in the perfumes on the night air.

Often at this time, a barn owl made its regular evening flight low over the woodland towards open meadows beyond. He would wait a few minutes, just in case.

Everything was quiet, with just the far away rippling sounds of the Clyde streaming through the rocky gully below his grounds. Replaying the evening's conversation, he was pleased to know Colin Campbell a little better but disappointed by his lack of enthusiasm for the finished Institute.

To Owen, the building was everything he hoped it would be and he was in correspondence with Joseph Lancaster regarding his latest papers on universal education. The more he read of the lack of opportunities to teach the children of ordinary working people, the more he wanted to press on with his own plans. He knew what he wanted to do and was confident in his plans to create a model school using Lancaster's methods which could then easily be reproduced across the land.

Wearing only his light shot-taffeta dinner suit, he began to feel cold and scanned hopefully across the sky above the trees before turning towards the house.

And then he saw it! A majestic barn owl gliding silently on heavy muffled wings, eerily pale, its round, flat face turning this way and that.

Owen smiled to himself and hurried on towards the warmth: his love of Nature never dimmed.

Having filled the day proving to Campbell the efficiency and production in the mills, he was going to spend the next morning discussing his plans for further improvement to the village. These included clearing ground above the buildings, making terraces and giving allotments to the workers. There, they could grow kale and potatoes or whatever crop they chose, dig the land and enjoy the soothing balm provided by the plants and animals all around them in the countryside.

'My dear man,' Campbell said, sighing and chewing on his morning pipe. 'You have very grand ideas.'

'They are simplicity itself!' Owen cried. 'When the school and Institute are fitted out our employees can learn to read, write and all manner of subjects taken for granted in the Grammar School up the hill. In the long light evenings of the

376

growing season they will have the satisfaction of harvesting vegetables for their tables, saving them money and also bringing the benefit of breathing fresh air. What is grand about these ideas, may I ask?'

'You are expecting the company to pay for this, I gather?'

'Only a small proportion of the profits. It works admirably in the village shop where the extra income, after costs are deducted, is put towards the school room.'

'I doubt Mr Campbell of Hallyards will agree, or Mr Dennistoun.'

Frustrated, Owen launched into a speech regarding the unrest which was being widely reported in the newspapers concerning the disgraceful working conditions in factories throughout Britain. He urged Mr Campbell to look at the broader picture, to see how their mills, New Lanark mills, could lead the way in better practices.

'The Institute is attracting much interest among the visitors who come here daily. At present, they have only heard in theory what I propose, when it is fitted out and they see for themselves the difference in this small community, the word will travel.'

'Let us wait until the war is over before expending any more money, eh? When cotton prices drop and markets re-open, then we can look at your philanthropic gestures.'

By the time Campbell's carriage pulled away from Braxfield House, the bonhomie of the night before had vanished and Owen bid him a stiffly polite farewell.

'Oh dear, I can see from your demeanour that all is not well,' Anne Caroline said softly when they walked back into the house.

'Mr Campbell is unable to understand what I am telling him, or refusing to understand. It is beyond tiresome!' He sat down heavily into a cushioned chair by the window, his eyes flitting over the garden, unseeing, still lost in the argument with Campbell. 'It was the same with Mr Barton and the Manchester company. Loud words of disgust at the deaths and sickness in the factories, declared horror at instances of children being worked to death and absolutely no action taken by them to rectify matters.'

'I will pray that my cousins will be of a fairer mind.'

'It is acknowledged that the factory system is now adopted widely throughout the land, where it never used to exist.

'If this method of manufacturing is to continue, and continue it must for it now provides such an important revenue, then it must have some *balance* ... the working classes are being cruelly abused and for what? The lack of a few pounds spent on their behalf and the will to change things for the better?'

'Dear Papa used to say the same, I fear he was right when he said it was the sin of greed which made men blind to the suffering of others.'

'Your father said many a true word, my dear. He stood by what he said, acted in good heart and with a sound, clear conscience.' Owen made to rise, aware he was already late for the office. 'I daresay Campbell will attend church tomorrow, showing himself to be a follower of an established religion where charity and doing good to your fellow man is preached. Yet, he prefers to have a few pounds more in his pocket each year than to help hundreds of others.'

Anne Caroline smiled ruefully, knowing he was correct.

She was surprised by Campbell's ostentatiously expensive jewellery and fine brocade evening clothes but even more taken aback by the rude way he treated the servants.

Still, the investment he made in the mills came at a time when her husband required new partners. None the less, she would pray to God to guide Mr Campbell away from his path of avarice.

***

A week before Fiona was due to have the new baby, Bessie moved up to Lanark to stay with her son, holding herself in readiness. In the Spring, when Fiona first realised she was with child, she sent Bessie a note asking her to be with her at the birth. Bessie wrote back saying she did not feel she was able; her legs were stiff, her eyesight poor and she lacked the strength which might be required. In short: she was too old. She did, however, have a friend, Morag, who was called to nearly every birth in the Parish, bringing a cheery smile and years of knowledge.

After several notes were exchanged, a compromise was struck.

So, when Fiona gave birth to a boy on a rainy autumn morning, both Bessie and Morag were beside her.

'He's an awfy bonny wee babbie,' Bessie whispered, 'Whit a lot o' dark hair! D'ye ha'e a name fer him yit?'

'Aye, Alexander. The weans chose it, if it wis a lad. It wis tae be Charlotte, efter the queen if a lass.'

'Posh names!'

'They learnt them in yon schoolroom ... thank the Lord it wis nae Napoleon!'

While Fiona was lying in her bed admiring her new son with a delicious glow of achievement, Owen was having a very different morning.

It started well with a letter confirming that Stanley Mills were now leased to Stewart Douglas, a Glasgow merchant. This was a massive relief and he was in an optimistic frame of mind when he settled at his desk after doing his usual rounds through the work rooms. Then Clegg knocked at his door.

'Mr Owen, sir, this letter's jist bin delivered. The man said it wis urgent.'

Recognising the handwriting and seal of Robert Dennistoun, Owen reached for his letter knife and rapidly lifted the blue wax. Scanning quickly over the contents, he leaned back in his chair and read it again, this time with close attention.

The tone of the letter was one of fury and outrage, also physically evident in the scratchy lettering and careless, hurried, splashes of ink.

It had come to Dennistoun's attention that his father-in-law, John Campbell of Jura, gave Owen a considerable sum of money to invest in the mills. There was no record of this investment in the accounts when the new partnership was formed and no mention of any interest payments being made in the annual reports. Both he and Alexander Campbell demanded a full explanation and requested a meeting with Owen, in Glasgow, at his earliest convenience.

It was obvious, for whatever personal reason, that John Campbell never made the investment known to his sons-in-law.

Owen was not planning to leave New Lanark in the foreseeable future but as Anne Caroline and the children were travelling up to Charlotte Street within the week, he would accompany them in the carriage.

He sent a short reply agreeing to meet Dennistoun then set his mind to this unexpected development.

He recalled the day when Campbell sought him out: it was not long before David Dale took ill and died.

John Campbell's manner was furtive. Tapping the side of his nose and saying 'strictly between us', he gave Owen a banker's cheque for £20,000 to be invested in the New Lanark mills.

Owen acted cautiously, following Campbell's request not to make 'a song and dance' about it. He did not feel it could be registered with the company under Campbell's name, as a shareholder, because it would have been open to public scrutiny. It was also such a large sum that it would have changed the proportion of shares and control in the company, which he did not wish to have happen with his Manchester partners.

Throughout the intervening years, John Campbell's money was used exclusively on the running and improvement of the mills, just as he expected it to be. However, it was held in Owen's personal partnership account. Or rather, *at one time*, it was held in Owen's personal account. The money had long since been used.

There was no problem in showing what the money paid for or where it went, of that Owen's mind was at ease. At no time did he consider it to be his own or fund any personal expenses from the capital. The difficulty lay in the fact that the money was not recorded as being invested in the business, which made Owen personally liable if Campbell demanded it to be repaid.

Prior to meeting John Campbell's sons in law, Owen paid a long visit to his solicitor, Mr Macgregor. Closeted in a dusty, book-lined little office over-looking the Trongate, the two men reviewed the situation in every detail.

How this confidential matter came to be known by Campbell and Dennistoun was unknown. After lengthy discussion, it was decided Owen should make it clear to them, in the politest of terms, that it was not their business: he was not accountable to them.

'This has the potential to be a very difficult situation,' Macgregor cautioned him. 'While I understand you acted in good faith by keeping quiet about this generous investment in the mills, as Campbell of Jura intimated, you could be seen to have taken the capital and used it as your own. Without the constrictions of a company board or shareholders to agree its dispersal, it looks irregular. Also, Mr Owen, my dear fellow, it must be remembered that you have not paid any interest out on this gentleman's investment.'

'He has not demanded it.'

'Yet! If a chap was to look at the case with a prejudiced eye, you could be viewed in an unflattering light.'

Owen left Macgregor's office and walked along the bitterly cold streets to the Tontine Rooms, bracing himself for the encounter ahead.

'Sirs,' Owen told the two belligerent men when they arrived to join him in a booth at the back of the coffee rooms. 'With all due respect, the issue of any sum of money which your esteemed father in law placed in my hands to invest, is a private affair between that gentleman and myself.'

Alexander's ruddy complexion darkened, 'This is outrageous! Anyway, why would he give you such a great sum?'

'You would have to ask him yourself,' Owen replied, equitably.

'We shall!' Dennistoun cried. 'You can be assured we will be looking into every detail of this whole affair!'

Their irascible manner and peeved, bitter expressions exuded bad feeling between the partners. Owen held his ground. He had done nothing illegal or immoral with the money but he was aware of the strong undertone of suspicion emanating from the men.

Perhaps their father-in-law was not of a mind to put capital in to their own ventures and they resented his faith in Owen? The investment had, indeed, been made in a clandestine manner. Were they offended at not having their judgement included in the decision? He did not know, but he felt a malevolent atmosphere tinge the remainder of the short meeting before they called for their capes and left.

***

381

Three days of violent stormy weather spanning the end of the old year and the birth of 1812 prevented the Hogmanay ceilidh from taking place. Those in the village with a superstitious nature looked back on the memory of branches being ripped from trees, chimney tops crashing and smashing to the ground and the dreadful, almighty roar of the Clyde churning through the valley and claimed it to be a portent of the future.

On the surface, day to day life carried on as normal. On the factory floor, Rosie continued to be rewarded with the white side of her Silent Monitor being consistently displayed. In her house on the hill, Fiona took full advantage of her time off work with baby Alex and Tom. She spent her days pickling and bottling and, when the frosts left the soil, digging and planting in her vegetable plot while looking after Sionaidh; revelling in her home and family.

Ailsa was now on Mr Owen's payroll in the carding rooms, proud to add her contribution to the family purse.

Every few weeks, Davey came home for a night, bringing tales of his carpentry and new friends. A lithe, animated lad, he was learning to play the fiddle and entertained them at the fireside with spirited songs and stories. Sometimes, he brought a present of food or seeds for the garden but, to his mother, having all her children at the table was the greatest gift he could bestow.

Despite the tightening of belts in Britain's deepening recession, Joe and Donnie managed to keep their business afloat, much to Joe's relief. Having spent almost all his savings to keep Donnie at home, he was reluctant to dip in to the money he made from the large building at New Lanark. Although he never regretted for one moment paying Clark, his personal plans and ambitions were now postponed until he could accrue more capital.

Still, they moved from week to week, keeping busy enough to pay the rent, keep Rusty shod and put food on the table: no mean feat with six children at home to feed. Apart from Sionaidh's illness, the Scotts were grateful for their lot.

In Braxfield House, Anne Caroline and her household passed the days pleasantly. The children enjoyed dancing classes, French classes and music with local tutors, riding their ponies and playing among the estate grounds at every opportunity.

Jean and her three younger sisters visited for a long spell in the spring, giving rise to an unlikely romance between Monsieur Lavasseur and Mary.

The desire came entirely from the handsome young French Lieutenant's side. Smitten with Mary Dale, who was now a refined, well read young woman, he accepted Owen's occasional invitations to dine with the family after the boys' French lessons.

Monsieur Lavasseur took extra care with his appearance for these dinners, his black hair slicked into stylish waves, cologne wafting at his every gesture. The change in their tutor was noted by his pupils until one day the Frenchman asked young Robert to pass a note to his aunt Mary.

The hopeful lover's note was not well received. Mary read the flowery, well intentioned lines with disgust and told Robert in no uncertain terms to take it back to its author and tell him never to dare to bother her again.

Owen was surprised when Mary asked him, with cheeks flaming, to withdraw the invitation to the French tutor to join their dinner table.

In the event, it was unnecessary for Owen to say anything because the poor, rejected young man decided to forego the agony of being publicly ignored by the beautiful Miss Dale.

The French lessons continued, however, he always made his excuses and departed Braxfield before Sheddon rang the dinner gong.

Beneath this apparently idyllic lifestyle, Anne Caroline was increasingly aware of a change to her husband's behaviour. He spent hour upon hour in his study and took long tours of the village, not to guide visitors around the mills, but alone or with Clegg: making notes, watching, assessing.

In May, the country was shaken by news of their Prime Minister, Spencer Perceval, being shot and killed in the lobby in the House of Commons. The Tontine Rooms and every coffee house and inn up and down the country buzzed with speculation; was this the beginning of an uprising?

However, within twenty-four hours more details were published, bringing the rumours of panic to an end. Perceval's murderer was a merchant who believed the government owed him compensation for being held captive in Russia. It was a purely personal matter and one which sent him to the gallows within a week of his crime.

Owen sympathised with Perceval's widow and their twelve children. Bad news seemed to be in abundance with increasingly despondent reports from the war and New Lanark's end of year trading figures being even lower than anticipated.

All attempts to persuade his partners to agree to finish the Institute were falling on deaf ears, either ignoring him or reiterating their position: they were cotton merchants, not educationalists. Besides, they ended their letters, 'the New Lanark mills make very good provision for their workers, so why pour more money into bettering conditions which are already streets ahead of their competitors?'

'They just do not understand!' Owen declared to Anne Caroline one evening. 'I have been working towards this point all my adult life and especially since coming here a dozen years ago.'

'The visitors have nothing but praise, my dear. You should be very proud of achieving such a clean, healthy factory.'

'It can be so much more than that! Yes, a successful factory is essential but it is the improvement in the population of the community which interests me. Look at the world! Just look around and we see and hear of beggars, thieves, murderers! Take Bellingham, who drew his pistol on Perceval to exact revenge for a perceived grievance. These people were not born that way, they were made that way by society.

'Here, in New Lanark, I can prove this point, on a much smaller scale, of course, but nevertheless, it can be demonstrated! By treating and educating children in a rational, reasonable manner the end product will be a rational reasonable society.'

Anne Caroline looked doubtful; they discussed this subject on numerous occasions.

'Caroline, my dear, you know from the first day we arrived in the village, I wanted to put my ideas and plans into action? Remember?'

'Of course, and you have ...'

'Oh, the simple ones, yes! Those which I could instigate without any need for agreement from my partners: fines for stealing or drunkenness, instead of dismissal or sending them before a magistrate. Keeping their homes clean, not beating the children ... or any of the workers!'

'And in the school rooms?'

'Only partly. That is what is so infuriating! I am so close to creating a village where the inhabitants live and work together in harmony. Where Roman Catholics and Protestants tolerate each other sufficiently to work together and even laugh together where they used to come to blows or trade insults. The managers and workers talk to each other with mutual respect ... believe me, Caroline, that is a very different practice than in the vast majority of factories.'

'It has been acknowledged, Robert. The many experts and inspectors which visit the mills have all spoken highly of your work.'

'It is not *enough*.' Owen wandered around the drawing room, his hands behind his back, an earnest expression on his angular features. 'You should hear some of the exclamations of amazement when people see how the mills can turn a profit without terrorising the employees or forcing tiny children to labour in stifling work rooms.' He turned to face her, 'Why ... why is it so hard for some people to just be *kind*?'

His words hung in the air like specks of dust swirling in a shaft of sunlight.

'Kind?' she asked, feeling his exasperation.

'Kind! You are a kind person, my dear. If you saw a weary, starving child, tripping and whimpering as it dragged a cart of raw cotton twice its size, would you not cry out! Go to the child's aid? Allow it to rest? Perhaps provide some water or food?'

'Of course!'

'It would be the right thing to do? Yes! Yet there are those men ... and women, whose job it is to whip and bellow at these infants, threatening them with dismissal if they do not carry out the job they are paid for!'

'Surely, it is the parent's fault ... the child should be cared for at home ...'

'Perhaps the child is an orphan? Or his parents are ill or have fallen on hard times and it is up to the child to earn for the family ... or more likely, the child's parents endured the same neglectful abuse when they were infants and see no wrong in repeating the behaviour. Wouldn't a kind person, someone who has been brought up to distinguish wrong from right, be appalled? Moved to cry out at the scene I described?

'And yet, that is what is considered normal. It is in *my* mills, *here*, in New Lanark, where they gasp and cry with wonder! The children are almost chubby, the overseers firm and expecting order but not violent and yet ... and yet, these mills produce good quality cotton, on time and for profit.'

Owen's irritation was growing stronger with every day he was blocked from putting his reforms into practice.

The following week he was taking the chair at a public dinner in honour of Joseph Lancaster, a man he long admired for his new system of effectively teaching large numbers of pupils with few teachers.

In preparation for the evening, Owen's thoughts and ideas for his Institute in the village were once again at the top of his mind. Whenever he walked past the towering, empty building, he was gripped by a feeling of rising impatience and intense disappointment at such a wasted opportunity.

Lancaster, a Quaker, came to the dinner plainly dressed in a dark grey knee length jacket, dark breeches and a white cravat, a stark contrast to the flamboyant, colourful outfits and jewellery displayed by the assembled men and women in the meeting room. He was a few years Owen's junior and many years younger than the majority of his audience, but did not appear in the least overwhelmed.

He was a solidly built man with ordinary brown hair neatly parted to one side, curling against his high collar. Although a slightly disappointing figure at first glance, his animated brown eyes immediately captivated all those he met. There was a passion within him to spread the word of how easy it was to provide a good education to the masses, without great expense.

Owen's enthusiasm and sincere belief in Lancaster's work provided a strong basis for his introductory speech.

He kept the address brief, maintaining that education was the primary source of all the good and evils, misery and happiness in the world.

'Consider,' he asked, 'the differences, bodily and mental, which are found between different races of mankind and different individuals in the same race. From whence do these general bodily and mental differences proceed? Are they inherent in our nature, or do they arise from the respective soils where we are born? Evidently from neither. They are wholly and solely the effects of that education which I have described. Man becomes a wild, ferocious savage, a cannibal, or a highly civilised and benevolent being, according to the circumstances to which he may be placed from his birth.'

He looked around the sea of interested faces, all eyes focused on him.

'Let us suppose, an exchange of any given number of children to be made at their birth between the Society of Friends, of which our worthy guest, Joseph Lancaster, is a member, and the loose fraternity which inhabit St Giles in London. The children of the former would grow up like the members of the latter, prepared for every degree of crime, while those of the latter would become the same temperate, good moral characters as the former.'

He paused, allowing this fact to be assimilated, then concluded: 'How momentous in its consequences for good or evil is the work of educating the youth of the nation!'

The speech met with rousing approval and by the end of the evening, Owen climbed into his carriage with a feeling of elation.

The next day, on the long drive back to New Lanark, he looked out upon the Scottish countryside in all its spring glory and came to a sudden realisation. He should find new partners. He was no longer content to manage the mills merely to raise the production figures and see the profits gobbled up by greedy merchants.

He recalled his early years of reading Rousseau and Voltaire, of debating Tom Paine's 'Rights of Man' and the earnest discussions on the French Revolutionaries' declared aims of Liberty, Equality and Fraternity. Adam Smith's statement came to mind, regarding the different talents in different men, arising not so much from nature as from habit, custom and education.

Invigorated from being in like-minded company, Owen decided he should seriously set about finding men who shared his vision. He thought he had made himself very clear to

387

Campbell, Dennistoun and Campbell, but this time he would write down his aims, then there would be no ambiguity.

Events, however, overtook him.

The United States of America suddenly declared war on Great Britain.

Thomas Jefferson's trade embargo had done little to dissuade either French or British naval forces to cease boarding their ships to seek out purported deserters employed on US merchantmen and press them into war service. This continuing problem was only part of the reason for the unexpected start of hostilities, the main motive being to expand America into the northern territories of Canada.

All along the border with Canada, the British not only supplied the Canadian militia and their Native American allies with guns, ammunition and information but they sent troops to fight alongside them. However, generally, the feeling from Britain's new Prime Minister, Lord Liverpool, and his government was that Britain was far too busy fighting Napoleon in Europe to be distracted by America.

The implications of further disruption to importing supplies from overseas added to the gloomy picture shown in New Lanark's annual reports.

Dennistoun and Owen's other Scottish partners sent word that they would be visiting the mills and expected Owen and Humphreys to be available for a meeting.

The men alighted from their carriage in colourful lightweight jackets and cream cotton breeches, stretching and admiring the immaculate village around them, baking under the summer sun.

Inviting them into his office, Owen offered refreshments, trying to gauge their mood. It did not take long to feel the animosity.

After a short preamble and stilted niceties, Alexander Campbell leaned forward in his chair and looked pointedly at Owen.

'The accounts for the last year are exceedingly disappointing, Mr Owen. However, that is not why we are here.'

Owen remained composed and looked expectantly between the four men in front of him.

Alexander Campbell, lean and dark bearded, Dennistoun, square faced, uncomfortably hot in his showy, shot silk scarlet waistcoat and Colin Campbell, pale faced, busily fiddling with his nails, his lips set in a tight, straight line between bushy side burns: they did not look pleased. Of all of them, Humphreys, his long time friend and under manager, appeared the most discomfited.

'We spoke of your underhand dealings with my father-in-law, John Campbell of Jura, for which you gave us no proper explanation or comfort. Now, another similar matter has come to light. I am given to understand that you made a private arrangement with Mr Humphreys. Am I correct? Whereby you will receive his share of the profits?'

Owen's eyes went to Humphreys who avoided his glance, instead reaching to refill his beaker with lemonade which Cooper prepared for the meeting.

'Sir,' Owen replied, thoughtfully. 'The affairs you refer to were not underhand. They were personal matters, agreeable to both parties. They do not impinge on anyone else, so I fail to see the relevance here.'

'They are irregular! Who else do you have strange, hidden dealings with? Eh? What will we discover next month? or next year, Mr Owen?'

'Everything you require to know which affects the business, you are already fully appraised of, Mr Campbell.'

'You went ahead with your buildings,' Dennistoun said. 'Yet, you knew we were not in full agreement.'

'And you knew that was my intention, from the very start of our partnership. I made no secret of my plans.'

'Your plans are grand in the extreme! These are hard times to make anything from the markets and you wish to squander money on a school? A public kitchen? Yes, Mr Owen, we know your plans and we do not agree with them, do we gentlemen?'

There was a mumble of agreement between the others.

Owen regarded them with barely concealed contempt.

'Alas,' he said with a sigh. 'I fear we have reached the same impasse as I experienced with your predecessors. You simply do not understand what I am striving to do here.'

'It would seem to us that it is *you* who do not understand what we are doing here!' Alexander Campbell said, aggressively. 'These are cotton mills, we are cotton mill owners,' each word was clipped, slow, as if explaining to a

child. 'In case you have not kept abreast of world affairs while
you are shut off down here in this picturesque glen, the country
is now at war, both to the west and to the east. Trade was
difficult, now it will be nigh on impossible ... and you want us
to sink money into *schools?*'

'We have different views of the village. I wish to achieve far
more here than temporary profits.' Owen quelled his rising
displeasure, 'Gentlemen, let us not argue. I propose that I
should find new partners, once again, and buy the company
afresh.'

'Oh! Do ye, by Gad!' Dennistoun exploded.

'Good God, Owen,' Alexander cried, 'the profits may be low
this year but these are the best mills in the country! I speak for
us all when I say that we do not wish to sell. No! It is *you* who
we cannot work with ... it is *you* who will have to leave New
Lanark. Regrettably, due to the abnormal business practices we
have discovered we are in a mind to fire you.'

The words hit Owen with the force of a bullet.

Leave New Lanark?

Leave the project he poured his heart and soul into for nearly
thirteen years ? It was preposterous, unreal ... a nightmare.

'You will step down from your position as manager at the end
of the month,' Dennistoun pronounced, grimly.

'I shall resign,' Owen said flatly, keeping his fury at bay, 'at
the end of this week.' He surveyed the solemn group, raising
his eyebrows. 'Who is to replace me? Humphreys? Mark well,
sir, you will now have to be on profit-share.'

'Colin Campbell, has agreed to do the task.' Alexander
Campbell said, waving his hand at his colleague.

Owen leaned back in his chair, silent, a myriad of expressions
gleaming in his intense eyes.

The men stood up to leave and Owen politely nodded to their
muttered good byes, still too shocked to gather his thoughts
properly.

'Mr Owen,' it was Alexander Campbell. 'We are sorry it has
ended this way. You have been here a long time and made it
what it is, but your plans are impossible. Your visionary ideas
are just that, ideas, but no one is going to give you financial
backing, you know. I should also warn you that my father in
law is growing very concerned at the prospect of never seeing

his capital again. He is talking of requesting its return, with interest.'

Campbell swept out of the door, leaving Owen alone.

After a long time, he stood up and went to the window, gazing out at the grassy slope to the mill lade, a timber wagon trailing up from the forge and the huge greystone facades of his towering mills.

It was unthinkable to see a future which did not include New Lanark. Yet, that's exactly what was staring him in the face.

He was out of work, out of New Lanark, had no income and all his money was tied up in the company.

Worst of all, they would not consider selling it to him.

He had lost New Lanark.

Chapter Eighteen

"Create all the happiness you are able to create; remove all the misery you are able to remove." **Jeremy Bentham**

Anne Caroline sat at her writing slope and dipped her quill in the ink well.

What to write?

'My dearest sisters, I trust this finds you in good health,' she paused, frowning with concentration.

How could she break the terrible news about Robert?

How could she broach the subject that their father's wonderful mill village, which they knew and loved since infants, was now in the hands of strangers?

Since Owen told her of the outcome from the partners' meeting, she prayed and cried in equal measures; always behind closed doors, out-with his hearing. She wanted to comfort him, be a steady, calming influence but she was at a loss as to how to help.

He was distant, deep in thought, only managing to regain some normality when the children were present.

It did not take long for the news to leak out to the servants that something was very wrong and Owen instructed Sheddon to speak to the household and reassure them that their jobs were safe. In truth, she wondered if this was indeed the case for his salary was severed and all his other assets were held in the stone walls and machinery in the village.

Two days after resigning, he appeared from his dressing room in the morning freshly shaved with a brisk, efficient air to his movements. In his favourite pale grey jacket and breeches, a deep blue and yellow printed silk cravat at his throat, he looked altogether more cheerful.

'My way ahead is clear to me, Caroline,' his voice sounded firm and energetic again. 'I am still the largest shareholder in the mills and I will *not* let them take this opportunity away from me. There are men out there who share my ideas and do not flinch at their responsibility to those less fortunate. I shall find them and together we will buy the village back.'

With the letter to her sisters still unwritten, Anne Caroline remembered his fine words, the eager expression on his much loved face, and felt a hard knot of compassion. Owen was no sooner picking himself up and tackling this mammoth task than he was hit by another blow.

That it came from her own relative, John Campbell of Jura, caused her great distress. No doubt, urged on by his sons in law, Campbell instructed his lawyer to demand immediate payment of six thousand pounds of unpaid interest on his client's initial investment.

On receipt of this alarming request, Owen rode to Glasgow with the letter and asked Macgregor for advice. The advice was difficult to hear and impossible to fulfil: John Campbell was perfectly within his rights to ask for the money, it was long overdue and should be paid forthwith to prevent further legal action.

'I do not have six thousand pounds,' Owen told him, flatly.

'Then we have a problem.'

'I am in the process of acquiring new partners and we shall put forward a good price and buy back the mills.' Owen omitted to mention that, at the moment, his current partners were not of a mind to sell.

'That will not aid you in your search for funds to pay Campbell of Jura. Perhaps, you should sell your shares to the present partners? Raise the money that way?'

'Out of the question! I aim to retain my share of the village, not throw it to the wolves! When I have it back I will prove to them how productive the mills are when run under my guidelines and generate this sum of money tenfold. However, at this moment in time, I cannot pay. I just need some time. '

'Then,' Macgregor said, tapping the plume of his quill against his cheek, 'I will reply to this request by saying you are not at present in a position to meet with the payment but the debt is acknowledged and will be paid.' He fixed Owen with a fierce stare. 'I have to warn you, sir, that Campbell will be advised to raise bankruptcy proceedings against you.'

Owen was a sickly pallor, grey shadows around the eyes, 'Meaning that they would take my shares in New Lanark ... for that is all I have?'

'Quite so. Let us hope you find wealthy partners before it goes that far, eh? Or can you borrow from the Royal Bank? You are thick with the agents in the city's branch, are you not?'

'Not as I used to be, but I have arranged funds to maintain my domestic life. Mr More is a strange fellow, I truly wish Scott Moncrieff was still at his desk.'

'And Mr Dale.'

'Indeed.'

When her husband returned from the city, Anne Caroline heard only of the decision to pay Campbell when the money was available. He did not bother her with the spectre of bankruptcy.

Unfortunately, the spectre materialised into reality before the end of the month when Campbell instigated formal legal proceedings to declare Owen bankrupt.

On that summer afternoon, with her pen poised, Anne Caroline discovered she could not bring herself to mention the dreadful position in which they found themselves.

Instead, she decided to recount a funny incident about the children and started to write again. The ink was dry in the quill-nib leaving a scratchy broken line on the paper. Snatching it up, she screwed it into a ball and hurled it into the cold fireplace.

Her eyes pricked with scalding tears. 'Please God, have mercy on us!' she whispered fervently. 'Robert may be ignorant of your love and forgiveness, but he tries his very best to help others and while he professes not to follow your word, does he not carry out your wishes in his every action? I pray for your merciful guidance to lead us out of this terrifying plight.'

Voices sounded in the hall and she hurriedly wiped her eyes, straightening her shoulders and assuming a quiet composure.

'Caroline, my dear,' Owen came into the room, 'At last! I have completed the Statement regarding the mills and Clegg is ensuring it leaves for the printers on the Edinburgh Mail coach today.'

Clegg was continuing in Owen's private employ as his personal secretary, an expense he could scarcely afford but felt was essential. Every day, he was receiving correspondence regarding his innovative work in the village, as well as from Glasgow and Manchester business colleagues and in his capacity as a Dean of Guild in Lanark.

'As soon as John Moir produces the pamphlet,' Owen continued, 'I will circulate it amongst the highest circles of wealthy enlightened thinkers and philanthropists. This time, there will be no misunderstanding as to my intentions for the business.'

Anne Caroline smiled with genuine relief.

'Oh Robert, I shall pray for its success.'

He put his arms around her, holding her close; her red rimmed eyes told all too clearly of her distress.

'Please, try not to worry so much,' he murmured, soothingly, as she pressed against him. 'I am completely tired of having partners whose only aim is to make money. Even before Campbell and the others visited, it was my intention to break from them. I have written to Mr Atkinson in Manchester, entreating him to persuade a vote to sell the works.' He tightened his grip around her, sighing. 'Oh, my dearest, there may be difficult months ahead but I have set my heart on the future of New Lanark. I have too much to carry out here, important work which will improve the lives of the working people right across the nation ... it will *not* be taken from me when I am so close!'

***

'Mr Owen's oot! He's left the mills!' Rosie cried, opening the door to Sarah and Cal's room.

'Whit?' Cal was shocked.

395

'Ye ken Ah telt ye Gerry heard a big row, a couple o' week's past? An' then Mr Owen's no' bin aboot sae much? Weel ... he's bin fired! Fired! Ah esk ye? Why wid ony yin want tae fire a grand maister like Mr Owen?'

'Why wis he fired?' Sarah asked.

'Och, hav Ah no' jist said? Ah din nae ken why!'

'Does yer man no' ken?'

Rosie sat down at the hearth, it was a warm evening but the coals were lit, glowing beneath a bubbling pan of oats. Automatically, she stirred the contents as she spoke.

'Naw. Yon toffs frae Glesgie were doon an' the next thing, Mr Owen's pitting a' his papers t'gither. Ma Gerry says he heard frae Clegg that the gents frae Glesgie fired him.'

Cal was plaiting long strands of horses' tail hair into a fine fishing line, 'Amounts tae the same thing,' he said gloomily. 'He's left New Lanark.'

'It's jist the worst thing Ah've heard since Mr Dale sold the place,' Rosie said sadly.

'An' mind, at first ye did nae tak tae Mr Owen at a'!' Cal grunted, 'Ye've changed yer tune!'

'Aye, Ah have, an' every yin in the village tae! He's an' awfy fair man, fer a' that he's a Sassanach.'

'Who's the boss the noo, then?'

'Gerry's bin stuck wi' auld baldy heid Humphreys fer days an' he's jist telt him tha' Owen's no comin' back as the manager, sae mibbee it's himself that's takin' the joab?'

They sat silently for a while, Cathy and Stephen lying on their beds, exhausted, waiting for their porridge before sleeping.

'There's a thing,' Sarah said, yawning. 'D'ye ken we need tae clean the hoose noo? Fer the inspections?'

Rosie gave a last stir to the thick oatmeal and knocked the spoon clean on the side of the pot with more force than usual.

'O' course ye hav tae clean the hoose! Yer a wee slitter, Sarah! Ah'll be daen ma roonds as usual an' sae will a' the inspectors. It wid be a disgrace tae gae back tae the middens some folk used tae call their hames.'

Cal said nothing. He liked Mr Owen and he liked the way the village was run: it was safe. No-one was beaten or treated harshly, the managers and overseers could only shout at you, and even then, only when Mr Owen was not around.

What was to happen now?

Cal pushed the question from his mind and carried on choosing the longest black hairs from the pile at his side, plaiting and straightening, plaiting and straightening.

He hated change.

***

Owen distributed his beautifully printed Statement of the New Lanark Mills to every person he could conceive might be interested in becoming new partners in his venture. It described the building stock, mills and machinery in detail and set out clearly what he wished to achieve in the community.

Despite many enthusiastic and supportive replies, he soon realised the weeks were passing and no-one was responding with offers of investment.

'I am going to travel to London,' he told Anne Caroline. 'Surely, in the capital, there will be a more enlightened society? I have several excellent contacts there, people I have been in correspondence with for years and hold the same views as I.'

'Will you be away long?' she asked, knowing the answer even before her words died on the air.

'I cannot say, but certainly no longer than I must for I shall miss you and our dear children bitterly.'

'Oh, and we will miss you ...' she caught herself, hearing a pathetic note in her voice.

Dear Robert, he was doing everything in his power to keep them at Braxfield House and retrieve the mills. She must show courage and allow him to go about his business unhindered by worries on her account.

'We will eagerly await your return,' she said instead, 'I am sure you will succeed with your search and, besides, it will be pleasant for you to meet and speak with those you know only through their writing.'

Downstairs, on the day of Owen's departure, Sheddon took particular care with his address to the servants after morning prayers.

'Our master is travelling on important business. I am sure we all wish him success in his endeavour. While he is away we will keep him in our thoughts and prayers. We will care for Mrs

Owen and all his family and the estate in readiness for his early return.' Sheddon looked at Murdoch who was pale with anticipation. 'We trust you will have a safe journey to London, Murdoch. It will be interesting for us to hear about the great metropolis on your return. God keep you safe, haste ye back!'

He gave his customary nod and slight wave of his hand, dismissing them to carry out their day's duties.

Straight away the servants rose from their seats around the table, bursting into their own personal farewells to the valet.

'It'll no' be like the Highland tour at a'.' Murdoch was telling them. 'Ah can nae say if Ah'm that taken wi' gaun tae England but ... '

'Mind the highway men!'

'Will ye see the King? Weel, no' the auld batty yin, the ither yin?'

The questions and good wishes followed him around as he gathered the last of his own belongings: Owen's trunks were already meticulously packed and on the carriage to take them up to the Stage Coach.

'Take care of yoursel',' Peggy said quietly, taking her leave of him in the servants' hall, 'and yer maister. All oor joabs and the wean's future depend oan this trip. We will be thinkin' on ye.'

Murdoch gave her an impulsive hug, 'Ah ken it's important, Peggy. Din nae fash yersel', Ah'll tak guid care o' him an' Ah reckon we will be hame afore ye ken!'

After Owen gave Clegg last minute instructions, everyone gathered on the gravel to wave the carriage away, the younger children jumping up and down with excitement, unaware of the gravity of the situation.

At dusk, when the bell swung above Mill One to end the working day, the news spread rapidly throughout the village: Mr Owen was trying to buy back the mills.

* * *

The weeks wore on and the pair of nesting ospreys Cal enjoyed watching from the forge started leaving. First the large, brown breasted female, then her two young, one after the other and finally, after treating Cal to a spectacular display of scooping a writhing fish from the Clyde right below Dundaff Linn, the male bird disappeared. The valley felt suddenly empty; they had all flown south for the winter.

Falling leaves sprinkled the ground, fungi gleamed among dying vegetation and the scent of wood and coal smoke was heavy in the damp air. Autumn was closing in around them, with the sun lying lower and lower in the sky.

On a dull, cloudy morning, Ruby, one of the women working beside Rosie, came to her machine late. She was breathless and flushed, giving excuses of a bad headache and dizziness. The Overseer berated her tardiness and set the gears working on her machine. Shouting over the racket that she would be getting a dock in wages, he saw her stagger and lunged forward just in time to save her falling among the leather straps and metal wheels as she collapsed in a billowing cloud of plaid skirts.

The other Overseer and several of the children ran to help. Between them, they carried her hastily to the relative space and peace of the corridor and sent for the doctor.

It was measles.

Within the week, more than a dozen cases were diagnosed in the village, with the market town of Lanark also reporting an increasing number of people being struck down.

Rosie was terrified she must have caught it because she worked so close to Ruby. Every day, she peered at the skin on her chest and arms, laying a palm across her forehead and wondering if she felt all right: too hot? too cold? Then, while she was asleep one night, she started to toss and turn, waking Gerry with her moans. He lit a candle and saw the angry red rash on her face, on her hands below the long sleeved night gown, transparent with sweat where it stuck to her body.

She was burning with fever.

He hauled on his jacket and trousers over his long night shirt, so distraught that it hung out like a skirt down the back of his legs, but he never noticed. McGibbon was not at home, but his wife took the urgent message and said, patiently, that when he returned from the other two newly infected villagers, he would come and see Mrs MacAllister.

The villagers were not the only victims.

On hearing cries from the nursery early one morning, Dora found Anne Owen showing all the signs of the disease. The eight year old was miserable, rubbing her eyes, blotchy with the rash and whimpering with the scorching pain of a dangerously high temperature.

Both Dora and Peggy survived measles and small pox as children and set about moving the little girl into a separate room, praying the others would not take it. Their prayers were not answered, over the following few days all the Owen children, except Richard, went down with the disease.

The lamps in the nursery wing of Braxfield never dimmed. Anne Caroline nursed them almost constantly, having to be helped to her bed on several occasions, exhausted but desperate to be at their bedsides. Miss Wilson, who was very fond of the children, offered her services and helped Peggy and Dora to make sure there was always someone watching the invalids while the others rested or managed to take a few minutes to eat Cook's sustaining food.

Slowly, one by one, starting with Anne, the children showed signs of improvement. When George, the young footman took ill, there was only baby Mary and David left in the sick room.

'Mary is past the worst,' the doctor told Anne Caroline, 'And your servant boy is a strong lad, I believe he has only a light dose, like your eldest, Robert, his eyes are clear already.'

'And David? He is very weak, don't you think?'

'Yes, I'm afraid David is still rather poorly.'

The icy chill of fear shivered up Anne Caroline's back.

'How shall we best treat him?' she asked, her voice husky.

The doctor prescribed some stronger medicine, handing her a small green glass bottle.

'Four times a day. I shall call back tomorrow but do not hesitate to send for me if his condition worsens.'

Anne Caroline's devoted nursing continued and slowly David started to improve.

His mother, however, was losing the flesh from her bones with worry. She could not sleep, except fitful, exhausted naps in the nursery chair and only managed a few mouthfuls of food at a sitting because her stomach was so clenched with terror.

Watching her children suffering broke her heart and opened memories of losing loved ones; torturing her with images of baby Daniel. She prayed endlessly, read from the Bible, beseeched God constantly in her mind, even while instructing the servants or murmuring comforting words to her son.

Eventually, the day came when David ate a whole bowl of porridge and his delightful, impish personality shone in his eyes once more.

'Thank the good Lord for that,' Miss Wilson whispered to Cook. 'As if it isn't enough for the mistress to be worried half to death about keeping her home, her husband's away at the other end of the country and she won't send for him.'

'What good would it dae onyway? He could be laid low wi' the fever too, an' then where wid we all be?'

'She's worn away to nothing. The dresses just hang on her and when she draws the shawl tightly around her, well, she's as thin and fragile as a twig.'

'Noo the bairns are on the mend, an' George is ready tae be oot his bed, Ah'll mak some beef broth.' Cook folded her well muscled arms. 'We'll soon ha'e them richt as rain agin!'

Three eldery patients died in the village, many more were bed-ridden for weeks but, slowly, Rosie recovered.

In all, she was away from the mills for a month and if Gerry could have persuaded her, she would have rested for much longer. He was grateful to Sarah for helping him care for her, bringing food and changes of night clothes to their room, but Sarah was too scared to cross the threshold. She couldn't risk catching it herself and kept her distance from everyone, even Cal, passing her wariness to her children. For the first time in years, they did not walk up to church for several Sundays, fearful of mixing with a congregation who may be carrying the early stages of the fever.

Fiona and Joe tried to carry on as normal, counting their blessings every day when they awoke to find the family healthy and without symptoms.

By the time the first frosts were sparkling across Clydesdale's rolling hills, the contagion was dwindling and finally every one began to breathe easier when a week passed with no new cases. It left behind it many who were irretrievably weakened, their eyesight and hearing impaired and, for the most unfortunate, eleven fatalities.

On waking one morning to see another dreary, overcast sky showing beyond the curtains, Anne Caroline decided that they all needed a change. Before dressing, she penned a letter to her sisters taking up their standing invitation to spend the darkest months in Charlotte Street.

She longed for company, close, adult company. Owen had been away for months and although he wrote frequently with accounts of the interesting people he was meeting and dinners he was attending, she was lonely.

Due to the measles outbreak, Jean and her younger sisters did not visit Braxfield in the late summer and she yearned to see them again.

She pulled the bell cord and turned her attention to making arrangements for travelling to the city.

Ramsay answered her bell, but her usual pleasant expression was drawn, her eyes shifty.

'I need this letter taken up to catch the mail coach,' Anne Caroline looked more closely at her maid. 'What's wrong?'

'Peggy said to tell you that Master Robert is unwell.'

'Unwell? Is it serious? Why have I not been told before?'

'It was only just this minute, ma'am.'

Anne Caroline fled along the corridors, her heart beating wildly, only pausing to try and calm herself before entering the nursery. It is nothing, she told herself, please God, let it be nothing.

Robert was lying curled on his side, breathing with difficulty, his soft brown curls wet against his forehead.

'Fetch the doctor, immediately!' she cried, sending Ramsay flying out the room. 'How long has he been like this?'

Peggy was leaning over his bed, a cold cloth in her hand.

'Not long, ma'am. He was up with the others earlier but said he felt sick after his porridge. I thought he was with William playing in the attic but found him in here ...'

'It cannot be the measles, he has just recovered ...'

The doctor was at a loss, suggesting it was a mild recurrence of the disease because Robert was not so badly affected the first time.

'It is certainly not mild,' Anne Caroline murmured, watching her son's laboured breathing. 'It is almost as if he is asleep but his eyes are open ... Robert, darling, Robert, can you hear me?'

The little boy swallowed and blinked, then closed his eyes. Throughout the children's previous illness, Anne Caroline chose her words carefully in her letters to her husband, telling him the children were coping well with the fever. Now, she discarded the note to her sisters and wrote instead to London, asking Owen to return.

Their son was seriously ill and she needed him beside her.

A week later, late in the evening, Owen arrived back at Braxfield and his first view of the house through the trees caused him to fear the worst. It appeared to be in complete darkness in the moonless, rain soaked air: had they gone to Glasgow? The post chaise clattered to a halt and within moments Sheddon swung open the front door, sending a shaft of light down the steps.

'How is he?' Owen called, jumping from the carriage.

'Holding his own, sir.' The butler bowed his head. 'Good evening, sir.'

Anne Caroline came rushing out of the drawing room, unashamedly throwing herself into Owen's outstretched arms.

'I came as soon as I could,' he held her tight. 'Tell me! How is the boy?'

'Oh my dearest, I am so pleased you have come home. He is still dangerously ill. Come, we will go up together.'

They were so absorbed in one another that they did not notice Jean and Margaret emerging from the drawing room. They were standing silently, not wishing to intrude, watching the tender scene. Julia and Mary were coming down the stairs, tying the sashes of house coats, their hair loose around their shoulders.

'My sisters came to be with me ... it has been the most terrible time. Oh thank the Lord you have come home!'

Sheddon left the family reunion and hurried downstairs, meeting Murdoch and the footmen carrying in the bags from the back hall.

'That's the master home,' Sheddon announced to the staff in the kitchen. 'He looks utterly exhausted. Please prepare a tray of supper for he may wish something to eat. Goodness knows how long he has been travelling.'

'Four days,' Murdoch said, wearily. 'Four of the longest days o' ma life. He's bin tha' worrid, an' would nae stop the night at the last inn. Rollin' an' rattlin' in the dark is an awfy thing, Ah pray Ah niver ha'e tae dae it agin. Forever worrying aboot highway men, even wi' a guardsman up wi' the driver.'

'Ye paur lad,' Cook cooed, 'it's lucky Ah've a fine mutton stew fer ye.' She looked around for the scullery maid, 'We'll pit it oan the table in a jiffy.'

'That'd be grand. It's richt guid tae be hame. Ah'll see tae the master, an' then Ah'll sleep like the deid.' Murdoch went to the range and held his hands out for warmth. 'How's the wee lad?'

'Och, it's bin yin thing efter anither since ye left.' Cook bustled around the room, directing the maids to stoke the fire and lay a tray, while ladling the meat into a pan to heat. 'He's mighty poorly, there's nae doubt aboot it. Yon doctor's bin applying the Spanish Fly, poor wee mite. They've kept the blister open fae days noo ... he can nae catch his breath tae greet, sae Peggy says the tears jist flow doon his wee face.'

'Whit's wrang wi' him?'

'They din nae ken. It's no' the fever, a' the ither weans an' George took the fever but it passed, thank Our Merciful Faither.'

'D'ye think he's gaun tae die?'

Cook stopped what she was doing, pursing her lips, 'We are praying he's spared, an' din nae gae sayin' ony thing tae upset Peggy or Miss Wilson, they're fair vexed aboot him.'

Whispered rumours spread through the village, 'Robert Owen's back at Braxfield, his eldest lad's dying ... may be already dead. Why else would he have come home with such haste?'

'Have ye heard ony mair aboot the Owen lad?' Joe asked Logan, walking together to a Lodge meeting.

'He's gie sick, yon doctor is up at the big hoose twice a day an' they can nae fathom whit's wrang.'

They turned a corner into the wind, leaning into it, coat tails whipping around their legs.

'Owen's havin' a rough ride, that's fer sure.' Logan continued, one hand gripping the brim of his hat. 'Humphreys is no' up fer the joab on his own, he's an assistant, no' a proper manager. We need Owen back.'

'Ah heard there wis anither manager, Campbell?'

'Pah! Ma horse could dae a better joab running the mills than tha' yin. All talk! He disnae ken a carder frae a twister! Ah remember the days wi' Dale, he knew his factory, every wheel, every nut an' bolt. Mr Kelly wis the same. By, Kelly wis a man! An engineer! He has his ane mills noo, on Bute.'

They turned again, this time into the lee of the tenements and a calm fell around them, their footsteps and voices suddenly loud in the still air.

'There's nothin' tae beat unnerstaundin' yer trade,' Joe said, solemnly. 'Ah used tae think Ah wid ne'er git ma ane business. All yon years o' toil ... but Ah ken it wis worth it.'

'Oh, aye, son. An' that's why Mr Owen is the manager he is. He's worked on the factory flair, he kens whit he's eskin' o' the werkers, no' like Campbell.'

They arrived at the door of New Lanark's St David's Lodge, No. 279, and were admitted by the Tyler, Alexander Tod, a man long known to Joe as a mill wright since the early years. Removing their hats, they left the freezing dark streets behind to enjoy warmth, a fine dinner and further discussions on ways to help the plight of the most needy in the local area. They helped each other, like brothers, but they also carried out charitable works, of which Joe was proud to participate.

During his years of involvement with the Freemasons he was very aware of the layers inside the fellowship. Their deep spiritual teachings were fascinating, opening an understanding of himself and his contribution to wider society and he was keen to learn more, move to the next Stage and become even more engaged.

***

Peggy stood very still beside the doctor, her starched white cap trembling, her hands pressed tight against her round stomach, creasing the front of the long apron. Opposite her, dark figures against the bright nursery windows, Owen and Anne Caroline were holding their breath while the doctor examined their son.

'Yes, you were right to send for me, there is a change in his condition.' McGibbon coiled up the rubber tubing of the stethoscope and laid it aside. 'Happily, it is a change for the better.'

Anne Caroline gasped, leaning forward to stroke the little boy's hair.

'Oh praise be to the Lord!' she cried. 'I was sure he seemed less fevered and the dreadful wheezing in his chest is less ... don't you think?'

'It appears so.' The doctor stepped away from the bed, allowing Peggy to arrange the blanket neatly over her charge.

'He is still very pale,' Owen said, with concern. 'He was always a rosy cheeked, sturdy lad, it grieves us to see him like this.'

'Start to feed him up. Give him plenty of molasses and weak ale, oats too and some finely chopped, raw red meat. You should see a difference soon.'

Thankfully, the physician's words were borne out and Robert's precarious condition began to turn the corner to recovery.

Owen had left very pressing affairs in London and was thrown into a quandary. His children were immensely important to him and quite apart from any feelings of duty as their father, he cared deeply. To leave Braxfield while there was a chance of Robert suffering a relapse was out of the question, but he knew he could not postpone his departure indefinitely.

There was better news from Dennistoun and the Campbells, possibly due to Atkinson's intervention. The partners were now in agreement for the mills to be sold, however, at present anyway, they would not agree to a private sale to Owen. It was at least a step forward to the stalemate.

Anyway, he was still seeking new investors, a decidedly difficult task. Great Britain was consumed by the soaring costs of fighting two wars abroad while struggling to contain the machine breakers in the north of England, a product of acute social unrest and poverty across the entire country.

Owen's latest project, directly inspired from the speech he gave at Lancaster's dinner, was an essay laying out his views of how a child's character is formed through early experiences and education.

This apparently simple principle, so easy to express while talking to friends, was much harder to communicate on paper.

When complete, it was to be printed and distributed in the same way as the Statement on New Lanark. However, this piece of work was a much more intense, enthusiastic paper, stating his views unequivocally. These were long-held personal beliefs and despite being aware that they may be thought extremist, he saw nothing to be gained by watering them down. Unless he stood up for what he truly believed in now, when could he? How much more desperate could his situation be? No, this was the time to speak up, bring his plans in to the light and place them before the eyes of every influential contact he could reach.

While writing this essay and mixing with men of learning from all manner of professions, he became more and more captivated by his vision of how society should be, *could* be, if the upcoming generation was educated properly.

It excited him enormously. If he could put across his plans sufficiently to gain support and put them into practice, the ramifications for the ordinary people of the country were staggering.

Every day he reviewed his notes, adding a slightly better word to use here, or striking out a phrase there. Nevertheless, his son's health took precedence and he bided his time at home until he could leave without tormenting himself with worry, not only about Robert but also his wife.

It was nearing December when he and Murdoch left Braxfield House one white frosty morning. Watched only by a cloud of cawing rooks winging their way across the silver sky, their carriage wound its way up the hill to meet the Stage Coach heading south.

Owen leaned forward, seeing the smoke shrouded roofs of New Lanark in the valley below. It was so much more than slate and stone buildings, wrought iron wheels and gushing water. It held such promise; ready, built, home to over two thousand men, women and children ... many already busy on the factory floor. Yes, they worked hard and brought in money for the merchants, but they should be fairly rewarded and lead full, healthy lives at the same time.

He slumped back into the cushions. No longer being the manager of the mills caused a physical wrench. He sighed, placating himself, all too aware of the tediously long journey ahead. He must set his mind to completing his essay and securing the required finances.

He *must* succeed.

Chapter Nineteen

"To train and educate the rising generation will at all times be the first object of society, to which every other will be subordinate." Robert Owen

The grave misfortune of Owen losing his position at the mills and facing bankruptcy was echoed by Nature's unusually cold, wet weather. Crops either failed entirely, withering in sodden soil, or were so delayed in ripening that some farmers were still trying to gather in their sparse yields after Hallowe'en.

Soldiers were deployed to break up ugly squabbles over bags of flour or potatoes, tempers flaring under the stress of keeping hunger at bay. Prices rose every month, shortages of basic foodstuff became common-place and money was of little use to the gentry when their desired luxuries were simply not in the country.

As an island, Britain was being increasingly cut off from even the illegal, smuggled trade with Europe and America. Its merchant ships bringing goods from further afield were constantly under fire and its meagre reserves being rapidly consumed.

In February, weeks of sub-zero temperature gave the perfect conditions for Frost Fairs to be held on the frozen Thames and Owen was persuaded to join a party of friends to experience the souvenir booths and entertainment set up in tents on the solid river.

One afternoon, Daniel Stuart invited him to a dinner where he met William Godwin, the celebrated social philosopher and author of *An Enquiry Concerning Political Justice*.

Godwin's work discussed the revolutionary ideals of justice, freedom and equality, subjects close to Owen's heart. Soon, he became a frequent guest in Godwin's home, sometimes arriving before breakfast and staying to take supper in the evening. Together, they mulled over Owen's drafts at length and in minute detail. Godwin was an excellent writer with a sharp brain, skilled in coaxing Owen into condensing his occasionally rambling, superfluous prose into precisely the right words to convey his radical ideas.

Godwin introduced him to other socially aware, enlightened thinkers. The two men regularly spent time at Charing Cross in Francis Place's personal library, an established meeting place for radicals. This unusual venue, located at the rear of Place's tailoring shop, drew bright young men to deliberate current events and Owen struck up a friendship with the Scotsman James Mill, a shrewd political economist who was currently absorbed in writing articles for the Edinburgh Review. During the ice covered days of London in mid-winter, Owen enjoyed many lively debates with these men, and many others, in their houses or by the fireside in Godwin's home.

In Scotland, the freezing temperatures allowed the popular game of curling to become possible again.

Impromptu sheets of ice were created on the outskirts of Lanark on the common ground and Joe and Donnie were among the crowd of enthusiastic players eager to practice their sport.

After a couple of days it soon became clear that the ice would remain long enough to hold a bonspiel. Hundreds of people came to both play and watch, enjoying some exciting entertainment after enduring the darkest months of the calendar.

'What are they doing?' young William Owen asked his mother, craning his neck to see out of the carriage window. 'Can we stop? Listen! I hear music!'

Anne Caroline knocked on the carriage ceiling and the horses were reined in to a halt.

'It is a curling match,' she said, looking out on the colourful, bustling scene. 'They push stones around on the ice. Your grandfather used to watch it sometimes, in the parks in Glasgow.'

They were returning from a visit to Lady Armadale and were warmly dressed for the winter's day so they alighted and strolled around on the crushed icy grass, keeping to the outside of the spectators.

Robert was still too unwell to leave the house so only William, Anne and Jane accompanied her, with Dora in attendance, the younger children not having been included in the Armadales' invitation.

Anne Caroline was in a lighter frame of mind for the first time in months. The sky was a brilliant blue, the sun a glorious golden light bathing the frozen landscape. Everything appeared crisp and clear, lively with voices and laughter. She breathed in the fresh air, catching scents of burnt sugar and charcoal smoke, narrowing her eyes against the glare to take in the spectacle.

Before leaving Braxfield that morning, their postman, Dunn, delivered a letter from Owen: he was coming home.

He wrote to tell her the welcome news that his essay was about to be published. He was obviously in a buoyant frame of mind and also told of staying with Mr Lancaster at Labrador House, and with the Borradales and the Coles, who Jane and Julia knew. He asked fondly after Robert's continued recovery and laid her mind at rest in regard to the content of his essay which she was concerned might appear too revolutionary. He assured her that it had been read and approved by highly respected men in London.

She hugged this precious news to her heart, but in particular, she remembered the warm, affectionate words: the personal messages to her and the children.

"My dearest Caroline ... to know that you are well is the greatest pleasure I have, except to hear that you are happy, as that includes something still more than health, and I now look with the greatest delight to my return ... with kind love and kisses to all our dear boys and girls ... with the sincerest affection, your truly attached husband ..."

Glowing from her inner thoughts, Anne Caroline did not feel the chilly air and was content to indulge the children with roasted chestnuts and toffee apples.

Joe saw the Owens from where he stood at the end of the rink. The young boy was juggling hot chestnuts in his cupped hands, grinning and hopping between his two little sisters,

411

teasing them. The girls' long ringlets swung around their heads, capes and petticoats dancing, giggling with an openness more usually seen in village children. Mrs Owen was laughing with them, her gloved hand holding the string of a sticky toffee apple at arms' length, away from her pale blue coat, a wide golden fox fur collar encircling her shoulders.

It was just a glimpse through the moving crowd, but Joe was struck by how at ease and friendly the family looked together. Even the maid was joining in with the merriment, swaying to the rhythm of the fiddle music from a nearby stall; smiling and passing words with her employer.

His attention returned to the game until, on winning that end, he was walking and sliding up the length of the rink with his brush when he noticed Mrs Owen and the children standing close by, watching.

He raised a hand to his temple and nodded, catching her eye and smiling.

She acknowledged him with a small dip of her head, the fur trim on her hat accentuating the movement.

'Who's that man, Mama?' William asked.

Dora was as keen to know. Her eyes were devouring the handsome blonde man and his son who were holding the attention of every woman present, and not for their curling skills.

'That is Mr Joseph Scott. He is a stonemason, my dear. He used to live in New Lanark and I first had cause to speak with him when I was just a child,' she surprised herself, 'not much older than you are now!'

'He looked very pleased to see you.'

'Oh,' she chuckled, 'I think Mr Scott's wide smile was because God has blessed us with this most beautiful day today ... and also because his team is winning!'

They waited to see the final end played and applauded with the cheering crowd when Joe and his popular New Lanark team won their match.

'Well played!' Joe cried, when all the players shook hands and he accepted congratulations from his opponents. 'A grand match!'

The freezing temperatures remained for weeks but few could spare the time from work to play on the rinks again before the thaw set in. Joe and Donnie stored their stones at the back of their shed, carefully unscrewing the brass handles to take inside. After giving them a thorough polish they laid them on the mantelshelf, wondering when the next opportunity would arise.

Thick lumps of ice were still bobbing in the pools below Corra Linn when Owen returned from London.

He was jubilant to be home, renewing his close relationship with all his children and marvelling at how they had grown. Robert was still causing concern for, while he was physically recovered from his illness, he was unnervingly sensitive to touch, crying out if any part of his body was accidently knocked. This intense sensitivity was also present in his mental state and he was moved to tears at the slightest provocation.

The servants treated him like an invalid and, sadly, that is what his parents were also being forced to acknowledge.

The strong, inquisitive and at times overly wilful child was no longer present. Robert spent his days in bed, pale and tearful, struggling to dress and sit in the garden, quite incapable of joining his father and William for walks or riding his adored pony.

When Owen was not attending to his family or other business with Clegg, he was actively seeking new people who might be interested in his essay and, ultimately, investing in the mills.

Having accomplished his aim of publishing a piece of work which declared his views to the world, he needed to spread it far and wide. He had not, however, put his name to it, feeling it better to let the ideas speak for themselves. To this end, it was published anonymously.

No sooner was he home and enjoying this relaxation with his family, than he received formal notice of imminent bankruptcy. The sudden change in his light hearted mood was noted straight away by Anne Caroline and he was forced to confide in her.

'The upshot of it is,' he concluded, 'If I do not pay six thousand pounds to Campbell of Jura within seven days, they will seize my assets and dispose of them in whatever way they can.'

'The house if not ours, Robert ...' she cried, perplexed.

'Perhaps the carriage and horses ... and I have a few pieces of

413

jewellery which you and Papa gave me over the years but all of those together will not raise such a sum.'

'They would take my shares in the New Lanark Mills,' he said, gently, trying to make the blunt statement sound less painful.

'Oh! Oh *no* ... that cannot happen! There must be a way of finding this money?'

'If there is, neither Macgregor nor I have found it.'

'If I, personally, possessed the capital, of course I would give it to you, immediately. I only had the dowry Papa settled on me before our marriage. As you know, his Will dispersed his fortune between my sisters and various charitable organisations.'

She stood up and moved restlessly around the drawing room, deep in thought. Although she was regaining her strength, she was a slim figure, her bracelets hanging loosely on her wrists. The straight folds of her Empire line dress, with her hair coiled up on her crown to show off her slender neck and shoulders, accentuated her thin frame.

Owen watched her. There was a fragility about her now and the little lines around her mouth and eyes were becoming more obvious. These did not detract from his admiration, if anything, they re-inforced his love for her.

'I have it!' she hurried towards him, placing her hands on his chest, brown eyes shining. 'My dear, we must confide in my sisters, they are each very wealthy in their own right. They have every confidence in you and love you dearly, I am sure they would feel bitterly rejected if we did not turn to them in our hour of need.'

'I could not ask them to pay my debts.'

'Please Robert, they have the means and would willingly do anything in their power to help you, especially where Papa's mills are concerned. Anyway, you will repay them as soon as this wretched business is over and you have new partners to take the mills back.'

Had he not been so dejected at his predicament, he would have smiled at her show of confidence.

They were still discussing this thorny issue when Peggy brought the youngest children down to the drawing room to say goodnight.

'We belong here,' Anne Caroline said softly, when they were alone again. 'If you are forced to let them take away New Lanark, where will we live?' The gravity of the situation needed to be voiced, 'how could we live? Our servants ... dear Sheddon and Miss Wilson?'

'I would find a position elsewhere, there are many around Manchester who would offer me a senior manager's post. Do not worry, my dearest, I would provide for you and our family whatever the outcome.'

Anne Caroline *was* worried, dreadfully worried. Before blowing out the candles late that evening, she managed to persuade Owen to travel up to Glasgow the next day and speak with her sisters.

As his wife predicted, Owen discovered Jean and her younger sisters were horrified to know of the possible loss of the New Lanark Mills. They were equally upset to hear this precarious situation had been going on for nearly twelve months and immediately offered assistance.

Having acquired their willing agreement to stand as guarantors for the outstanding capital, Owen walked briskly through the city streets to see Macgregor, his mind rapidly creating an achievable and structured repayment plan to appease Campbell.

He entered the lawyer's cluttered office in high spirits but was soon brought crashing down once more when he was advised of a newly arrived missive from his current partners.

'They've devalued the company!' Owen cried in alarm. 'This is monstrous! The New Lanark Company is worth at least eighty thousand pounds, if not half again as much and now they are valuing it at a mere forty thousand ... they are playing a dangerous game here.'

'I fear they have caught wind of your affairs and are acting to cover their backs, should they have to pay out, or more probably, buy in, your shares.'

'Caught wind? It is Dennistoun and Alexander Campbell who are behind this storm that is designed to blow me out the water! These shares are my security for the bank! They have halved my collateral with a strike of their pen. It is outrageous!'

It took Macgregor a while to calm his client down and hear the more positive news regarding the Miss Dales' offer of help to stop the bankruptcy petition.

'We will require a formal contract with my sisters in law,' Owen told him. 'Both Miss Mary and Miss Jean are, I am given to understand from my wife, most probably about to become engaged into marriage. Everything must be done very properly and securely for them, especially as their future husbands may wish to take over their wives affairs following the weddings. I owe them a deep debt of gratitude and shall repay them as soon as possible.'

'How is your search for new partners coming along?' Macgregor asked.

'I am delighted to say that I have been very well received in London. Indeed, there is already such heart-warming and confirmed interest that I am in a mind to offer to buy the mills back right now! Play them at their own game and use their figures! As I sit here today, I am sure I can raise sixty thousand from my Quaker friends. Please write with this offer straight away. We will turn the tables on those scoundrels yet!'

For all that Owen was his client, Macgregor held a certain sympathy for Dennistoun and Campbell. It was common practice in these dark days of the war and volatile markets to devalue a company and especially when a major shareholder was seen to be in a critical financial position. So, he did not agree the business men were necessarily behaving like 'scoundrels'.

In any event, the offer was rejected but a ray of light pierced the gloom shrouding the future of the mills: the partners were considering putting the whole mill village up for public auction.

Although he was heavily burdened with paperwork and strategies for the future, Owen was forced to push his problems to one side and receive his brother at Braxfield for an unexpected and hastily arranged visit.

'For years I have wanted to show William my mills and my family,' he uttered on receipt of the news of his imminent arrival. 'He has never taken up the invitation and now ... of all the moments to choose ... this is most inconvenient!'

Anne Caroline was delighted to finally meet a member of her husband's family and found William very agreeable. Surveying him subtley while they talked, she was intrigued to note similiarities between the siblings in their high cheek-bones, arched brows and the line of their jaws. William was considerably older, his hair streaked with silver at the temples but he was in robust good health and of a cheerful disposition. After welcoming him to their home and introducing his wife and children, Owen was keen to get back to his desk. However, not wishing to appear unfriendly, he took his brother for a walk around the gardens before suggesting he might like to rest after his journey and they should meet again in the drawing room before the main meal of the day.

'Why, Robert! This is a magnificent place!' William exclaimed, enjoying a glass of claret before dinner. 'You live like the Lord of the Manor!'

Anne Caroline bowed her head, embarrassed.

'We do not own this estate,' Robert said, quietly. 'I have rented it for our use due to its close proximity to the mills.'

'And the mills are doing well?'

'They are holding their own.' Owen changed the subject. 'And what of your news, William? I had hoped we would be meeting your wife?'

'Alas not. Dinah sends her most affectionate good wishes and hopes she will have the pleasure of knowing you both soon.' He paused for a moment then hurried on, his words rushing together. 'We have a son! William! It is a fine and wondrous event in my life because I once believed I would be denied the blessing of a child of my own. You may recall, I wrote to you some time back? When I married Dinah? She brought me the joy of having a warm home life along with two infants from her previous marriage. Of course, it was a tragedy for her to lose her husband and we pray he is with the Lord. The little children suffered severely from their father's death but I have taken them as my own.'

'My goodness, it must be a great change for you.' Robert was taken aback. He jumped to his feet and shook his brother's hand. 'Congratulations on the birth of your son!'

While they talked it became clear that William was still as unsettled in his life as he had been when they met years before.

It was not until the next evening that the true reason for his journey to Scotland became clear.

'We are looking to make a new life,' William told Robert in the privacy of the study. 'A new start, if you like. You have these fine mills and I wondered if you were in a position to repay the loan I made to you when you were starting out in Manchester?'

'Ah,' Robert's mouth drew into a tight line. 'This is very unfortunate timing.'

Taking a moment to marshall his thoughts, he sat back in his chair and looked candidly at William.

'Had you asked me this a year or so ago,' he said, slowly, 'yes, I would have gladly written a cheque for the full amount, with interest. Your loan of one hundred pounds started me out on this grand adventure and it will be repaid. However, my current situation is not all it appears.'

For a long time William listened while Robert told him about the predicament he found himself in and the reasons for it. He described at length his desire to create a model community which would stand as a shining example of good practice, both as a factory and as a way of conducting day to day life for improving happiness and health for the lower classes.

'Why can you not just content yourself with managing a successful mill?' William cried, 'That was what you wanted when I gave you the first capital. Why do you always want more?'

'Money and status have no meaning to me, you know that, William. I can run a mill, of course I can, I have proved it again and again. No, I wish to make a *difference*. Look around you, look at the poverty and the cruel practices across our land. The vice of greed pushes all else aside! By doing nothing about it when I am in the prime position to change this offence, I would be colluding with all that is wrong and complacent. No! I aim to show that making money and caring for the workforce are not incompatible. It can be done! Why should children labour all hours of the day ... or only learn to read if their fathers have money? *All children* should have that right, even the poorest.'

'You are dreaming! Wake up to the reality around you before you lose everything, I beseech you! Speak to your partners and take back your old position, forget these notions of expensive schools.'

'That would not do at all,' a perplexed expression furrowed Robert's brow. 'You do not understand. Wherever I go, whether it is here at New Lanark or at another manufacturing enterprise, wherever it is, I want to implement my ideas. It is *vitally* important to me. I have already made such a difference here, I have no wish to leave now so I will find new partners ... I will buy back the mills and, yes, William, I shall repay you as soon as I can.'

'This is folly!' William stood up and paced around the room. 'You have a wife and children, you owe it to them to be responsible ... not bankrupt and unemployed! Why are you always so stubborn? Eh? Always believing you can do what you want, regardless of others telling you it is not possible?'

'It *is* possible. It will benefit the whole community and has wider ramifications. I shall show you!'

'What with?' William was aghast. 'You tell me you have no money and are no longer employed by the mills!'

'I hope you can understand,' Robert said calmly, despite heightened colour on his cheeks, 'I cannot go through life seeing all that is wrong and not doing something to put it right.'

Exasperated, William laid a hand on his brother's shoulder. 'I wish you well, but I fear for you. These days of war are not the time for grand gestures of philanthropy. I know you, Robert, you will do what you wish, I cannot persuade you otherwise but I will pray for your wife and family.'

When William left Braxfield the next day, the brothers shook hands in a formal farewell. Each fervently wished the other could understand their point of view yet knew this was unlikely to happen.

It was a wet, cool summer but there was plenty of amusement to be found for the children indoors, allowing Owen to see them between the long periods he spent dealing with correspondence. He especially enjoyed joining the older children for several hilarious afternoons in the drawing room in the company of the ostentatious dance tutor, Mr Dodge, who came up from the village school twice a week to instruct deportment and dance.

Then, briefing Clegg on all his current affairs, Owen set out for London again, determined to have partners ready, with their funds in place, when a date for the auction was set.

***

Fiona sat on the edge of her bed, a smile on her face, listening to the boisterous voices filtering up from the parlour. How many times had she looked out the little cottage window at the scene below? She loved it in the spring and summer when the hillside was bright green, ferns rising in spikes from their mounds of last year's golden foliage, flowers of every colour peeping amongst the lush grass. She loved it in the winter, white and blue, every twig and stone laid bare or shimmering under snow and ice. But autumn: autumn was her favourite.

It was the last Sunday in October and she gazed out onto every colour imaginable. It was a long time since she last painted a picture, probably before she was married? The desire to translate the view from her home to a sheet of pure white paper became all consuming.

However, this was not the reason for her satisfaction, it was knowing Davey was at the table downstairs. These rare Sundays when he walked across from Carluke were high points in Fiona's life.

She finished brushing her hair and deftly plaited it before coiling it neatly on her head and pinning it in place. Tying her prettiest lace bonnet in place, she stood up, smoothing her dress and taking a moment to acknowledge the pleasant feeling of simple domestic comfort and peace.

She was even coming to terms with Sionaidh's illness. For years she carried an anxiety which spoilt her enjoyment of everything in life, waiting to pounce and gnaw away at any happiness. Their daughter's distant, difficult behaviour and sudden fits were now accepted by the family. It was just the way she was, for whatever reason.

They all knew she would never work in the mills or any other job, but they loved her, treated her with as much patience as their weary lives allowed and protected her from the outside world. Their only fear was that she might hurt someone. At one time or another, all of them suffered from being hit in the face or bitten when she was upset, but they forgave her whereas an outsider might cause trouble.

Today, Sionaidh was surrounded by family who all understood her ways. Today was a safe day.

'Yer lookin' bonnie,' Joe said, when Fiona joined them.

'An' Ah'm feelin' bonnie, ma darlin'!' She kissed him on the lips in passing and wrapped an apron around her waist, ready to tend the meal.

After eating from wooden bowls for the last twenty years, they recently purchased a dozen patterned china plates and Joe made a rack for them and screwed it securely to the wall. Now, they were already neatly laid out on the table for the family meal with a centrally positioned jug full of sprigs of bright red and gold leaves taken from the trees on the lane.

Davey and Donnie were sitting on either side of the range, their legs stretching across the hearth rug, making it difficult for their mother to reach the fire.

'An' how long can ye stiy wi' us?' Fiona asked Davey, her eyes flicking over his long brown hair, noticing some of the strands were plaited, interwoven with leather. It was a habit amongst the Highlanders and she was quietly pleased. The older he grew, the more he resembled her brother. There was no denying it now, making her look more closely at his profile, his straight, short nose, dark brows and the way he used his hands when he talked.

Distant memories of her childhood rustled like autumn leaves against a closed door.

'Weel,' Davey said, 'efter Hogmanay, Ah din nae ha'e a joab, sae if Ah can nae find anither yin afore then, can Ah kip here fer a while?'

'O' course ye can!' Joe laughed. 'This is yer hame lad, wherever yer Mam an' Ah live, ye ha'e a hame. Mind that.'

Davey raised his tankard of ale, smiling gratefully. 'Tha's a comfort, Da. Ah've bin huntin' fer werk since Mr Selkirk telt me, but there's nuchin' aboot. They're layin' men aff, no' takin' then on.'

Fiona was already wondering how they could fit everyone in to the cottage. It was fine for Davey to sleep on a makeshift mattress for one night but living with them would be different.

Sarah, Lily and Cathy arrived at the door, followed by Gerry and Rosie, the latter carrying a parcel containing a fruit loaf.

Everyone tried to squeeze around the table, leaving the younger children to find a space to eat from a bowl on the floor.

421

When Cal arrived, there was a brief pause in the gossiping and laughing while Rosie said Grace, then the noise erupted again.

'Sae where's Stephen?' Fiona enquired, passing around baked potatoes to eat with their stew.

Sarah shrugged, 'He did nae want tae come ...' she gave a dismissive wave. 'He's no' bin gaun tae his werk either, an' Ah can nae mak him. He's a big lad, fifteen years noo, he should ken whit he has tae dae if he wants tae earn. Cal caught him skulkin' doon by the forge the ither day when he wis supposed tae be in the store rooms.'

'He comes tae the school room a'richt,' Fiona told her, knowing from Sarah's expression that she was more worried than she was saying. 'The evenin' lessons. Some times Ah'm werkin' late an' see him. He's a bricht lad. His readin' an' numbers are awa' better than mony o' them, an' he's no' bin at the school lang.'

The chatter moved on and the subject of Tam Murdoch's father dying came to the fore.

'An' noo Tam an' his brither ha'e a hoose!' Joe told them. 'His Ma' can nae live on her ane, sae Tam's wantin' tae stiy there an' buy his brither oot.'

'That's an awfy ramshackle wee hoose,' Rosie said.

'Aye, mibbee, but his Da' paid fer it an' Tam's lookin' tae fix it up. He esked me tae tak a look an' whit's nae fallin' doon has damp crawlin'up.'

'Does he still hauld a caunel fer wee Melanie?' Fiona put in.

Joe and Donnie roared with laughter,

'She's no' sae wee these days, ma love!' Joe grinned. 'She could eat Tam an' no' look ony different. She's a grand baker, mind, a great lass, but Ah can nae see Ewing ever agreeing tae tha' match.'

'If he has his ane hoose,' Fiona said, 'perhaps Mr Ewing would look at him?'

'Tam needs a builder, eh, Da'?' Donnie winked.

'An' a joiner!' Davey winked back at his brother.

'Now a' we need is a roofer!' Joe smiled at his sons, turning in his chair.

'Din nae look at me, Da!' Robbie said, cheekily, chewing on his food. 'Ah'm fer the looms. Nice an' warm indoors while yous are oot there freezing!'

'Weel Tom!' Joe called across the heads of the children clustered around the bowl on the hearth rug.

The little boy looked up, 'Whit?'

'Ye fancy bein' a roofer? Pittin' thatch or tiles on the roof?' Joe waved his hand to the ceiling.

'Away!' Fiona admonished him, affectionately. 'Leave the bairn alane.'

The gathering broke up before it grew too dark and Joe went round to the shed with the boys to check Rusty for the night.

Sionaidh was fractious and tired so Fiona left Ailsa to clear up and helped her other daughter up to the bedroom.

It had been a lovely day; fun and full of laughter. She sat on the floor beside the low bed and sang soothing Gaelic lullabies until the child grew calm and eventually fell asleep.

'*Goodnight, my darling,*' she whispered, tucking the blanket over her shoulders and standing up to tip-toe out.

Then she paused, listening.

Footsteps were running up the lane towards the cottage, fast. The latch sounded on the door and Cathy's voice called out.

Fiona hurried down the stairs, 'Whit's happened?'

'It's Stephen! He's gone!' Cathy's pretty face was ravaged with tears. 'Mammy's in an awfy state ... Uncle Cal telt me tae let ye knaw ... Stephen's gone!'

Joe came through the door, catching the last of her words.

'Gone where? D'ye ken?'

'Aye, he left a note. Mammy couldnae mak it oot sae she esked me an' Uncle Cal tae read it, he said he's gone tae America tae find Da'.'

Fiona looked blankly at Joe, ushering Cathy towards a chair by the fire. 'Whit's got in tae the lad? His Da's deid.'

Joe shook his head, laying a hand on Cathy's shoulder, 'Naw, Sean's no' deid. He went tae America.'

Fiona sank down into the other chair, 'America?'

'Aye,' Cathy reached for Fiona's hand, 'it's a secret. Da wanted Mammy tae gang wi' him, all o' us, tae gang wi' him, but she wid nae ...' There was a long pause before she continued. 'Stephen's ne'er forgiven her ... he swore tae me the nicht Da left tha' he wid find him an' Ah wid see him agin, we wid be a family agin. An' ... noo he's gone.'

'But, how can he gae tae America?' Fiona gripped Cathy's hand tightly, 'we're at war wi' them,' she glanced up at Joe, 'aren't we?'

'That's why Mammy's in sich a bad way.' Cathy started to cry, stammering over her words. 'The note says he's gonnae join the Navy.'

***

On the 24th December the Glasgow Herald newspaper advertised the sale of the New Lanark Mills by public auction at the Tontine Rooms on 31st December.

Owen was ready.

He had made many useful contacts during his long sojourns in London and the reception to his essay on the Formation of Character was gratifying.

Four of his new partners were members of the Society of Friends. They were already supporters of Joseph Lancaster's education system which Owen advocated using at New Lanark. A fifth partner, Michael Gibbs, was a member of the Church of England but was sufficiently enthusiastic in Owen's stated aims to improve the lot of the working class that he wished to pledge money towards the purchase.

All his new partners were strong believers in the need for social reform, however, another gentleman who Owen greatly admired and hoped would join the company was Jeremy Bentham.

Bentham was famous in the London philosophical and legal circles and Owen was very pleased when mutual friends, James Mill and Francis Place, arranged an exchange of correspondence with the respected man. This lead to a private meeting between them at Bentham's home which Owen felt went extremely well.

By the week of the auction, however, although Bentham gave every indication of wishing to be part of New Lanark, matters were not formally settled.

Owen planned to stay at Charlotte Street the night before the auction but the day before leaving Braxfield he rode down to New Lanark to take a last look round.

'It's Mr Owen,' Gerry said, peering out of the office window as the distinctive cream coloured mare clip-clopped slowly along the wet cobbles.

Humphreys was already up in Glasgow, being entertained by Dennistoun, so Gerry and his junior clerks threw on their capes and hats and went out to speak to their former manager.

'Mr Owen! Sir!' Gerry, not normally effusive, ran awkwardly after the horseman.

'Mr MacAllister! Good day to you!'

A fine curtain of rain misted the village; heavy grey clouds smothering the sky.

'Ah speak fer us all here in the village, Sir, we wish ye all the very best o' luck.'

Owen smiled down at him, droplets of water dripping from the brim of his top hat.

'Well, thank you. I shall do my very best, you can be assured of that.'

He rode on: past the empty hulk of his planned Institution, down in front of Mill One, along between the mill lade and the towering grey walls of the other three mills, past the new school and down the steep, slippery incline to the forge and dyeworks.

The Clyde was in spate, deafening him with its incessant, splashing roar, rushing through the trees on the island. Branches and huge fluffy blobs of foam dipped and rose in the churning brown water, moving rapidly downstream in the current.

Reining in at the furthest point, Owen looked back at the village. It was midday but so dark that lamplight glowed from every window and at the base of each structure the massive iron wheels, the mechanical heart of the mills, were all turning, spraying out cascades of white water.

The buildings were impressive, the machinery and products from the factory admired both at home and abroad but it was the people, the living, breathing residents and workers which now held his attention.

Eventually, soaked and thoughtful, he rode home.

***

On the morning of the sale, Owen left Charlotte Street in the company of his solicitor, Alexander MacGregor. Three of his proposed new partners, Allen, Fox and Gibbs had travelled north to Glasgow for the event and would be meeting them at the Tontine.

'I've heard the opposition have arranged a celebration meal,' Macgregor told Owen as they rolled through the streets in Owen's carriage. 'A public one, to boot!'

'They must feel themselves very sure of success,' Owen said, quietly. 'Clegg was informed that Robert Humphreys has been promised my position.'

'Well, we will have to see about that. As far as we can tell, Dennistoun and his partners are spreading around the rumour that you have no money nor support. Presumably their spies do not have acquaintances south of the border.'

They arrived at the elaborate, carved stone portico of the Tontine Rooms and joined the throng of people gathering to enter the building. The sale was causing a stir among the merchants and bankers of the city, many of them friends, customers and colleagues of Owen, who clapped him on the back or called out their good wishes when he passed.

Clegg was hovering at the inner door, 'Sir,' he stepped forward into the stream of people. 'I have seated the English gentlemen at a table at the back, as you asked.'

Owen turned to Macgregor, shaking his hand. 'I will thank you in advance for I am sure you will follow my close instructions.'

'I am at your service, Mr Owen. I will not deviate.'

The two men exchanged a direct, understanding look before Macgregor turned away. Owen watched him push his way through the crowd to the front of the packed room, choosing his place several chairs along from where Dennistoun's party were seated.

'Well, Clegg,' Owen said, with a calmness he did not fully own, 'let us join our friends and let the auction commence.'

Having valued the mills at forty thousand pounds yet rejected Owen's offer of sixty thousand, Owen had insisted on the upset price being set at sixty thousand and after a brief preamble, the bidding began.

'Sixty thousand pounds.' Alexander Campbell announced his opening bid.

A murmur sounded through the audience.

'Sixty thousand and one hundred pounds,' Macgregor called out.

Sniggers came from Campbell's side: so the rumours were right, there was very little money at Owen's disposal.

'Sixty one thousand!' Campbell cried.

'Sixty one thousand and one hundred pounds,' came Macgregor's clear voice.

'Sixty two thousand!' from Campbell.

'Sixty two thousand and one hundred pounds.' from Macgregor.

Slowly the bidding went up, each time Campbell raised the price by one thousand and was countered by Macgregor adding one hundred pounds.

At eighty four thousand and one hundred pounds, Campbell asked for an interval and took his partners out a side door and into a huddle in the corridor. Members of the assembly took the opportunity to visit the water closets or order drinks from the porters; the ladies gathering in cliques to giggle and share gossip.

Clegg disappeared for a few minutes and came back smiling.

'Mr Dennistoun's snorting snuff and Mr Campbell's huffing and puffing in close debate with Humphreys.'

The auction continued, rising again by a thousand from Campbell and another one hundred from Macgregor. At one hundred and ten thousand and one hundred pounds, there was another delay.

'Aha!' Kirkman Finlay told his party, 'Owen's going to win the day!'

Owen overheard the vote of confidence and wished he could be sure of success. There was only a further ten thousand pounds more to offer and Allan, Fox and Gibbs were sweating and looking very glum.

The bidding resumed.

'One hundred and eleven thousand pounds!' Campbell said decisively.

Macgregor added one hundred more.

Now the room was silent, merchants and clerks alike, leaning forward in their seats, apprehensive.

When it reached one hundred and fourteen thousand, Owen swallowed heavily and reached for his cup of cold coffee.

Macgregor cleared his throat and said, 'One hundred and fourteen thousand ... and one hundred pounds.'

Dennistoun jumped to his feet in a rage, dropping back into his creaking chair as Campbell's voice could be heard above the clamour.

'We are done!'

The crowd exploded into a spontaneous cheer.

Owen and his partners rose to their feet, exclaiming with relief, clasping each others' hands, beaming and sharing congratulations.

At the front of the room, the defeated partners were in an ill humour.

'Confound that Owen!' Atkinson muttered, 'he has bought it ... and twenty thousand pounds too cheap!'

'Come, gentlemen,' Campbell growled, 'we must put a good face on it, the dinner tables are laid for us and it has all been paid for ... so we must comfort ourselves with the sirloin and drown our sorrows in the excellent claret.'

'Clegg!' Owen stepped aside from the excitement, his assistant hurrying to his side. 'Please send the news to my wife. Engage the fastest horseman in Glasgow,' his eyes shone with elation, 'she must be told as soon as possible!'

The messenger arrived at Braxfield on the third horse of his relay, in a shower of gravel and galloping hoofbeats. The commotion alerted Sheddon and Anne Caroline at the same time and they met, hurrying, in the hallway.

'A message for Mrs Owen!' the messenger shouted, dismounting and running to the steps. 'Mr Owen and his partners have won the day! They have bought the mills!'

Within the hour, the good news reached New Lanark and their jubilation could not be contained.

'Mr Owen is returning! He has bought back the mills!' Logan declared to an urgently called meeting of the floor managers. 'Inform all the employees immediately and grant them the rest of the day off! We must all celebrate this momentous day! Praise be to God!'

The Hogmanay celebrations were already in preparation but the thought of having Mr Owen back in charge filled everyone with further relief and excitement. In the gathering dusk of the December afternoon, Logan left the sounds of merriment and music behind him and marched up the hill to Joe's house with a lively bounce in his stride.

'Mr Owen's managed tae oust auld Humphreys an' the Glesgie men!' he shouted along the road, seeing Joe and Donnie un-harnessing Rusty in the lane.

'My, that's jist grand news!' Joe called back.

Breathless from the climb but still grinning, Logan leaned a hand on the pony's back, 'Ye should see the delight on every face in the village! We need tae prepare a welcome fer him. Come tae the Lodge tomorrow evening ... and spread the word o' this joyous outcome!'

On the Tuesday, four days after their triumph in the sale room, Owen travelled down to the mills with his new partners so they could view their purchase. It was bitterly cold and the coach was driven by a postillion, carefully assessing the frozen ground in front of the horses on the icy rutted roads.

'We are nearly at the old market town of Lanark,' Owen told his companions after hours of bumping through Lanarkshire. 'Only a few more miles and we will plunge down into the valley and you can take your first sight of the mills.'

Suddenly, the horses dropped their pace and William Allan, facing forward, gave an involuntary cry.

'Good Gracious, may the Lord have mercy!' his face was panic stricken, 'There are men running towards us!'

Owen stuck his head out the window to see a crowd bearing down on them, waving and shouting. Then they were engulfing the carriage and he saw their cheerful smiles, the laughing children skipping at their sides and he raised a hand to wave.

'They are friendly!' he shouted above the din, the horses now at a standstill. 'I believe it is a welcoming party!'

'Extraordinary!' Gibbs said, shakily, more used to being attacked than celebrated.

The carriage started to rock and tilt forward, a group of men were pushing and pulling at the harness.

'What's happening?' Fox cried in alarm.

'They are ... uncoupling the horses!' Allan replied with a mixture of awe and trepidation.

A team of brawny men pulled the leather traces away from the shafts and hefted the weight of the carriage onto their shoulders. Gripping the polished wooden poles they boldy marched forward.

Owen leaned from the carriage, beseeching them to stop, 'Please! The working classes have too long been treated like brutes ... beware of injury!'

His pleas were to no avail and a flag was placed at the front as they were dragged ceremoniously through Lanark's streets. Leading this triumphant procession, arranged by the Freemasons, was a loud, colourful pipe band, the pipers swaggering and bellowing with a fervour which carried the sound far across Clydesdale. The carriage made slow progress surrounded by waving, jubilant townsfolk, all wishing to catch a glimpse of Owen and add their personal congratulations.

The teams of men changed several times over the miles, drawing the carriage down to Braxfield House where they persuaded Anne Caroline, Jean and Mary, who were forewarned but still nervous, to climb aboard.

The carriage was then uncovered and the whole party took off again amidst more music and drums, flag flying, to be paraded through the swarming streets of New Lanark.

'Heavens above, Owen! This is an incredible place!' Fox exclaimed, his red face glowing with excitement. 'I would not have believed this possible! How many people live here, did ye say?'

'There's about one and a half thousand working in the mills, so with their families that's over two thousand residents but some of the people here ...' he broke off to acknowledge a group of children jumping and waving at the carriage door. 'As I was saying, I can see many on the streets who are from Old Lanark as well.'

'Look at the mills and the high stone dwellings!' Gibb said in astonishment. 'There are flags and people waving from every window ... they love you!'

Owen put his arm around Anne Caroline; the moment was too special and invigorating to restrain his emotion.

Caught up into the high spirits, she kissed him warmly on the cheek, whispering in his ear, 'This is all for you, my dearest, you have won their hearts and their trust.'

The Scotts were amongst the crowd when it streamed up Braxfield Road to return the mill owner to the big house. Joe and Donnie were part of the last team of men hauling the carriage, sweating and straining until they came to a halt in front of the magnificent front door.

Sheddon and the household servants were gathered on the steps, warmly wrapped in their Sunday best, the Owen children muffled to the ears in woollen jackets. Mrs Cooper had been invited to join them for the occasion, standing nervously between Miss Wilson and Senga, her hawkish face surveying the spectacle with bewilderment.

Owen stood up in the carriage, holding his hands up and begging for quiet, incredulous at the out pouring of friendship and respect he was being shown.

'Whit's he sayin'?' Fiona asked, pushing through the rabble, pulling Sionaidh behind her to reach the front.

Rosie and Sarah squeezed up beside her while a never ending wave of villagers surged up the drive and thronged on the gravel and lawns.

At last, a quiet descended.

'Thank you! Thank you, every one of you!' Owen shouted across the assembly. 'This is a joyous day!' He paused, his lean face flushed with the thrill of the occasion.

'I now have partners whose hearts and minds support what I wish to accomplish in our mills. I have been called a philosopher,' his voice rang out, 'a visionary! People say my ideas are all very delightful and very beautiful in theory, but visionaries *alone* expect to see it realised.

'To this remark, only one reply can or *ought* to be made, that these principles have been carried most successfully into practice ... *here!'*

A cheer rose up, dying away when he began to speak again.

'I am not an idle visionary who thinks in his closet and never acts in the world.

'I am back ... and eager to continue the work I started. Together, we will show the world how much better society can be. I aim to improve your lives and those of *all* workers across the nation. I have much to do, we *all* have much to do! We will prove to the politicians and the doubters how every child can be educated and lead a happy, healthy life while *still* working in the factories. It *can* be achieved without suppression and cruelty and it *will* be done! We will show the world a new view of society! Thank you!'

'God bless Mr Owen!' someone shouted and everyone chorused his blessing, whistling and hollering until he disappeared into the house.

It was growing dark, snowflakes tumbling around them to form a white carpet on the frozen ground. Davey hoisted little Alex onto his shoulders and the Scotts turned for home with the slow-moving, mumbling crowd.

Fiona and Joe were walking with their arms around each other's waists and she glanced up to catch his eye, drunk with exhilaration.

'It's braw tae ha'e Mr Owen back,' she told him, 'an' Davey wi' us agin. We jist need an end tae the war an' we can stoap worryin' aboot Sam an' wee Stephen.'

'Ye alis need summat tae be concernin' ye, lass!' Joe scolded, affectionately. 'Ah din nae ken whit this year has in store fer us, but richt noo, Ah ha'e ma sweethairt in ma airms an',' he raised his head to look ahead up the white road; snow silently covering every twig and blade of grass, turning the dusk landscape into tones of grey and white. 'Ah can see all ma family, an' they're a' weel, an'...' he kissed the top of her snowflake speckled bonnet, 'tha's aboot as guid as life can git!'

She giggled, girlishly, 'Mr Owen says he's gaun tae improve oor lives!'

Joe laughed, 'That we'll have tae see!'

*

The New Lanark Trilogy by C A Hope
Based on the true story of the
New Lanark Cotton Mills.

NEW LANARK
SPINNING NEW LIVES
The First Book

Meticulously researched to blend real people and
actual events, these novels take you back in time to the
1780s. Follow the remarkable journey of three young
people bound together by David Dale's pioneering
community. Set against the turbulent backdrop of the
French Revolution, Highland Clearances and the
dawning of the Scottish Enlightenment.

NEW LANARK
IN SEARCH OF UTOPIA
The Third Book

With Britain engaged in wars with both Europe and
America, the villagers of New Lanark prepare to live by
Robert Owen's philosophy. The winds of change bring
unforeseen consequences, especially for Anne Caroline
and the Scott family as they experience an era destined
to leave a living legacy for the future.

Real Life Characters

Prime Ministers (mentioned) over the period:
  Henry Addington, William Pitt the Younger,
  William Grenville, Spencer Perceval, Robert Jenkinson.
Armadale, Lord Justice. Sir William Honyman m Mary McQueen
Alexander of Ballochmyle, Claud, mill owner (wife-
  Helenora, sister- Wilhelmina)
Atkinson, Mr, partner of Owen in the Chorlton Twist Co.
Bayley, Thomas
Barton, Mr, partner of Owen in the Chorlton Twist Co.
Bentham, Jeremy 1748-1832
Braxfield, Lord, Lord Justice Clerk, Robert MacQueen
  1722-1799
Brown, John, banker
Burns, Robert, poet 1759 – 1796
Campbell, Alexander of Hallyards, Glasgow businessman
Campbell, Colin, Glasgow Businessman
Campbell, John, of Jura
Carrick, Robert, banker, Ship Bank
Clegg, Mr, Owen's clerk
Craig, Mr James, manager of Stanley Mills
Currie, Dr, friend of David Dale
Dale, Anne Caroline "Carolina" (wife of David) 1753-1791
Dale, Anne Caroline, (1778- 1831) Mary, Margaret, Jean
  and Julia - Dale's daughters (died in infancy –
  Arabella, Christian and Katherine)
Dale, David 1739 - 1806
Dale, Hugh, brother of David 1741- 1794 (wife - Margaret,
  son – David)
Dale, James, half brother of David 1753-1819 (wife -
  Marion Haddow)
Dale, William, 1784-1790 son of David Dale
Davis, Dinah, second wife of William Owen, 1772-1854
Davidson, Major Christopher, 26th Rifles, Cameronians
Dempster, George, 1732-1811 lawyer and MP for Perth
Dennistoun, Robert, Glasgow business man
Dodge, Mr, dancing teacher
Donne, Dr James, of Oswestry
Dunn, James. mill worker / postman

Drinkwater, Peter
Finlay, Kirkman, mill owner and businessman
Gibbs, Michael, businessman
Godwin, William 1756-1836
Graham, Sir Thomas, 1st Baron Lyndoch 1748 - 1843
Hilgrove-Turner, Colonel Tomkyns 1764-1843
Hamilton, Gilbert 1744–1808, businessman,
Humphreys, Robert, under manager New Lanark
Kelly, William, clockmaker, engineer and mill manager
Lancaster, Joseph, educationalist 1778-1838
Lavasseur, Monsieur, French prisoner of war, tutor.
Logan, Willie, Freemason of Lanark
MacIntosh, Charles, chemist 1766-1843 (m. Mary Fisher)
MacIntosh George, businessman 1739 - 1807
McGuffogs, drapery shop owners
McKenzie, Rev, Lanark minister
Methven, Lord Justice. David Smythe 1746-1806
Methven, Lady Euphemia b1769
Mill, James political philosopher 1773-1836
More, John
Moore, Sir John, 1761 - 1809
Muir, James, Glasgow hop merchant, father of Thomas Muir
Murray, Matt, Freemason of Lanark
Lawson, Bob, Freemason of Lanark
Owen, William, eldest brother of Robert 1764-1837
Owen, Anne, sister of Robert
Owen, Robert 1739-1804 m. Anne Williams 1735-1803
Paterson, Archibald, businessman
Percival, Dr Thomas, 1740 - 1804
Pitt, William, 'The Younger' 1759-1806
Place, Francis 1771-1854
Ross, Lady Elizabeth Lockhart
Ross, Lady Mary (of Bonnington)
Sandeman, William, partner in Stanley 1722-1790
Scott, Robert, artist
Scott Moncrieff, Robert, banker businessman 1738-1814
Sheddon, William, Owen's butler
Stephenson, Captain Thomas (of *Egyptienne*)
Tennant, Charles, chemist 1768-1838 (m. Margaret Wilson)
Turnbull, Hector, partner Luncarty Bleachfields
Wilson, Miss, Owen's housekeeper at Braxfield House
Young, Dr Thomas

Guide to the Dialect used in this Novel
aye – yes
auld lang syne – old, long days ago: days now in the past
bairns – children
bàn – blonde / fair skinned (Scottish Gaelic)
besom – a naughty, cheeky or bad girl/woman
bin – been
brèagha – beautiful (Scottish Gaelic)
brither – brother
buildseach – witch (Scottish Gaelic)
cannae – cannot
caunel - candle
chap – knock (chap ma door – knock on my door)
cheerio - goodbye
cla'es – clothes
cludgie - toilet
crabbit – bad tempered, snappy
cry him – call him (his name)
cuddies – horse, pony or donkey
dinnae fash yersel' – don't upset yourself
dinnae ken – don't know
disnae – doesn't
dour – glum
douth – depressed, gloomy
driech – dreary, wet or depressing
drookit – soaked
efter – after
gae – go
gaun – going
gowd – gold
gowping – giving pain, hurting
greetin' – crying (tae greet – to cry)
grun - ground
guid - good
ha'e – have
haud – hold
haun – hand (gi'e me a haun – give me a hand, help me)
havering and footering – prevaricating

heid – head
jennies – engines (spinning jennies – engines for spinning)
jist - just
kens – knows (ye ken – you know)
lummock – clumsy, lumbering
mair – more (onymair – anymore)
mind – remember
mon – man
mony – money or (in context) many
muckle oota a mickle – (making) much out of a little
neb - nose
neeps – turnips
neònach – strange, weird (Scottish Gaelic)
nicht – night
noo - now
nuthin' or nuchin' - nothing
ony – any
oot - out
richt – right
sgriosail – dreadful, damnable (Scottish Gaelic)
skelpit erse – smacked bottom
slitter – untidy, dirty person
stoater – great, brilliant
tae – to
tatties - potatoes
telt - told
thocht – thought
t'morra – tomorrow (tomorra)
vennel – narrow lane, close
weans – small children
wee - small
whaur – where
wheesht – shush, be quiet
whit – what
wid – would
yin – one
yon – that or there

Bibliography
Owen, Robert Dale, *Threading My Way,* Trubner & Co, 1874, reprinted in the Classic Reprint Series by Forgotten Books 2012
Owen Robert, *A New View of Society,* Everyman's Library
Cooke, Andrew, *Stanley,* Perth and Kinross Libraries
Cooke, Andrew, (1977)The Stanley Extra Mural Class, *Stanley Its History and Development,* University of Dundee
Royle, Trevor, *Cameronians, A Concise History,* Mainstream
Donnachie, Ian and Hewitt, George *(1993) Historic New Lanark,* Edinburgh University Press, Edinburgh
Whatley, Christopher A *(2000), Scottish Society 1707-1830,* Manchester University Press, Manchester
New Lanark Trust, *The Story of New Lanark Living in New Lanark The Story of Robert Owen*
McLaren, David J *(1990) David Dale of New Lanark,* CWS Scottish CO-OP
Griffiths, Trevor and Morton, Graeme (2010) *A History of Everyday Life in Scotland 1800 to 1900,* Edinburgh University Press
RCAHMS *New Lanark Buildings and History,* Broadsheet 15
Morgan, Giles (2007) *Freemasonry*, Pocket Essentials
Podmore, Frank, (repro of pre 1923 book) *Robert Owen: A Biography.* D Appleton & Co 1907.
Sinclair, John, *"Old" Statistical Account of Scotland* (and many other pamphlets, papers and Owen family records)

Grateful thanks to:
Clifford Owen
Lorna Davidson
Robert Owen Museum, Newtown, Wales
New Lanark Trust
Cameronians Museum, Low Parks Museum, Hamilton
AK Bell Library, Perth
Mitchell Library, Glasgow
Pioneers Museum, Rochdale
Stanley Mills, Historic Scotland

Lightning Source UK Ltd.
Milton Keynes UK
UKOW06f2355280416

273202UK00016B/418/P